PRAISE FOR
ENGAGED IN WAR

Historically precise to the era, a tale delineating the strength of the will to survive despite the horror of combat, death, and uncertainty, filled with rich details, fully fleshed characters, and twists and turns, the reader is kept turning the page to learn what will happen next. **—The Midwest Book Review**

Engaged In War is as entertaining as *GONE WITH THE WIND,* as riveting as *SAVING PRIVATE RYAN,* and as heartwarming as FORREST GUMP.

—Geraldine Ahearn, Author Reviews

As the Allies liberate France, *Engaged in War* answers some of the questions posed in *Virginia's War.* It kept me riveted to Will's tale of survival and finding that perfect someone – even if they can barely communicate with words. I'm now impatient to read what's to come next. **—Dear Author**

London has crafted an intriguing tale filled with rich details, fully fleshed characters and plenty of twists and turns to satisfy the reader who enjoys character focused historical fiction. *Engaged in War* relates the chronicle of Captain Will Hastings, enmeshed in the Normandy D-Day landings. Within a span of a few lines of text; the scene is set by a hard-nosed major with a yen for revenge coupled to a God complex. Historically precise, *Engaged in War* is a tale delineating the strength of the will to survive despite the horror of combat, space, death of loved ones, and even uncertainty regarding the future. From the prologue to last page the reader is kept turning the page to learn what will happen next.

—Molly Martin, The Compulsive Reader

Awards:
London Book Festival, Silver Medal for General Fiction
Author of the Year, Military Writers Society of America
Stars and Flags Book Award, Silver Medal

FRENCH LETTERS

BOOK TWO

ENGAGED IN WAR
Normandy, 1944

Jack Woodville London

Vire Press, L.L.C. ✦ Austin, Texas

Published by
Vire Press, L.L.C., Austin, Texas
www.virepress.com

Editor-in-chief: Mindy Reed
Book design: The Authors' Assistant, Austin, Texas

ISBN paperback: 978-0-9906121-7-9
ISBN eBook: 978-0-9906121-5-5

Cataloging-in Publication Data

London, Jack w. 1947–
French Letters, Engaged in War/Jack Wooodville London

p.   cm.

I. World War II–France   II. Historical Fiction

Fic Lon   PS642 L86 2010

Dedication

I dedicate this story of a young doctor in an uncertain world to my father, Dr. John V. London.

ENGAGED IN WAR

NORMANDY
1944

CHAPTER ONE

June, 1944

The aerodynamics of a Duncan yo-yo in flight are such that with just over 60 degrees of vertical angle, and a thrust of no more than ten or fifteen times the weight of the yo-yo, it will fly over the hull of a landing ship (tank) and disappear into the English Channel.

"This is called sleeping." Antsley said it aloud but no one heard him. The landing ship was loud enough just idling at the docks but now, on the high seas, loaded with tanks, guns, and medical crews on the way across to France, it was deafening. Even if anyone had been able to hear Antsley, they most likely wouldn't have been listening anyway because most of the triage medics were sitting on the deck against the starboard hull watching Cheadle take their money with card tricks at a dollar a guess.

"Okay," Cheadle said to the half-dozen farm boys and conscientious objectors sitting in a circle on the deck, "pick two cards. Okay, what've you got? Don't show me." A boy who had just joined the bow ramp triage team in Southampton picked two cards, a six of spades and a nine of clubs. "Got 'em? Got 'em?" He had them. "Don't forget 'em. Okay?" He wouldn't forget them.

Antsley sat on his helmet in order to be high enough off the deck to put the yo-yo to sleep. The boat bounced hard on a wave, the diesel engines roared as the propellers cleared a trough for a few seconds, the boat landed hard again. Antsley put a heavy top spin on the yo-yo, flipped his hand palm up, and the wooden toy raced down the string, bottomed out, and spun on its own for fifteen or twenty seconds before he jerked his hand up. The toy raced up the string and settled in his palm.

No one paid any attention.

"Okay, spread the cards out. Spread 'em out, that's right, make a fan of 'em. Good. Okay, I'm gonna pull out your two cards." Cheadle made a good show of touching the backs of the cards, concentrating with his fingertips on the telekinetic identity of the possible choices, then lifted his hands. "No good, Watson. They ain't in here." Cheadle pointed to the deck, shrugged, and went on. "You must've palmed 'em. They ain't in there."

Everyone had seen Watson put the two cards right in the middle of the deck and take his hands away. They also had seen Watson go to mass at the middle-deck service a couple of hours before and knew he would not likely throw away his heart-felt pre-battle absolution to cheat on a card trick for a buck. And they knew Cheadle.

Cheadle left the cards on the deck, leaned back on his haunches, and said, "What'd you do with 'em, Watson?"

"Nothin'! I put them back in the deck. You saw me. Everybody saw me."

"Well, I'm tellin' ya, it was the six of clubs and nine of spades, right? And they ain't in there!"

Watson was dumbfounded.

"How'd you know what they were? You haven't even seen the deck!"

"Well, because they're right here!" Cheadle did a very workmanlike job of reaching across the deck, beyond the pile of cards, to Watson's army boot, then moving his hand over to snatch two cards out of the cuff of another medic's fatigue pants. Cheadle held them up. "What'd I say? Six of clubs, nine of spades!"

The triage boys howled in laughter. No one thought Watson had cheated. They just thought Cheadle had pulled off a great magic trick which, in a way, he had: he had transformed one of Watson's dollars into one of his own dollars.

"How'd you do that?"

Ten feet away, on his helmet, back against one of the hull stanchions, Antsley said, "This is called walking the dog." He flipped the yo-yo onto a jacket on the deck, a foot or so in front of his hand, and let it crawl across the jacket, then flipped his wrist and the yo-yo popped up the string and up into his hand. No one paid any attention.

"Magic. I just knew what cards you picked and then I teletransported 'em into Jacob's boot. Pretty basic. Give me a dollar."

2

Watson handed over the dollar and asked again, "Come on, Cheadle, how'd you do it? Magic?"

"Naw, it isn't magic," Antsley's voice punched through the noise and into Watson's question.

Anstley didn't know then and never knew for the rest of his life why he said anything. He liked Cheadle. He had given Cheadle three or four of his own dollars at magic card tricks, some on the boat from New York, some in field training at Shrivenham, all without resentment. None of them really thought they were going to survive the landing anyway, so he didn't mind Cheadle having a last laugh with the guys. But, for some reason, when the dog crawled back up the yo-yo string and into the dog house of Anstley's hand, the words just popped out. And for some reason, the landing craft had at that moment gone quiet, like it does in church the second someone's stomach cuts loose. He kept on.

"It wasn't even the six of clubs and the nine of spades. You picked the six of spades and nine of clubs. This is called giving the dog a bone." He flipped the wooden toy one more time and, as it landed on the jacket, Cheadle scuttled the ten feet over to where Antsley sat with his back against the hull, grabbed the yo-yo, and put sixty degrees of arc under it with enough thrust to put the last remnant of Antsley's boyhood over the side, where it disappeared ten miles from the coast of France.

"Oh shit, Antsley. I'm sorry."

Cheadle himself would wonder for the rest of his life why he had thrown Antsley's yo-yo over the side a half hour before the boat was supposed to crunch up on the beach to unload tanks and take on casualties. Their job was to be the first medics a wounded soldier would see when he got on the ramp, to assess how wounded he was, then get him to a triage doctor to keep him alive long enough to send him to the middle of the boat for treatment or on up to the ward deck for surgery. Standing on the wide-open front ramp of a huge boat, completely exposed to the raging battle, was not likely to be very safe. Cheadle didn't want his buddies' dollars. He just wanted to do what Antsley was doing, keep his mind off his impending baptism with a bit of fun. "Oh shit, I'm sorry. I didn't mean it. Hey, come on," he continued, seeing Antsley's face turn bleach-white and his eyes well up as the little wooden comet, its string tail behind, climbed, peaked, and disappeared forever. Cheadle knew that this trick was a lot dirtier than any he had ever done before, and didn't know how to undo it.

3

"It's all right," Antsley said. It wasn't all right, but he had been raised that when someone does something wrong, you not only forgive them, you make them feel it wasn't important. "It's all right." And Antsley was grown up enough to believe that all of them on triage up at the wide-open bow of the landing ship, even the doctors, were there because they had been put on an Army shit list made up of people who could be replaced if they got shot.

That was when a line snapped back at the mid-deck, at the very end of the rows of trucks.

The trucks were hitched to howitzers and the broken line set free a gun carriage that whipped around on the rough seas and smashed the gun barrel into a sailor's face.

The other thing Antsley would not understand for the rest of his life was why he left his post to try to help. The sailor was the Navy's casualty, not the Army's, and he was closer to the mid-deck team, not the triage teams at the bow. But Antsley jumped up and sprinted past the built-in crane towers and life-boat stanchions, between the tanks and the trucks and guns, and threw himself onto the deck underneath the still-rolling howitzer, trying to crawl to the maimed sailor, yelling 'I'm here. Lay down, I'm here. I've got you.' The most Antsley could say in his own defense was that not only did the mid-deck medics and doctors stay where they were but even the sailor's ensign and deck hands froze when the boy was struck. Antsley slid under the thrashing gun barrel and tried to reach far enough to swab at the boy's face, to see if it had killed him. That snapped everyone on deck back to life.

"YOU! HELP THAT MEDIC," the ensign shouted at a pharmacist's mate. "You two, get on that gun! Get something under the wheels."

Antsley heard the officer shouting but couldn't see him because the line was whipping around just above his head, threatening to finish what the loose cannon had not. A glob of the boy's blood gushed onto the deck and hit Antsley in the face, causing him to jerk his head and look upward, just in time to see Sergeant Gill and Major Halliburton jogging down the companionway ladder to the scene.

Uh oh.

But there was no turning back now. He wiped the blood off his face, stretched as far as he could, got an arm under the sailor, and began to drag him away from the gun.

In a matter of seconds the swabbies got the gun's carriage blocked enough for Antsley and the pharmacist's mate to get the screaming boy onto a litter, just as the major and the sergeant set foot on the tank deck. A couple of Sergeant Gill's mid-deck crew had edged closer to the scene.

"Thank God you're here, Major," the ensign shouted with evident relief. "You," he continued, to two medics. "You two men help carry this litter up to the ward deck. What surgery do you want him in, Major? MOVE!" The soldiers budged but Major Halliburton didn't. "Get a move on for God's sake. This kid is hurt." The medics stopped in their tracks.

The Navy ensign looked again at the Army major, then realized that Halliburton was neither permitting his men to carry the sailor nor doing anything else.

"Easy, Ensign," Halliburton said, his voice steady and clear, somehow making itself heard above the diesel engines and the thunder of distant shelling. "Easy. I've got him."

It didn't look like Halliburton had him.

"Sir, this man is—"

"Ensign, stop. I said we've got him." Halliburton turned with the calm demeanor of a headmaster, ignoring the ensign and facing his sergeant. "Sergeant Gill? Has anyone triaged this casualty?"

Even Sergeant Gill could have triaged the sailor; the muzzle of an eight-foot-long howitzer barrel had smashed his face in. To compound the problem, the boy's leg appeared to have made a right-turn midway between his knee and hip.

"Triage, sir? He's got a broken...."

Halliburton ignored him and stared at the hero of the rescue, who was scrambling to regain his footing on the bouncing deck.

"Who do we have here? Ah, Private Antsley? Get up off the deck. It seems you've left your post." Halliburton paused to be sure he was understood. "Well, Anstley, go back to your post and bring one of the triage surgeons here. NOW!"

Still, neither Antsley nor anyone else who was huddled around the litter quite grasped what was happening.

"Sir, he's...."

Antsley didn't even finish the sentence; Halliburton's glare was all the order he needed. In the meantime, Halliburton ordered the pharmacist's mate to stop what he was doing as well.

"Step back, there. Step back," Halliburton directed the pharmacist's mate. "Sergeant Gill, tell your medics to control the patient until he is triaged."

"Major, listen—we saw it happen. That gun hit him in the face. Get him up to one of your surgeries before he bleeds to death, for God's sake."

Halliburton ignored the ensign. The only thing that seemed to respond to his plea was the ship itself—the diesel engines had revved up and the hull vibrated like a drum as the LST picked up speed. The men and the arms on the tank deck, the tanks, the trucks, the howitzers hitched to the trucks, all began to shake. Everyone on deck could sense that the landing ship had entered shallow water.

"Stand by, all of you. Sergeant Gill, get your men to their posts. Ensign?" Halliburton turned to answer the ensign, "Ensign, this is my deck. You may return to your duties."

"Your deck, sir? Not until we land..." The ensign was young, but no coward. And it was his man who was bleeding all over the deck, not the major's.

"No, Ensign. I'm afraid you're mistaken there. This became my deck the moment your cargo cut loose. Landing Special Order Seven: When the secured armament on deck is freed, the deck will be readied for medical transport under the command of the Army medical administration. I am Army medical administration. Your secured armament is loose." He gave a nonchalant nod to the howitzer that was still bouncing out of control and the two sailors trying to chock its wheels without getting crushed. "So, this now is my deck. Go on about your duties, Ensign."

Halliburton dismissed the Navy officer without another word or glance, then returned to Sergeant Gill. Gill had retreated ten yards backward into the midst of the mid-deck medics and treatment doctors, most of whom had known better than to leave their assigned places to try to help. The sailor gushed blood onto the steel deck.

Although no one entirely grasped what they had seen, least of all the ensign, neither did anyone argue. They resumed their duty stations while the sailors secured the gun and began to brace for the landing. Only Gill and Halliburton waited for Anstley to return with a triage doctor. When he did, they bent over the sailor.

"Let me check his airway, Antsley. Get his chin up just a bit there."

Antsley lifted the sailor's chin; the sailor coughed a wad of clotted blood onto Antsley's uniform.

"He's breathing, Major. Nose is crushed, for sure, face is cut up, but he's breathing." Captain Blackwell gently touched the boy's face. "Eye sockets might be broken, cheek grossly intact. Hard to believe he's even alive after that gun hit him." The ship bounced harder on each wave the closer to France it got. "Leg's shattered."

Blackwell looked in his eyes, tried to get a pulse, put his head on the sailor's chest and listened.

"He's in shock, lost a bunch of blood. I've got to get a splint under here, Major. Then we can get him up to the OR without moving his leg. Get me a splint, will you, Sarge? They're in the number two field kits over there." Blackwell pointed about ten steps away to a box secured to the hull, a large red cross painted on the outside, and the Number 2 stenciled on the front. "Splints and bandages should be right on top."

Sergeant Gill took a step in the direction of the field kits when Halliburton stopped him.

"Captain, are you forgetting something?"

Blackwell looked up.

"Is there anything else wrong with this sailor?" There wasn't; the shattered leg and mashed face were all that could be seen without moving the boy. "If there isn't, your work here is done. Turn the casualty over to the mid-deck team for treatment and further assignment. Sergeant Gill?"

Gill held his breath and waited for Halliburton's order.

"Sergeant, go mid-ships. Tell one of the deck doctors to join us over here." The mid-ship doctors were not more than fifteen feet away at their stations, waiting for the landing. They had heard every word. "The triage doctor has assessed a facial injury and a broken leg. Oh, yes, and shock. If one of your deck doctors assesses that this sailor needs surgery and is more urgent than any other casualty on board at this time, he will find me ready to assign the patient to a surgery on the ward deck. I'll be at the companionway."

Halliburton paused, then turned to Antsley and Blackwell, still on their knees trying to comfort the sailor.

"Captain Blackwell, you just had a trial run and you failed. You skipped steps on the conveyor belt. 'Triage, assign, treat, assign for surgery.'" The chill began to sink in. "This sailor is no worse off for waiting. Learn from this. If you don't, you're going to kill some brave men, casualties who've already been wounded, because you failed to follow orders and assign

7

them where they belong, when they belong, on the conveyor belt. It probably will be a soldier who should be in surgery but won't be because you knocked him off his place on the assembly line." He spoke to Blackwell but he glared at Antsley. The scar on Halliburton's forehead turned redder than it already was, the ragged suture points glowing like little beacons on his patrician forehead. "Once the treatment team arrives, you two are dismissed. Return to your posts."

Halliburton turned and walked the ten or twelve steps to the companionway ladder, his own designated post, the place on ship where he would receive the worst-injured soldiers from the deck doctors and approve, or not, their admission to surgery. At that moment the ship's diesel engines throttled back to avoid driving the craft halfway up the French beach to the bluffs on the far side. And, for just that moment, the ship was almost quiet. Halliburton heard the hushed comments of his two triage soldiers.

"You get a look at his face, Captain?" Antsley whispered. "Looks like that guy we seen on the newsreel, that guy Joe Louis cut up like a salami. That's what his face really looks like."

Neither Antsley nor, for that matter, Captain Blackwell, gave a moment's thought to whether Major Halliburton could hear them.

Halliburton didn't give a moment's thought to whether they might be talking about the sailor. Instead, he felt his own scar to see if his helmet visor covered it; it didn't. Until then he had made no effort to hide it. It was a man's scar, a soldier's scar. There were only a couple of Army men on board who had been at Shrivenham when he had come back from London and they never said a word. But Halliburton had heard the Navy boys chuff about it when he passed by and they thought he was a war hero. *There's that major who caught it. Bomb hit. Couple of months ago. Look at his scar. Tough bird.* All true, as far as it went, and Halliburton approved of the sailors' judgment of him. Now he heard the version being whispered about, the *cut-up when-someone-beat-him-up* version. He had to make a decision, and did.

At that precise moment LST 556 scraped onto Omaha Beach. The moment of silence ended and the war intruded, the shelling suddenly very close by and heavy. The ship's diesels roared as their transmissions geared down to control the landing. The engines on the tanks and trucks on deck revved up, the bow doors sprang apart, and the landing ramp went down. There was an urgent, methodical sequence of Shermans clanking forward and of deuce-and-a-half trucks lunging toward combat. Swabbies swarmed behind them, emptying the deck, clearing away the web of restraining ropes. Deck hands and medics leapt into action to ready the ship for three hundred wounded American soldiers whom LST 556 was expected to receive before closing up and racing back to England within fifteen minutes of getting the gun off the boat. Antsley and Captain Blackwell braced against the hull at the open bow doors, holding their breath with the rest of the triage teams against the moment when German gunfire would fill the air.

LST 556 was on the beach a lot longer than fifteen minutes, and Antsley and the triage teams watched more than they triaged. Neither the Navy nor the medics thwarted Halliburton's medical conveyor belt—it was the Germans. The men stared around the ship's doors and squinted through the hinges only to see soldiers wounded on the beach, then wounded again as they tried to get to the ship. Hundreds of men lay within a hundred steps of the open ramp, pleading for medics, but the Germans fired down on them as fast as they could see them. The army medics on the beach finally began to drag the wounded away from the boat and toward the sea wall rather than try to get them on board.

Antsley felt a hand grip hard on his shoulder.

"Listen up!" It was Gill. "Major wants a triage team to volunteer up on the surgery deck. Antsley! You're one. This your triage doctor?" He pointed at Blackwell.

"No, Sergeant, I'm— "

"Major wants Antsley and his doc up on deck. Who's your doc, Anstley?"

Before he could answer, another skinny kid, not much older than the medics, raised his hand and, it seemed to Gill, smiled.

"That's me, Sergeant. I'm on Anstley's team." He was Anstley's team; there were just the two of them.

"Major says they's too many teams down here, sir, so Major wants you two up on the surgery deck. Now!"

The other triage teams, Blackwell and Cheadle and the others, all watched in envious disbelief as the men followed Gill. Two hundred litter cots had been set up across the deck, rows and aisles squared in an orderly way so that the doctors and medics could move easily between patients to bandage, splint, administer fluids, or carry a man up to the ward deck as needed. It was past these cots and up to the ward deck that Gill led the men. They climbed Halliburton's ladder, then edged along past the waiting surgeries and halted at the commander's stateroom.

"Here, sir," Gill called out. "Go on in, sir. Major wants you." The triage doctor entered; Gill grabbed Antsley by the neck. "Not you, Antsley. I said SIR. You ain't no sir. Stand at attention while you waits." He shoved Antsley up against the outer wall of the cabin where, for the first time, Antsley could see over the hull of the landing ship and beyond to the entire length of the invasion beach.

Oh my God. When he began to grasp what lay in front of him Anstley forgot to breathe, so much so that a full minute went by before he realized that Gill had disappeared and that he was overhearing every word that Major Halliburton was telling his doctor/team captain inside the cabin. *Oh my God.*

"Hello, Hastings."

"Sir."

"I have a change of assignment for you."

"Yes, sir. I wondered whether you might do that once we landed."

"Well, you were right for the job. Triage doc. Not married. As I remember, you don't even have a girl back home. Is that what I remember?"

Hastings ignored him. "Where do you want me? Enemas? Catheters?"

"No, no, Hastings. I have something much more important than that. I'm assigning you to swap doc." Halliburton waited for an argument, a smart remark, anything. None came.

"Yes, sir. What exactly is a swap doc?" The young medical officer had never heard that term before. There was a chance he had missed it in training, but not a very big chance. It was better to ask.

"Listen carefully and do not screw this up. The engineers have cleared the beach."

Antsley heard the rustle of a map being rolled out; he looked over the hull to see what Halliburton meant by 'clearing the beach.' The beach didn't look very clear.

"There are medical stations here," Halliburton pointed to random Xs on the map where the beach gave way to the sand dunes.

"Yes, sir."

"And there's a clearing station here," he pointed to a third spot, about half-way up the sand dunes between the beach and the town. "Do you remember that?"

"Yes, sir. I suspected the day might come when you would find a need to put me on the beach. I paid particular attention to where the medical aid stations are supposed to be set up."

"Good. Your orders are to go to them. All of them. After you've checked in with every medical unit on the beach, you are to go on up the draw to the clearing company. They'll have a field surgery set up there. Now listen up—if any of the doctors already on the beach is incapacitated, you send him back to the boat. You will stay and take his place. Understand? "

Halliburton's voice was almost apologetic, but in a way that sounded rehearsed.

"I understand, sir."

"If you do swap out with one of the doctors on the beach, someone will replace you tomorrow when the LST returns. So go, and take your field kit with you."

"I have it, sir."

"Good. There'll be plenty of medical supply dumps on the beach, no worry about that. All is planned. But take your own things." He paused, working to keep his face commander-like. "I didn't want to do this, Hastings, you know that. But I put too many teams on triage at the LST ramp. My fault. And it looks from up here like we need docs out there more than up at triage. Sorry."

They both knew it was a lie. A major could lie to a captain, and often did.

"I understand."

"Do your best." Halliburton paused one more time, unable to contain his theatrics. "Oh, and take Antsley with you."

"Antsley?"

"Antsley!" Halliburton snarled. "Don't mess with me, Hastings. I know you two are buddies. I know what you're up to. Get him and get out of here." Halliburton's ragged stitches bulged, not much, but enough that Hastings understood. There would be no rumors going around about Halliburton, not on this boat.

"He's just a medic, David. What in hell do you think he did to you?"

"Get out, Hastings. I want you two off this boat in one minute. That's an order. And take that little shit with you. Out!"

Halliburton waited less than a minute, then followed Hastings to the ladder. He stared at the tank deck, watching Hastings drag Antsley along to grab his field pack and jog to the bow of the landing craft, then sprint down the ramp and on to the beach.

He looked out from the top of the ladder and saw what Antsley had seen. A haze of black smoke hung over burning tanks and smashed artillery pieces littered the beach. Germans up on the bluff fired down both on the vast fleet of landing ships and also on the men trying to sprint across the sand. Bodies, dead and dying, littered the ground from the water's edge to the low sea wall at the foot of the sand dunes. The draw was visible a quarter mile away but finding a medical station there or anywhere else on that beach would have been impossible. *I don't see a single medical flag up anywhere. Oh, well, the best laid plans of mice and men,* he thought. *Hope they find the medic units.*

Then he saw Hastings, Antsley in tow, sprinting across the shingle, running from one smoking hulk to the next, zig-zagging toward the draw, dodging things too small for Halliburton to see. Halliburton took his binoculars and studied the draw that led up to St. Laurent. *Must be behind schedule,* he thought. *Should be a field surgery up there by now, but looks like the krauts still have it.* He lost sight of Hastings and Antsley a hundred yards from the water's edge, running toward a cluster of men huddled behind an overturned tank. And then he spotted what he had trained for—litter bearers, tens of them, dozens, bringing wounded to his landing boat. It was time for Halliburton to swing his hospital ship into action.

He spotted Sergeant Gill as well, and motioned for him to come.

"Sergeant, time to get in the driver's seat. They're coming." He pointed at the rising tide of wounded, men on litters, men in tatters, flooding across the bow ramp. "You short-handed?"

"How you mean, Major?"

"I thought you had a standing order—none of your men was supposed to leave the ship."

"Yessir. They all know it.

"Look, there." Halliburton pointed to the beach. Gill had trouble making out what the major wanted him to see. "Looks to me like Captain Hastings has commandeered one of your men, Sergeant. He clear it through you?"

"Who, Major?"

"Antsley. He's one of your medics isn't he? What's he doing there on the beach with Captain Hastings?" He pointed again, and Gill spotted the two soldiers diving into a shell crater for cover.

Gill sputtered a furious denial.

"I ain't given nobody permission to leave the ship, Major. It's all I can do what with being in charge of them layouts on the deck, sir." Gill puffed up sufficiently to display that he had not been at fault in the matter.

"Well, get on back to your deck, Gill. You can deal with your medic later."

"Yes, sir."

"If he makes it back, Sergeant."

"Yes, sir, that's right. If he makes it back."

"Enough of that. We've got wounded coming on board. You've got fifteen minutes to sort them, move the surgicals up here, and start primary treatment for the casualties on deck. Then we push off. The conveyor belt is now ready for action."

Gill saluted and ran back to his station. Halliburton glanced once more at the beach. Then, with his formidable talents for planning and revenge, he turned to orchestrate his medical teams and so begin his war.

CHAPTER TWO

"D_{AMN!}"

For the third time Lieutenant Carter, Shorty, had put his head out the pillbox door to shout at the men outside and, for the third time, banged his helmet on the way back in. Shorty was at least six feet, four inches tall. "You guys are gonna get us killed if you don't keep a blanket over the door." Shorty was so tired that he didn't really direct the last sentence at anyone in particular, nor did anyone inside the pillbox pay any attention to him. He did notice that Captain Garth was still on the floor, curled up and reciting passages from a military handbook on field surgery.

"Debridement is to be achieved to prevent suppuration established by decomposition of tissue and hematoma in dead space, accomplished by destruction of bacterial flora by...." Garth's cadence sounded like a Latin mass.

"Shorty, make him shut up. Garth? Please? It's okay. You're gonna be just fine." It was Captain Collins who ordered them around from a makeshift operating table where he and Captain Murphy, the anesthetist, were hunched over a soldier, trying to splint a shattered leg by flashight, without a splint or pain killer.

Shorty figured that it had just about come full circle since the field hospital had made its way up from the beach and taken the pillbox over from the infantry platoon or squad or mob, whatever it was, in the late afternoon. It had begun hours before when he saw billowing smoke and the crumpled barrel of a German antiaircraft gun flop downward out of the slit window. Shorty had yelled to his field hospital section, huddled behind the sea wall. "Stay down here, I'm going up to the pillbox." No one had tried to follow him. "I'll signal for you as soon as it's cleared out."

14

When he got to the pillbox, the infantry was herding some dazed prisoners down out of the trench while dodging fire from above. One soldier was on his knees, praying over two dead Germans.

"You in charge?" Shorty had asked. "Nope." "You?" "Nope." "You?" The soldiers had ignored him, intent on not getting shot themselves. Two men who didn't appear to be anything more than a couple of privates seemed to be telling the others what to do, and the others seemed to be following their orders, but no one admitted to being in charge. When Shorty had asked where their lieutenant was one of them had snorted and jerked his thumb toward the blasted pill box door. Their platoon leader was inside, not dead, just huddled over on the floor, back against the cement wall, sitting in a tangle of shattered telephone wires and ammunition crates, ten or fifteen feet behind the loader of a wrecked anti-aircraft gun. It didn't take a doctor to see that the shaking lieutenant was scared to death and couldn't have led a box of kittens to a bowl of milk.

"He's kind of afraid, sir," a Private Rogers had said to Shorty.

"We caught it getting off the boat, Lieutenant," added another private whose name Shorty couldn't remember. "Lieutenant Campbell thought we was going to find the company there on the beach, but we never did." Once the lieutenant had gotten scared his squad had taken over, letting him tag along while they fought their way up the draw and took out the pillbox.

"You keep him, sir. He ain't okay. If you're putting your field hospital in, well, he's better off here with you." One of the men, a grizzled fellow without a single stripe or even a unit patch, basically had ordered Shorty to take Lieutenant Campbell off their hands. Before Shorty could sift through the idea of an infantry private ordering a medical corps lieutenant to take charge of his infantry lieutenant, the soldier was on to other work, ordering the rest of the men to reload and follow him up the draw. The man whose name he couldn't remember had gone inside the pillbox and plucked Lieutenant Campbell off the floor and led him out, telling him it would be all right and just to stay close to him, they were just going up the draw to find the rest of the company. Ten minutes after he arrived at the pillbox Shorty was the only one still there who was alive. Now, eight hours later, Captain Garth was sitting hunched over on the floor exactly where Lieutenant Campbell had been, and just as shaken, all from Shorty having agreed to let Garth go back down to the beach for supplies. *Which he didn't find*, he thought.

The unit clerk had draped a white flag with a red cross across the gun slit so that their own ships would stop firing on it, and they did. Unfortunately, the Germans on the bluff couldn't see the medical unit flag from their side and another hail of machine gun bullets clattered off the domed roof, then an artillery round hit the pillbox and shook the dune beneath it. The doctors jumped at the impact and jerked their patient around, causing him to scream at the top of his lungs.

"Listen, Shorty, this isn't working. We can't see what we're doing. Garth's less help than a dead man. Get the medics and tell them we're pulling out."

"Sorry, Captain. No can do. We're not pulling out."

The 261st already had that argument. The doctors, all captains, wanted to pull rank on Shorty, a lieutenant, to order him to shut down the field hospital and head back down to the beach.

"We're out of everything, even clean water. No generators for light. No clean surgery kits. Nothing to irrigate with. Not even any splints. Damned sure no morphine. We can't stay here."

Collins and Murphy had tried to put it up for a vote, too, but Shorty had said no, it wasn't a democracy, and the only reason they were captains was so they could order people to submit to medical treatment, not to order their unit commander to lead a retreat, even if he was just a lieutenant.

"We've been ordered to set up here and we're staying put. KEEP THE GODDAMNED DOOR COVERED!" Shorty shouted again. Garth chanted medical homilies. Collins and Murphy grumbled.

"Shorty, there is no way we can do this. Morph's trying to do my job and I'm trying to do Garth's job and we're going to snap this kid's leg off if we don't get a better look. Morph, just hold him still while I, hell, I don't know what I'm supposed to do—we don't have a splint."

"Hey, you! You're blocking the light."

Someone had stumbled across the debris in the darkened ex-gun pit.

"You need a splint?"

"Of course I need a splint. Hey, who said that?" It became quiet for a moment, the men waiting to see who had spoken.

Shorty made out that someone was wandering around in the dim light, stepping carefully over the wires and clutter between the doorway and the makeshift tabletop where Collins and Morph were working.

"You—go outside and wait with the wounded. Find a medic."

"I'm not wounded." The soldier waited a moment, then continued. "I'm supposed to find the field hospital. Is this the 261st?" He looked around in the dark and saw Garth sitting on the floor, mumbling about exteriorations. He then focused on Collins and Morph working on the patient. The boy's leg was bent and had lost most of its color, ragged folds of bleeding muscle dangling across the exposed bone. His boot had been cut free and was lying on the cement floor.

"So, do you want a splint?" the intruder asked.

"Do you see a box of splints around here? Jesus, we don't even have clean water, much less splints."

"I'll get you one." The soldier ducked outside, then returned a few moments later, using his fingers to push out a rivet to separate the legs of a bipod that was still attached to an automatic rifle. He wrenched them back and forth for a few seconds, then pulled them free and handed them to Collins.

Collins wasn't impressed.

"Great. Hey, Boy Scout—is this a splint? How about going back for some k-ration spam, call it morphine! And dirty socks, for bandages." Collins took the bipod legs in each hand and waved them around, then chucked them out the slit window.

"I was just trying to help, sir." The young man stiffened with the insult, then tried again. "If you want a real splint you need a Number 2 medical chest."

"Hey, you, whoever the hell you are—do you see a Number 2 medical chest? If we had a Number 2 medical chest, do you think we'd be watching you tear up a bipod? Shorty, get this guy out of here."

"Well, sorry, Captain. If you wanted a real splint I'd need to go get a Number 2 chest." Hastings could tell that talking with Collins wasn't getting anywhere; he turned to face Shorty. "They're all over the beach, sir. Well, not all over the beach, but there are some down there."

Hastings's apologia was enough to make Collins stop shouting and to make Shorty ask:

"Who are you? What are you doing here, anyway?"

"I'm from the LST. Well, I was from the LST but it pulled out and headed back to England. I'm supposed to check on the medical installations here and—"

"So what's this about you knowing where the medical dump is?" Shorty had maneuvered close enough to the flashlights to see the medical corps insignia on Hastings's collar; he was a bit surprised to see a doctor that young, and in combat dress.

"It's not exactly a dump, Lieutenant. It's more of a truck that got blown up. The Number 2s are scattered around it on the beach."

"Forget it. I sent a couple of men down there a couple of hours ago to bring back anything that had a red cross on it; nearly got my bone man and my translator killed." Shorty pointed to Garth, who was still on the floor, muttering. "Hey, Fouquet! Come here."

A medical technician came through the curtain and appeared at Shorty's side.

"Fouquet, where'd you look for the medical dump? How long ago was it you saw the Number 2s, Captain? Still daylight?" It was. "Yeah, forget it. They're gone by now."

"Probably not, sir. They were inside a minefield."

Carter paused to consider what the visitor was telling him: not only had he seen medical supplies, which an army doctor might be expected to notice, but he had seen them inside a minefield. None of the doctors Shorty knew could tell a minefield from a football field.

"Look, Captain, how'd you know they were in a minefield?"

"Because we went inside it. My medic, he and I opened one of the boxes and took out the bandages and splints and what-not to run them over to the aid station by the seawall. You do kind of need to watch your step."

"You walked into a minefield to dig out a bunch of first aid stuff? Are you crazy?"

Hastings nodded that, yes, he had, and added that he and Antsley had re-stocked their own field packs, too. Shorty wasn't sure he believed him but he was sure that if something didn't change Collins was going to continue making them all more miserable than the Germans were doing.

"Listen, Captain—What's your name? Listen. Can you just tell Fouquet where they were?" He spoke to Captain Hastings but he looked at Private Fouquet.

"Oh, no, not me, Shorty," Fouquet chimed in. "I went down there once and I'm not going back. You can court martial me, I don't care."

"I'll take you down there, Private. It's pretty easy." Hastings didn't seem to display any particular concern about the minefield or, for that matter, the gunfire up on the bluff.

"No, Captain, uh, what's your name? No, I don't want any more officers going down to the beach on a supply run. Can you just tell Fouquet where the Number 2s are?"

"Sure. They're one hundred and forty, maybe one hundred forty-five steps east and thirty to thirty-five steps south of the entrance to the draw, the gap in the sea wall. On a straight line between the 14th Evacuation Company tent and, I think, an LCI that was shelled there at the low tide line. It might have been an LCP. They look a lot alike, especially when they've been shelled."

Carter and Fouquet both blinked at the flood of precise information.

"It's a little tricky, though, what with the minefield. Let me show you what I mean." Hastings reached inside his field jacket and fished out a note pad and pencil. He paused for a moment, then began to sketch. He drew back and forth, methodically, studied his sketch, added some lines. Next he jotted some words onto the page, then ripped it out and handed it to Fouquet. "They're right beside the truck. There."

"Jesus, sir, this looks like, I don't know..." Fouquet was astonished; without another word he handed the drawing to Shorty. "Take a look at this."

"Christ, this looks like you traced it off a picture—how the Hell did you do this? I mean..."

The sketch could have been an artist's study of the battlefield below Les Moulins and St. Laurent, drawn as a landscape looking down toward the sea. Hastings had drawn the pillbox with a curvilinear shape and cross-hatched lines for texture. Next to it there was a nuanced rendering of the Les Moulins draw, a gap between the sand dunes that led from the hamlet of Les Moulins at the top of the bluff to the beach and sea wall at the base. The sea wall was drawn in three dimensions to separate it not only from the sand dunes and the shingle beach but also to identify where along its length, for a couple of hundred yards in either direction, there had been set up several aid stations, a clearing station, and an evacuation hospital. Instead of squares, he had correctly sketched the aid stations as canvas shelters, the clearing station as a cathedral tent, and the evacuation hospital inside a garrison tent, hidden behind an open-faced cavern between the sea wall and the sand dunes. Hastings had given each of them their militarily-correct unit designation.

Beyond the sea wall and the medical installations there was a layout of the beach as he had last seen it. Seven tanks were drawn exactly where they had been shelled and lost their tracks. Two wrecked jeeps, five trucks, and a bull dozer were placed at various spots between the sea wall and the water's edge. Among the other debris of war he had sketched four different piles of boxes, one adjacent to a vehicle.

"That's the one you want, Corporal. These others, the ones close to the 115th Aid Station, those aren't medical supplies. Mostly ammunition. I think there is one box of—I don't remember, but it isn't medical." He looked up to see them gaping at the details, both of the map and of his memory. "This is what you want, here." He pointed at a different group of boxes, placed inside a dotted line on the beach. "These are mines. That's what the truck ran into. Watch out for the engineers' tape to get you through; just go around and come up from the ocean side and follow the tape to the burned-out truck, then bring the boxes back out the same way. You know there aren't any mines there because the truck already blew them, but don't get off to one side or you might step on another one."

Carter and Fouquet waited a moment, each wondering whether Hastings was an army doctor or, more likely, an artistically inclined coward fleeing from battle in someone else's uniform.

"You want Antsley to go with you? He'll remember, I'm pretty sure."

"Who's Antsley?"

"He's my medic." Hastings had edged back to the doorway, then stuck his head through the blanket and yelled. "Off the landing ship. Hey, Antsley?" Antsley made his way in and stood next to Will. "Take this guy down to the beach for those Number 2s."

Shorty studied the two of them, wondering whether they really were medical corps or, just possibly, deserters. They sounded too much like country boys to be German spies, even the one with the captain's bars and the caduceus on his collar. And Shorty needed the Number 2s.

"Okay, Fouquet. Get a jeep, get going. But Captain—you're not going. Got it? Good. You two—get!" He waited long enough for Antsley and Fouquet to exit the pillbox. They could hear Fouquet complaining and Antsley replying that, yes, it was scary all right, but Doc hadn't gotten him killed, not yet. Then Shorty whirled to face Will. "I want to know what's going on, Captain. Tell me, how exactly did you find us?"

"It was easy. Well, no, I missed it a couple of times. This guy down at the evacuation hospital told me he thought the 261st was up and running at the top of the draw, so I came this way. But I was looking for a full field hospital and went by here a couple of times before coming in."

"What are you doing here?"

"Well, you're on my list. I'm supposed to check in with every medical unit on the beach. All those on Dog Red, anyway."

"Why?"

"Swap doc. If somebody's short a doctor I'm supposed to take his place." Hastings paused a moment, then steeled himself for disappointment. "You need a doctor?"

"Swap doc?"

"Yeah, swap doc."

"I've never heard of a swap doc. Is that a real job?"

"I don't know. I never heard of it either. I think the major just wanted to get rid of me."

Shorty again considered the two men who had stumbled into his unit. Anstley looked like he was fourteen years old. Hastings said he was a doctor but couldn't have been much older. *And that story about being like some kind of a refugee from a landing ship.* Anybody could have picked up a helmet with a red cross on it.

"You got any actual orders on you, Captain? I mean, you know..." Shorty didn't know why but he wanted to believe them. *And I'm short-handed; he can't make things any worse.*

The question made Hastings pause; it hadn't occurred to him until that moment that by following Halliburton's order he, and Antsley, were flitting around in a combat zone without any orders, even without a unit. He didn't know why, but he decided to trust Lieutenant Carter.

"No, not really. We're not AWOL, I mean, who would go AWOL to go into combat?" he asked. Someone exactly like me, he said to himself, but he didn't want to make an even bigger mess of it. He could tell, however, that Shorty had to have some kind of explanation. "I mean, Major Halliburton, he's medical admin on the landing ship, he just called us up to the bridge there on the LST and told us to get off the boat. That's the long and short of it." He stopped and waited, expecting Shorty Carter to tell him to go away. Shorty didn't.

"So, seems to me, Captain, like you're in a mess. What started all this, anyway?"

Will's powers of perception did not extend to subtleties of the abstract. Being in a mess covered a lot of his life.

21

"Well, it really started back when I was going out with this girl back home. Her father kind of ran the town and one time her brother caught us skinny dipping and so her father thought I was getting into the family jewels. So, he and Doc Pritchard..."

"No, Captain, I meant how did you get into this mess? Your major ordered you off your boat—it seems to me like sending a guy onto the beach and telling him to go here and there and everywhere, asking if he can trade places with somebody, well, it seems like it would have been hard to come up with a better way to get a man killed. You must have really pissed him off."

Will decided right then that Shorty Carter understood how people work. Even so, he only told Shorty the end.

"Well, yeah. The major caught one about six weeks ago, in London; there was a bombing. Anyway, I was there and so I stitched up his mouth and forehead, closed some cuts over his eyes. I guess the stitches don't look too good. He kind of liked the way he looked before, better."

"That thing you do with the drawings?"

"Yeah?"

"Not as good with stitches?"

"No. No, I'm not. I just do one stitch, really. The cross-stitch." The scars on Halliburton's forehead and mouth looked more like cheap shoe laces than sutures. "I haven't been out of medical school all that long—the Army got me before I could intern anywhere. I went through Belfast, of course, and the DMO sent me off for a couple of weeks to a country doctor in England until a class formed at Shrivenham." Dr. Atkinson's little practice had mostly been earaches and pregnant women, not combat wounds. Hastings didn't tell Shorty that. "Not much surgery, that's for sure."

"I CAN NOT DO THIS!" Collins exploded from across the pillbox. "THERE IS NO LIGHT. THERE IS NOTHING STERILE...NOTHING! HOW THE HELL CAN I OPERATE WITHOUT IRRIGATING?"

Collins and Morph had wrapped the boy's leg and put him aside to start on a nineteeen-year-old whose stomach was hanging out in bits. Even Garth had gotten up from the floor and edged over to the makeshift table. The men were working with the last sterile kit they had, digging out bits of shrapnel by flashlight, mopping up blood and tissue faster than they could close it. Collins was furious.

"SHORTY—THIS IS NUTS. WE'RE GOING TO DO MORE DAMAGE—"

"You guys need a truck," Will volunteered. It set off Collins like a rocket.

"NO SHIT. Hey, Shorty, where'd this know-it-all come from?" Collins ripped off his mask, backed away from the patient, and handed his forceps to Hastings. "Here, Whiz Kid! You're so damned smart, you do it." Collins lit a cigarette, then blew smoke in Will's face and stalked out of the pillbox.

"Sorry, Lieutenant. Didn't mean to make him mad." Hastings had never been surprised when people treated him badly; he was not surprised now. But, as far as he could tell, the 261st was his last chance to stay off the LST. "I was just saying you needed a truck."

"Hey, Shorty, this guy's going bad," Morph said in a hushed voice. "I can't keep him going." The pillbox was small enough that everyone could see the soldier's color was draining away; he seemed not to be breathing at all. They felt helpless.

"A truck. Right. Good luck with that—we're just a section hospital."

"Well, someone left a truck up at Les Moulins. Well, not there, exactly, but about a hundred meters farther on toward St. Laurent." Hastings said it as clearly as he could, and everyone listened. "No idea what happened to the crew. Sure isn't a field hospital up there."

"A truck? A hospital truck? How the hell do you know that?"

The men stopped what they were doing. Garth, Morph, even the medics who had been clearing up after the last casualty, all waited to hear him out.

Will didn't say anything, not with words, but instead headed for the door, turning around only to show Shorty something that he had fished out of his field pack. Then he disappeared into the dark.

"What the hell was that?" Shorty asked, to no one in particular.

"It looked like a distributor cap, sir."

"A what?" Shorty had heard correctly but didn't believe it any more when he heard it than when he had seen it in Will's hands. "What's he doing with a distributor cap? I've got three doctors who are out of everything and then this guy shows up with a sketch pad and a distributor cap?"

For neither the first nor the last time in Shorty's war he wondered whether there was any chance of the 261st going on. He was almost ready to agree with Collins and give up the pillbox when, as if in answer, Fouquet and Antsley made it back.

The jeep slid to a halt in the sand, four Number 2 medical chests perched in the back. Fouquet was shaking; Antsley was not.

"Jesus, Shorty. These guys are nuts," he growled. "You ever try to walk around a minefield in the dark? With guns going off? I quit."

"We found 'em, didn't we?" Antsley said, helpfully. "We got 'em up here, didn't we? Help me with this box. Where's Captain Hastings?"

Shorty didn't answer, did not put Fouquet under court martial arrest, and did not question why God had decided to resupply the 261st field surgery. Instead, he helped the privates carry the wooden crates into the pillbox and began to pry off the lids.

"Listen up, docs—surgery's open for business," Carter called out. "Here we go. Plasma? Who needs plasma?" Captain Collins stormed back inside and commandeered the bottles. "Okay, we've got splints. *Splints, assorted, collapsible, three.* You ready to go back to work? Captain Murphy, we've got your dope." He held a container pack of morphine sulfate up above his head. "Iodine. Iodine. Field surgery packs. Typing paper. TYPING PAPER? What are they thinking? Jesus H Christ." Carter dropped the paper where he stood. Each of the four boxes was marked: Number 2 Medical/Field. In one of the boxes there was a typewriter and hundreds of medical report forms.

For fifteen minutes the 261st was, if not a field hospital, at least an emergency room. Collins and Morph pumped enough plasma into the dying soldier to keep him alive. Garth settled down to dig metal out of a leg, then splinted it. Antsley quietly eased out to the front of the pillbox to help triage, which he was doing when a Dodge truck chugged and lurched its way down the ragged draw between the sand dunes and huffed to a halt outside the pillbox.

"Hey, Antsley, go tell those guys they've got a truck," Hastings yelled from the cab.

The truck part of it wasn't much of a truck. There were bullet holes in the hood and windshield. One of the rear tires was flat. But the field hospital part of the truck was intact and Hastings had no difficulty in pulling out the resuscitator and suction equipment and hauling them in through the open pillbox door. He lugged them to the working doctors and turned them over to a startled Captain Murphy.

"Where you want your light, sir?" Even Collins was speechless, but Will ignored him, spun around, then returned moments later dragging a generator light stand into the pillbox and flooding them with enough light to do surgery. "So, you've got light, pentothal anesthesia portables, and clean tools, Captain Murphy." He turned to face Collins: "And you, sir? These are for you. Anything else you want to bitch about?" He held out to Collins a green Army sock with something weighted down inside. Collins, to his credit, shook his head, then returned to his gut-shot patient.

It was Shorty who broke the silence.

"Okay, who exactly are you? Stop messing with me. And where'd you get the truck?"

"It was up at Les Moulins. Well, not there, exactly, but about a hundred meters toward St. Laurent."

"You're nuts—you know that?"

"I was already up there twice. Like I said, when I was looking for you, I was looking for a full field hospital, so Antsley and I went up on the bluff as far as St. Laurent." He waited for Shorty to say something but Shorty seemed overwhelmed. "It's not too bad up there—you just have to keep an eye on where you're going." That was all Will had to say about having walked into the most forward combat zone, where he and Antsley had bandaged soldiers in a shattered town square until their supplies ran out. Somehow, inexplicably, they had not been shot themselves. "Anyway, like I said, I knew the truck was up there. Don't really know what happened to the crew."

"So you saw their truck and took the distributor cap off?"

Hastings nodded, yes.

"Jesus, Captain. What the hell are you doing in the medical corps? You should be in the fucking magic corps. Is there anything you can't do?"

"Well, yes. I'm just in the medical corps because—"

"So what's the sock for?"

Will still held it in his hand. He reached down inside the sock and dug out one of the bipod legs that Collins had thrown out the window. He also fished out a green ration can.

"He," Hastings said, pointing at Collins, "asked for some spam and a sock, and here they are. I think that the gelatin in this can of spam is going to ease his pain and he can use the sock for a bandage, just like he said. And he's going to need 'em to clean up the cuts he's going to have after I stick this bipod up his ass, which I'm going to do as soon as he's through working on that soldier."

The pillbox went quiet. Everyone stopped. Hastings had made his way right up to the table where Collins was standing and, by getting up on his toes, stared right into Collins's face, three inches higher and ten years older than his own. Shorty made a grab for Hastings to take him down but Collins reacted first—he burst out in laughter.

"You're okay, Whiz Kid. Hey, Shorty? Whiz Kid here's supposed to be a doc. So put him to work, for crying out loud." And with that, Collins went back to sewing his patient up.

Shorty Carter turned back to the whiz kid: "Well, Captain—you say you're a swap doc. Are you a surgeon?"

"No. Like I said, I'm just barely a doctor. You want me to help out?"

"Well, yeah, sure, as long as you don't beat anybody up. We're already short-handed. Got it?" He paused, then went on. "I'm putting you down as a surgeon. Got it?"

"Yeah. Sure."

"What's your name?"

"Hastings. Will, really. Will Hastings."

"Well, Will Really Hastings, I'm Shorty. If we ever get a radio working I'll send a twix to division and tell them that you've signed on here for the time being. Captain Garth, put him to work."

"He's your bone guy?" Will asked.

"Yeah. Garth, Captain Hastings has volunteered for you to teach him about bones and stuff." Shorty pushed them to the same corner of the pillbox. Garth nodded; Will let his breath out.

"Thanks, Lieutenant." Will peeled off his field jacket and went to work.

"I'm Garth." Garth nodded, and then turned away, picking up a splint and reciting, maybe to Will, maybe to himself, "Fractures of the femur are to be evacuated from field units to the forward hospitals in the Army with half-ring splints using the litter bar, ankle strap, and five triangular bandages."

"I'm Will." He moved toward the patient's boots and looked at Garth for direction.

He stayed for four more days.

It was not until June 10 when the message came that Captain Hastings was to return to the landing ships that he had time to think about what Antsley had whispered to him, that he had seen someone that first night on the beach.

"Hey, Captain," Antsley had said. "Hey, Captain. I saw Douglas. He's up there with the infantry. I saw him bring a wounded guy down here, then he took off."

Will had told Antsley it couldn't have been Douglas—Douglas was dead.

26

Antsley had said it had to be Douglas but Will had repeated himself. "No. You're tired. All these soldiers look the same in the dark." And to forget about it, after all, Douglas was dead.

Will had almost forgotten about it himself until they trudged back to the landing ship. Then, when he saw Halliburton up on the bridge deck, he remembered what Antsley had told him and wondered whether it might be true.

CHAPTER THREE

A wooden plate, hung by a string to the doorknob, read: 29th Inf. Div. Med. Ofc. Bureau Personnel. A smaller scrap of paper tacked to it said the duty officer was Lt. Col. Nagel. They knocked and, from the other side, were told by a cheery voice to enter.

"Well, doctors. Have a seat. Blackwell, Hastings. You're from 556?"

"Yes, sir."

"Have a good journey?"

"My first time off the boat, sir. Captain Hastings was on the beach most of the time."

"You men been drinking?"

They lied and said they had not.

"Too bad. You could probably use a drink. You both look pretty banged up. Well, let me get your files. Oh, yeah. You're the men who Major Halliburton... Oh, well, let me say, your reputations do precede you, yes indeed. Okay, I'm Lieutenant Colonel Nagel. I'm in charge of reassignments. Give me a sec here." He bent over the folder, studied it, occasionally looking up at the two doctors, then bending down to study again. He finally closed the folder and sat upright in his chair, hands together in a steeple.

"Well, this is something. As best I can tell, you, Blackwell, were assigned as bow ramp triage for five crossings to the combat zone and handled six hundred thirty-five casualties evacuated from the beach, ranging from Class 1 to Class 6 casualties. Fragments out, wounds stitched down, burns debrided. That's a long week. Stand by." He put Blackwell's file down, picked up Will's file, and began to read. "Oh, this is very good. In the meantime, you, Hastings, made one crossing, managed one patient, and were AWOL for four days." He paused. "And pilfered medical supplies off the boat.

28

"Sir, we can explain—"

"This is rich. Listen to this." Nagel stopped to read something. "Captain Blackwell—under 'Admin Obs' Major Halliburton wrote that you 'exceeded time,' 'did not follow Manual of Therapy,'—actually, it looks like he didn't know how to code that one for the first day or two, then wrote 'dnfManTh' for the rest of the week. We have a couple of 'doubtful exteriorations,' which I assume means you triaged someone and left their bowels hanging outside instead of packing them back inside, and then triaged a couple of others by 'should have exteriorated,' which I gather means you left someone's intestines on the inside rather than leave them out. Or does it mean you triaged them but didn't tell the next guy down the line what to do?"

"I was just triage, sir. Major Halliburton didn't always like my triage. I didn't operate on anybody or God only knows what he would have written."

"Now, as for you, Captain Hastings? Let me see—one, two, ah, I have it—one each day that you were on the ship, that's it. Listen to this: 'Suspect medical officer is diverting military equipment to personal use.' He then notes that everything from clamps to scalpels to a box of 3-0 silk sutures were missing. That's a new one. Anyway, it looks like for the entire twelve or so hours that you were on the LST and not AWOL, Major Halliburton wrote you up twenty-four times. These are amazing. 'Officer delayed in following orders to depart vessel as designated exchange medical detachment.' What the hell is that, Captain, a 'designated exchange medical detachment?'" Nagel didn't wait for an answer. "And then, 'Officer did not exchange with designated shore medical officer.' Then, 'Officer did not appear timely at'—and he has down what appears to be a list of every collecting station, aid station, clearing hospital, and field hospital on Omaha Beach. That's good—you were late to all of them. Then, today, 'Officer elicited medical personnel to abandon post.'" He looked up at Will and asked: "Who did you try to get to jump off the boat today? For Christ's sake, why would someone want to jump ship on the way back to England? Hell, you'd think a guy would jump off on the way out, not on the way in? All while stealing surgical tools from inside closed operating rooms on a closed war ship in combat in the middle of the English Channel, one which, I might add, you weren't physically on, since you were on the beach in France but not at any medical facility in the entire 29th Division zone. Wow!"

"Sir, I don't think it's fair to blame Captain Blackwell for any of this."

"Blame him? No one's blaming him for anything. Well, maybe he wasn't as creative with Blackwell as he was with you but I daresay I've never seen a write up like yours, Hastings. It'll go into some kind of book somewhere. Damn, your name rings a bell."

"Sir?" Blackwell intervened. "Sir? The major made up that stuff about the designated exchange doctor or whatever you call it. There's no such job. Captain Hastings was ordered to go out onto the beach to see if anybody needed replacing. He got stranded when the landing ship pulled out and wound up doing surgery on the beach for five days."

"We know that." Nagel seemed slighted, as if Blackwell was giving away the punch line before he had told the whole joke. "We do get reports here; he was at a field surgery in St. Laurent most of the time. Don't you think those guys have clerks and radios? Jesus, what kind of army do you think we're running? So, what did you guys do to Halliburton? Or what did he do to you?"

As his last act as their commander on the LST Halliburton had charged the entire triage crew, every officer and man, with dereliction of duty, demoting the enlisted men to private and threatening the officers with court martials. Will and Blackwell had watched the enlisted men file out of his stateroom, white as ghosts, before Halliburton had ordered them inside.

"Hastings, Blackwell, close the door." They had. "You're being reassigned." It was hard for Halliburton to contain his glee. For their part, the doctors breathed easier, a sign not lost on Halliburton. He glared at them.

"Where to, Major?"

"I don't know Blackwell, and frankly I don't care, but I wouldn't be too gleeful if I was you—I'm referring you to the judge advocate general for review. Whatever happens to you, I hope it results in making you less likely to further injure the men than what you showed me over the last five days. You two get your gear and get off my boat. Report to the Division Bureau of Personnel. It's somewhere on the docks. Dismissed."

Blackwell had left the cramped stateroom and shut the door behind him but Will had remained inside.

"I said dismissed, Hastings. Get out."

"One moment, David. You've got no gripe with Blackwell; he was stuck next to me on my two crossings. And as for Antsley, you ordered me to take him..."

"Listen to this, Hastings, and listen well. Antsley has you to thank for his predicament. He should thank me that I'm not sending him up for desertion. But you? You're a detriment to the medical corps. I watched you trying to do wound care on the return today and I'll tell you this—you're worse than no doctor. And you've gotten Blackwell in over his head. I've spent half of my time in the Army getting rid of you and now I'm done. Get out!"

They gave Colonel Nagel an abbreviated version of Halliburton's dismissal. He seemed dissatisfied.

"Hoped there was a better story in there." He paused to see if they would tell him more; they didn't. "All right, here's what we need to do."

He put the papers down on his desk and looked at the two doctors sitting across from him, again made a steeple with his fingers, and began.

"The order came down that any of you men who served on the LSTs would get first dibs on medical jobs in the Zone of the Interior. That means here, in England. I'll have a list up tomorrow of what's available. You can have any posting that you're qualified for, or might be. Nothing much good left, though, I'm afraid. Anyway, if you see something you want, just tell me and I should be able to get you assigned there. Actually, I did get an opening in Yorkshire this morning, little hospital for some commandos in training. Anyway, just tell me where you want to go and I'll see what I can do."

"Sir?"

They seemed dazed.

"I'll see what I can find for you. You've got three days before I send you off. Here's a couple of chits. Go find the BOQ's; they're a couple of houses on the edge of town. Run up to London if you want but it'll be tight getting on a train and you don't want to be AWOL coming back this time or I can't help you. Anyway, clean up, get some sleep, find someone to do your uniforms. And unless you're teetotalers, for crying out loud, go find a pub. You can come back tomorrow if you want but I don't think the assignments will be much to choose from. All the units expected shortages after the landings so the doctors in reserve for them were still here and they beat you to the punch. Nor do I expect it to be any better tomorrow or the next day. Anyway, I'll do up your orders on Thursday and you'll be off to someplace new by that afternoon."

"Sir? Is there some kind of mistake? What about—?"

"What about what?"

31

"About the judge advocate general? About Major Halliburton's write-ups? Aren't we...?"

"Aren't you what? In trouble? Oh, God no. We thought the write-ups were hilarious. The men loved 'em. I showed 'em to Colonel Seacum and thought he was going to bust a gut. Not too much to laugh about these days. Major Halliburton's very good at what he does, keeping his conveyor belt flowing and all, but outside of that, let me just say he's got a reputation at the Division Medical Office. His LST had the biggest patient load, his casualties got loaded faster, unloaded faster. Halliburton knows the rules and he gets things done. I think when I get all the numbers together we're going to see that you boys on 556 did more kinds of emergency surgery than anybody in the whole shebang, and that includes that hospital ship they tried out there for a few days. But between us, Halliburton's a bit crazy. Writing you up for triaging men with their guts hanging out, stealing needles and threads. Not to mention the 'peter cases.' What the hell was that all about? Never mind. Anyway, we all had a good laugh."

Colonel Nagel took the write-ups out of their files and tore them up, then handed them to Will and Blackwell to throw in the trash can for themselves.

"That's it?" Blackwell asked.

"Yep, that's it. Where is Major Halliburton, anyway? He's known for a couple of days that the division wasn't going to use you docs on the LSTs after today. We've got some real field surgeries over there now, all up and running across the whole front. And an airstrip—they started flying the worst cases out of France this morning. I figured he'd be over here by now demanding his rights to some cushy job in London."

That son of a bitch—telling us he was firing us when he already knew our temporary duty was over. What a jerk. Will thought about Antsley and Cheadle and all the others Halliburton had delighted in demoting as his last act as their commander.

"He was standing alone in the middle of the tank deck," Will said, "under a sling of wooden crates marked 'High Explosive,' sir. Suspended five feet above his head." Halliburton had stood on the LST, ordering the Navy to stop loading while he methodically ordered each patient to be reassessed to determine in what order he would be taken off.

"He's the Navy's problem now, or at least he is until the last casualty is off the boat. He'll show up here soon enough. Take these." He handed them some temporary housing vouchers. "You got any money? Doubt if you spent much on the boat."

They didn't need any.

"Alright. Dismissed, see you Thursday. Good work, men."

They saluted, turned, and left. Fifty feet down the bleak hallway they broke into a laugh.

"That was too good to be true. Come on; I'm buying you another beer."

They had their hands on the handle of the door leading back out to the dock when Lt. Colonel Nagel reappeared.

"Captain Hastings? May I see you for a moment? Forgot something."

"I'll wait out here, Will."

"Come with me, Captain. Sorry I forgot while you were in the office. I'm afraid I have some news for you. Some bad news. It's about your brother."

Peter Hastings had been assigned to a glider squadron at Aldermaston. Will walked across the hangar floor and spotted a mechanic who promptly ducked his head down to stare at a parts tag on the counter top. The mechanic waited until Will was ten steps away, then pulled a pencil from behind his ear and made a mark on the parts tag before deliberately turning away to look at the wall behind him. Will waited until the clerk turned back to the counter and made another mark on the parts tag.

"Excuse me. I'm looking for the Fourth Readiness Support Squadron."

"You found it, sir. Be wit' you in a minute." The clerk made another jab at the paper tag, then turned away again and began to wander back and forth between the counter-top and the wooden cubbyholes that lined the wall separating the parts counter and the maintenance floor at the rear of the hangar. He pulled a ladder to the cubbyholes and started to climb.

"Excuse me, Private. I'm looking for the Fourth Readiness Support Squadron..."

"Be right wit' you, sir."

"Major Hampton. He sent for me."

The clerk stopped.

"We ain't got no Major Hampton, sir. Nobody here by that name."

"I'm Captain Hastings. Major Hampton sent me this note. It's about..."

The clerk scrambled down the ladder. Will handed him the note.

"You're Captain Hastings?"

"Yes. Yes I am. I'm looking for Major Hampton. It's about my brother's things. He is, he was, Lieutenant Hastings. He was assigned here."

The clerk stopped, then looked carefully around the parts room to see if they were out of the range of others.

"Can you come wit' me, please?"

He opened a gated barrier for Will to pass behind the desk. Through a window Will saw into a vast hangar where men in military fatigues and soft caps performed indistinct repairs on distinctly damaged airplanes. Wings stood on end from the floor. Motors were affixed to stands. Chain hoists suspended propellers above engine nacelles. Will saw it all, but took in very little of it. The clerk led him to a solid metal door, knocked on it, opened it, and asked Will to wait while he left, "to find somebody what might help."

A few minutes passed by before a second airman knocked on the door, entered, looked at Will, and almost passed out.

"Jesus, sir. I thought there for a minute...." He stopped to catch his breath, then started in. "See, sir, it's like this. It's... well, I come in here and you looked like the lieutenant. I mean, you guys could be twins."

Even though Peter was almost two years older than Will, both were slender and almost six feet tall, with jaw lines that were smooth and led toward strong cheek bones that when they were younger, caused each of them to be called "Chipmunk." Sandy blond hair hung down below the brim of Will's garrison cap, drooping over a high and straight forehead which itself led to firm, clear eyes. Will liked it when someone told him that he looked like his brother. He loved Peter and had wished more than once that he had been able to learn to fly.

"Sir, I've got your brother's things. I put them in a foot locker, if you'd like to see them."

"I'd like to see Major Hampton first, if I could. I got a letter from him, a twix, which said he could tell."

The clerk listened, patiently, until Will ran out of words. He went to the door, opened it, looked out, came back in, and closed it again.

"Sir, there is no Major Hampton."

"Is this a joke, Private? I can tell you I..."

"No, sir, it's not a joke. I didn't say that right. Listen—I'm Major Hampton. Well, I'm not, you can see that, but I was the one who, well—I sent the twix to you, sir. Lt. Hastings asked me to."

"What do you mean Lt. Hastings asked you to?"

"I'm sorry, sir. Pete, that is your brother, the lieutenant, he gave me his letter. He told me to get it to you. His letter, sir." He paused to see if Will understood. "Pilots write out a letter so if they don't, well, you know, sir. Anyway, he gave me his letter to get to you. In case he didn't come back. Which he didn't."

"Why did you say you were Major Hampton?"

"It's a clerk's code, sir." The clerk spoke in a hushed voice. "All the clerks know it. If we twix a signal and sign it 'Major Hampton,' that means it's a big deal, sir. The clerk who gets it knows what to do. I figured Douglas would get the twix and get it to you."

"Douglas?"

"Yes, sir. Isn't that his name? I set it up a couple of months ago. For you and your brother to meet up in London. Wasn't your medical clerk a guy named Douglas? Douglas knows Major Hampton."

"I'm afraid Douglas is gone, too." It hurt Will almost as much to think of Douglas as to think of Peter; Douglas had been with Halliburton near the Picadilly tube entrance when the bomb exploded.

"Sorry, sir. I just figured, well, it seemed like Douglas was your buddy. Lt. Hastings, that is your brother, sir, well, he was my buddy. He was a really good guy, sir, knew I'd do anything for him. He was real clear about it when he asked me to hold his letter. I told him it would be an honor. He was real straight with me about it. Give this to my brother and put it in his hands. And I promised I would."

They left the airless supply room and Will followed him across the tarmac to a storage building.

"We keep all the air crew stuff in here, sir. In case they make it back. We had a guy in last week who'd been gone six months. Got out through Spain." The clerk immediately regretted having said it.

"If you have crews that go down and then make it back, how do you know for sure that Peter? You know, that he....?"

There were photographs. Reconnaissance aircraft had circled the landing zones over and over in the last week. Peter's glider had missed the landing zone and smashed into a hedgerow. The antitank gun inside his glider had come loose and killed everyone aboard. Will tried to sort out exactly when it had happened; it seemed that Peter crashed at about the time that

Will had been helping Blackwell get over seasickness on the tank deck before the LST got to France.

"Would you like to open his chest, sir? Happy to do it."

Will thought about it. Peter's chest would have his dress uniform and shoes, his military medical file and orders, and not much else. *If I understand it, he would have worn his flight suit and a set of combat boots on the plane. He probably didn't have anything else. If I open it and there's a letter or two, picture of some girl I don't know, I'll never get it out of my head.* Will had seen it happen before. Some of the men got a Dear John letter or some bad news, obsessed about it, and couldn't shake it. A girl back home, a parent who died, a brother missing, a guy would reread the letters and stare at the pictures and then unravel. Will didn't want to unravel.

"No, thanks a lot, no. I'll wait to open it when I get home."

"You want Major Hampton to send it home for you, sir? I think he can get it on a boat. Just tell me where."

Where. The Army was always asking him to write down his hometown. On his personnel file. His medical file. His dog tags. His Serviceman's Life Insurance. Hometown paper. Hometown church. Always some Army form with a space for 'Hometown.' It was like a trick question. He wondered what town Peter had written down. *I never knew how to find him or when he'd turn up, not until we got drafted. If they hadn't sent me to live in Tierra, Peter never would have known where to find me.* 'They' was the Texas orphan agency. *The truth is, I probably would have quit going back to Tierra myself if it hadn't been for Doc. Doc and Poppy. They kept saying Virginia was going to come around.*

That is what they had told Will, the first time she had quit Will, in college. *She'll come around, Will. Just go on and finish school. You two are too young now anyway.* Poppy and Doc repeated themselves the second time, and the third, and all the other times she had quit him. Virginia hadn't written Will since February. But there wasn't anyone else he would trust with Peter's things, especially Poppy Sullivan or Doc Pritchard. He would send the box to Virginia.

"Let me write this out for you," Will said. "We really didn't have a home town, you see. But this is where I went to school and that's where we last saw each other. So I'm going to ship it to myself, but in care of someone there. She'll keep it for me until I can go get it."

Will wrote out his name in care of Virginia, to be delivered at the Tierra train depot.

"And thanks, thanks a lot. I can see why you were Peter's buddy. When he took a liking to someone, they took a liking to him. He was right to count on you, and I appreciate it."

There was a more or less direct train from Aldermaston back to South-ampton, with only one change. Troops jammed the cars and every platform was crowded. Women and children were taken off trains to give places to soldiers. Cars sat on sidings. Bren guns poked over sand bags at every crossing and station. Somewhere between Aldermaston and Guildford Will opened the brown envelope the clerk had given him. There were two things inside. The first was Peter's letter.

Dear Will,
   I've been thinking about that tree outside the Fort Worth Masonic Home where we'd go hide when they were trying to find us. That and how we used to slip out the dorm window to go swimming in the Trinity down by the fairgrounds. Those were good times. I'd give anything if the orphanage hadn't sent you off to Tierra. I never had any idea it would mess up our lives so much, but I guess by now you know that. I wish we had hooked up in London. There was so much to talk about but if you're reading this, it won't matter. Anyway, this stuff happens and no matter how upset you are, you're my brother and I love you and I'm gonna wait for you back at that tree, you hear? Listen, this is for you—always think about where you are, where you're going, and how to get there. Right now, I want you to live through this war and go ...

At that point the letter was smudged. Peter had written something, erased it, and written over it.

...back to Tierra. And take care of Virginia. She'll need you. That's what I want.

                   Your loving brother, Peter

The second thing in the envelope was a map, a pilot's silk escape map of France. The cloth was almost two feet square and showed the coast of

Normandy. Roads to Cherbourg, St. Lô, St. Malo, were connected by thick red lines. Rivers, the Vire and others, were in drawn in blue. It was clean and new and appeared to have never been opened.

And then he saw it. A small mark, no more than a single pinpoint, a dot on the road between Bayeux and Valognes, between Cherbourg and St. Lô. Carentan. That was all the map disclosed, the single word. Carentan. *A map–showing me where to go. How to get there.*

He folded the map and Peter's letter and put them back in the envelope. They and the photograph of Peter standing by Virginia on her porch, the picture Shirley had mailed to him, they were all that he had to prove that there ever had been a Hastings family.

What was in the box? he thought. *I should have opened it.*

Will thought about what was in his own barracks bag, what Peter would have found if it had been Will who was killed. A couple of sets of uniforms. Faded orders. The transportation voucher that had got him on the ferryboat from Belfast to Stranraer and then onto the train to Shrivenham. *That was hilarious, waking up with a hangover to find myself handcuffed to Bell, or Douglas, whatever his name was.* His field surgeon's kit. The stethoscope Doc and Poppy had given him when he graduated from medical school. Three old letters from Virginia. A faded postcard that Johnny and Hoyt had sent from Hawaii. A Hemingway novel he had stolen from the book box at the USO club in Swindon. *Was that the same day Halliburton went after that girl?* The twix Douglas had given him to meet Peter at the Rainbow Club in Picadilly. The photograph. None of it was worth anything to anyone but him. None of it proved that he belonged anywhere or to anybody.

What would Peter have that's any different than mine? Uniforms, personal things. Gillette razor blades. Brylcream. Ipana toothpaste. Pilot things. Some letters. Would they be Dear John letters or letters from some girl he left waiting?

Will swallowed hard, admitting that he wanted to be exactly like Peter but knowing that he was not. There would not be any Dear John letters in Peter's foot locker. Peter charmed everyone. He could laugh, dance, tell a joke. He was dashing. He could fly a plane, read a map.

The troops ignored the only Yank on the train. The enlisted men, the other ranks, clustered in threes and fives and tens, singing *Hitler has only got one ball, Goering has two but both are very small....* They were as drunk as their sergeants let them get before entraining for the last piece of England many of them would ever see. Their officers sat in twos and threes, whispering through youthful mustaches stories of missing sub-lieutenants with whom they had gone to public schools and of girls who had told them they would wait but who probably would not.

Will remembered for the rest of his life that he had never been as alone as he was that night, in the crowded train. Hoyt and Johnny had died at Bataan. Virginia was dead for him too, or at least her love was, if she ever had loved him anyway. The only two letters he had gotten since February had been surprises; one from Shirley Fleming, now this one, from Peter. He took out a tablet and pencil and began the letter to Virginia. When after six hours the train braked to a stop he had finished.

> *14 June, Portsmouth: Virginia, Peter is dead. A major in the 8th AF confirmed it to me as Peter's next of kin. He crashed somewhere around Carentan. I don't know more than that.*
>
> *I don't know what will happen to me next but Virginia, I've had to make a decision. Peter is gone and I'm alone. That's the plain truth. I love you with all my heart but I know you don't feel the same about me—you haven't written in months. The only one who told me you were waiting for me was the voice in my head and now the voice finally told me to grow up and quit thinking you were waiting. You never really said you would and seven years is enough. I'm going to stop looking out the bus window to see if you're there. I've got to do something useful with myself. I love you, and that's why I'm not asking you to wait anymore. You're free.*
>
> *– Will*

He read the letter a final time, then tore it out of his tablet and signed it.

It was done.

"Good Morning, Colonel."

"Captain Hastings, good morning." Lieutenant Colonel Nagel looked up from his desk, stood, and offered his hand. Will took it. "I didn't really expect you back this morning. Anything I can do for you? Would a couple more days help? I can put you on sick leave if you like."

"No sir, thanks. I'm not going to get any better sitting around."

"Need anything taken care of?"

"No, sir. Major Hampton was pretty decent. He said he'd get everything taken care of. I think I should go back to duty. Is that possible?"

"It is, although, like I said, I'm afraid there isn't much I can offer. Have you looked at the postings?"

"No, sir. Well, yes, I looked on the wall, but they were all pretty much the same to me. I don't know anything about any of the unit numbers or places."

"There might be one thing. I have an opening for a back-up surgeon at an exhaustion center at Castlemans. That's pretty near to Shrivenham, if you liked that part of England. I'm afraid it won't be a very challenging job."

"Well, actually, sir, I'd like to go back over. To a field hospital."

Nagel thought Will was kidding, and said so.

"No, Colonel. I don't have any reason to stay away from the front. I'm not married, no family. Better me than somebody else. And after the beach, well, it'll be all right. What I've been thinking about is there were these guys up on the beach at this field surgery. They were always one guy short, always ten more casualties than there were docs to take care of them. Anyway, it seems to me like I should be in a place like that. What I didn't learn by the time I finished the Army course in Shrivenham, well, the 261st taught me there on the beach. Army surgery is pretty much cut open, probe, stop bleeding, take out bullets, sew up holes, take out sponges, sew up—"

"And leave it for the general hospital to come in behind and clean up after you." Nagel thought he was joking but quickly realized that it must have sounded pretty rotten, coming from someone who had spent the invasion behind a desk. "Sorry, Hastings. Just kidding. You're serious about this, aren't you?"

"Yes, sir."

"Anywhere special?"

"I was with the 261st on the beach, good group of men, they could use some help. But my brother's plane went down somewhere near Carentan, so any unit around there would be all right too. If you can do it."

Nagel knew what he could do and what he could not: no matter how honorable the motives, Carentan was the one place he would not send Will. Nagel also knew what Will did not; the deal to give the LST doctors a pass to stay in England had been a mistake—the Army needed doctors everywhere because doctors were getting killed as fast as the rest of the troops. A dozen medical officers had died on the landing beaches or within a few miles inland. More than fifty were unaccounted for from the parachute and glider landings. Even the LSTs had been in danger; a number of them, without medical teams, had been sunk.

"Let me see what I can find, Captain. Come back tomorrow morning. You can change your mind, if I've got anything left for you to change to."

"Sir? One of the medics off the boat—I guess it's not my place to volunteer them, but if they—"

"Let me see what I can do. I'll see you tomorrow at 0800, Will."

"Oh, sir? One last thing. Would you put this in the mail for me? I'd sure appreciate it."

"I'm going to find him." Will sat on the bunk and unfolded the silk map.

Blackwell sat across from him, elbows on knees, a bottle of Four Roses and two glasses on the footlocker.

"You're going to find him?" Blackwell said, doubtfully.

"I don't think he's dead. They said there were pictures, but they were recon pictures. There weren't any soldiers, inside the plane or out. Just the front of his glider smashed open."

"Listen, Will. If, and I'm just saying if; if an antiaircraft gun went through the cockpit—"

"They didn't have his dog tags. I'm just saying, that's all. I've got this feeling, I don't know how to explain it, but it's like I know he's still alive. I used to get it when he'd show up at the orphanage. I got it when he showed up in Tierra at Thanksgiving. I just—feel him—that's all."

Blackwell knew. He'd seen it, just like Will had. A letter from home. Girl ran off with some other guy. Death in the family. Cousin went down in the Pacific. What Will felt wasn't Peter's extrasensory connection, it was grief. The reaction to grief was to unravel and Will was unraveling.

"If he is, well, you know, then I want to see his final resting place. That's all. Will you help me?"

"Help you?"

"You know, get to France, to Carentan. Find the plane. Just to make sure."

"Sure I will. Sure. Here." Blackwell measured out two more glasses, then screwed the lid down on the bottle. "So, what did Nagel say when you turned that job down?"

"He said I was crazy. Maybe so, but who wants to be a backup surgeon an an exhaustion hospital, somewhere in England?"

"Yeah," Blackwell answered. He lay back on the bunk, tilted his head and sipped. "Yeah. Who would want that?"

By four-thirty Thursday afternoon Will was formally posted to the 261st Medical Battalion of the 29th Infantry Division. The division was still scattered all across Normandy but its field hospitals were reorganizing near Vierville.

"Report to the regimental adjutant. He'll get you to the 261st, Will."

"And the team, sir?"

"Antsley will go with you, Will. Captain Blackwell has been assigned elsewhere. Sorry."

Will was surprised that Blackwell was not going, but who was he to blame Blackwell?

"Not everybody's an idiot, sir."

"Maybe so, Will." Nagel handed Will his transfer orders and posting. "Give these pages to the unit clerk—they'll get you on the boat. Then give them to the regiment when you get to France." Instead of waiting for a salute he reached across the desk and shook Will's hand. "And good luck."

"Thank you, sir. See you after the war."

"See you after the war, Will."

Just before five in the afternoon there remained only one officer from LST 556 who had not picked up his orders. He appeared in the outer office of MedPers and waited.

"May I have your posting?" The clerk turned to the officer and held out his hand for the officer's document. It was not handed to him.

"Stand up and salute when a superior officer comes in, Corporal."

The clerk looked up to see a very angry major. *Jesus Christ,* the corporal thought. *Napoleon himself. That prick isn't more'n five four and a hundred and forty, counting how much the cob up his ass weighs.* He stood.

"Didn't anyone teach you military etiquette, Corporal? Straighten your shirt, Corporal. Button your sleeves. And 'stand at attention' means legs straight, back straight, thumbs on the seams of your pants, Corporal! The real troops in France aren't getting shot at so you can sit over here behind a desk and forget that you're in the Army."

"Yes, sir. May I have your posting, please, sir?" *SSDD*, he thought. *Good old Army. Same shit, different day.*

The major handed the first four sheets of paper to the clerk. They were carefully inscribed: *Per Temporary Regulation 6.8.44, Fifth Medical Hospital, by order of the CMO: Para 2.2: Leave: Men returning from combat zones or from exposure to enemy fire during the invasion phase shall be eligible for three days exhaustion leave. Para 2.3 Assignment: For exceptional performance medical corps officers may, upon return to UK, be assigned to the zone of the interior at a general hospital or station hospital within the MOS of the medical officer....*

Halliburton handed the clerk his posting. He had written a request for three days leave in Oxford, which had been granted, then assignment to hospital administration at Fifth Surgical General in Cheltenham. It too had been granted.

"Do you believe you can handle this posting, Corporal? Or should I ask Colonel Nagel if you might be better able to handle a job at a unit where proper dress and salutes are not as urgent to the mission? In, say, an infantry unit?"

"No, sir. I can handle your posting, sir. It'll be my privilege. May I just review it for your transportation, sir?" The clerk read it, then resumed. "Sir, your transportation will be here at 1600 hours. On Sunday, sir. Just outside this office, sir. Are your temporary quarters adequate until Saturday, sir? Do you need more ration allowances or meal chits, sir?"

"Very good, Corporal. And yes, I do require an allowance." The working ladies of Oxfordshire had taken Halliburton's remaining cash; their counterparts in Southampton did not accept meal chits or ration coupons. "Temporary Regulation 5.30.44, Paragraph—

"Yes, sir. The finance office, Deputy, P-1, is in the fourth building down, sir. They do this for every man coming out of the line who needs a pay boost."

The major stiffened, his signal to the clerk to salute. The clerk saluted. The major wheeled about and marched out of the Medical Personnel office and onto the docks in search of the pay office. Back inside, the clerk looked across his desk to the other clerk, a nineteen-year-old pimply youth who could type seventy correct words per minute.

"Hey, I forget. Which of these two trays is for postings in the zone of you-don't-get-shot-at and which one is for posting to the combat zone?" He dropped Halliburton's file into the tray marked 'France—4th Infantry.' "Hope I got it right. The Army shouldn't trust anyone as dumb as me to do this."

The pimply typist cracked up.

The clerk continued. "We've got to get a move-on if we're going to get this office cleaned out today. I used to think moving MedPers somewhere else was a pain in the ass; now I think it's a pretty good idea. How far is it to Weymouth, anyway?"

"No idea," the pimply typist replied. "But I'll bet you one thing—I'll bet you can't see Weymouth from here on Sunday, at 1600, when the only transportation off this dock is on a boat to France."

They looked out through the windows to the dock. They saw, a hundred steps away, Halliburton dressing down some sailors who had walked by without saluting. The clerks saluted each other, then laughed again.

"Enjoy France, Major Asshole."

CHAPTER FOUR

July, 1944

"*H*alte."

The rifles clattered, safeties clicking off, straps and clips slapping against wooden stocks and trigger guards. The women froze.

"*Gesperrt die brücke! Mit Verlaub!*"

One of the soldiers, a boy of seventeen, aimed his rifle squarely at the forehead of the tallest of the women, the one who stood out from the others on the end of the bridge. His corporal directed another of the soldiers to clap the lid of the machine gun's plate feeder; the metallic clink rang across the stones and rails and struck the women's ears.

The three women knew what it was; they had seen a machine gun at work in St. Lô and, once, near the farm. They backed away, one step at a time.

"What did he say?"

"I think he said that the bridge is closed. It was open two hours ago."

"Why did they close the bridge, Niece? You said it was open. Is there something happening?"

"I don't know, Aunt. Let me."

"Hey, Fritzie!" her sixteen-year-old sister yelled at the soldiers. "Is that you?" She snatched her beret off her head and waved it like a railroad man with a red lantern, then turned her back on the Germans and flounced her way off the bridge, skirt flapping, shoulders swinging.

"Hush, Sister! Do you think they're flirting with you?" Géraldine suspected that, away from the farm, Claudine had used her adolescent beauty to tease the schütze, once a sport, not any more. *This is no time to taunt them, Sister.* She tugged their sleeves, Claudine's and Aunt Julia's, and nudged them another step back away from the bridge.

"Do you speak French?" she yelled to the corporal. Some of the Germans spoke a little French; she paused to see if her question would help. "I was allowed to pass two hours ago. I came to get my aunt and my sister. Our farm is just five kilometers past the bridge. May we go home, please?"

The corporal was one of the newer troops, a fighter, not an occupier. There were more like him now since the Americans had begun to fight their way inland. He shook his rifle barrel at the women, three or four more times, and said again to go away, then ordered the privates to aim at them until they did. The youngest soldier, the one who had aimed at Géraldine's forehead, watched the women walk away through the mud until they were out of sight. The others relaxed at their posts, joking about how easy it now was to have French girls, so many that now they had to run them off at gun point, the kind of jokes soldiers make.

"How are we going to get back to the farm? Route de Carentan is the only way through," Aunt Julia whispered. The road bridged the river and passed through Pont Hébert, then continued north to Carentan. Their farm was a few miles along the way, tucked on a hillside between the road and the river.

"They closed all the other roads. Route de Carentan is open just because they have to drive their tanks and trucks out there."

"How do you know that, Sister?" She was afraid that Claudine had learned how to flirt but was too much of a coquette to have learned how to stop. "Do you follow the little German boys around so they can whistle at you? Is that what you were learning at school? Is that what she learned, Aunt?"

Their aunt fretted but had no good answer, not in the rain and mud. The women wrung out their shawls and stepped deeper into the mud that had pooled in the rutted road. Géraldine felt badly for having fussed at them; she had been sent to bring them home, not torment them.

"I'm sorry, Aunt. We'll walk. It's not far. "We'll find our way through the farms to Le Déversoir." Le Déversoir was on the river as well, the Vire, and there was a concrete spillway, a barrier the girls had used a hundred times to skip across the river. "It's only a few kilometers from home. If we just follow the river."

"We can't, Niece. We'll drown trying to walk across. It's too narrow. I can't do it. It's raining. I'll fall."

"Do you want to go back to St. Lô?"

46

It was not a serious question but her aunt was even more afraid of what she did not know than that which she did.

"We could go back, Niece. The Germans are letting everyone go down inside the caves. We could stay there."

"What caves?"

"Under the market square. There are tunnels in the rocks. The Germans cleaned them out for bomb shelters. We could go back."

Géraldine was not going back; a German had just aimed his rifle at her forehead.

"No, Aunt. The closest crossing is the spillway at Le Déversoir. Or we can walk all the way to Ste. Marie du Vire and ask someone there to row us. Claudine must come with me. Besides, our parents would be very unhappy with me if I left you alone."

Géraldine led them several hundred yards further away from the bridge, then turned into a farm lane that seemed likely to lead in the general direction they wanted to go.

"The river winds back and forth all the way to the Manche. The spillway can't be more than one or two kilometers from here. We'll just walk through the farms until we find it, then go along the bank until we get to Le Déversoir."

The lane was not particularly inviting, a mud track sunk between hedgerow embankments. Thick foliage grew across the lane, making it almost as dark in daytime as at night. The evening's light and the rain made it impossible for them to see more than a few hundred steps ahead.

"You can have my shawl, Aunt. I don't need it." She took her wool wrap and offered it to Julia.

"No, Niece, you'll catch a death. I don't need it." Her aunt took it anyway, wrapping it around her shoulders and over her head, making herself look like the peasant women she had chosen to not become, her features disappearing beneath the layers of wool. "It isn't the wet, Niece, it's the mud. Well, the wet is the mud, of course, but I could walk just fine if I didn't sink into the mud. Maybe we should go back."

Claudine broke a small limb from a bush.

"Take this, Aunt, she said. "Stick it right in front of you, one step at a time, right there on the path. It will keep you from stumbling. At least you'll know how deep the mud is before you step in it."

Claudine was no more worried about teasing her aunt than teasing

German boys. She seemed to glide as she walked, light on her feet, almost dancing in circles as she roamed along the hedgerow lane. A dog barked.

They froze.

Géraldine made them wait, then shushed them off the lane and into the thick hedge at the base. The dog barked louder but didn't come through the hedgerow at them. There were no commands, no rifles clicking or machine guns bolting to the ready.

"Hello?" She ventured. She waited. "Hello Doggie? It's just us, Doggie, we're not... "

From seemingly nowhere a figure appeared, then another. A third glided out from behind a tree. There were women, women and girls, and they formed a huddle around the three.

"Shh! Quiet!" one of them hissed at the three, then waited. "Where are you going? Is it safe where you came from?" She glanced around, behind her, back up the road, then to either side. The dog settled down.

"Is it safe?" Géraldine answered. "They wouldn't let us cross at Pont Hébert. It's not safe there so we tried here. We're trying to cross the river, that's all."

"You can't go this way either. There are more Germans. They have the road blocked, maybe a couple of hundred meters ahead."

"And you?"

The women were no different; they were all trying to flee from the looming battle. They had set out hours before; the Germans had turned them back everywhere.

Géraldine began to have second thoughts. *Maybe I should take them back to St. Lô, to the cellar or the tunnels. Something is happening, an attack, a counter-attack, I don't know, but I don't know how to get past.* Then she made another decision.

"We'll just go back to the main road, then see what we should do. We don't have to decide before then. It's just a little further back there and whatever is happening with the soldiers is probably something just around here, close to Pont Hébert, that's all. We'll find a way through."

"I have an idea," Claudine said.

"What?" Géraldine suspected it would not be a very good idea, probably to do with flirting their way past a guard somewhere.

"We'll go back to the main road, like you said, then walk a little of the way toward Martinville. It's in the other direction, on the Bayeux road.

48

Then we try again."

"And if it's closed?"

"It's open."

"How do you know?"

"Schützes who flirt with the girls, that's how. Their officers took them away to load the trucks that are going to the other side of Martinville. I saw them."

"That doesn't mean we can go there."

"We can go look. If they're driving their trucks that way then the road is open. We just have to walk off the road a bit."

Géraldine didn't say anything but thought that for once her sister might be right.

If the Americans could push the Germans back this far from the beaches, the Germans must not have enough soldiers. There would be a hole in the line somewhere, some farm or orchard, and they would just walk through it and come out at the river.

"Then it's decided. Let's try the road to Martinville," she said, aloud. "Let's just go and see. We don't have to decide before we get there."

She didn't intend to decide for the other women, or even include them, but they had accepted that Géraldine was in charge, and they were content to follow. The group grew, and would continue to do so.

Claudine was right. The road leading to Martinville was jammed with German trucks, their lights extinguished. Tanks, half-tracked lorries pulling guns, and troops rushed along the battered route that led to a hamlet and ridge three miles away. By walking inside the fields along the road, rather than on the road itself, the women escaped notice. Before arriving at Martinville they came to another farm lane, blocked from the main road only by strands of barbed wire. The Germans had put it up and left it. It was not manned.

The women quietly made the turn back toward the Vire and resumed their trek. For an hour they walked quietly, cautiously, resting, walking again. The women had become comfortable with a practiced silence. No dogs barked at them, there were no startled cattle or goats. They found nothing between them and the Vire but empty meadows. At last, deep in the night, they heard it, the water rushing over the concrete spillway. There were the dim outlines of the first buildings on the edge of Le Déversoir. They had succeeded.

"*Halte!*"

The women froze. A few began to cry.

The command was punctuated by the metallic clang of rifle bolts slammed home. "Stop there. Let me see you."

"Sir? There are three of us. Three." She wondered if the soldier spoke French as well as his command had implied. "And some women who joined us. We are..."

"Let me see you." He repeated himself but, despite his clear voice, the women could not see him. "Now!"

"Where are you?" Géraldine called back to him. "We can't see you? We don't know where to walk so that you can see us."

"I can hear you, walking in the mud. Come this way, another ten steps."

The women did as they were told.

"Stop now; I see you. Are you alone?" They were. "How did you get here?"

Now the women heard another soldier, hidden somewhere, who began to mimic their wails in pidgin-French. The corporal told him to shut up.

"You must go back. Turn around, now, and walk back down that road. And hurry."

"They would not let us pass at Pont Hébert. We have to get across the river. We live on the other side. Please, how may we get across? "

"I don't know. Just leave. You should not be here. Go! Now!"

He barked the last phrases. The women still could not see the Germans but felt their eyes in the dark. They turned, slowly, and began to walk back.

There weren't any Germans along the way for almost an hour, Geraldine thought. *It's only a few hundred yards back to another meadow. We'll go back there, then try for Ste. Marie.*

Géraldine believed, for just a moment, that she would get everyone safely away. We're going to make it. She led them back down the path they had come from and toward a pasture. *We're very close, maybe just one more field. We'll sleep in the field until morning; then they can see it's only us, and they'll let us through.*

But one woman, a woman she didn't know, could not bear it any longer and began to run.

"*Halte!*"

Then, a single shot, and the woman fell.

CHAPTER FIVE

D{.r} Genet walked out of his wrecked clinic. He glanced toward the fountain, then back in the direction of the church. The town square was still a shambles. He began to lock his door, then remembered. *I'm like that idiot,* meaning the priest. The church was never locked because there was nothing in it to steal. *Nothing to steal here, either.*

That much was true. The shells that had knocked the steeple off the church and cracked the village fountain had wrecked Genet's clinic as well. There were no windows intact. The sturdy beams that supported the walls and floors above his examining room had bowed in the blast so that plaster fell and contaminated everything. His sterilization equipment was broken and the medicine cabinet destroyed. Ste. Marie now had even less of a clinic than when the Germans had strutted around taking what they wanted. *Not that I'm complaining,* he added. The priest was outside. *At least they're gone,* meaning the Germans. He had not decided yet what to make of the Americans who took their place.

"*Bonjour, Genet. Ça va?*"

There was no avoiding Father Jean. Apart from them being among the few men the Germans had left in the town, the priest earnestly believed they shared some kind of ordained healing power, the doctor's physical and his spiritual. Genet thought the priest was a pest.

"How's the belfry, Father?"

"Coming along, Doctor. Coming along." The priest had coerced the able-bodied to haul the rubble out of the chancel and dump it behind the school. He and the mayor had used some long-hidden carpentry tools to clear out beams and tiles from the fallen bell tower to cover the exposed opening. It still was necessary to build something to enclose the gaping hole into the church through which rain now fell in sheets. "I may ask the Americans."

51

Genet didn't encourage him. The Americans were different.

He had cheered along with the rest of the town when they appeared out of the woods in the meadow down by the river, then methodically set about firing their mortars and light field pieces to scare the Germans out. No one had been killed, at least not any of the villagers, and the Americans had given chase, following the Germans out the other end of town. Everyone in Ste. Marie, mostly older women and some children, had danced on the little square, drunk a year's worth of Calvados, and promised each other undying mutual assistance in the repair of the fountain, the clinic, the church, all the venerable structures on the square.

Then, before anyone was sober again, more Americans had arrived and set up a field hospital inside the regional apple cooperative barn down by the dock. It seemed like they were going to stay. For two days Genet had watched as their jeeps roared into the village from the hedgerows, sped around the square and on to the apple barn where they unloaded their wounded and hustled them inside. Several times a day their bigger vans, red crosses painted on them, roared away from the apple barn and back up toward Isigny where, he had heard, the Americans had put up a five hundred bed hospital in tents. Between the ambulances and the jeeps and the coming and going there was a regular procession of ordinary army trucks, all of them filled to the top with boxes marked with big red crosses.

Genet figured the Yanks were good for one good deed and he didn't want it wasted on the priest. Father Jean was exactly the kind of cleric who would bow and scrape and pester the Americans into helping him straighten out the church before Genet could get them to restock his medical clinic. *God's been hanging around that church for centuries; He'll take care of the priest when He feels like it. But the Americans aren't going to hang around here any longer than it takes to push the Bosches out of St. Lô.* Genet guessed that it would be a week or two at most.

"Have you been down there, Father?" He meant the apple barn, which was now a field hospital.

"I have not, Doctor. Have you?"

"I have not."

That was mostly true. Genet had wandered into the barn and looked around, hoping that he could pass for a bumbling local with a proprietary interest in the apples or distillery before someone in authority ran him off. It had worked. He had sputtered out phrases to do with apples and crops and preservation of the regional heritage for Calvados brandy. A young man, he thought a lieutenant, had politely shunted him to one side while directing the others to clean the place up.

He had been astonished by the Americans. They had put up screened partitions and laid out the wounded on cots faster than a French doctor could have taken a patient's temperature. They had divided one part of the barn into two surgery rooms with adjustable tables, a generator to power the portable lights, and a canvas floor to limit the dust.

But it was American ingenuity that had impressed Genet and drove his plans. There was a truck inside the barn which, he could see through its open side, had an x-ray machine, a laboratory, and a wall of banked blood and plasma. He had never seen so much advanced medical equipment and could only imagine how most of it worked. He didn't know if the field hospital was Heaven-sent, as Father Jean claimed, or had just dropped in Genet's lap for a more terrestrial purpose, but the village doctor had a plan to get his hands on a bit of it before the Americans moved on.

"Let's wait a day or so until they're better settled, Father. We don't want to be in their way. We should let them get organized." He wanted the priest to believe that the Americans would happily give them anything if they would just be patient before showing up like poor guests, hats in hand.

He waved goodbye to the priest and began a tour of the village. The bakery was intact, the green grocer less so, not that the Germans had left either of them much to bake or sell. The post office and telegraph were not in bad shape but there was no mail to anywhere nor any wires left to the outside world. Some of the homes on the east side of the square were wrecked. The roof on the school had several holes in it but it wasn't so bad that the newly homeless couldn't sleep in the classrooms for a while. He skirted around the one-block center of town to re-enter his clinic and home through the back door. Once inside, he retrieved his fishing tackle, the only piece of important equipment that still worked, and sneaked back out. The priest was nowhere in sight.

Genet wandered down the cobbled path to the apple barn, an ancient half-timbered structure. It had been built close to the river for the convenience of moving the apples downstream on barges, yet it was far enough from the village that no one would suffer either the odors of fermenting fruit or the risk of the alcohol distillery blowing up in the night.

It seemed to him, in the rain, that hospital traffic had slowed. It was hard to say because the village was off the direct road between the coast and St. Lô. The constant artillery barrages on this side of the river were always a few miles away; those across the river boomed farther to the north. It was never clear exactly where the front line was but there weren't as many jeeps and ambulances as there had been the first two days. He had no way of knowing that the allies' temporary harbors had been torn apart in the storm, thus slowing the American attack for want of being able to unload the machinery and supplies of war. Even so, after fifteen minutes, Genet decided that if there was ever a time when he might be able to talk to the commander, this was the time. He walked into the barn.

"Sir?"

"*Bonjour.* He was uncertain about the strange ranks and stripes; the man at the front door could have been a sergeant, a captain, anything. Genet dived in. "*Your commander, please. I have some business.*"

Genet had no idea what the charge desk clerk said; he only knew that in impenetrable English the man cocked his head and yelled. Another soldier came up, spoke, left, and then a third came. Genet knew this man was undoubtedly a sergeant, partially because of the stripes on his sleeve, partially because of a certain bulldog look to his face and a suspicious glint in his eye.

"Whatcha want, sir? I'm Sergeant Prior." Prior put his face somewhat closer to Genet's face than was comfortable. Genet repeated in French his request to speak to a commander. The sergeant responded with a yell that sounded like "fuckit."

Another soldier arrived, this one with only one stripe on his sleeve and a look of frustration on his face. Genet thought that here was an underling, a man he could do business with.

"Fuckit!" Prior exaggerated his mis-pronunciation of Fouquet's Cajun name, "What's this guy want?"

Fouquet, in addition to being Shorty's errand boy, medical chest-finder, and midnight setter-up of tents for the field hospital, was also the translator. His French was correct, albeit Louisiana Acadian and, accordingly, ancient.

"My sergeant demands that I inquire how mightest I aid thee?" Fouquet asked.

"What?" Fouquet's French sounded to Genet as if he had come from the seventeenth century.

"Doest thou have an inquest for my sergeant?"

This required tact. The bulldog was a sergeant, the translator a decent youngster limited by vocabulary and rank. Genet thought how best to answer the poorly-put question, then decided to be direct.

"Yes, thank you very much. I do. Please inform your sergeant that your army destroyed my medical clinic."

"Thy medical clinic?"

"Yes. In the village. My clinic. It has been destroyed. I have no criticism of your bombs; it is only that they smashed into my examining rooms and," here Genet stretched a bit, "my surgery."

Fouquet did his best to understand, then translate, what Dr. Genet had said. Prior understood even less than Fouquet and said, "So what?" Fouquet did not need to translate so what, Prior's expression being enough for Genet to understand that he had been presented with a philistine.

"Tell your sergeant that I see your boxes of medicines and supplies, more than I have ever seen anywhere. You have more than we had before the Germans came." He paused, Fouquet translated, Prior stewed. "I must have some of your supplies to care for the people who live here. Many of them were injured in your attack on Ste. Marie."

"Not only no," Prior barked back, "but Hell no. We ain't a French medical warehouse. We're damned sure not going around handing out stuff to every guy with a fishing creel. He don't look like a doc to me."

That was true enough. Genet should have left his rod and reel outside. It also impaired his cause that he didn't look like a doctor—he was dressed in a faded blue canvas jacket and worn corduroy pants. It was difficult to see his feet under the cuffs but, whatever he wore for shoes, they were caked in mud. Fishing flies were hooked in the brim of his battered hat. He looked like a fisherman, not a doctor. Not even Fouquet appreciated that it was by fishing that Genet and half the town had anything to eat.

Genet, however, was not entirely unprepared. He produced a list and showed it to Fouquet. Prior looked at the list over Fouquet's shoulder.

"*I do require these things. They are necessary. There are other medical devices and compounds that we can add later but these I must have now.*" Whether because of Genet's tone or Fouquet's limitations is unknown but Prior misunderstood him to express in French the unfortunate sentiment that there could be no discussion about it. Genet proceeded to read from his list:

"*Sang.* Blood. A, B, and O, *tous les classes*, all types." Fouquet translated.

"No." Prior answered.

"*Plasme.*" Plasma.

"No."

"Penicillin."

"No."

"Sulfa."

"No."

"Iodine and antiseptics."

"No."

"*Seringues. Scalpels, utensiles chirurgiques.*" Syringes, scalpels, surgical instruments.

"No, no, and no. Doesn't he understand no? What's the French word for we don't owe you French a damned thing, you owe us?"

"*Non!*" Genet said something else that Fouquet thought best not to translate.

"He's asking if he can talk to the commanding officer."

"NO!"

It didn't matter at that point; Prior believed that he personally had saved France's butt and there was no circumstance in which he would give one of its teeming ingrates so much as a band-aid.

To Genet, the game had only played its first hand. He gave a formal nod of the head to Fouquet, turned, and left, walking not toward the village but instead, somewhat incongruously, in the rain, across the meadow, toward the laundry hut on the banks of the Vire.

The laundry hut was open to the river on three sides. It had a tidy slate roof and a scrub shelf where the village women washed their clothes and aired their gossip. Ignoring the rain, Genet laid out his fishing tackle, eyeing some perch that were rising to the bugs in the reeds upstream. Out in the river there was a large rock, big enough to climb on, which the village boys used for diving. For the time being the laundry and the rock were the domain of a flock of ducks, motley things with white and brown bodies, green necks and heads. There also was a young American sitting on the floor, gazing across the still water. He appeared not to notice Genet's approach. Genet studied him.

Will's magic show had changed. He still disappeared into thin air at night but it was no longer to look for boxes or trucks. Shorty had never caught him, not exactly, but everyone knew that after he rejoined the 261st Will sneaked off in the night to search for his brother's glider. Once, near Isigny, Shorty had found Will wading out of the river; Will had said he just went swimming. Another time, at three in the morning, Shorty had waited inside Will's tent for an hour before Will came in, dripping wet. "I swapped with Garth, Shorty. I don't mind." Garth had backed him up.

They had different ideas about the matter. From Will's view, he was just searching through the countryside for proof that Peter had, or hadn't, really died in the glider crash. "Where's his dog tags? If he's dead, where's his dog tags? A grave? Something?"

Shorty's side of it was that if everyone had a patient on the table and an emergency came in, it was not all right for Will to be absent without leave, wandering around the French countryside in the dark. "You're a field surgeon, not a sleuth. Besides, if someone catches you slipping around five or ten miles from where you're supposed to be, they'll charge you with desertion. And with all those drawings and maps you've got stuffed in your pockets they'll think you're a spy and put you up against a wall."

Will had said he understood. He had promised Shorty that he would not 'go swimming anymore,' but Shorty hadn't let it go. Before the 261st pulled out of Isigny the scuttlebut was that Sergeant Prior had been told to sneak around to see if he could catch Will going AWOL. Will had not been caught again.

Will had never missed being where he was supposed to be, nor in six weeks had a single casualty gone without Will's medical treatment, not until that morning. To make it harder for Shorty, Will had made a habit of volunteering to trade Collins's and Morph's turns up at the combat aid stations so that they, and Garth, could stay behind at the field hospital. By the time they set up the surgery in Ste. Marie du Vire, everyone knew what he had been doing.

Then, that morning at about the same time that Genet had been dissembling with Father Jean on the town square, Sergeant Prior told Shorty he hadn't been able to find Will. Collins needed help with a gunshot stomach and didn't get it; the boy died on Collins's table. When Will appeared from behind a portable screen near the back door of the barn Collins had shouted at him for not pulling his load. Will had shouted back that all Collins had to do was yell for him; he had been helping Garth set a fracture. Garth backed Will again, but only barely—he had finished the fracture fifteen minutes earlier, then told Will to knock off. But Collins and Sergeant Prior had put a bug in Shorty's ear; Shorty had pulled Will out of the barn and into the cab of an ambulance and locked the doors.

"All right, Will. It's just the two of us. If the surgeons can't trust you, the men won't either. Then you're no good to anybody. It's time for you to stop being mad and start acting like a doctor. You're hurting us."

"Mad? I'm not mad, Shorty. Collins was right. I could have helped him when I finished splinting that kid with Garth. I just don't like Prior and Collins accusing me of disappearing when I'm right there in the field hospital. It's not that big of a barn."

"Not that kind of mad, Will." Shorty lit a Lucky Strike, then inhaled deeply. "I mean mad like you're cracking up. You don't sleep. You don't talk to anyone. You sit with the other guys but you don't eat. I see that kind of thing. I'm no shrink but I know when a guy's cracking up." Shorty cranked down the window an inch to let the smoke out, then continued. "It's about your brother, Will, isn't it? Tell me, when was the last time you saw him?"

Will had dug the photograph out of his pocket and passed it to Shorty; Shorty had seen it before, they all had. He passed it back. Will held it.

"Back home, at Thanksgiving. We were supposed to meet up in London, Peter and me, in May, but we didn't pull it off. Peter sent me a note, 'Let's meet at the Rainbow in London.' I had this friend, Douglas, a clerk, and he went through this secret army clerk network with a guy in the Eighth Air Force and they got it set up for Peter to get a pass. We go to London. We find Piccadilly. We sit in the Rainbow Club. We wait for Peter until closing time, but Peter never shows up. So, the last time I thought I was going to see my brother, he doesn't make it."

Shorty hadn't heard that story before. He decided it was better to let Will talk, and he waited.

"We finally give up but then this major shows up, the major who threw me off the LST. He was from the school, too, back at Shrivenham. I did a favor for him once. So he shows up at the Rainbow and says he wants a girl. He always wanted a girl, that's neither here nor there, but he starts in on us to take him to the Windmill Club, a couple of blocks away. 'Hey, bet your brother got it mixed up, went to the Windmill, a lot of pilots go to the

Windmill,' like he knows. So we start out to walk over there and BOOM! A bomb! The Germans drop a goddamned bomb and it lands right smack on the Windmill Club. Not only does Peter not make it, neither does Douglas. That's the end of him. BOOM! And Halliburton gets all cut up, then blames me for his scars. Halliburton—he's the major."

Shorty didn't know what to make of the story. Will's voice didn't break off with emotion or clench up in fury; it was calm, like it always was, and polite, like it always was.

"It's just the war, Will." He paused and thought for a moment, then made a mistake. "You think you should be out here, Will? On the line? I can get you a couple of days back at the evacuation hospital, if you want. You know, not as much constant, you know, shelling and surgery, surgery and shelling. Some order in your life. Just for a while."

Shorty knew as soon as he finished that he shouldn't have said it; instead of consolation it sounded like he was trying to get rid of Will.

"You want me out of here, don't you, Shorty? I've been in this war one month and I've lost everything. Seven months ago I had everything, my girl, my brother, right back there in Tierra, at Thanksgiving. Then I lost my girl. I lost my buddies. Then, whatever Hitler hadn't already done to me back home, or at the Windmill Club, he finished off in the first fourteen minutes of D-Day—he killed my brother! You can say I'm angry, may even be mad. But don't tell me it's the war, or that everybody loses somebody in the war. I didn't lose *somebody*, Shorty. I lost everybody. You know what I've got left, Shorty? This field hospital. That's it."

"Then if this is all you've got left, Will, you better take care of it."

"Are you going to take this away from me, too?"

"Like I said, Will, you better take care of it, Will. You, not me, not Prior, for damned sure not Collins or Garth or the casualties. If you want to keep it, you better take care of it." Shorty had rolled down the window for the last time, flicked his cigarette out into the rain, and hated himself for being so hard on his friend. That had been an hour ago.

Shorty had gotten out of the truck and, without another word, walked back to the field hospital in the barn. Will had wandered away in the rain and now found himself sitting on the floor of the village laundry shed, watching the ducks.

The rain, for Will, was France. England had been tidy fields and warm beer. Belfast had been a grim hospital and a sickening ferry voyage across to

Scotland. France was rain. He didn't understand why but he found himself thinking about the quarry, back in Tierra, about Hoyt and Johnny and Virginia, and wishing he could have gone back to do things differently.

He gazed across to the far side of the Vire and tried to make out what little he could see through the rain. The river was lined with the same trees and shrubs as the dense hedgerows where the troops were fighting one field at a time. The opposite bank, thirty or forty yards away and obscured by reeds, was perhaps ten feet above the water level, a path worn across its face. He wondered how hard it would be to climb up the bank, then dismissed the idea.

The rain eased up and, for just a moment, Will glimpsed something beyond the opposite bank. Several hundred yards distant there was a building, gothic, like a church, rising high above an enclosure, a long, high wall that extended all the way across a small clearing. There was a steep gabled roof and a single tower, most of it obscured.

It's beautiful, he thought. *It's like...*

Will had not had any particular expectations of France. There had been ancient churches, a few crumbling castles in England. He had assumed without thinking about it that France would be more or less the same, except wrecked by the war, and that was pretty well how France had been. But this was different, whatever it was, perfectly proportioned, serene even, as if there were no war. Then the rain pelted down and it disappeared, restricting his view to the river and the boulder nearby. His thoughts returned to the quarry.

It hadn't been much of a quarry. The government had dammed up a little rain-weather creek so it could dig out stone for a road base. The bulldozer had dug too far into one of the banks and unearthed a huge rock that rolled right into the middle of the water. He and Hoyt and Johnny had skinny dipped in the quarry hundreds of times, jumping off the diving rock and nearly drowning them all long before the Army got to them.

Will closed his eyes and saw scrawny Johnny and burly Hoyt, ragged hair and gangly legs, yelling "wahoos" as they jumped off the diving rock, arms flying while they splashed into the quarry. Then he saw himself a couple of years later, sitting on his bed in the medical school boarding house, reading the newspaper clipping Shirley had mailed to him. *Tierra Soldiers Lost at Bataan*. Doc wrote to tell him that it had driven Old Bradley so nearly crazy that he was afraid he might wind up sending him to that hospital in Lubbock where he had put Emma Sullivan. That seemed like a hundred years ago. He sensed that someone else had walked out of the wet meadow and into the laundry shed, and expected it to be Sergeant Prior.

"*Bonjour.*"

Will looked up to find that he had been joined by a Frenchman, his hat so soggy it draped against his ears. His faded canvas coat flopped open to reveal a wicker creel slung at his waist.

"*Pêchez-vous?*" The Frenchman showed Will his fishing rod.

"Hello." Will stood up. The startled ducks jumped away and waded out into the river. Will smiled at the man, courteous, and made room for him to set his creel on the scrub shelf.

"*Ma pêché. Des poissons,*" the man whispered. He pointed toward his wicker creel and indicated with his free hand that Will should open it. Will drew out two rubbery fish, one struggling, the other very alive but staring up at him, wide unblinking eyes, submissive. "*I just came from your army hospital, there in my apple barn,*" Genet said in French, smiling, gesturing back toward the field hospital. "*Your sergeant is a gangster.*" He assumed Will would not understand a word he said, and he was right. He began to un-tie a fly from the line and select another, then noticed the caduceus on Will's collar. "*Are you a doctor?*"

Docteur was sufficiently close to English that Will picked up the one word and nodded, yes, he was a doctor.

"*Moi aussi. I'm a doctor, too.*" He deftly tied the fly and tested the knot, then pointed at himself and °repeated that he was a doctor. "*Do you like to fish?*"

Will smiled, nodded, shook his head, and tried to express that he didn't understand a word. He hoped he wasn't bothering the fishing doctor. "Am I bothering the fish?" He gestured at the river, made a few swooping motions with his hand, and imitated a cast of the rod and reel.

Genet thought Will wanted his rod and reel and offered them to him. "*Voulez-vous pêcher?*" He extended his rod and reel for Will to take. "*Attrapez-la, oui?*"

Will declined. Genet shrugged, not understanding. He stepped just outside the laundry shed and made a cast into the slow-moving river.

The rain ebbed and flowed and, from time to time, the gothic building reappeared through the downpour. Will took out his notepad and pencil. He sketched the roof first. Beneath the roof there were high windows and

61

stone tracery. As the weather permitted, he added the graceful tower, then the curtain wall. Within just a few minutes he had completed the sketch, adding a thick forest flanking the buildings and a tidy meadow leading down to the river.

"*Le monastère.*" Will looked up; Genet had come up behind him and was looking over his shoulder at the sketch. "*Good drawing. I didn't think America had any artists.*"

Will misunderstood that he had been told he was a very good American artist. Genet understood that Will wondered what he had drawn.

"*It's a monastery. There's nobody there now. The monks all left when the Germans came. Fritz emptied their cellars, all the wine, their meat and grain. And the cheese, ah—the monastery was famous for its cheese. The Germans took it all. Then they took a few of the monks. The rest ran away. That was in 1940, maybe 1941.*"

Will understood only that it had been a monastery and he was not perfectly certain of that. He had an inspiration, and asked.

"Carentan? Is Carentan over there? Or the road to Carentan? Road? Route? That's the French word, isn't it, route? Route to Carentan?" He pointed across the river and in a northwesterly direction.

The fishing man understood as little of Will's rambling English as Will had of his meandering French—one word: Carentan.

"*Well, Carentan, that's a long way. Maybe, I don't know, fifteen kilometers, as the crow flies. I went there once; there's nothing there. The war is worse there than it is here. Well, maybe not worse, but the Germans over there, they're fighting like mad men.*"

Even though he didn't understand a word, Will paid close attention to whatever Genet said about Carentan, a fact not lost on the old man. Why this American was interested in the other side of the river was his own affair, Genet thought, but he definitely wanted to know something about Carentan. And, he reflected, he had tried the correct approach to request that the Americans replenish his medicines, and the Americans had presented him with a blockhead. Now, he thought, if he politely acted like a tour guide, this little Yankee might ease his path to the supply truck. It was worth a try.

"*There's just the monastery. Then there's a farm on the other side of the monastery, Chateau Dupré. They call it a chateau but really it's just a small farm, some cows and an orchard. Maybe once it was part of a chateau, I don't know, it's not so old, maybe two hundred years. The Germans didn't bother it much. See that row-*

boat?" He pointed to the far bank, at the reeds. Will noticed the wooden bow of a very small rowboat hidden in the rushes. *"That was the monks' boat. I don't think the monks use it so much, now. But Dupré's children used to swipe it to row around, swim in the river. That was a few years ago. No one goes about in the country any more now; it's not safe. I haven't been over there in a long time. Now do you want to try to fish?"*

That was Genet's best diplomacy. He again offered his rod and reel and offered to show Will a few casts. Will was too embarrassed to try; he had never picked up a fishing rod in his life. They shook hands. Genet packed his creel and walked away in the rain.

Will leaned against the back wall and closed his eyes. There were Johnny and Hoyt jumping off the diving rock, Peter swimming in the Trinity River a mile or two from the orphanage. He gazed at the rock in the middle of the river, then beyond to the veiled sight of the monastery on the Carentan side of the Vire. He knew that he was on dangerous ground; his urge to slip into the water was almost uncontrollable. He had no fear of being followed by Prior. Instead, he was afraid of being needed and not being found. Shorty had had enough.

He put the drawing in his field jack, then forced himself to pull his helmet down to cover him from the rain and walked back to the field hospital.

"Dr. Genet? Is that you?"

"Father Jean?" The doctor looked up to see the priest watching him as he made his way up the cobbled street. He could have been walking home from the river. He could have been walking home from the army hospital. He stared right into the priest's accusing eyes.

"Catch anything?"

"I did, Father. A couple. Do you have anything to eat for dinner?"

The priest did. He also believed that Genet was not telling him everything he caught.

"I caught more than enough for me, Father." He held the creel up in case the priest wanted to poke his nose in it. "I have all I need. For tonight." He smiled and waved goodbye, leaving the priest in the middle of the dilapidated village square while he slipped into his own little house behind the shuttered clinic.

And my catch just might turn out to be a big fish, Genet thought. For the first time in a very long time he was lighthearted. He began to hum, then whistle, while he took up a long-unused scalpel to clean his catch. *That little officer—there's something he wants, something on the other side, maybe in Carentan. What is it? I don't know, not yet, but I'll find it. And when I do, he'll get it. And when he does, I'll get a box or two of whatever they have stacked up inside that field hospital of theirs.*

CHAPTER SIX

The rainfall and the hedgerows combined to make it so dark that the troops hadn't seen the sun in days. A mile south of Ste. Marie du Vire the sunken farm lanes were knee-deep in mud. The foxholes were filled with water. Captain Deere had ordered Campbell's platoon to post two-man teams every twenty yards facing south in the general direction of St. Lô. There they huddled.

"*Calvaire*. C- a- l- v- a- i- r- e. *Calvaire*." Rogers had learned six or seven French words, all religious, in the month since they had gotten off the invasion beaches. "That's what they call the crosses, like that one outside the village. Ste. Marie du Vire—funny name for a town." He puzzled for a moment over the village's name, then returned to his running commentary about its symbol. "Do you know why they call them *calvaires*? It's because they name them after the cross where our Lord and Savior died. The cross of Calvary."

"You got any mystery meat?" Newton had peeled the lid off a ration can of particularly vile sauces and gray solids. "If I eat one more can of spaghetti I'll have the runs so bad I won't have to wait for the krauts to make me mess my pants." Rain dripped off his helmet visor and into the can.

The rain was a blessing. As miserable as the men were, the rain had kept the Germans from counterattacking on foot. Even their little spotter airplane had been grounded.

"Hear that?" Newton continued. An artillery battery to the east fired a random salvo. They counted, *one thousand one, one thousand two, one thousand three*. There was no follow-on salvo, nor did the Germans shoot back, suggesting that the battery was just firing honesty rounds toward St. Lô. "Krauts'll sometimes lob a few rounds back to keep us on our toes but as long as the rain keeps up no one gets shot at. You got any goddamned fruit? I'll trade you some cigarettes for a goddamned can of fruit salad."

"I wish you wouldn't use the Lord's name in vain," Rogers replied. He meant it as a tutorial rather than a challenge, but began to dig through a soaked box of C-rations in search of a can of fruit. "I've got some Spam left. You want it? What'd Sgt. Altgelt say?"

"He's taking Curtiss down to the river. Fuckin' CO said we had to cover the flank all the way to the river. CO's never been to the river and he thinks one platoon can fill a hole a mile wide. He cracks me up." Newton snorted, then opened his canteen and took a long pull on the Calvados he had sneaked in from their last bivoac on the other side of Ste. Marie du Vire.

"I don't get it."

"The CO told Captain Deere who told Lieutenant Campbell who told Sgt. Altgelt to stretch our line all the way to the river. Sgt. Altgelt's moving Curtiss over to the end of the line. He'll be back in an hour or so."

"Why?"

"Latrine orders. Soon as the rain stops we're going to push off. What's 'latrine orders?'"

"Rumors." Newton not only thought Rogers was a Bible thumper but a stupid one as well. "*You know—We're going to push off to Pont Hébert. Push off to St. Lô. Come out of the line for training. Lead the charge up that hill. Ike's going to send Patton back to the States. Ike's going to give Patton a new command.* Rumors, just rumors. Get some sleep. My stomach's too fucked up to sleep."

Rogers crawled into a space created by the split trunks of a cluster of trees. He fixed his bayonet onto the sight ring at the end of his rifle barrel, then used the bayonet tip as a fence pole to make a roof of his poncho and keep the rain from dripping directly into his eyes. He leaned back and tried to go to sleep.

"Hey, Newton, you all right?" Rogers could hear Newton's gastric dysfunction right through the rain and the poncho. "You're louder than a .105."

"Fuckin' C-rations are killing me. You ever try a mixture of spam, spaghetti, and mixed fruit? Cover me a minute."

Rogers crawled out from under his poncho and slid back into the foxhole. Newton slithered out of the mud and across the lane into the field behind them. He found a bush and tried to assume a latrine position under a ring of tree branches. Rain poured onto him.

Wonder if Jerry can hear my stomach? I need some real food. These rations are murder.

To emphasize his point, Newton picked through his C-ration box for toilet paper and discovered the lidded remains of the vile pasta, cutting his thumb on the jagged edge of the tin can lid.

"Shit!"

He consciously chose to disobey a standing order, took the can, and hurled it as far as he could into the bushes.

Clink.

He froze. The tin can dropped back into his lap and fell into a puddle of mud at his feet. He slowly reached to his side, took his rifle in his left hand, and drew it across the front of his body. He grasped the trigger guard with his right hand, then swivelled it up to a shooting position. He slowly rose to a standing position, looking across the field, to his right, to his left, and peered into the rain, then cautiously took two steps to his left and hit his head on a wheel from the bent landing gear of a wrecked plane that had crashed into the trees.

It was not immediately obvious that it was a plane. There was no motor or propeller. The landing gear was stuck about six feet above the meadow, lodged in the branches and trunks of the ancient hedgerow. The wings were nowhere to be seen. Some of what had been the cockpit was still attached to the left wheel. Wing struts and a wing spar were twisted all through the highest branches. The heavy growth of the hedgerows, the rain and dark, made the wreckage all but invisible.

"Rogers! Hsst." Newton, his intestines forgotten, slithered back across the road and dropped into the foxhole. "There's a wrecked plane inside that field."

"Anybody alive?"

"Couldn't be. If it wasn't twenty feet up in the trees I wouldn't have even thought it was a plane."

"Ours?"

"Probably. It's a glider."

"Think we should tell the lieutenant?"

Newton thought about it for a few moments, then decided.

"Let's wait till Altgelt gets back. It's probably been there a month. A couple of hours won't make any difference."

"It will in Heaven."

"I don't get you."

"If there's men back in there—it could be the doc's brother even—they need to be given last rites. You know, prayers."

"If the doc's brother or anybody else is up there in that airplane you won't find enough pieces to pray over. Altgelt can call Graves Registration to come look for them." Newton had become averse to touching bodies, G.I. or German; they littered the battlefields all the way from Saint Laurent to Isigny to Ste. Marie. "Blacks are better with the dead anyway. Leave it."

"What if it is the doc's brother?"

"There's not anybody there. Leave it alone."

Rogers said okay but decided that at morning light he would go over and look, just to be sure. Even if it wasn't the doc's brother, if there was a soldier in the plane, someone needed to ask the Lord and Savior to guide his soul up to Heaven. He pulled his poncho back over his helmet and said a quiet prayer, just in case.

Six hundred meters further down the line Sergeant Altgelt and Curtiss crept out of the hedgerows and into a weed-choked lane that led to a wrecked farmhouse.

"Hoot."

"Owl."

"It's us, Witt." They could hear Witt, but not see him. Witt tossed a stone toward them; it splashed in the mud at their feet. They looked up and, hidden in the wrecked stack of the farm house chimney, saw the figure of a G.I. They made their way over to him.

"CO says we've got to cover all the way to the river, Witt. How far is it?" They took out the sketch Sgt. Altgelt had made from Lieutenant Campbell's topographic map. "Just past the ruins." Several dots on the map indicated the presence of ruins, an old castle, a church or something. "You seen any ruins here?"

The only ruins were the farm itself, at the end of the lane, beyond the last hedgerow. Curtiss had expected a crumbling tower but it was just a farmhouse wrecked by artillery shelling. The walls and chimney had collapsed beneath a caved-in thatched roof. The doorway and windows had fallen inward. It was hard to tell how long it had been since anyone had lived in the place.

The other landmarks on the map were a tool shed, misspelled *tuils*, a church, a mill, and the river itself, beyond the *tuils*. A road, more of a cart track, veered off from the lane. Across the road, approximately where the map said *tuils*, there was an old Norman half-timbered barn, shell-damaged but not so badly that it couldn't be used. Remnants of plows, a broken-down cart, hay rakes, apple baskets, and ladders lay scattered about.

"That's the tool shed, Sergeant. The men I relieved said Jerry put up a rear guard here yesterday." Witt pointed out bullet holes that pocked the wood and whitewash of the walls. "The river's just over there."

A levee rose some forty or fifty yards beyond the tuil shed. A water gate cut into the levee and opened into a sluice. A clean, well-formed aqueduct ran from the water gate back to the barn. Across the lane an apple orchard spread out in the direction of the village.

"That's the windmill." Witt pointed to a dilapidated contraption jutting at odd angles out of the river bank, cloth debris flapping in the rain and wind. "I guess it's more like a Dutch windmill than one of ours. I wouldn't have known it was a windmill if the lieutenant hadn't told me."

A marsh had formed between the orchard and the aqueduct. They didn't see a church, as marked on the map, but no one had crawled beyond the windmill to look for it. Anyone moving past the marsh would have been exposed.

"Funny how the river chokes off here. It's a lot wider back at Ste. Marie du Vire. There's a dock there and everything. How far is it from here?"

"About a—"

Crack!

From out of the rain they heard a single rifle shot. They dropped behind the crumpled chimney, crouched to their knees, and readied themselves for Germans to pour out of the meadow and up over the river bank. They tapped the magazines of their rifles, mechanically ran their hands over ammunition pouches, tugged at grenades, and waited.

No one came. A full minute later, from hundreds of yards back down the lane, they heard a single voice crying out.

"MEDIC!"

"Jesus! Who was that?"

"Not sure, sounded like Rogers," Altgelt answered. "Witt, come with me. Curtiss, find a place for covering fire as close to the river as you can get and keep your head down. Send a flare if..." Altgelt and Witt left, jogging through the mud in the sunken lane.

Curtiss, now a one-man flank, outpost, and listening post, wondered about the rifle shot. *Germans? Warning shot? Rogers? Could be anything.* He tried to focus on the zone in front of him. The artillery had died down. *That's usually when an attack comes.*

He waited a half hour, peering into the reeds, sighting his rifle on the flapping cloth of the windmill, jerking around prepared to shoot at the barn, the orchard, the farmhouse, whenever the wind blew. There was no attack.

The reeds waved in the gentle morning breeze, rain drops falling on them and on the marsh. The diffuse light, the rain, the flat colors made it difficult to see and Curtiss thought he should crawl forward, just to make sure. The site didn't quite match what should have been there and he wondered if Lieutenant Campbell hadn't made another hash of reading the map. He remembered the screw-up at St. Laurent. *Lieutenant's come a long way since then*, he thought. *Everyone's come a long way; longest twenty miles I ever covered.*

He stared at the horizon for another long minute, then retreated into the *tuil* barn and pulled his pants down by one of the milking stalls. It was the first time Curtiss had been alone since the troop resupply truck had dumped him on the division's beach back in England a couple of weeks before the landings. He let his breath out and tried to go to the toilet.

Goddamn Rogers, he thought. *He's gonna get me shot someday.* Rogers was not a particularly bad soldier; Curtiss had seen bad soldiers in Sicily, and Rogers was not one. Instead, Curtiss's concern was that Rogers was going to keep pecking at him until the lieutenant or Captain Deere started asking the same questions that Rogers asked: *What unit were you with before you got here? How come a soldier as good as you doesn't have corporal's stripes? Or a unit badge? Or the big one: Where's your personnel file? It should have shown up by now.* He knew that the main thing was to keep his name off the daily report of wounded, missing, or sick until he could get a personnel file together and slip it into the battalion's records. *If I don't get shot first.*

Curtiss' personnel file, a work in progress, was still buried in the bottom of his barracks bag back in England. *Just a couple of more hours and I'd have finished my file and I'd have been a medical clerk somewhere.*

Instead, the replacement depot had put him in the 116th Infantry Battalion before Major Hampton finished typing it.

It was going to be a good personnel file, too, much better than the first couple he had made up for himself. He had even found a guy in the big personnel office at Birmingham who could press a new set of dog tags for him in swap for a case of bourbon and a box of rubbers. *I was that close to a foolproof ID. That's all right—I'll sort it out, with a little time.*

Then Rogers had scared him. Rogers had been running on about where he grew up.

"Me, I'm from Aspermont. Do you know where Aspermont is?" Rogers had yammered away about some little dirt town north of Abilene. The school was real good. It seemed a man couldn't get more than about a dozen head of cattle on a spread because it just wouldn't hold the grass between rains so now they're trying cotton. Four churches, two grocery stores.

"Rogers, will you be quiet for Christ's sake!" It was hard enough to sit in the rain and peer across the meadow trying to spot the Germans, who also were sitting in the rain on the other side, trying to spot you, without Rogers going on about his churches and sisters and idiot cousins.

"Well, four churches, if you don't count the Holy Rollers. My mother says they're not Christians at all, just some kind of crazy people. Do you know what they do? Sometimes we'd go out there to the Holy Roller church and sit under the windows and peek in and they'd be jiggin' around in there. Like dancing, except not, I don't know, like shaking more. And the preacher he'd say some things I didn't get because they were talking in tongues and his eyes would roll back in his head and people would shout out. It was real loud, but I didn't understand any of it. Well, when I have kids, they're not going to be talking in tongues and rolling their eyes back in their heads in church. You got any kids?"

"Two boys."

The question had caught Curtiss off guard. Ever since he had landed in the platoon he had been asked where he grew up, where he lived, what he did before he was drafted. Some of the men asked where he had learned to fire a mortar, how come he knew how to reload a German machine gun. It didn't matter because Curtiss kept to himself. But no one had ever asked him if he had any kids so, when Rogers slipped the question into a long description of cousins and ugly sisters, it had sneaked up on him.

"Two boys," he had said before he could stop himself. He almost choked as the words came out.

"What do you call them?"

"Ronald. Ronald and, and Albert," he lied. There was no reason to tell Rogers their names. He had to be more careful.

"They look like you? My mother says you can look at a boy and see who he looks like. Girls you can't do that but boys they always look like somebody else. My aunts say I take after my dad but my sister she favors my mother, on account of they're both kind of bony in the face. But my mother she's real nice, although my sister, well, she'll make a good wife but it's gonna be hard for her to get someone what with that bony face of hers. And I have this cousin he lives over in Spur and he has the reddest hair you ever saw. Man is it red, but no one else has any red hair. He don't take after anybody. And he's pretty tall too. How old are they?"

"Who?"

"Your boys? Ronald and Albert."

Twins ran in their mother's family, Opal had told him. His boys had been three years old when they sent him to the workhouse, four when he came out, five when Opal took off. They had moved back up to where her people were from, a little town near Amarillo. He couldn't blame her; he hadn't been very good at providing. He had flubbed the job at the bank, then the job at the insurance agency. He had started to go after her but the sheriff went after him first, then gave him another choice—the workhouse again, or the Army. Now the twins were six years old.

"Three. And two." Rogers didn't need to know they were twins. *Now that's two more facts to remember. Damn, it's hard to keep straight what you tell everybody. It's always better to keep your mouth shut.* The constant vigilance of combat had worn Curtiss out, and Rogers had gotten through his defenses.

His ears picked up. Through the rain he heard something, not like a Panzer or one of those little PAK guns the Germans had, more like something crashing through the water. The rain made it hard to tell the direction of the noise. He tensed up, looking toward the barn door, watching, listening for someone to come over the dike or out of the river.

Nothing happened. He had no machine gun, not even a BAR. His choices were to conceal himself in the barn or try to crawl forward to get a much longer field of view.

I wonder what the boys are doing now? It's July—they should be playing up in a tree house, maybe fishing or something. He wondered if they were any good in school, if Opal's brothers had taught them how to ride a bike or to feed pigs and chickens. *I should have been home to do all that.* Every get-rich-now idea he had told her about had fallen on its nose. He could type, but not sell stocks, not in 1937, not in Amarillo. He could talk, but not sell insurance. He could drive, but not sell oil leases. *I should have just gone on up to Bridle with her and become a dry land farmer.*

He wanted to write home, not for the first time, or the last, but knew he couldn't. He would have had to put his name on a V-mail letter and some censor in the personnel office would see it. Nor could he expect to receive a letter; he hadn't heard from Opal since he was in Sicily, a couple of weeks before he had filled out a form to report himself as taken prisoner of war, right before he hid in the crowd of First Division troops going back to Northern Ireland.

He snapped out of the luxury of being alone, of the daydreaming that got people killed, and pulled up his pants. Curtiss slipped out of the barn and crawled on his stomach to the edge of the marsh some fifty yards away. He had begun to edge into the reeds when he heard them.

Click.

Splash.

There they were. He could just make out their heads through the heavy rain. They crawled under the derelict windmill, then slipped on hands and knees into the tall grasses of the marsh. He unlatched his safety and checked his remaining grenades. When the first one stood and looked at him he sighted down his rifle barrel and put his finger on the trigger. Then they began to shout at him, and to run. The next thing he knew he was overwhelmed.

Just as the first one got to him, he set off a signal flare and tried to keep them off.

Newton had awakened at daylight to find himself alone in the foxhole. "Hsst! Rogers!"

Rogers hadn't answered. Probably went to take a load off, Newton thought. He pulled his poncho over his helmet, then lit a cigarette. He took a deep drag on it, squatted down in the foxhole, and exhaled slowly so that there would be no big cloud of smoke for anyone to see. It had become morning, the dull light of a rainy French morning cloaking the battlefield. In Normandy, in July, the dark of night was never quite dark and the rainy days were mostly dim. Trees and tanks and people did not have sharp outlines, farm buildings dissolved against the backdrops of orchards and fields. It scared Newton to think back how many times he had walked right up on top of some krauts before he spotted them. It had happened almost every day that they had been engaged, and that had been almost every day since they had gotten off the beach, except when it rained so hard.

He couldn't see any Germans in the line of trees on the other side of the meadow but, if they were there, neither could they see him. He edged slowly to the backside of the foxhole, peered out and down the farm lane. Rogers was nowhere to be found.

"HSSST! ROGERS!"

He heard a slow crashing of trees, not the abrupt snap of trunks or branches but a slow, creaking leafy sound, a groan of tree limbs that had finally given up and were going to break and fall under weight. He knew immediately that Rogers had slipped out of the foxhole and gone to see the crashed glider.

He hated Rogers. The man never broke rules, not exactly. And, when fighting broke out, Rogers wasn't any more scared than the next guy. Rogers carried his share of ammunition boxes and lugged the mortar plate around, even carried the field radio. He didn't complain when the lieutenant volunteered him for listening posts or rear guards. But the only thing worse than Rogers' religious talk was his religious deafness. He remembered Altgelt once telling Rogers to slow down and think before he ran off into some torn-up village. "You idiot—there's Germans hiding in every one of those houses. You're exposed," Altgelt had yelled at him. "I ain't afraid to meet Jesus," Rogers had answered. "I'm not afraid of your meeting Jesus either," Altgelt had yelled back, "but I don't want you taking me along for your introduction." He knew that Rogers had gone off into that field to see if there were any bodies that needed praying over.

He weighed whether to stay at his post or to slip across the lane and find Rogers. James and Baker are over there with the .30 caliber machine gun, he thought. And the new guy, what's-his-name. That meadow is fifty or sixty yards across. If something pops they'll open up and I can be back here in ten seconds. That goddamned Rogers.

He tried waiting, hissing out Rogers' name, and even throwing a few rocks at the hedgerow on the other side of the lane where he had crawled through and found the glider. Rogers made no response.

But if the dumb son of a bitch is trapped under that plane or broke his leg or something. He thought through the problem of getting Rogers out of the field and back to the aid station, or leaving him in the field and manning the position alone, or explaining to Sergeant Altgelt why Rogers was not at his post. The rain poured harder. *Krauts'll never attack in this rain.* In the end, he decided that he should fetch the zealot before Rogers got them both in trouble.

Rogers was in trouble, although not very serious trouble. Newton found him trapped under a tangle of branches, leaves, landing gear struts and control cables, parts that had been wedged in the trees until Rogers had poked at the wreckage in the dark. The forward section of the glider had broken away from the rest of the plane.

"What in hell are you doing, Rogers? Are you hurt? Jesus Christ!" Newton poked around in the tree limbs and flapping debris. Rogers' head and left arm rose out from between a wheel strut and a cracked limb. His helmet was shoved forward over his face and was pushed against his head by a small leafy branch.

"I'm all right. Just help me get this branch up. And please stop using the Lord's name like that."

Newton slung his rifle over his shoulder and across his back and stepped into the clutter, then grabbed at a thick limb with both hands and began to lift. Rogers used his left hand to push against the smaller branch and tried to stand up for better leverage. A control cable that had gotten snagged between some frame tubes and tree branches popped free. At the moment when their combined forces lifted enough of the mess away from Rogers to let him take a step, the cable snapped forward, whipped against Rogers' suddenly-freed right arm, and caused him to slam his rifle butt against the branch.

The rifle shot went right into Newton's calf muscle, a sting so sudden that he didn't believe he had been shot until he found the hole in his pants leg which, quite apart from the shock and the ballistic crack of the cartridge, began to bleed. He crumpled to the ground.

"Oh, Newton, you okay? I'm sorry, Newton, you okay? Tell me you ain't shot. Oh goodness, I'm sorry. I'm really sorry."

Rogers watched Newton's face, the cascading looks of surprise, then pain, then shock as he fell back across the tree branches and onto the soaked meadow. Rogers grabbed him, took his face in his hands, and shook Newton by the shoulders, but he knew that he had done something really, really stupid.

"MEDIC!"

75

Newton was not very large and Rogers had grown up throwing cattle onto their sides for branding, helping his family to build corrals. Even so, the mud, the weight, and the darkness inside the meadow were more than Rogers could handle. He failed to get Newton out of the field before Altgelt and Witt arrived from where they had left Curtiss. Antsley had heard the call at the company command post and arrived at more or less the same time. They asked what Newton had asked.

"Don't exactly know, Sergeant. All I know is that the rifle went off and hit him in the leg."

The medic laid Newton longways on the muddy lane, checked his airway, looked for a pulse, and made sure he was breathing. "He's in shock and he's not real happy about it either. Where is it, soldier? Where is it?"

Newton made a half-hearted gesture with his hand and pointed to a muddy fold of his pants leg. The medic pulled the trousers out of Newton's boot, lifted it up, and quickly found the bleeding wound.

Rogers' mind was not as good as his aim. *I shouldn't have gone over there to that airplane*, he thought, *but if there was souls in there, it was my duty to pray over them.* He felt sufficiently righteous to stand for punishment against the charge of trying to do the Lord's work but, in the absence of any bodies, it would be hard to prove that he was doing the Lord's work by poking around in a wrecked plane. *Maybe I shouldn't have poked up in that tree.*

"You have trouble with the safety, Rogers? A lot of these M-1's do that." It never occurred to Sergeant Altgelt that Rogers hadn't told him the whole story.

Rogers knew that if his safety had been on, or at least if the cable and the branches hadn't knocked the safety off, Newton wouldn't have been shot.

"Yes, Sergeant. Safety came off somehow."

"What'd Newton do? Go over there to take a shit?"

"Yep. He sure did." He didn't clarify that Newton had returned two hours earlier, or that Rogers had left the fox hole while Newton was asleep.

"I need to get him up to the aid station. He's got a pretty good bleed going." Antsley ripped open a package of sulfa powder and dumped it in Newton's wound. He wrapped a compression bandage above the wound, then broke a morphine syrette and jammed it into Newton's leg for good measure. "You'll be all right, soldier. We're going to get you back to the aid station."

They lifted Newton to his feet and tried to help him limp away on the medic's arm but the bullet hole and the morphine teamed up to make it hard work.

"Okay, Medic. Go find a litter and get him out of here."

Antsley returned fifteen minutes later with two more men and a litter. They put Newton on it, cleared his rifle and sent it with him, then carried Newton away. Altgelt ordered Rogers back into the foxhole and told Witt to stay there and take Newton's place for the time being.

"Oh, Sergeant?" Rogers had stopped worrying about Newton and resumed worrying about the souls who might have been in the glider.

"What."

"Newton found a plane over there."

"What do you mean, found a plane?"

"One of ours, Sarge. Up in the trees."

"Anyone in it?"

"Don't know, Sarge."

Sergeant Altgelt began to suspect that there was more to the story than Rogers had told him, but at that moment the new guy, a replacement whose name he couldn't remember, came rushing up the lane to report that Curtiss had sent up a flare. Altgelt took out the walkie-talkie.

"*Lieutenant Campbell? Sergeant Altgelt. Over.* "

"*Go ahead, Sergeant. Over.*"

"*Listen, we got a flare from Curtiss. Something brewing at the flank. Over.*"

"*Get down there. Take the machine gun team. Mortar team, too. Over.*"

"*Already got 'em, sir. We're moving out. Oh, and sir? That gunshot was Newton's. Medic's bringing him up now. Out.*"

"*Get to the flank. Report back ASAP. Out.*"

Altgelt deployed the mortar team to the chimney of the wrecked farmhouse. He sent the light machine gun team into the apple orchard to cover the flat land between the barn and the river dike, then cautiously worked his way to the marsh. It was there that he found Curtiss.

Ten or twelve women, partially hidden by the tall reeds and grasses, stood huddled together in the flooded pasture at the base of the dike. Their clothes were filthy and torn, soaked from crawling through the marsh. They had taken off their shoes, some leather, some rough wooden shoes, and were holding them high overhead as if that might keep them from getting as soaked as their clothes. Curtiss stood between them and the water gate, alternately peering through the rain to the stretch of flat land on the other side, then back at the women. Altgelt skirted the group and sloshed through the muck to reach Curtiss.

"Who the hell are they, Curtiss?"

"No idea, Sergeant. I don't understand a word they're saying."

"What's over there where they came from? Any sign of Jerry?"

"I don't know. I can't see more than fifty yards through the rain. I tried to ask them about 'krauts' and 'boches' and they pointed back toward the hedgerows. I don't know if they were trying to say the krauts are holed up over there or not. I think they're trying to get away from the bombs." He handed a leaflet to Sergeant Altgelt. "One of them gave this to me."

They had seen the leaflets all over Normandy. Ike's pilots had scattered them before the invasion. *AUX HABITANTS DES ZONES DE COMBAT.* In smaller letters someone had put a pencil mark where the words *bombardiers alliés* were written. The leaflets told the French to flee the towns.

"Probably came from St. Lô. Morning reports say that we, which meant American and British air forces, already bombed it to rubble. But there's not a soldier in the First Army within three miles of it."

Curtiss shrugged.

Altgelt slipped back down the dike to look at the women. They shivered where they stood, the rain drops plinking into the shallow pond at their feet, reeds brushing them, their cloaks and coats draped about their shoulders, all soaked with water. Their eyes were hollow with fear, staring into space, yet darting in every direction and startled by every sound and movement. All of the women were covered by sores. There were children, grandmothers, school-age girls, young women, old women.

He slung his rifle and put away his walkie-talkie, then waded toward the women to extend a hand to them, inviting them as much as he could to come out of the marsh and follow him to the old barn. One-by-one they slipped and trod and floundered toward sturdier ground, holding hands and leading one another, and made their way out of the weather and into the old structure. He called one of the men from the machine gun team to trade places with Curtiss at the dike. When Curtiss arrived they tried to question the women.

"Listen, ma'am, you're safe now. Where are the Germans? Can anybody tell me where the Germans are?"

"We St. Lô."

One of the women, a determined-looking girl of twenty or so, tried to answer through her wet face and in her meager English: "We no German." She was emphatic. The other women let her act as the group spokesman, although it was unclear whether this was because of her half dozen words of English or merely that her energy was greater than her fear.

"What'd she say?"

"'We St. Lô.' I think she's saying they've walked here from St. Lô."

The girl then pointed at one of the other women.

"Blessé. Sor? Her blessé." The girl, a note of urgency in her voice, pointed to a woman who had slumped down against the mucked floor of the barn. Two other women rushed to prop her up, clucking feminine concern.

"Blessed? Huh? Is that what you said? Blessed? I don't—" Altgelt had no idea what the girl was trying to tell him. The woman in question did not appear to be a nun or otherwise obviously blessed.

"Blessé." She repeated it slowly and in a louder voice. "B l e s s é!"

The woman in question let out a painful moan and, when the others helped to turn her over, Altgelt could see that she was bleeding through the back of her dress, a ring of blood spreading outward from a small caliber hole near the middle of her upper back.

"Curtiss—give me your med pack. Put some sulfa on this lady's wound." Sergeant Altgelt took the sulfa, then gave it to the girl. "Medicine!" He pointed to the wounded woman, then mimed the action of tearing open the packet and dropping it into the wound. "Medicine!" He handed it to her. One of the other women nodded and began to help the wounded woman to her feet, then to walk her to a milking stall where there would be more privacy for the removal of upper garments.

"Ask her where's the Germans who shot this woman." Altgelt assumed that since Curtiss had found them he should talk to them.

"Where Germans? Where?" Curtiss, not unreasonably, abandoned pronouns and adjectives and adopted the strategy of speaking slowly. "Where?"

Géraldine held up two fingers, then three, then shrugged that she didn't understand him. Curtiss repeated 'Germans' and mimed a look of inquiry, pointing at the river, the trees, south in general.

Altgelt, frustrated, looked at her, then at Curtiss.

"Where the hell were they when this woman got shot?" He pointed first at the injured woman, then back across the dike, tried holding up fingers to count miles, or kilometers, or anything. Altgelt's pidgin French was worse than Géraldine's pidgin English. By the end of the exercise all he knew was that there were five somethings, whether Germans, tanks, the distance to St. Lô, he had no idea.

"Whir de coes." Géraldine waved in the direction of the rest of France. Altgelt sighed.

"Germans here?" Sgt. Altgelt pointed to the barn, pointing out the bullet marks on the half-timbered walls. "Germans?"

"*La-bás! Touts les allemains sont la-bás!*" She pointed back in the direction of the hedgerows, perhaps toward St. Lô. "*Wit coes! Pres du Le Déversoir.*"

"What'd she say?"

"I think she's saying the Germans are somewhere over there, where there are cows. "Farm? This farm?" He pointed to the ruined house, the barn, the apple orchard. "You?"

"Non, Sor. *Ferme* me there." She pointed across the river. "We go *pont*. We *ferme!*" she repeated, followed by a make-believe kablooey. "*Ferme* PLOOSH!" She pointed back to where they had come from and repeated the sound of a farm blowing up, emphasized by the rapid raising and lowering of arms and hands, fingers spread, eyes blinking, the universal pantomime of something exploding. "PLOOSH. *Ferme!* Dere. Coes. Coes. Mooooo. Coes!"

Curtiss understood. Cows. Farm. The Germans were somewhere back in the farms in the direction of St. Lô. St. Lô was five kilometers away. The Germans could be five kilometers away; they could be just beyond the nearest hedgerow.

Altgelt sent Géraldine and the medicine to help the lady in the barn while he and Curtiss rushed back to the dike. Dawn had yielded a bit more light and the rain had eased slightly. Still, the visibility was so poor that neither of them felt exposed, even standing on the dike and peering as far in the direction of St. Lô and the Pont Hébert road as they could.

"Look, Sergeant."

"What?"

"This isn't the river. It's a canal."

Curtiss was right. In the rising light they could see that the dike wasn't a river bank but, instead, merely a tow path. Beyond the sluice the canal made a gentle turn, then flowed another forty or fifty yards before it disappeared into a line of poplars and emptied into the Vire.

"Jesus! We still haven't got the flank covered. Curtiss, head that way."

Altgelt motioned for him to make haste on down the levee and take up a position that would, at last, close the flank as they had been ordered to do hours earlier. Curtiss took off at a run while Altgelt unpacked the walkie-talkie to report back to Lieutenant Campbell.

As he trotted along the path Curtiss tried to sort out the confusion. The map symbols showed ruins, a church, the river, and the tuil shed, something so insignificant that it would hardly be printed on a military map. There was the river, the ruins of the farm, the barn and tools. But it was more of a milk barn than a tool barn, defended and abandoned by the Germans a few days before. He remembered the women taking the wounded lady toward the stalls where he had relieved himself half an hour before. Then he knew.

It was too late, he knew it was too late, but he screamed back at them anyway.

"NOOOOO!"

For a fraction of a second Curtiss saw as plain as day his platoon ser-geant in Sicily, kicking at a door. *Never kick a door with anything you don't want blown off.* The sergeant had kicked, the door had exploded, the ser-geant's face had a look of surprise, then anger, then death, all while his foot and boot flew off the end of his leg and the remainder of his body pitched backwards out of the doorway and onto the cobbled street, all in the same instant that the explosion inside the tuil barn blew the stall door off its hinges, killing the already-wounded woman and puncturing Aunt Julia like a pin cushion.

The booby trap had blown wooden splinters into the women who had taken the blessé into the stall to pour sulfa powder on her wound. Sergeant Altgelt found them, a bleeding heap where they had been knocked back-ward twenty feet. Splinters, dirt, cow dung, hay and blood had blown over all of them. Clouds of dust and barn debris rose from the stall and dirt floor and choked off the air. The women screamed and backed against the walls and beams and waited for more booby traps to kill them all.

Sergeant Altgelt turned to face the river to see whether the explosion had brought the Germans down on them. He signaled the mortar team and machine gunner to adjust their weapons and bracket the dike while the cluster of women panicked. Then he realized that Curtiss was no lon-ger on the dike, and grabbed his walkie-talkie.

"*Lt. Campell! Altgelt! Over.*" The urgency in the sergeant's voice came through louder than the static and crackle of poor reception.

The lieutenant answered, asked if they were under attack.

"Not yet, sir, but we need a medic pretty bad. A bunch of refugees came up out of the marsh over here. Booby trap went off. One of them's dead, some wounded. And Curtiss, sir. Over."

"What about Curtiss? Over."

"He took off, sir. Running. I sent him to cover the approach, but when the barn door blew, he took off. Just ran like crazy. And disappeared into the rain. Over."

"Curtiss ran away?"

"Ran, sir, but not *away*. He ran *south*." It was hard to describe, harder to understand, but Curtiss had taken off at a dead run across the meadow; if there were any Germans, that's where they would be. "Not *away* from the Germans—*toward* them, wherever they are. It's more like he attacked, sir. Sir, I need you to get on down here."

CHAPTER SEVEN

—◦∞◦—

Sanders helped Antsley get Newton out of the jeep and into the barn. He removed the information tag tied to Newton's shirt and handed it to Jefferson to type into the casualty report form, then asked what had happened.

"So, what's going on with you?"

The morphine had further reduced Newton's already-limited capacities such that his answer came out *Rogers* SHOT BY *accident* AIRPLANE *fell.*

"You were shot by an airplane?"

Newton nodded.

"Hey," Sanders whispered. "This guy says he was shot by an airplane. Antsley just brought him in. There ain't no airplanes out there, not in this rain. Jesus, you think he, you know?"

"You know," meant, "shot himself." Colonels were convinced that there was an epidemic of privates shooting themselves in the leg to avoid Germans shooting them in the head. The Division daily reports routinely directed all medical units to report suspected cases, which 'will be dealt with severely.'

Antsley didn't know. Antsley hadn't seen any airplanes. Newton was not making complete sense. The bullet hole in Newton's calf angled downward. Captain Collins was the surgeon on duty.

"Hey, soldier? How you doing?" Collins stood over Newton and glanced down at his leg, read the medic's note tag. "Says here that you got shot by an airplane. How'd you get shot by an airplane? It's raining Noah's flood out there; I haven't heard a plane in three days."

"There was this plane," Newton slurred up at him. "I went to sit in the bushes, no, it was Rogers, he disappeared, no, well, I found him. And then the airplane." Newton's eyes narrowed, he took a deep breath, then tried

83

to point at his leg but instead poked Antsley in the eye.

Antsley rolled back Newton's fatigue pants, then paused while Collins looked at the wound. The bullet hole, small and round, congealed blood and sulfa, was quite fresh.

"Hey, someone get me some light. And some gloves." They were provided and Collins began to probe. Newton abided the procedure by mentally composing a garbled prayer that the wound would disable him enough to get him out of the front line but not enough to cripple him after the end of the war.

"It is a gunshot wound," Collins commented. "Small caliber. A booby trap would have torn everything up 'cause most of the mines take off a foot or a hand, tear up a leg. This one's just a nice clean hole. See here?" He invited Antsley to inspect. "Round hole. Straight line." He rotated the metal probe around in the bullet hole to demonstrate.

Sanders came back to the treatment table. "Let me get your dog tags, there." He lifted Newton's metal identification tag and chain, copied down his name and blood type, then his service number. "Want a priest? Want a chaplain?"

Hope not, Newton thought to himself. It came out as a snorted laugh. *More I'm around religion the closer I come to getting killed.* He laughed until Collins hit the bullet with the probe. "God DAMN!"

"Found it. We'll have you up and running in no time." Collins tapped on the probe a few times to be sure he was hitting a slug rather than a tibia, each time bringing Newton half way to a scream and a sitting position.

"You want me to prep him, sir?" Antsley asked. Collins said no.

"This isn't much of a hole. I'll do it here. Get me a sterile kit." Both Antsley and Sanders raised their eyes but they didn't say anything: the skin around the wound was well-defined and Collins was their superior officer. They thought it was lucky that the bullet had not gone deep enough to hit a bone. "So hey, soldier, you seen any good-looking French girls out there? This is the third town we've been in—hold still and I'll just pop this right out—and I'll be damned if I've seen a one. Now England, never saw anything like it. Girls all over the place. Hold still, you won't feel a thing."

Newton had not seen any French girls in the muddy foxholes and wrecked farms where he had been fighting for six weeks. A technician came; Collins changed gloves and adjusted the light, told the men to help Newton hold still.

"Hey, soldier. You see that over there?" He pointed to a metal vat across the barn. "That's a still. Calvados still. If some guy owned a still like that back in the States they'd elect him king of Kentucky. Hold on, this is going to stick for just a second." Collins pushed a syringe-full of procaine into Newton's leg. "We're going to let that sit for a second, then scrub you up a bit. So, you know what Calvados is? Fruit brandy, apples, pears. Strong as lightning. Best anesthetic I ever saw. What we don't rub in, we drink. Ha ha ha. Where you from?"

Newton lost the sensation in his leg.

Collins began to extract the bullet, a process which Antsley watched with curiosity. Collins did not apply a tourniquet, merely gouged around with the probe and forceps. Before too long he extracted a lead slug from Newton's calf muscle.

"*Voilá*," Collins said, holding the missile up for all to admire. He passed the slug to Antsley, then to Newton. "Show this to your grandkids," he said, ignoring the hole he had left, now twice the size of the hole he had started with. It was while he cleaned and bandaged the wound that they heard an explosion.

"Thunder?"

They waited to see if the generators failed. They didn't, nor did any lightning flash across the rainy landscape outside the barn doors. The rain continued. The thunder did not.

"What was that? Someone get on the horn and see if they're pushing off."

Sanders came back in a few minutes to report that the combat units were still dug in. "They think it was something on the flank. They're trying to get some intell to be sure the krauts aren't trying to do an end-around. They'll let us know." A few minutes later he came back.

"Hey, sirs. We might have some customers. Battalion says what we heard was some kind of mine blew up in a barn, messed up some civilians pretty good. They're sending them in. Probably take a half hour or so; it was deep in the woods, right at the end of the line."

"Tell 'em I've got someone on the table," Collins said. "Garth can do the next one."

Will had seen far less of France than Sergeant Prior believed Will had seen. Prior had taken Shorty's comment to mean he should spy on Will.

85

Thus, for days, Prior had clumsily hidden at corners and stood behind trees in an effort to catch the snot-nosed young doc going AWOL. This in turn led to a unit-wide game of hide-and-seek in which all the enlisted men, who hated Prior anyway, sent him off on goose chases to see if he could catch Will in the act. For two days there had been reports of Hastings running off into the woods, Hastings swimming across the Vire, Hastings drunk and disorderly in a village *estaminet* some way back up the road. Prior's suspicions were fueled by his discovery of several exceptionally well-drawn pencil sketches of places he had never seen, depicting for the most part imaginary towns, the fictitious ruins of fictitious battles, and several views of the monastery as it might have been seen from different angles, all drawn entirely by Will's imagination, each planted for Prior to find. The game did keep Prior out of everyone's way. Fouquet saw him lurking at the edge of the abandoned tile factory, a crumbling tin building with the word Tuils barely visible on the faded sign.

"Shhhh."

"What's up, Sarge?"

"I've got him!"

"Who?" Fouquet restrained a laugh. He wondered what Prior had done in civilian life.

"Captain Hastings." Prior almost spat on the word captain. "He's over there, where they wash clothes." He held one finger to his lips to indicate the need to be silent, then pointed with his free hand to the laundry shed a couple of hundred yards distant. "I've been waiting; sooner or later he's going to give it the slip and get across the river."

"Sorry to wreck the plan, Sarge. Shorty told me to go get him; we've got a jeep coming in with a couple of wounded refugees. Garth's already scrubbing." He could feel Prior's aggravation radiating from his hiding place behind the tile shop. "Maybe next time." He went on his way before having to listen to any more of Prior's invective about snot-nosed officers.

Will heard the steps on the grass before he ever got to the laundry.

"Is that you, Fouquet?"

"Yes, sir. How'd you know?"

"How's Sergeant Prior? He followed me all the way through town, out past the stone cross on the St. Lô road, then back around behind the apple barn and over to that old tile factory. I had to slow down a couple of times so he could catch up. Here, drop this where he can find it." Will handed

Fouquet a modestly drawn sketch of a wall-enclosed French farm. In the background there was a longhorn bull walking along behind a John Deere tractor in a ripe wheat field. Prior was from Brooklyn. "What's up?"

"Well, it seems there's a bunch of refugees, sir. Hurt by a booby-trap a mile or so away. Medics are bringing 'em in, radio says one of 'em's pretty bad, sir. Captain Collins has someone on a table and Captain Garth, well—"

"Okay, I'll be right there. Tell Garth to.... never mind, I'll be right there."

Will had spent a lonely hour sketching and wondering whether he should have told Shorty more than he had.

Will had managed to get Halliburton out of the rubble of the Windmill Club and back to Shrivenham. There he had stitched up Halliburton's face, bandaged his ribs and applied analgesics to his cuts, good deeds that Halliburton punished by ordering Will to do short arm inspections on the enlisted men at midnight. That had gone on every night for almost six weeks, right up until the day they were shipped off to go aboard the LSTs.

As for Douglas, there had been no trace of him in the bomb debris, not so much as a boot. Will had been saddened, not surprised, that it had come to that. Douglas's exit had been as mysterious as his entrance, months before, when Will had awakened on a train to find himself hand-cuffed to the man who would talk him through the loss of Virginia.

Now, both of them, once friends, were gone, as much out of his life as Hoyt and Johnny. There was nothing for it. Shorty didn't need to know everything.

Will put away his sketch pad. He pulled a poncho on over his uniform, put on his cap and steel helmet, laced his boots. He looked once more at the grainy snapshot that Shirley Fleming had sent to him, Peter standing next to Virginia on the Sullivan's porch, both of them grinning. He had tried to remember when Shirley took the picture but couldn't. It was no matter; he was grateful for her having sent it. It was the only thing Will had that looked like his life used to look.

He didn't pay much attention to the ragged women huddled inside the door of the barn except to perceive that they were extremely anxious. Sanders cleared a path for him and he walked right by Claudine, who stood next to Géraldine, then went to the back to scrub. Through the flood-lit screens he made out Morph at the head and Garth at the side of the operating table. They didn't appear to be doing anything.

"It's a bad one, Will," Garth called out over the screen. "She's in shock but Morph went ahead and started her. Collins is tied up."

"What are you waiting for?" Will came in and looked the scene over. It wasn't clear that Aunt Julia was still alive but someone had placed an intravenous line in her arm to run blood. Morph had snaked a tracheal tube down her throat so that he could run anesthesia. Otherwise, Garth was doing nothing to start surgery.

"Jesus, Will," Garth answered. "This is a little more than a broken arm or a bullet in the leg. She's got holes in places where most people don't even have places." Garth drew a deep breath. "And we're not supposed to be doing this."

"What do you mean?"

"She needs a lot more than we're supposed to be doing here, especially on a civilian. This isn't some 'splint the leg' or 'ectomy the bullet' and send her back home." He paused to see if Will agreed; Will did not. "*Field Hospital Memo Number One*: we're not fixers, just cogs on the assembly line, Will. I've got to send her back to the 'vac at Isigny."

"Don't worry about that, Garth. If you don't start doing something now she won't make it to the evacuation hospital." Morph was watching her signs drop. Morph also was aware that Garth had become belligerently timid since a couple of days ago when a nineteen-year-old rifleman, wounds not much different that Aunt Julia's, had died on Collins's table.

"We can't do her, Will," Garth repeated.

"You think we can just wrap an army blanket around her and put her in the ambulance? Jesus, Garth, she looks like the pig."

All the combat surgeons had been given a pig, in Belfast, for practice. Few of the pigs survived. When Will lifted Aunt Julia's drapes she did look like his pig—blood everywhere and thick barn door splinters sticking up out of her mid-section. The medics had tried to remove some, causing more bleeding, and left others in her pelvis and abdomen. There was more. Will continued.

"There's blood seeping out of a hole in her chest. Two gashes in her stomach. Those splinter holes further on down look like a basketball net." He gently touched her abdomen to see whether the flow was sensitive to pressure; it was. She didn't breathe so much as rattle up and down as the oxygen dictated. Her heartbeat, when they found it, was borderline. "And her right leg is wrenched at a pretty good angle." He turned to the instrument cart and chose a scalpel. "So, here we are, Garth—lead, follow, or get out of the way."

"What do you think you're doing, Will? Jesus? You don't know how to..."

"You're probably right, Garth," and without another word, Will sliced Aunt Julia from her navel to her sternum, then spread open a surgical field and dipped his hands into her mangled organs. "Morph? Can you breathe her a bit while we figure out out where all this bleeding's coming from?" If she couldn't breathe during anesthesia it wouldn't matter where the bleeding came from.

Garth watched, paralyzed at seeing his inexperienced assistant wade into the surgical slough he had himself been too timid to try.

"Lots of holes in here, Garth. Sure could use some extra hands." Will had begun to probe behind one of the huge splinters; a gush of blood flowed out. "Can you at least hand me a clamp?" He looked Garth in the eyes.

"God damn, Will! Do you know what you're doing?"

"No idea. Never saw anyone this bad, not alive anyway. But all we really do is open, poke, clamp, clean, and close. Anybody can do that." He clamped off the first hemorrhage, then began to unfold intestines, finding more bleeders than he knew what to do with.

"Listen, Will. Even if you don't kill her, what are you going to do with her? We can't keep her. You're going to get us..." There was something of a plea in Garth's voice. He didn't want to do this.

Morph, who never chatted during surgery, broke in:

"Take a look at her, Garth. Look real close. See her clothes?"

Aunt Julia's clothes consisted of nondescript remnants of a ragged blue dress, stiff leather shoes that probably had been fashionable at one time, and patched and worn undergarments. Géraldine's shawl had been dumped on the floor.

"She looks to me like some kind of soldier, you know? French Resistance, whatever they call it here." Morph paused to let Garth absorb his tale. "So she's Allied. That qualifies her for the evacuation hospital. If you two don't kill her first." Morph had never told the surgeons what to do but, then, Garth had never refused to operate. This was new ground, and it was slippery.

Garth found a clamp, handed it to Will, then looked for a retractor.

"What'd you do before med school, Will?"

"During the winters I worked for Doc Pritchard. In the summers I worked at the slaughterhouse behind the butcher shop. I was the guy who cleaned up after they killed the pigs. One of the Sanger brothers would put a .22 rifle up to their heads and shoot. The pig would flop down right there on the concrete, bleeding, shit all over the slab. Sometimes they died. Sometimes they didn't."

"That qualified you for medical school?"

"It did. They weren't too picky in Tierra. Doc Pritchard was getting kind of old. Can you hold that, just a bit to the right? There." He waited for a moment to see if the clamp held, then to think about whether he should keep his mouth shut. The clamp held; his mouth didn't. "So, when I graduated, the town kind of raised the money for me to go to school."

"You must have been one hell of a student. Here."

"Not really. The thing was that Doc Pritchard only had so much malpractice left in him before Poppy Sullivan would have killed him. Poppy owns the paper. Swab there, please. Good. Actually, Poppy owns the town. So Poppy either had to put up with Doc or get rid of him. I was the solution."

"Why'd they pick you? Look, Will, you can't just go rooting around in there. Use the retractors to lift below the wound, then probe up. Jesus."

"Because Poppy Sullivan said so. He said I was going to go to medical school and, after I did, I was coming back to Tierra. It was as simple as that."

It hadn't been quite that simple. Poppy had picked Will because Virginia had picked Will. Poppy had indeed told Will that there was a scholarship to send him to medical school; a couple of years passed before Will figured out the rest. It came out during one of Doc's drunks that the scholarship was just money Doc had wheedled out of the cotton farmers and Shirley Fleming's dad at the bank.

"All right, Will, enough. Move over." Through a combination of watching Will attempt to put Aunt Julia's intestines back together with enormous cross-stitches and a brief wave of all-for-one esprit, Garth succumbed. "If the Germans didn't kill her it would be hard to explain that I let you do it. Move." He edged around the table, then transferred a clamp from one hand to Will's left hand. When Will lifted his right hand Garth selected a forceps probe and stepped into the fray.

"The sheriff had already explained to me everything I needed to know.

90

Okay, let me get a sponge down there, Garth." They paused in the storytelling long enough to get the bleeding back under control, then Will resumed. "What he said to me on the way to the newspaper was he was taking me over to see Poppy Sullivan and I was going to do whatever Poppy told me I was going to do. Or Sheriff Hoskins was going to cut my balls off."

"Uh, Will, did it ever occur to you that Tierra, Texas might not be the best place for you to go back and heal mankind? That might explain why you like this war so much."

"There was a little more to it than that. When the sheriff picked me up at school, I thought he was taking me to jail."

"Jail? What the hell for?"

"Virginia. Poppy's daughter."

There had arisen a question of Virginia's honor. Not precisely, but Poppy Sullivan would not have known about the technicality of the question; he would only have been told that Will had been caught with Virginia at the quarry, both of them, in the water, naked. "So here I was getting ready to offer to marry his daughter and instead he told me that I had been awarded a scholarship to medical school."

"So, did you? Offer to marry her?"

"I did. It kind of aggravated him. All he said was 'Of course—why'd you think I had the sheriff bring you over here?' Poppy had emphasized the word 'you.' The sheriff had already used his recruiting system on my buddies, Hoyt and Johnny. But by the time Poppy was through with me, I didn't care."

"So, you going back? You need to exteriorate the whole thing, Will. All of it. Slowly. After the war? You going back to marry the girl and save the town?"

Will had asked himself the same question. In the end, the answer had been no. It would have been one thing to go back to Virginia, but Douglas had made him ask himself the hard question: would he go back if there were no Virginia? "*Seven years of not saying yes sounds a lot like no, Will. Why did you ever believe she was in love with you anyway?*"

That's what he had decided, even before Peter was killed—he would not go back to Tierra. Before he could tell anyone else, though, Morph brought him back to the operating room:

"Full stop, Docs. Her pressure's dropped. She's crashing."

CHAPTER EIGHT

Genet returned to the Calvados barn to press his claim for medicines and implements. It had occurred to him that presenting himself to Sergeant Prior as a fisherman had not helped his chances to restock the medical clinic. He now wore a faded blue suit, a rumpled white shirt, an ill-knotted tie. Despite the umbrella, by the time the soldier in charge of quarters had located Prior and told him that the Frenchy was back, both Genet and his clothes were wringing wet from the continual downpour. Prior stood in the doorway, arms crossed, knees locked, jaw clenched, and listened to Genet's entreaty.

"*Plasme.*"

"No."

"*Antibiotiques.*"

"No."

"*Teinture d'iode.*" Iodine.

"No."

"*Pansement adhésif.*" Adhesive bandages.

"No." Prior hadn't even bothered to yell for Fouquet; he didn't need a translator to say no. The only reason he might want Fouquet was to tell the little French guy to stop coming back and bothering the field hospital. He opened his mouth to yell for the unit translator but was stopped short by a sight that seemed to trouble Genet as much as himself.

A wiry little priest approached, stomping down the cobblestones toward them, water splashing with each step. A priest could mean trouble. To Prior's relief, the priest walked right past him, pivoted, faced Genet, and began to berate him.

"*Genet! What are you doing here? I thought....*" The priest thought they had

92

agreed to share equally in their attempts to fleece the Americans.

"*Ah, bonjour, Father Jean. I couldn't find you this morning. Well, no matter....*" Genet had no compunction about lying to the priest; it was a great convenience that the priest would have to forgive him if he went to confession, something he did only when caught lying to the priest. "*I came on down to try to meet their commander so that we, you and I, we may bring to their attention the needs of the town. The clinic...*"

"*The clinic? You put your clinic ahead of the church? Have you forgotten the church?*"

"*No, no, Father, not at all. But you do seem to be able to hold mass without your belfry. I can't do surgery without a clinic. And it seems to me the Americans have settled in. Let's start now.*"

The priest had no doubt that Genet had been trying to get to the Americans first. It was as a victim that he turned to Prior and began to press his own case, the necessity of American carpentry to restore his belfry from the damage done by American artillery.

"*Good morning, American commander.*" Father Jean had never figured out how to tell which German soldier was in charge; he understood even less about American uniforms and ranks. "*It is my church whose bell tower you have blown down with a very strategic and accurate bit of artillery, succeeding in routing the German garrison which, God be with us, had occupied Ste. Marie for four years. We give you our thanks. However, Man proposes, God disposes.*"

"Huh?" Prior had developed a false sense of security with Genet's one-line medicinal demands; the priest sounded more like a rapid-fire pest. The sergeant was completely befuddled and again started to yell for Fouquet; again the priest cut him off.

"*As you can see, American soldier—what kind of soldier is this man, Genet? General? Colonel?—that while God was willing to let His house be used in this battle for the purpose of liberating us from the Huns, it is now time to give thanks to God and restore His house. Therefore, I have come on God's behalf to inform you that you may send a team of carpenters, carpenters and masons, to rebuild my bell tower.*"

Father Jean had not spent the Occupation listening to the BBC on a clandestine radio hidden in the forest; he spoke no English. He trusted his Employer to see that Prior would understand French. He was mistaken.

"*So, come with me, General. Let's walk up to the church.*" Father Jean made the mistake of grabbing Prior by the arm, not rudely, but in the way French people do, to point him in the direction he wanted Prior to go. "*You could see it from here if your good soldiers had not blown the belfry down. Of course, if your men had not blown the belfry down, you would not need to come with me."*

The priest thought it was a good jest; Prior thought it was the last straw. He shook off Father Jean's hand and was drawing back his right fist to slug him when Shorty appeared.

"No! Stop! Jesus Christ, what the hell's going on out here?"

"I don't rightly know, sir." Prior really didn't know, a fact that made him unsure of which lie to tell the lieutenant. There were two of them, it is true, the old coot and a priest, but even Prior sensed that it would be hard to explain to Shorty why he was preparing to assault either one of them. "This one shows up every day trying to free-load; this other one," by whom he meant the priest, "he's new. Don't know why he was trying to do." Prior's lack of clarity ended in a sputter.

"Either of them speak English?"

"Not rightly as I can tell, sir."

"Enough, Sergeant. You three are making more racket than the rain on the roof. They with the ladies waiting on the refugee?"

"Don't rightly think so, sir. This one was here yesterday. The other one," and he jerked his head toward the aggressive old priest, "he come walking down from the village."

"All right. You know what to do, Sergeant."

Prior knew and, in his best sergeant's voice, yelled:

"FOUQUET!"

Newton screamed, too, not because he thought a priest had got hold of him, but because he thought God had. Newton believed he had died, and screamed. The sound was not speech but, instead, a primal surge, loud, a wail that overrode all other sensations. In Newton's mind he was clear: *No, God, not me, not now, I'm too young. It was just a little bullet. I'm afraid, God. I don't want to die. I didn't mean what I said to Rogers, I...* In his vocal chords, however, it came out as a guttural NEEAAOOUGHHH, all initiated by the gentle refrain of "Moonlight Serenade" and the vision of one of the most beautiful faces Newton had ever seen. He thought the former was celestial music, the latter an angel. As usual, Newton got it wrong.

Claudine jumped back.

Unable to sit still for four hours and surrounded by dozens of hardy young Americans, Claudine had become bored by the wait for news of Aunt Julia's surgery and slipped away to explore the apple barn. She was impressed by the portable laboratories, the x-ray machine, the generated surgery lights and abundant trays stocked with medicines and bandages, things and amounts not seen on the farm or even in St. Lô. It was nevertheless a different piece of equipment that had drawn her deeper into the field hospital—a phonograph. She located it in the recovery ward just as the Glenn Miller Orchestra slipped its way into Newton's head through 78 scratchy revolutions per minute. Fouquet, hearing Newton's garbled shouts about angels and deals with God, knew better and came to the post-op ward on the double.

"Hey, soldier. You're okay. What's the matter?" He bent over Newton's cot and checked for a pulse and heart rate. "You're okay, soldier. Have a bad dream? How many fingers am I holding up? Thirsty? What's your name?"

Newton rose slightly off the cot. He took in Fouquet, the apple barn, the smells and the thin Army blanket, and was relieved to find that he was not dead. He smiled, inhaled sharply, and descended back to the cot.

"Hey, medic. I was having this great dream. I was dreaming about this angel but she was like a girl, a real live girl." Newton muddled through his vision of a slender, tallish, olive-skinned enchantress not much younger than he was, all wide eyes and dark hair falling forward as she bent over him. Like his bargain with God, very little of what he said was clear. Even so, he was convincing enough that when Fouquet heard the word girl he turned to look where Newton pointed.

Looking back at him, leaning against a post, Claudine Dupré so startled him that Fouquet, too, wondered whether an angel had crawled out from behind the Calvados distillery.

"Who are you?" He looked at her, momentarily forgetting Newton, then realized she was a French girl. He switched to his stilted translation: "Who art thou?"

She laughed.

"I'm Claudine. I'm waiting. For my aunt.."

"Medic? Hey, medic?" Newton, pleased to be alive, wanted some attention.

"Yeah, Buddy, what's up?"

"Found her, medic. Mine. Oh, and leg hurts."

"*Thou waitest? Upon whom?*" Fouquet's French sounded like that of an illiterate acolyte, a church urchin forced to follow one of the priests around at the endless masses and prayers at the convent school in St. Lô.

"*My sister. We are waiting for my aunt.*" She spoke slowly, as if to a child, and found Fouquet's admiring gape to be as pleasing as any the German soldiers had expressed. "*What's wrong with him?*"

Fouquet stopped staring at Claudine long enough to examine the gunshot wound. It was red, swollen. The stitches strained to close the bullet hole and Collins's repair. The whole area was ragged with fingernail scratch marks.

"You scratching at it, Buddy? Looks like you're clawing at it."

"Itches, medic. That's what woke me up. And the girl."

"Just leave it alone. I've gotta put another dressing on there." He cut some gauze and tape, then turned back to Newton. "Sometimes the penicillin causes a little itching. It'll go away. The girl's going away, too. You get some rest."

Newton was not happy with either bit of news but, he conceded, he was still better off than when he woke up and thought he was dead.

Then Prior's yell boomed through the barn: "FOUQUET!"

Even Newton heard the shout.

"Fucking sergeant," Fouquet muttered.

"That's how they make sergeant, Medic. Only thing you gotta have to be a sergeant is a big lung and a little brain."

"FOUQUET!" roared through the barn a second time; even Claudine jumped at the sound. This time, however, it was more than Prior. Shorty's voice came through the musty air as clearly as the sergeant's. Fouquet knew it was time to go.

"*Accompany me, Miss. We must depart.*"

Fouquet took Claudine by the arm and nudged her out beyond the post-op screen and away from the phonograph. She would have preferred to stay, as would Fouquet. Newton certainly didn't want her to leave. His parting view of her back was incentive enough to make him want to get well.

He lay back on the cot and tried to listen to the phonograph but the itching had returned with a vengeance. He bent forward to dig a finger under the new dressing but failed to reach it. Even though the itching wound was becoming more than Newton could bear, he gasped and coughed, then panicked because of the difficulty in getting a full breath of air.

If it ain't one thing, he thought, *it's another*. Then he passed out.

Garth went to rest; Will went to check on a few men who weren't hurt badly enough to be sent to the evacuation hospital. Prior and the medical technicians had set aside a space where the lightly wounded could recuperate before going back to the line. Six or seven soldiers lay on cots, their twisted ankles wrapped, bullet grazes cleaned and dressed, burns salved.

"Let me take a look at you, Corporal. Hand okay? Let me see you make a fist." The corporal made a fist; it was swollen. "Let's put a hot water bottle on there and see if that does the trick."

He checked on another soldier, a seventeen year old who had been a bit slow in getting his hand away from a mortar tube. "Sulfavitin doing the job? Tell you what—Captain Collins is headed back to Isigny in the ambulance; I can keep you here overnight if you want." Collins thought most lightly-wounded soldiers were goldbrickers. The boy did seem to react to the idea of a night on a cot, with clean blankets and warmish food. "Your skin's going to burn for a day or two, but that's about it. Your squad got you covered?" Will knew intuitively what Collins did not—that the best medicine for a wounded man is to go back to the line, to be there for his buddies, no matter what. The boy sighed and said he was ready to go back to his unit whenever the doc was ready to send him. "Can't screw my squad just so's I can sleep in a dry barn." Will told him to rest another hour.

Cot by cot he checked their pupils, respirations and blood pressure, cranial nerves two through twelve and pulse rates, encouraging each of the soldiers to take it easy until he felt ready to go back to duty.

"*Excusez-moi de vous deranger,*" she said. It broke his concentration and he glanced up.

"Beg pardon, ma'am?"

She was fifteen or twenty feet away, standing between two folding cloth screens that were the walls of the makeshift recovery room. It was hard to see her in the dim light; the barn was dark anyway, and the ward was kept dark so the wounded men could rest. He did not get up off his knees but, instead, continued to check the pulse of a private who had been hit by a large tree branch when a German shell shattered it. She did not go away.

"*I want to know about my aunt. Can you take me to someone who can tell me how she is?*"

97

"I'm sorry, ma'am. I'm afraid I don't speak French. We've got an interpreter. Fouquet. He's pretty good." He relaxed again, then turned back to the soldier. "Sorry, buddy. I've got to start again." The patient told him to take as long as he wanted. He looked at his watch, counted for a full minute. His pulse was still racing. The kid was still scared to death two hours after they brought him in.

Will finished and turned back to Géraldine. "All right, ma'am. I'm sorry to make you wait. Do you speak English?"

"*Non*," which was not completely true. American was not the same as English, not the bits she had heard now and then on the BBC. "*Can you tell me what they have done with my aunt? It was the middle of the day when they took her away. Is she still in surgery?*"

"Wish I understood you. Let's go find Fouquet. Guys, don't leave, I'll be right back." A couple of the men chuckled from their cots. Will nodded at the young woman and led her away. Garth was still in his surgical gown when they walked past him on the way to the front.

"*Le chirurgien?*" The surgeon?

"Is he the surgeon? Is that what you're asking? You're here with that lady who had a lumber yard coming out of her stomach, aren't you?" There was more light in the barn as they approached the front; he saw more clearly that not only was she a French woman but a ragged, wet, young one, with a shawl over her shoulders and a thin wet muffler around her neck. Her hair was covered by a scarf, her outer clothes the worse for having been in the rain for a couple of days. He realized that she was one of the women he had noticed when he had passed through the front of the barn on the way to surgery. "I'm Will"

She was not pretty, not exactly, but her haggard expression didn't disguise that if she bathed and put on some clean clothes she would be pleasant enough to look at. He suspected she was a farm girl. He waited for her to reply.

She did not tell him her name. Instead, she tried again to say what she wanted:

"*Is that man the surgeon? We were waiting for my aunt; she was operated on. I want to know her condition.*" Then she, too, heard the phonograph, along with Claudine's cheery voice floating over the top of the partitions, as flirtatious with Americans as she had been with Fritz at the bridge.

"*Claudine?*" She called out.

"Claudine? Is that your name?" Will pointed to her. "Claudine, you?"

"*No, je ne suis pas Claudine. Claudine est ma soeur.*" She realized that she was being brusque but wanted to find her sister and find someone who could tell her about her aunt, not chat with a hot water bottle plouc.

Will nodded, then turned her around to lead her back into the barn in the direction of the music. When they got there Glenn Miller was wafting above Fouquet's head, Claudine standing on one side of him, Antlsey on the other. The two medics wore silly grins; Claudine's striking smile greatly exceeded her dirty face.

"Ma'am, this is Fouquet. He's the translator. He can tell you what you're asking. Hey, Fouquet? Who've you two got there?" Will couldn't blame them for the grin; unlike the grumpy one, Claudine was a sixteen- or seventeen year old version of everything that the men had heard about beautiful French girls.

"Don't exactly know," Fouquet replied, "but I've got a gun-shot-to-the-leg back there in post-op. He woke up and saw her and thought he'd died and gone to heaven."

"You don't have a gun-shot leg back there," Antsley chimed in. "He's mine. You weren't even supposed to be there. Go on back to the post-op. I'll take care of her."

"So if he was your patient, where were you when he started screaming?"

"Where were you when I brought him in from the hedgerows?"

"Down, tigers," Will told the two. "Claws in, paws flat. Yours is a little friendlier than this one but I wouldn't bank on her picking either of you two to go to the prom. Anyway, I think this one wants to know about that lady we did who hit the booby trap. Tell her that her friend is in the recovery room. She'll be there a while."

Fouquet translated it for him.

"She says the lady is their aunt, Doc. She wants to know exactly her condition. What do I tell her?"

"She's critical. Tell her I think if she makes it through the night we hope to take her to a better hospital tomorrow. Tell her that." Fouquet translated. Géraldine's expression did not display much gratitude. "Tell her it's a question of keeping a constant eye on her blood pressure and her respirations. If anything drops, well...."

Fouquet did his best.

Géraldine was not impressed, and said so. *"Thank the nurse's aide for me. He can go back to his blankets and hot water bottles,"* she said, nodding at Will. *"I would like to ask the surgeon. Can you take me to him please?"*

That took the smile off Fouquet's face. Sometimes it's better to not understand, he thought. He equivocated: "She says that she wants me to take her to the surgeon. She seems to think you're not a doctor or something."

"Tell her never mind. She wants to see Garth, so take her to see Garth." He started to add, 'and no need for her to wash up on my account.' Instead, he said, "And you two—keep the pretty one close by. Maybe Prior'll give you a pass for a couple of hours."

"FOUQUET!"

"Why's Sergeant Prior yelling?" Garth asked when Fouquet brought the girls to him. "And what are you doing here? Why didn't Captain Hastings talk to her?" Garth didn't know where Will was and he didn't know why Fouquet and Antsley, and two dirty moppets, were pestering him when all he wanted was a canteen full of Calvados and a nap. "I have no idea if she's going to live; Morph's in charge of post-op." Garth also didn't know why he had stood over the lady with Will for hours, hoping she wouldn't die before they could get her to Isigny. "Listen, tell her if the lady makes it through the night, we'll send her to a better hospital tomorrow. Then go away. And find out why Prior's yelling for you." Garth shut his door in their faces, the door being a portable screen that separated his bit of apple barn from Will's.

Fouquet took the hint and walked the two sisters outside, only to find Prior glaring at the Ste. Marie du Vire negotiating team.

"Goddammit Fouquet, I've been calling you. Who are they?" Even Prior was sufficiently impressed by Claudine that he paused long enough to look her up and down. Géraldine, used to being overlooked, was indifferent. Prior resumed: "Fouquet, this guy's back." He cocked his head toward Genet. "And he brought a priest with him. Tell them to go back where they came from and don't come back. I ran 'em off yesterday, this one anyway, trying to mooch." He singled out Genet as the freeloader. "So now this other one shows up trying to—don't really know what he's trying to do." Father Jean had aggravated Prior so much that he had been saved from a punch in the jaw only by Shorty's arrival.

"*Oncle?*" Géraldine walked right past the sergeant and directly up to the diminutive physician. "*Oncle? C'est toi?*"

Genet nearly fainted. He was prepared for Prior to tell him to go jump in the Vire. He was prepared for Prior to take a poke at the priest. He was prepared to go home empty-handed. What he was not prepared for was the sight of his nieces materializing from inside the American army hospital. He lifted his bent spectacles, peered, lowered them, and peered again.

"Géraldine? Is that you? What are you doing here? And is this Claudine?" He looked at them as if they had been resurrected from the dead.

Even Father Jean was surprised—the Duprés had not come to Ste. Marie for years. He seemed to remember something about one of the girls, but it escaped him.

Géraldine deflected the here part of Genet's question; she couldn't remember whether her uncle knew that she had been away, but to explain why she was back was too complicated for the moment, certainly with a priest present. She settled on answering as if here only meant being inside the apple barn.

"Yes, it's me, Uncle. And Claudine, grown up a bit. We're here because Aunt Julia is hurt, pretty badly. She's inside."

"Hurt? Aunt Julia? How? And why are you here?"

"Very hurt. I don't know how badly, they won't tell me anything. We were trying to walk home from St. Lô and we went into a barn and...."

Even Prior was quiet at the bedraggled family reunion, the two skinny young refugees and the old guy dressed in his suit. He stood aside while Genet led the girls to the bumper of a near-by jeep where they could sit together and pour out the entire story. Géraldine, however, was not temperamentally disposed to public displays of family worries so it was only a matter of minutes before the old doctor returned. He walked directly up to Fouquet.

"These girls are my nieces. It appears that the injured woman who was brought here is my relative, the sister of my brother-in-law. Would it be possible for me to see her? I'm a doctor."

Fouquet asked Prior, who didn't believe the story. The priest didn't help. "Genet? Well, he was a doctor until the Germans came. He ran out of medicine and so for the last couple of years we've all taken care of ourselves. I guess he sets a leg now and then." Fouquet told Prior that Dr. Genet was the only doctor for miles around. Prior told him to ask Lieutenant Carter. Shorty said to Fouquet that he didn't care but to ask Captain Hastings.

"Sure," Will said. "Bring him back with me."

They led Genet back to the post-op ward where Morph and one of the technicians stood vigil over Aunt Julia's mostly-dead form. Will made Aunt Julia's condition plain:

"Fouquet, can you tell him that, technically, we removed wood splinters from her large intestine, her chest cavity, and her stomach. It missed the aorta. We had to insert a drain and perform a colostomy. We shortened her bowel by about a foot and exteriorated most of the remainder. There are draining lacerations in her abdominal wall that have to be checked every few minutes for rupture or infection. Oh, and her pelvis is broken."

"*The physician relates that thy kinswoman has been sewn through her stomach and organs. From many pieces of wood that pierced her.*"

"That didn't sound word-for-word, Fouquet."

"I'm not sure of the French for, what did you say, 'shortened her bowel,' sir? Or most of the rest of it. I said you sewed up her stomach and organs from splinters. A lot of splinters."

"*How much blood, please? And morphine?*"

"Tell him I think we used about four units of whole blood plasma. Morph? Is that it?"

"She had 1500 mils and, as of now, she's in for about 160 grains of morphine over six hours. She's so out of it that if she dies we won't know it for a couple of hours."

"Don't tell him that. Just say four units."

"*Four things of blood. And some seeds of morphine.*"

Genet asked permission to observe her blood pressure and count her respirations; neither was encouraging. They left Morph as they found him and accompanied Genet back to the front.

"Does he recognize me, Fouquet?" Will pointed to Genet, who translated:

"*Sir, he inquires do you recognize him.*"

The brighter light of the front of the barn did for Genet what had earlier been done for Will—he got a better look at who he was with.

"*My goodness, no, I didn't recognize you in the costume. Would you like to try some fishing?*"

Will did not speak French, not even enough to fumble his way past good morning and hello and the name of the apple brandy that everyone pilfered. However, in the odd way of languages, the first thing Genet had ever said to him at the river had stuck in his head, and he answered.

"*Pêchez-vous?*"

It delighted the old doctor. "*Maintenant? Oo la la!*" "Now? Whew!" The girls heard both of them.

"*Uncle! Why are you talking about fishing with the bedpan nurse? Did you see Aunt Julia? And what did the surgeon tell you?*" The sisters stood in the doorway, avoiding the rain. Géraldine had to raise her voice just to be heard.

"*I did. She doesn't sound very good. She lost a lot of blood, so it's a problem of her blood pressure. And her respirations.*" He paused to see if she understood, then finished: "*The doctor says if Aunt Julia survives the night they may be able to take her to a better hospital.*" He nodded at Will.

"*That's what this one said to me. But what did the doctor say?*"

"*The doctor? That's what he said, niece. You ask him.*" Genet turned, expecting Will and Fouquet to confirm what he just said. Will, however, had walked away and was already across the road, talking with a soldier, the boy whose hand Will had dressed a couple of hours earlier.

"Hey, sir?" The soldier lifted his field pack back over his shoulders and pulled his helmet onto his head. "I'm headed back. Thanks."

Will took the boy's dressed hand, looked at it, turned it over, then helped him get his shoulder harness adjusted and his web belt slung properly and buckled.

"You're going to be okay, Private. Just take care of yourself and keep one eye on the cows. They know where the Bouncing Betties are." The corporal laughed, said that was a good one. "No, seriously. The cows watched the Germans bury them so the'll step around them. Of course, if you see a cow with it's legs blown off, you better walk somewhere else."

The boy burst out laughing. Will reached inside his field jacket; he took out a small flask and slipped it into the boy's hand. "And here's a first aid kit. If you get wounded, pour half of it on the wound and drink the other half. If it's a big wound, put the cork in to stop the bleeding. You take care of yourself, hear?"

The soldier, still scared but no longer feeling quite so alone, began to laugh. They shook hands and he walked over to the medic's jeep and climbed in. The boxy little truck trudged into motion. It was only a mile or so back to the hedgerows where he had been wounded and the racket of intermittent machine gun fire could be heard against the echo of artillery. Nevertheless, the boy stood up in the jeep and, when it bounced past the front of the barn, waved a cheery goodbye. Will waved back.

Genet was impressed, and said so.

"*He's very good, isn't he? With the soldiers.*"

"*It is a true fact that in the army soldiers agree to this doctor,*" Fouquet answered. "*He does not have many years but hurt privates arrive to the hospital for to inquire in particular of Captain Hastings. His shirt is not full. They return to the combat smiling for what he says always.*"

"*He isn't very old, is he?*"

"*I do not consider it, sir, but you have reason. Why dost thou ask if he goes to the fishing?*"

Instead of returning to the dry barn, Will crossed the cobblestone road and continued across the meadow, letting the gentle rain fall on him. They watched him walk to the laundry hut, then disappear inside.

"*I think he does not to fish, sir, but goes to the distant small house to be alone. Our lieutenant says we may leave him there when there is no patient for the surgery.*"

"*Is he a nurse in your surgery?*" Géraldine asked. She had been quiet until now, watching Will buck up the soldier's spirits to go back to the line. She had listened while Fouquet explained in his broken Louisiana French that the men would do anything for that doctor because he didn't act like he was any better than the next guy. They had not been aware that she was listening, less aware that she had watched Will walk off alone through the wet meadow grass.

"*A surgery nurse? No, miss.*"

"*Just an aide, for thermometers and water bottles, then?*"

"But no, he is a doctor, miss. He is the one who made the surgery on your aunt."

Géraldine was quiet by nature and quiet as she sorted out the fact that Will was not a hot water bottle *plouc*; both Fouquet and Genet had to strain to hear her as she said the French equivalent: "*Uh oh.*"

They watched Géraldine turn to walk across the meadow, her sturdy shoes and rough skirt swishing across the thick wet grass, leaving a trail to mark her path toward the laundry shed. The rain fell lightly on her scarf.

"*I think better if she dost not go to him,*" Fouquet told Genet. "*He rests not often.*"

Claudine spoke up for the first time: "*Let her go. She has to repent.*"

"*Repent?*"

"*She thought he was just a plouc. So, she thinks she has to apologize to him.*"

"*Did she say that to him?*"

"No, but she thought it. That's enough for Géraldine. 'Oh, I judged him wrongly, I must make amends.'" Claudine rolled her eyes and put her hands together in mock prayer.

Fouquet didn't think it was much to repent for but also didn't want to be part of making it a bigger mess than it was. "I may not leave here to go translate her words to him, miss. I must remain here." Genet concurred. Claudine, however, knew Géraldine better than either of them.

"Don't worry. Géraldine doesn't need your help to repent," she told them. "She'll find the way."

CHAPTER NINE

Click

"Shhhhhh."

"Ich bin nicht bei irgendwelchen Lärm. I'm not making any noise."

"Gott verdammt! Ein Vogel landet auf einem Zweig, und wir sind bereit zu schießen."

God Damnit! A bird lands on a branch and we're ready to shoot.

"Sei friedlich! Be quiet."

They were quiet; outpost duty was harder in the daytime because there was a lot of motion and sound. It was easier at night when no one was permitted out of doors; every sound carried at night and from their observation post they could easily see before they were seen. Now, in the morning, the hamlet was awake, the villagers walking in the rain back and forth between their outhouses and their huts, down to the river or the sluice to try to catch a fish or rinse their clothes.

Click

"Shhh, ich sagte."

"Ich habe es bereits gesagt, war ich nicht. I told you, I was not."

Fritz didn't say another word. He had never had a rifle barrel at his neck before but he knew exactly what it was, and he froze. The steel muzzle pushed into the base of his skull and he lifted both his hands, slowly, apart, and hoped it would save his life. When his hands were as high as he could lift them, he slowly turned his head to the right and saw what he expected he would see: Hans, too, had his hands raised. Fritz turned his head to look; the only difference between them was that whereas he had a gun to his neck, Hans was under the point of a bayonet.

Neither of them had the least idea where Curtiss had come from, but they knew that their war was over.

It wasn't as difficult as Géraldine expected it to be. Will was sitting on the floor of the laundry hut when she walked in, and he stood when she entered. She drew herself up straight, took a slight breath, and looked directly at him.

"Géraldine," she said, slowly. "Je m'appelle Géraldine. Dupré." She even made a very fleeting curtsy, which caught him off guard. "Je m'excuse de la pensée que vous étiez un plouc." This succeeded only in making him laugh.

"I'm not laughing at you. I'm laughing because I don't understand a word you said." It was true, literally, but it was plain that she was trying to apologize for something. And he did understand her name.

For her part, when she saw his shy face and his own flustered smile, her rigid embarrassment gave way to curiosity. She looked at him more openly and saw that he had kept his hand inside his field jacket; he was hiding something. For the first time in her quiet life Géraldine willed herself to act less like herself and behave a wee bit like Claudine.

"Qu'est-ce que vous cachez dans votre veste?" What are you hiding in your jacket? She pointed at his concealed hand; he understood. "Chocolat?" The Americans were famous for chocolate, chocolate and chewing gum.

"No," he answered, still cloaking something.

"Calvados?"

"No," he stammered.

"Un thermomètre?"

He broke out laughing, to which she reacted by walking the two or three paces across to where he stood, then reaching to take his hand out of his field jacket. For the rest of her life she would remember looking at his face, there in the laundry hut and in the rain, an hour after she had first seen him, wondrous that it could not have been more perfect.

It wasn't a thermometer. Instead, Will was trying to hide a small note-book and pencil, both of which popped loose and fell. They almost bumped their heads together, but did not, as each tried to rescue it before it got wet on the stone floor. She reached it first.

It was a drawing, a small but detailed sketch that was well on its way to completion. It was a profile, only, of a young woman with a shawl over her shoulders and a thin wet muffler around her neck, bits of her dark blond hair poking out from underneath a scarf. She was not pretty, not like other young women were pretty, but there was nothing to disguise that she was very pleasant to look at.

And she was gripping a hot water bottle.

Genet and Claudine found them when they reached the laundry shed. They were sitting on the floor, with the drawing, and laughing like two school children.

That is how they met.

Click.

The hair on Lt. Campbell's neck stood up. He switched off his safety and motioned to the squad to maintain absolute silence. Seven rifles, a Browning automatic rifle, and a light machine gun immediately took aim into the meadow directly in front of the lieutenant, through the trees at a spot that was all but invisible on the other side of the hedgerow. Campbell drew in his breath and hissed.

"Hoot!" He paused.

"Owl!"

"Who's there?"

"It's me, sir."

"Curtiss? What the hell are you doing out there? Where the hell have you been?"

"Sir, I could use a little help." He waited for an answer; no one said a word. "Sir, I've got prisoners. I've got 'em covered but if someone could just come over here for a second and help me get 'em through the thicket. Then they're yours."

Within a half hour everyone in the company knew that Curtiss had reappeared in the line, from the German side, complete with two prisoners, their .42 caliber German machine gun, all their ammunition, their potato-masher hand grenades, and a German field map. Lieutenant Campbell had been startled; Captain Deere was astonished. For the first time since the battalion had waded onto Omaha Beach he was speechless, sitting for five full minutes with his back against the earth works at the base of a hedgerow, his rifle trained on two teen-aged scutze in *feldgrau* army uniforms, wondering how on earth Curtiss had captured them.

"It was mostly a matter of finding them, sir. We knew they were out there. I just didn't know where."

"How did you know they were out there?"

"The ladies at the barn. That one lady had been shot; if it had been any more than a couple of hours, she would have been dead. And the map, sir."

"The map?"

"Yes, sir. I don't know exactly what's wrong with it, our map, but something's wrong. The river, it's not really the river, sir. It's just a canal that leads to the river. And the tool barn, sir. Why would they mark a tool barn on a map? And then spell it tuil? So, I figured we weren't dug in where we thought we were, and we probably had a gap on the flank. Then, when the barn blew, I ran until I found it. Then I closed it."

"How'd you find your way back?"

"Their map, sir. They have a pretty good map. They know where we are, that's for sure."

"So why'd you take off like that? You're crazy, Curtiss, did you know that?"

"Yes, sir. I do know that. But that lady who was shot by the Germans, well, they had to be pretty close. And I couldn't see that there was much more than a dike between us and them. I figured if we didn't find them first they'd come marching right back into our lines."

"I should court martial you, Curtiss, you know that? Taking off like that without a word. What the hell do you think Sergeant Altgelt's for? Why didn't you tell him?"

"Don't know, sir. I thought he was right behind me, it all happened pretty fast. But when I looked up, it was just me."

"So, where the hell did you find these guys? They look starved to death."

"They were about two kilometers further on, sir, south of the farm. There's a hamlet where the river bends back toward the southeast. There's kind of a spillway and the hedgerows on this side are pretty straight. Once I saw how much pasture there was between the hedgerows and the real river, I figured that's where they must have set their outposts up, to cover the pasture. I just kind of slipped through the trees until I heard them."

Deere took the prisoners back to the battalion command post. In the way of armies everywhere, word of Curtiss's adventure arrived before he did. The executive officer had a German translator waiting. They took the Germans' map, their machine gun and ammunition (*"How the hell did he get a couple of POWs to carry their own machine gun? And ammunition." "I don't know, sir. Curtiss is, well, he's not like any soldier you ever saw. Sometimes I just don't ask."*) and fed them. They were pretty sullen but ate everything in two boxes of k-rations, even the spaghetti. And they admitted that during the rain days the Germans had retreated all the way back to the paved road.

"Oh, Deere?" The executive officer thought his company commanders had a right to know what he knew, partially because they needed to plan, partially because no one knew who might have to take his place. "Deere?"

"Sir?"

"Heads up. I just came back from the village. The women in the barn? They walked there all the way from St. Lô. They had hell getting out of there and the krauts blocked them at Pont Hébert, but they made it back to the Bayeux road before taking off across the farms. You know what that means?"

Deere had no more than a vague idea of where St. Lô was and no idea of the road to Bayeux. His war had been fought one field at a time.

"It means there's a gap in between St. Lô and the Martinville Ridge. That's the hill up there where they're pounding the shit out of us with their .88s. This stuff Curtiss brought, the two prisoners, it all fits. And you do know what that means."

"Yes, sir." It meant that it was time to go on the attack. "I'll tell the men."

"Not yet. This is just a heads-up. We've got to find those ladies and see if they can show us how they got here."

"How long?"

"I don't know, couple of hours. The old man went nuts when he found out they didn't hang on to them at the hospital. But they're around." He paused one last time to consider what he wanted to tell Deere. "You did good, Deere. Curtiss must be a little crazy, but after a month here, who the hell isn't?"

"Yeah. Who isn't?"

An hour later the executive officer briefed the battalion and company commanders in front of Rogers's *calvaire*, three hundred yards from the apple barn. They discussed the details of supply and movement, of objectives and tactics.

"Put your men on one-hour alert. Tell them to draw three days ammunition and reserves, rations for at least three days. We're the right flank; 115th is on our left. At the command we push off to the main highway, Road 174, secure it, then wheel south. Our objective is the Bayeux road two hundred yards west of Martinville. That's the hamlet on the map. Saddle up. We won't be coming back."

"When's push-off?"

"Now plus FTG."

"FTG?"

"Find those girls. Soon as they show us where they came through, we go. We're bringing them in right now."

The company commanders called up their platoon leaders. "We push off as soon as the rain lets up. Everybody saddle up. Eat now, then draw full munitions and rations. Tell your men to pack their gear and leave it for the service company. And Lieutenant Campbell?"

"Yes, sir."

"I know you're extra short without Newton, but so's everybody. Make do. Battalion says we're going to get a medical attachment. I'm going to put it with your platoon. They can bring Newton back with them if he's okay."

"Yes, sir."

The platoon leaders gathered their men. The men took a careful look at the ruined village, the church and fountain, and the calvaire. It had always been just a matter of time before they left St. Marie du Vire and began to creep back down the sunken lanes, into the hedgerows, and across the open meadows. Most of them just wanted the rain to continue, but even the most optimistic among them could see the breaks in the clouds.

CHAPTER TEN

⸻⸻⸻❦⸻⸻⸻

Géraldine was awake.

She had expected to sleep much later; her body, long accustomed to working with her hands but unaccustomed to walking for days in the rain or hiding in farms, ached from every muscle. However, it was not her body that had caused her to wake up; it was Claudine. Géraldine had dreamt that her sister had been walking along Rue Torteron, in her school dress, a grey skirt, black shoes, dark jacket, beret. There may have been other girls, the dream wasn't clear, but as they neared a dark building Claudine was alone. She had carried her books in both hands, across her chest, and walked with the slightest sway to her legs, then looked up very slowly with a sultry smile, crooking her forefinger in a come-hither gesture to someone Géraldine could not see. Then she had begun to remove her clothes. Géraldine had tried to stop her, had shouted STOP! but the harder she tried to reach Claudine, across the street, across the sidewalk, across something, the more Claudine laughed and the less Claudine wore. *Hey, Fritz, is that you?* Then there were men, soldiers, boys, strangers, pointing, first at Claudine, then at Géraldine, who suddenly felt exposed herself. She couldn't decide, in her sleep, *cover Claudine, cover myself, cover Claudine, cover....*

Then she woke up. She found herself in her own bed, sweating, her chest pounding, the dim morning light beginning to eke through her window.

From the light she judged it to be around seven in the morning. The rain had stopped and, for the moment, so had the distant thunder of the guns on the other side of the river. She had never actually seen any of the guns. There had been anti-aircraft guns hidden behind broken walls in St. Lô but she had not paid much attention to them. And, of course, at night they saw the flashes as planes flew overhead. She had heard the big

112

guns, everyone had, but they were always out of sight, miles away, and as frightening for not being seen as for being heard. She never got used to it. She uncovered herself, down to the shift she slept in, then climbed out of bed to be able to see out the window.

From her upper-floor bedroom she could see, on one side, the farmyard of Château Dupré. An ancient barn occupied the far side of the yard. It was the oldest structure of the chateau, a tall half-timbered grange enclosed by the chateau walls on three sides but open on the courtyard side. She and Claudine and Jean-Claude had played there, years before, climbing over the hayricks and up into the rafters when the hay was stacked. The barn was tall enough to store grain and the threshing they had bundled for feed, dry enough to hold the apple crop, and secure enough for the cows and goats to huddle in the winter. She had walked over to the barn yesterday, before dinner, to be sure that all was as before she had been sent off to find Claudine. It was unchanged, huge cross beams and wooden timbers filled in with stone and plaster wash, a dirt floor for the carts and rakes and a worn threshing machinee. Despite the musty smell, the dairy stalls were still as clean as before the war.

Her gaze lingered over the yard. Between the barn and the chateau, the family home, several smaller buildings filled most of the space inside the walls. There were poultry coops, a dovecote, and a garden shed. A one-room house was built against the wall, next to the main gate and facing the orchard to the west. It had been a tool shed, a storage room and, when Jean-Claude was a boy, a bunk-house where he and the cousins slept when they stayed the night. She said a quick prayer for him. They had decided, her parents, Claudine, and herself, that they wouldn't talk about Jean-Claude. *Back in the Great War there was this boy Luc, and he went off with the rest of us. After it was over we kept saying 'Luc will be all right, Luc will be along,' but it was ten years before they found him, in a trench, just his identity disk and some boots.* Now, after they had taken Jean-Claude away, her father said that it was bad luck to talk about the missing. Hércule barked.

She looked around the yard to see if a fox had got in, or some crows. The geese were quiet and Hércule himself didn't seem too agitated. He barked again, but half-heartedly, and walked from the porch toward the postern gate, the door that led to the meadow and on toward the old monastery. Then she saw it.

The door to the postern gate creaked as someone lifted the string latch.

It swung slowly inward, then, through the shadow, a man emerged, quietly. She grabbed the curtains and stared as the intruder began to make his way across the farmyard.

"Shhh, boy. Down. That's a good boy. It's just me. That's a good boy."

He crossed the barnyard, slowly, the dawn light dimming some of the features. *Curious*, she thought, *as soon as the rain stops, the guns stop. And someone comes to the farm.* No one had been there since the Germans had made their arrangement and left, coming back for whatever they wanted, the milk and cheese, some cider. He sat down on the band of steps that led from the courtyard to the front door of the chateau, and waited. Hércule circled him on the steps, then lay down next to him, his days as watchdog and shepherd past. The door burst open.

"You! Go away. Get out of here. Hércule! Sic 'em. Sic 'em!"

Géraldine saw it unfold before they did. Her father had come out on the porch. The man stood up and raised his hands. She thought her father was going to shoot him before he recognized Uncle Genet in the dark. Both men heard her shout, "NO!" and looked up, saw her, then saw each other, and finally threw up their hands and embraced.

"Âllo, Dupré. That's a fine way to welcome me. Down, boy, that's a good dog." Genet stood, turned, and gave a somewhat scruffy smile to his brother-in-law. "I thought the Germans took all the guns. Put that down before I get hurt."

They sat in the Dupré kitchen and drank thin *tisane*. Genet missed the taste of verbena, long absent from Ste. Marie, and wondered what Madame Dupré might have hidden in her cellar, then decided it was none of his affair. They had offered *tisane*, he drank it, and began to tell what was happening across the river.

"I don't know," Genet began. "Sometimes there are a dozen jeeps in front, sometimes nothing. Trucks come and go. I never saw anything like it. It seems like they can do any kind of surgery within minutes of a man being shot. Even after the Bosch stole everything in my clinic they didn't have anything like this. But the Americans—they're rich! The number of tanks that come through the woods, and soldiers, thousands of them. It shouldn't be much longer." He tried to act nonchalant about the bread but failed; he took a second piece, cut it, and put as much butter on as he could get away with.

"Tell us about Julia." The Duprés didn't care about the Americans; he was a doctor, not a spy, and they wanted to know what he knew.

He told them.

"Here. You won't believe it." He handed Madame Dupré the drawing. It was only a sketch, five inches by seven, but in astonishing detail.

Madame Dupré was shocked, then transfixed, by the sketch of a figure partially clad by a sheet, her lower parts draped, her upper parts mostly so. The exposed center was an intricate detail of open wounds and tubes. Thin lines had been drawn to connect jagged wooden splinters to the corresponding parts of Aunt Julia from which they had been removed. To remove any doubt, or simply because he could, Will had sketched Aunt Julia herself, her face quite recognizable.

Madame Dupré studied the sketch, then placed it on the table and pushed it away. Claudine took it up, shook her head in dismay, and put it back down. Only Géraldine was able to study the drawing.

"Who could do such a thing?" she asked.

"Who? The wounds? The Germans, of course. You were there. The surgery? The Americans—it's a miracle. I don't know what to tell you; if it had been in my clinic, even at St. Sauveur, she wouldn't have survived."

"And now?"

"It's not easy to know. Too many vital wounds. She may not survive anyway. She must have lost a great deal of blood; with that and a lung injury, well...."

The three women, Claudine, Géraldine, and their mother, clucked and sighed at the implications of such injuries.

"And they gave this to you?" Madame Dupré touched the drawing, then pulled her hand back. "Why?"

"I don't know. Actually, I do." Genet already had decided to tell a soft version of the truth. "They don't have a very good translator. He couldn't explain to me the technical terms; he left and, after a little wait, he came back with a doctor. Nice boy, doesn't know anything about fishing. He gave it to me." He decided to take an indirect approach on the remainder of the truth. "How goes the war over here, Dupré?"

"No idea. We're hidden, thank God. No reason to come back here. But a couple of miles away, it's like the Great War, but worse. No trenches, just collisions. Tanks, guns, attacks. But the Americans are pushing them out."

"And?"

"I don't know. They've taken Cherbourg. They have most of the Cotentin. I think they're going to push past St. Lô to get out of the hedgerow farms. We stay here and don't put our snouts out."

The war was not being fought at Château Dupré, not yet. Out of the way, on the road to nowhere, it lay in a bend of the Vire where an oxbow framed the meadow on the Ste. Marie side and the convent fields on the west side. Hedgerow lanes bordered the chateau outside the walls on the south and, to the west, on the ridge above the apple orchard. The Carentan road was two kilometers away. That was where to find the war, not back in a hidden bend of the Vire.

"The soldier who gave me the drawing?" They nodded to show they knew which one Genet meant. "He wants to know about Carentan."

"Why?"

"The translator said his brother was a glider pilot. The Army told him that he crashed, he thinks at Carentan, and was killed."

"*Requiscat in pace, dei gracia, amen.*"

"*Amen.*" They crossed themselves, and Genet continued.

"I thought we should offer, you know. To show him. It seems he was the one who did the surgery."

Géraldine still found this hard to believe. The army doctor was not much older than she was. He was nice to look at, not in a handsome way, but like a boy who had grown too fast. He had a long face, smooth, and when he had taken off his cap and mask she saw that his hair was brown but with a glint of red. She had not mentioned it to Claudine.

"Take him to Carentan? Are you crazy?"

Genet was, but like a fox.

"Well, we have to thank him. He saved Julia. They didn't have to do that. Can you imagine the Germans, a mortally wounded française brought to them, would they have stopped what they were doing for a surgery like this?" He emphasized "like this" with a thump on Aunt Julia's beleaguered torso. "Carentan is just a walk in the country, ten kilometers at the most."

"No. Absolutely no." Monsieur Dupré had no doubt about it whatever. The man who hadn't hesitated to send his elder daughter to St. Lô to fetch his younger daughter was not going to send anyone sneaking through combat zones to look at what might be left of Carentan. "No."

"What, then? Nothing? For saving Julia?" Genet wondered whether he had himself been learning the art of guilt from too much time with Father Jean, but he wanted his clinic restocked. He pressed his point. "I have another suggestion. I think this will be quite proper, and please them. The doctor, and the unit too."

He explained what he had in mind.

Claudine pouted. Géraldine wondered why Genet had proposed that she be the one to go back with him, but did not disagree. She left to put on a more suitable dress and, a half hour later, she and her uncle rowed back across the river to the field hospital.

CHAPTER ELEVEN

"Morning, Lieutenant." The major got out of the jeep and walked right into the barn as if he knew everyone there and knew where everyone was located. "I'm Major Popper."

Shorty saluted; Popper saluted back.

"So, what can I do for you, Major?" Shorty looked at the soldier standing in his doorway. His uniform was dirty, face needed a shave, but so did everyone's. He wondered how the major had gotten past the front desk and concluded that Sanders had been as intimidated by the major as he was. *The guy is impressive*, he thought. When he squinted at his branch insignia he saw that the major was a doctor, too. "I don't suppose you're on the way in, are you? We could always use a couple of extra docs."

"Naw, but if there's some coffee I could get a hand around, that'd be okay."

They walked back to the mess; Shorty told Cookie to boil some of the morning's grinds for them.

"So, I'm looking for trouble, that's all. Need to borrow Captain Hastings for a while. Thought we'd run up to the CCA for a while." The CCA was the aid station closest to the battle. "You mind?"

The hair on Shorty's neck went up. He knew it had to do with the personnel action message; he should have taken more time with it.

"What's up at the aid station?" he asked, hoping he didn't sound too anxious. Shorty wished he didn't like Will so much; Will never made a big mistake, except, of course, when he had gone AWOL looking for gliders, before they got to Ste. Marie. The men liked him, except Prior, and Morph liked him, although Garth had been skittish since Will had pressured him into working on the French lady. Collins was of two minds; Will always volunteered to swap out with him when it was his turn to go to the battle zone, to Collins's relief, but the men all knew it, which Collins resented.

"Aid station's fine. Here's the deal. We've got all these reports back at the division medical office, twenty-five or thirty cases where Captain Hastings supposedly is butchering the troops up for supper. One report said something like 'found sponge in surgical field,' another was 'splint on wrong leg.' Stuff like that. Too much morphine, not enough morphine, un-treated hemorrhages, all kinds of stuff. But most of them had to do with stitches. In fact, nearly all of them said one way or another that after he was through with some guy, he sewed him up with poor surgical technique, like a zig-zag sewing machine. We didn't find a thing."

"I don't get it. What do you mean, you didn't find a thing?"

"I mean, all the surgery complaints turned out to be on patients who were already back in England. Or patients who had died. Nobody would say a word. So the Colonel said 'Popper, go take a look.'"

"What about the doctors who signed the deficiency reports?"

"New policy—they aren't signed anymore. Somebody decided it was more important to find out who was causing a problem and get rid of them than to get into a long drawn-out swearing match. Just like back home— Army doctors won't ever sign a malpractice report against each other, no matter how bad."

"So he sent you to do what?" Shorty wanted to say "spy" but that was too strong a word. Snitch also came to mind but, even if Popper wasn't in his chain of command, the colonel was. "... what? Supervise? Inspect?"

"I think 'spy' would be the right word. I'm supposed to act like I'm being sent to the line as punishment for something, then slack off and let Hastings do all the work. I'm going to keep an eye on him for a day or so."

There wasn't anything Shorty could do or say. He led Popper away to find his problem surgeon. They found him in the post-op room with Morph and Aunt Julia. Will didn't seem troubled in the least.

"Only thing is, this lady's looking up, blood pressure holding, heart rate a bit fast, respirations around 17 or 18. She's going to start coming off the morphine and when she does, she's better off at Isigny. If you've got an ambulance, let's send her."

Ten minutes later they were lifting her into the back gate of the big Dodge when two figures came walking out of the meadow and across the cobblestone road to the barn.

119

"*Bonjour, Docteur. Bonjour, Lieutenant.*" Genet called out a cheery greeting, puffing slightly from carrying a small wooden box in both hands. "*We've come to see if Mademoiselle Martel is better.*"

"Bonjour, Doctor. Bonjour.... ma'am." Will's French was no better than the day before but the sight of Géraldine improved the rest of him, to his surprise. "Wish I knew what else you said."

"He said they came to see if Mademoiselle Someone is better." Popper answered for them both. "Don't you guys have any soldiers for patients? Is this Mademoiselle Someone?"

"Do you speak enough French, Major, to tell them that we're sending the lady back to Isigny?" He did. "Tell them that she's stable for right now and they can take a lot better care of her than we can."

"I can tell *them* that, but I can't tell me that. Why are you sending this lady anywhere? She's not a GI."

"She's Resistance, Major. She spied out a leak in the German lines. That's how she got hurt." Will was perfectly willing to stick with Morph's story. No one in the field hospital wanted her to die; he didn't want her to die in front of Géraldine and Genet, and said so. "You can ask them, Major. They'll tell you." He shrugged with more confidence than he felt, particularly when Popper did turn to ask Genet if Julia was a member of the Resistance.

"*Resistance? Vache têtue, c'est certain. Elle s'est caché a St. Lô jusqu'à ce que les Allemands ferment tout.*" Resistance? Stubborn old cow, that's for sure. Stayed hidden in St. Lô until the Germans sealed it off." Genet beamed; Géraldine laughed, whether at the idea of Aunt Julia being in the Resistance or at the idea of her sneaking past German lines, each being equally untrue.

"Good enough for me. I didn't come here to tell you how to run your hospital anyway. What's this?"

Géraldine had taken the box out of Genet's hands and walked up to Will. "*Un cadeau. De ma famille. Nous vous remercions pour tout-ce que vous avez fait. Pour ma tante.*"

Popper and Shorty were amused but Will was caught completely off-guard—no one had ever brought him a present, never in his life. The closest thing he could think of was a fleeting memory of Doc Pritchard going out to the 'dobes to deliver a baby or set a broken leg, returning with a basket of beans and a pot of chili. He had to scramble to find words.

"Merci, ma'am, Docteur. Thank you very much. This can't be for me, everybody here took care of her." Even so, he lifted the cloth towel to peek inside the box. There was a bottle of wine from the Dupré pantry, a small round of mouldy cheese, a loaf of hard bread that was almost too large for the box. When he lifted it for Shorty to see he sensed that Géraldine turned her face to avoid looking at him. "I'm about to go up to the line. Is it okay if I leave this until I get back? I've never...."

Shorty took over. He took the box from Will, then led Genet to the doors of the ambulance, opened them, and told him to take a look at Aunt Julia. "Isigny." That's all he said, but Genet understood. "Isigny. Hospital there. Okay?"

"*Okay.*"

Then he pointed at Will and added, "He'll be back tomorrow, ma'am. Tomorrow."

"*Demain.*"

"Tell her thanks, Major, if you would. If she wants to come back tomorrow and share it..."

"She understood, Captain. Okay, time to go."

They closed the doors of the ambulance and slapped their hands on the body panel to tell the driver to pull away. They shook Genet's hand and expressed a polite nod to Géraldine, who nodded politely in return.

She stood with her uncle and watched the jeep drive away. Will and Major Popper headed off toward the town and, she had no doubt, on to the hedgerows, where the sounds of fighting echoed a mile or so away. Shorty waved goodbye. Géraldine and Genet turned around themselves and walked away, just missing Captain Collins who came out to demand that Shorty tell him what had happened with Newton, who was missing. By the time the division intelligence officer and the battalion executive officer arrived looking for Géraldine, she and Genet were already back across the river.

The next morning, when Géraldine got out of the row boat and tied the docking line to the laundry shed, two intelligence officers were waiting for her. One of them spoke very good French:

"Ma'am, we need you to come with us."

"Pardon?"

"We need your help, ma'am. We have a report that you walked here from St. Lô. Is that true?"

"Yes. I walked from St. Lô to Pont Hébert, but then they stopped us. We finally had to pick our way across the farms to Le Déversoir. We were trying to get here, except that there was a mine in a barn that exploded, and...."

She understood that it would do no good to ask them to let her go across the meadow to the field hospital. What she did not understand was why she had come back herself. Her uncle had said it was important to keep her word. "You said you would come back tomorrow, Niece. You have to do it." She also wondered why it had not taken much persuasion for her to agree; she had wanted to come back, even though it was hard to tell her parents exactly why, now that Aunt Julia had been moved.

Their jeep had cut deep ruts in the meadow where before only the laundry ladies had walked, they and Genet and, of course, Géraldine herself, and the young doctor. The officers were not rude but they were firm and, without another word, they told her to climb into the jeep.

"Where are we going?"

"Back to that barn, ma'am. We need you to show us something." The jeep rattled past the field hospital, up to the square in front of the church and her uncle's empty clinic across the town square, then out past the calvaire. The boxy little vehicle bounced along over farm lanes, past a row of men who manned foxholes and small guns aimed into fields. They passed an open tent with a red cross painted on the roof and she tried to not be obvious in looking to see if he was there. A half-mile beyond the tent they came to the end of the road, the shelled farmhouse, the canal, the barn, and Curtiss.

"We figured if you and Curtiss, this soldier, could show us how you got from St. Lô to here, well, it'd help, ma'am. If you could show us on the map."

They laid the map on the hood of the jeep and Curtiss pointed to Le Déversoir, then to the river. She didn't understand what he was saying but she did understand that the map seemed wrong. From where they stood she could see that there was no river, there was no tile factory, and the cross on the map was where she thought the calvaire was.

"I think this is not here, sir. I think this is Ste. Marie. We are here." She pointed to a canal south of the village.

The French-speaking intelligence officer explained what she said to the others; Curtiss explained something back to him and pointed to the map. Géraldine looked where he pointed, then explained:

"That is Le Déversoir. It's really a hamlet, not a village, and we didn't go all the way there. We were only going to the spillway, to wade across the Vire. That's where we came out of the farms and ran into the Germans. That is where they fired the rifle at the woman who had joined us."

Someone's lightbulb went off. Le Déversoir was not the name of a town; it was only the word for spillway. The way was open to the hamlet. The way was closed from the hamlet to the spillway, or had been until Curtiss slipped through and kidnapped the outpost.

"Then where, ma'am?"

"I will show you."

CHAPTER TWELVE

P opper told Shorty that there hadn't been anything to spy on. "He did just fine. Except for one thing."

There was always one thing with Will. Shorty decided that nonchalance was his better option, and said nothing, waiting for Popper to drop the hammer.

"We got kind of slow for an hour or two so he asked if I would mind taking over the CCA for awhile. I said 'Okay, what's up, want to take a nap?' He said 'No, I'm going to walk this guy back to the line, take a look for myself.' I thought he was crazy but he takes this kid, boy couldn't have been more than eighteen, tops, scared shitless, Hastings had cleaned up a pretty good scrape on him and put on a field dressing, told the kid, 'Hey, if you like, I'll walk back up to the hedgerows with you, I need to check on the medics anyway.' It was a lie, of course."

Of course. Will had wanted to sneak off to go looking for his brother. Shorty had figured it was just a matter of time and here it was—Will had broken his promise.

"So I said, 'Oh, okay, how long you gonna be?' and he said, 'Not long.' So I look up and he takes off and walks this kid across an open field. You getting this? An open field, in broad daylight. He puts his arm around the kid, helps carry his field pack so the kid can put both hands on his rifle, and they walk, back and forth like, all the way across this wide open meadow to the tree line on the other side. I thought, *This guy is off his rocker!* Well, of course, we hear all this shooting and I think, *Well, there go two more,* but a little while later Hastings walks back, only this time it's along the tree line. So I say, 'Jesus, Captain, are you nuts?' And he says, 'No, it's safe, I've been studying that pasture all day.' Then he whipped up a sketch of the pasture and showed

124

exactly where the gates were, some thinned-out trees at the far corner, a stone cistern. It was exactly like all those drawings he sends back to the evacuation hospital, except instead of it being some guy's descending artery or something, it's a pasture, and he's figured out from the trees and angles and all why Jerry couldn't have any guns trained there." He fished the sketch out of his jacket pocket and unfolded it. Shorty studied the drawing a moment and chuckled; he had seen dozens of Will's sketches before. The enlisted men had a stash of them that they used to drive Prior crazy. He handed it back. "It's like he's got nine lives or something. Never saw anything like it."

"So, what have you got for Division?"

"I'm going to tell the colonel that Hastings is just fine and the deficiencies are a crock. My guess is that somewhere along the way he pissed some guy off. That and I'm going to give him the drawing. The colonel loves this stuff. Got to go. Tell you one thing, though, if that temporary duty thing from Fourth Division comes back up after St. Lô, you ought to give this kid a rest. I don't think he ever sleeps. He could use a week off."

"Where is he?"

"He stayed back at the CCA, said we sent so much work back here that his replacement wouldn't be free yet, so he'll do another hour or two."

Shorty was not quite sure what to make of that. Will would not be waiting for a replacement from the 261st because Shorty wasn't scheduled to send another doctor to the front line until the following day, and then it was Collins's turn. Collins would be angling for someone to cover for him. Shorty decided he didn't want to know; with Will it was always something.

"See ya, Lieutenant. Oh, here's this."

Popper handed Shorty a string of messages from the division, then drove away.

To:	Major Popper, 29th Infantry Division, Division Medical Office, V-Corps Evacuation Hospital, Isigny, France
From:	Major Hampton, 4th Infantry Division, Division Medical Office, Cherbourg, France
Subject:	Personnel Action: Division Medical Office (Admin) to Commander (Acting, Admin) 261st Field Hospital (surg. det.). Sister Unit trying to locate Captain W.W. Hastings for temporary duty on special assignment. Advise.

Major Popper had endorsed the messages before he gave them to Shorty; Shorty read them and shook his head, wondering how Will had gotten someone in the 4th Division around Carentan to pull off a request like that.

But he and Will had made a deal—Will had promised Shorty to stop disappearing in the night to go looking for gliders in the French countryside, and Shorty had promised that as long as Will kept his word, he wouldn't kick him out of the field hospital. A deal's a deal, Will. You aren't going anywhere.

Shorty's reply went back in the next ambulance headed to Isigny:

Subject:	Personnel special mission—Captain Hastings:
	Regret 261st understaffed for corps attack on St. Lô. Captain Hastings essential to this unit and to evacuation hospital (surgical drawings). Request do not re-assign for special mission at this time; will advise when officer available.

Fouquet and Antsley unloaded the medical supplies at the aid station and went back to work under the tent, wrapping sprained ankles and bandaging cuts. An hour later another medical officer showed up to relieve Will. Fouquet was still in the aid station when the intelligence officers rolled to a halt in their jeep.

"You got a Captain Hastings here, Private? Promised this lady she could say howdy to him." The officer in the passenger seat jerked his head to indicate that he was talking about the same woman they had seen the day before. They both raised their eyebrows and grinned.

"He's over there, sir. Inside the field." Fouquet pointed across the lane to a gap in the hedgerow behind them.

Lieutenant Campbell had been told to tighten up the line in preparation for the jump-off. He and Rogers had stopped at the CCA to see if any of their platoon had been sent back to the aid station; none had. That had been a quarter of an hour ago.

"Hey, medic," Rogers had said to Antsley. "Remember what happened here? Right here is where you saved my buddy Newton. How's he doing?"

Antsley had answered that Newton wasn't doing so well. "I sure wish," Rogers had continued, "he never found that glider."

The word glider struck Will like an electric wire, jerking him up so urgently from the litter where he was working that the wounded replacement soldier had to catch the suspended plasma bottle that Will knocked over as he bounded across a twenty-foot wide tent. Rogers found himself staring into the face of the anxious medical officer.

"Found a glider? Where's a glider? Did you say Newton found a glider?"

Rogers offered to take him across the road to show him. Campbell said no, they had to get a move-on.

"Sorry, sir, thought you knew." Antsley trailed off; by the time he had gotten Newton to the field hospital the soldier had been so full of morphine that his raving about being shot by an airplane had sounded like drunk talk. Then, by the time Will had finished Aunt Julia, Antsley had discovered Claudine and forgotten all about Newton's ravings. "I thought Captain Collins had said something to you, sir."

As soon as his replacement showed up Will walked across the lane and disappeared into the field behind. When Géraldine arrived, two medics pointed the way for her, and she followed him.

The glider was almost unrecognizable. The wings had separated in flight and the glider had dropped straight into the trees. Limbs and branches had punched through the fuselage and ripped the fabric skin away. The landing wheels had sheared off at odd angles and the cargo had broken free and crashed through the cockpit. The wreckage was covered not only by branches but by the mud of the last two weeks' downpour. Will had no idea Géraldine was there.

She watched him pull glider remnants from the brambles. He laid out pieces on the ground, a wheel here, some windscreen there, bent wing struts on either side, wheels in front of them, body parts behind. Of wings and tail there was little to assemble, little more than mud and grass in the space he stepped off to allow for the missing pieces. He was indifferent to the sounds of battle a half mile away. Géraldine watched in silence.

He located the instrument panel, a wide piece of black sheet metal that looked as if it had been whacked by a very large mallet. He removed it and carried it into the clearing. She watched him study the broken dials and bent metal and pick away at rust and torn fabric. He stood up from time to time, gazed at the sky, northward toward the Channel, back up at the treetops. At the last he pried off a small metal number plate and put it in his jacket, then sat on the ground and bowed his head.

Fouquet had told her the story, that the doc was different from the others. 'Mistake thee not,' he had said. 'In appearance he may look like a student but there is much about him you do not see. At the beginning he searched his brother, a dead pilot. In June, now in July, he has no family.'

In daylight she saw Will clearly as he lifted his helmet and wiped a hand across his face. His face was smooth, but with lines, a gentle mouth. His eyes were weary. She wondered whether Will was going to cry. Instead, he looked up, and saw her.

"Bonjour," he said. It didn't sound very French.

"Âllo, Capitaine." She replied in a gentle, almost whispered voice. "I came to the hospital. Like I said I would. Yesterday morning. To say thank you."

Will didn't understand anything beyond âllo, least of all what she was doing in the combat zone.

"But some officers took me to Le Déversoir, to show them how we walked from St. Lô. They let me stop here, and I saw you."

He realized that she had watched him. He walked away from the reconstructed glider to the berm where she stood. She wanted to comfort him, that was all.

"I just heard about it," he said. "I...I don't know. I thought maybe I should take a look."

"I thank you," she said. Her English startled him. Even though it sounded like "tank you," it had not occurred to him that she or anyone else in Ste. Marie spoke a word of English. "I thank you fur de chirurgerie." He stopped and looked at her, fully, in the face, and told her she was welcome.

Antsley watched them walk back across the lane to the aid station.

"Sir, you can take the jeep back. We've stocked the CCA and, to be truthful, we're probably going to pick up and move pretty fast." Antsley told him that the buzz was that the regiment was about to try again to punch through to St. Lô. "Shorty, that is, Lieutenant Carter, sir, he said Captain Collins is due up here tomorrow. When he comes he needs to bring the jeep back, stocked up. This could be it."

"When, Antsley? When's the big push-off?"

"Oh, nobody knows. Now, two hours from now, tonight. Same old stuff, sir, hurry up and wait."

"I'm going to walk back, Antsley. It's just a couple of kilometers.

Fouquet, you take the jeep back to the unit. Tell Collins I'll be along in a few minutes, you'll can restock it. I'll be there before you're through. I just need to clear my head."

No one, least of all Fouquet, objected to going to the rear. He got in the jeep and started the engine.

"Take her with you," Will said. "I don't know who brought her out here, but she can ride with you back to the barn." He stepped to one side so that Géraldine could get in the jeep. She stepped back.

"No. I walk," she said. "I walk."

They didn't talk much. He didn't know what to say to her and, if he had known what to say, there still was the matter of the artillery. It was loud now, much louder. *The buzz about going to St. Lô's probably true*, he thought. *That battery over there's firing ten times as much as normal.* Further down inside him he admitted it: *No one could survive a crash like that.*

She didn't say much to him, either; it was enough for her that they stumbled along the farm lane, getting out of the way as a convoy of trucks rumbled by, stopping to check which of the crossroads led north to the village instead of east to the next battalion. It was not until they reached the *calvaire* in sight of Ste. Marie that she spoke.

"You brother." That was it: 'you brother.'

"Peter," he replied. "My brother's name was Peter."

"*Desolé.*" She bit her lip, unable to remember the English word for 'sorry,' and said the closest thing she could imagine. "*Desolé* you brother, *pilote.*"

It occurred to Will that someone had told her about him, even about Peter. It was normal for the guys to know things like that. Everyone in the unit had someone, a friend from high school, a cousin, somebody who was in danger. Shorty's brother was a mechanic in the Pacific, Collins's sister was in the nurse corps. They all knew about Peter. But how would Géraldine know? Did someone just gossip about him? Or had she asked?

"Peter went down on the first day. Somewhere near Carentan. I thought maybe this glider was his, you know, off course, that sort of thing. I think it's only ten or fifteen miles from here, across the river. So, I thought, maybe this was it. But it wasn't. Not this glider."

Will's story was too much English, and too fast. Like her uncle, she only understood 'Carentan.'

"Carentan. Close my *ferme*," she said.

Yesterday he would have asked, 'How close?' and 'What direction?' Even last night or this morning, while patching wounds, he would have asked, 'How far to Carentan?' and tried to calculate a way to get there. Not anymore, now that he had seen what happens to a glider when it crashes. He now got what Shorty had been saying, that there was no reason to go to Carentan to look for Peter. There wouldn't be anything to find. There wouldn't be anything to talk about.

"He was a really good brother," he went on, unaware that for the first time he was speaking of Peter in the past tense. "We don't have any parents. They died when we were little boys. Parents. Dead too. Orphans." He waited to see if she understood; she probably didn't, but she listened, picking at his words. They walked past the *calvaire* and up the lane that led into Ste. Marie. "The state separated us when he went to high school; I was in the eighth grade. But he always knew how to take care of me. Taught me to throw a football. Taught me to swim. Taught me how to sneak out at night. I loved him. A lot."

Will caught himself telling her more than he had ever said to Shorty, or Antsley, even to Douglas. He understood, instinctively, that with Géraldine it was safe to talk, not because she understood him but because she didn't. He could say things to her that he couldn't tell anyone else. Shorty would have given him advice. Garth would have said he needed to listen to himself. Collins would have said Peter was dead, move on. Géraldine just listened.

"You have any brothers and sisters? Guess so, huh, the girl who was with you at the field hospital. That it?" He walked on. "You know, Peter came to Tierra right before I got sent over. He was about a month or six weeks behind me. He was training other glider pilots back in Texas; his unit was going to send everybody over at once. We were going to meet up in London, but never did. Then when he crashed it was like.... " He began to leak, not exactly crying, just tears rolling slowly down his face. "We were going to have a time together. Paint the town. A big one before D-Day. All that. He said he had something really big he wanted me to know. I think he was going to tell me he had a girl, but I took it for granted it could wait 'til next time." Then he couldn't go on, not out loud. He had said all he could.

She took his arm.

It was a natural thing, just reaching her hands over and under his arm and taking it. If someone had seen them it would have looked like they were walking to church, or window-shopping, a boy and his girl, strolling aimlessly. The act itself was more natural for her; French people did stroll arm-in-arm, and it didn't mean they were a couple. It was not so natural for Will; it had been almost a year since he had felt the touch of any woman. She might not have been able to explain it either, why she took his arm. That was not something Géraldine did, not alone and not with a man she barely knew. She held his arm closer, not against her body, but close enough.

He didn't pull away.

When they reached the village square Genet was there, watching them.

"*Géraldine?*" The question was enough. It may have been normal for French people to stroll arm-in-arm, but it was normal only when they were *familiers*. Genet would not have been surprised if it had been Claudine, but there had never been the least degree of coquette in this one. He raised an eye, not in a mean way, but as her parents would have expected him to do.

"*What, Uncle?*" 'What indeed?' she thought. 'I'm not the one trading a niece for a few boxes of iodine and petroleum gel.' "*I thanked him. We walked. He told me about his brother. I understood some of it.*"

Whether Will understood or not, Genet was not going to speak to her in front of him about her being alone, walking with an American soldier; that would be a family matter, at most. Instead, Genet tried to answer the question of the glider that they had seen an hour before. He, too, wanted to put Will's mind at rest.

"*Not his brother,*" Genet said, a note in his voice that it was his place, not hers, to talk with the American.

"*What do you mean?*"

"*It was not his brother, not in that glider.*"

"*I know that, Uncle. His brother crashed close to Carentan. Not here.*"

Genet realized she knew more than he did but, nevertheless, felt it was his place, not hers, to explain. He turned to Will: "*Pas ici.*" Not here. "*The glider here wasn't your brother. The pilots in this glider were British.*" Will didn't understand, not even when Genet repeated 'pilotes' and 'Britannique.'

Genet led them into the cemetery that lay alongside the damaged church. They passed between the old graves, some crosses, worn headstones with indecipherable names and dates. At the rear of the churchyard there were two mounds of earth, unmarked, settling from the rain but decidedly recent.

"*Pilotes, Britanniques. Du planeur.*" British pilots, from the glider. "*Pas votre frere.*" Not your brother.

Genet was sure Will would be relieved, and Will did gather that Genet was trying to ease the fear that his brother had crashed right there at Ste. Marie. Unfortunately, at that moment, Father Jean intruded, his black robes flapping in the wind.

"*Oui, les pilotes Britanniques. We buried them here. When the Germans shot them.*" Then, to Geraldine's dismay, the priest emphasized by gestures what he could not have gotten across with words. He lifted his arms to pantomime the holding of a rifle, said, 'Pow,' said it again, then walked over to the ground and aimed the imaginary muzzle at the imaginary heads of the two unimaginably helpless British fliers. "*Pow. Pow. The coups de grâce. Shot them. In the head.*"

That was clear enough, French or no French. Will understood. He also understood that, even if the crash might not have killed Peter, then the Germans had.

"*Pow!*" The priest grinned, removing any remaining doubt of his being an idiot. He paid no attention to the effect he had on Will. "*I took it on myself. I gave them the sacrament, right there in the field, while the Germans stood over their bodies. Me. I did it. And then took Madame Vuitton's cart and brought them here. I buried them. Me.*" He grinned again, his pinched face aglow with the drama of trying to make the others believe he had always been for liberation.

Géraldine saw it. Will's face went from soft to hard, his eyes became steely. He continued to behave, quietly, and with respect, and she didn't know whether he would try to say anything. He did not. Instead, he shook Genet's hand, and the priest's, then looked at her for a very long time, almost reaching for her, but stopping himself. He then turned and walked away, down the last cobbled street that would lead back to the field hospital.

She could hear the priest mutter something to Genet, some question about her conduct, but it was not important to her what they said. She ignored them and stood, gazing, waiting until she could no longer see him. Will was not like any boy she had known before, boy or man, not that she had known many, and for the first time in her life, she did not know what she was supposed to do.

To:	Major Hampton, 4th Infantry Division, DMO
From:	Major Popper, 29th Infantry Division, Division Medical Office, Admin, V-Corps Evacuation Hospital, Isigny, France
Subject:	Special Mission, Joint w/ 29th DMO
Message:	Capt. Hastings' skills appropriate for mission but unit commander will not release for temporary duty before conclusion of present enemy engagement

Sergeant Gill took the message from the division medical office wire. It required only fifteen minutes before his major gave him the reply to transmit:

To:	Major Popper, 29th Infantry Division, Division Medical Office, Admin, V-Corps Evacuation Hospital, Isigny, France
From:	Major Hampton, 4th Infantry Division, DMO, Cherbourg, France
Subject:	Personnel Assignment
Message:	Noted. Subject officer best for special mission. Request you assign ASAP.
	By hand of Division Commander

The message decoder in England realized that he was handling something exceptional. That night, at the pub, he acted nonchalant with the other decoders. "Got a good one today," he said. "Can't tell you what, but something's afoot." He tilted his glass and waited for someone to ask him the question. "Something big, don't know what. But they're lining up the best doc they can find to go along. Sounds like somebody's gonna get hurt. Stay tuned. Cheers."

Hércule barked.

She sat up in bed, awake, not quite sure she had ever gone fully to sleep.

It hadn't been much of a bark, more like a yelp that the dog made when he rolled over on a bad hip, or stepped on a rock. It had not been an alarm bark, or a challenge.

She closed her eyes and tried to sleep. There had been no problem rowing back across the Vire, or walking with Genet past the monastery to the farm. He had come in for a glass and stayed for dinner. He had lied about the gifts, said the Americans had thanked them, and assured them that Aunt Julia was doing well. There had been no artillery fire, she realized, not for a couple of hours, not nearby.

Hércule barked again.

She got up and walked to the window, drew the curtain aside. The dog was at the postern gate, standing, and she looked more carefully into the shadows that the wall cast against the meadow in the moonlight. *The moon is out*, she thought. *That means they'll start the fighting again.*

A shadow moved.

She stared into the darkness, across the meadow at the tree line. It was nothing, a fox perhaps. Whatever it was had come and gone. She gazed off to the left, up past the apple orchard to the lane on the top of the ridge line, then back again toward the monastery.

She knew that it was just a fox. Nothing else, no person, certainly, would be out like that in the dark, not with a battle going on a few miles away. There were only two places to go from there anyway, down to the monastery and on to the river, maybe across to Ste. Marie, or, in the other direction, the Route de Carentan.

"I hope he'll be all right," she said, startling herself, speaking aloud in the dark bedroom. Claudine stirred and asked what she said. "Nothing, Sister." She waited to see if Claudine woke up; she would say she was thinking about Jean-Claude. "It was just a fox. Go back to sleep."

CHAPTER THIRTEEN

"Hey, Captain. What are you doing here?" Antsley was surprised to see Will instead of Collins.

Will had driven the jeep across the fields and canals to Le Déversoir, then followed the rutted paths inland, weaving back and forth until he made his way into the 116th's line. He found Antsley burrowed into the earth berm at the base of a hedgerow. The big red cross on Antsley's helmet was the only thing to distinguish him from the rest of Lieutenant Campbell's platoon, now spread along a farm lane, obscured by the trees and brush of another hedgerow.

Of the twenty-five men still in Lieutenant Campbell's platoon there appeared to be mostly riflemen left, with one or two light machine guns and maybe one bazooka. Except for the two new replacements, most of the men looked like un-wounded versions of the gaunt, exhausted soldiers who had been arriving at the apple barn around the clock for the last two days. The drive to St. Lô was killing the two battalions.

"Captain Collins is sick. I swapped with him. Guess I'll always be a swap doc. You doing okay? What's the story here?"

"Get the hell down, medic! You want to get shot too?" Sergeant Altgelt jerked Will down into the fox hole. Almost immediately a brace of machine gun rounds ripped the trees just above their heads. An overturned Army truck burned in the lane and, for the first time, Will noticed the legs of a G.I. crumpled beneath its wheels. He squirmed further down into the fox hole.

"They're on the other side of that pasture, maybe fifty yards over there. No idea how many there are but when Lieutenant Campbell says the word we're going through the trees. Stay down."

Antsley did not doubt that Collins was sick; Collins shook visibly every time Division called Lieutenant Carter and told him to send one of the surgeons up to the line for the next mission. What Antsley doubted was that Lieutenant Carter had sent Will up to the line. A rumor had got around that Will had slipped out of the apple barn again and had not come back until after sun up. The sound of a tank a hundred yards to the east made him look down the lane.

"Look at that, Captain." He pointed the tank out to Will. It was a Sherman, rocking back and forth crossways in the farm lane, then ramming forward to punch straight at the base of the hedgerow. Heavy steel prongs had been welded to its front and the tank was gouging the berm apart rather than crawling up and over it, shoving dirt and branches aside, indifferent to the anti-tank shells crashing into the trees. The tank knocked away at the berm. Several mortar rounds dropped close by, scattering shrapnel, but no one got hit. A minute or two later a second tank chugged along the lane and pulled up about twenty yards from Sergeant Altgelt who, with hand signals, directed it to smash at the hedgerow directly in front. The flying dirt settled onto their helmets.

"You thought Shorty wouldn't let me come up, didn't you? We couldn't find him when the jeep was stocked, so I left him a note with Garth and came on up here." He could tell that Antsley was not convinced; Will didn't care.

"Did you take a look at the glider, sir?"

"Just glanced at it. It was pretty torn up. It's been there more than a month." Will looked up and down the farm lane at the tanks. The men burrowed in, waiting for the command to attack. "It was British, went down on the first day. Germans shot the crew. They're buried in the village, behind the church."

Antsley heard something new in Will's voice. He had never seen Captain Hastings angry before but he had seen an awful lot of other angry G.I.s. He wished he had told Will about the glider a week ago and blamed Collins's taste for Calvados over the duty to take a patient history. The nearer tank surged almost all the way through the berm; it would be only a matter of seconds before the men would be told to follow it into the pasture and attack whatever was waiting for them on the other side. Sergeant Altgelt hissed at them:

"Listen, docs. You guys keep your heads down. We're gonna need you.

You see that high ground over there—that's Martinville Ridge." Altgelt pointed at a hill about a half mile beyond the field where the Germans were dug in. "Those krauts over there shooting at us, they're just the perimeter. The hill's the thing. When we go, the Major says we're not coming back, not until we get into St. Lô."

There was no gun fire in either direction for a couple of minutes. Altgelt's walkie-talkie crackled and Lieutenant Campbell's distorted voice barked through it loudly enough for everyone to hear.

"Yes, sir." Altgelt signaled to the squad leaders. A relay of hand communications went up and down the line. In another minute they relayed a hand signal back to him. The tanks' engines surged and their tracks kicked dirt and brush underneath and out the back. They broke through the trees and revved up their engines, and the assault began.

"The light machine gun's going to cover us. Sit still, docs. Do not follow us." Altgelt rolled over on his back, took three deep breaths, made sure his ammunition clip was in place and his grenades ready. He stood up as close to the tree as he could, patted his helmet, and sprinted out into the open meadow to follow the nearer tank. A few yards away Rogers, Witt, and a dozen other men sprang up to run behind him. Will and Antsley watched from the foxhole.

The soldiers sprinted back and forth and were three-fourths of the way across the meadow before the first German shot was fired at them. The tanks fired machine guns back at the distant puffs of smoke but did not slow down. Will and Antsley stared, wide-eyed, at the crash of German rounds fired at them from the distant tree line. Alongside them the light machine gun crew fired a burst over the tops of the running troops and into the far hedgerow where the Germans had hidden in the trees. The tanks raced across the field, firing their main guns and smaller machine guns, then disappeared into the distant hedgerow. Men began to fall.

Witt went down, then Hansen. Rogers broke away from the protection of the last tank to run toward them, and he fell as well. A stream of tracers zipped the tufts of grass alongside them and kicked up at the fallen men just as the last of the platoon got out of the pasture and disappeared into the trees.

A dozen more shots were heard, then silence.

"MEDIC!"

"Come on, Antsley." Will stood up to run across the meadow. Antsley

137

grabbed him by the arm.

"Get down, sir. You can't go." Anstley grabbed his musette bag with his right hand, then cleared the berm in one jump. Before Will could respond Antsley had broken from cover and sprinted across the field. The red crosses on his armband and helmet were almost the only parts of Antsley that Will could see and he focused on them as Antsley pumped his arms and ran as fast as he could.

Will saw Antsley reach Rogers and Witt, then flop down to his knees. Another shot. Antsley's head jerked. His helmet flew off, and then he fell.

Will was not aware that he had broken cover but as he began to run he saw the machine gun rounds cut into the far trees. His legs pumped in the wet, soft grass and, across the meadow, he saw a feldgrau uniform tumble down out of the tree branches. He smelled the cow patties and the dandelions and the sweat from his headband, and saw his friend on the ground next to Witt.

"ANTSLEY! WHERE ARE YOU HIT? ANTSLEY?" Breath heaving, heart pumping, Will broad-jumped the last yards, his field bag in his hand, and collapsed in a heap beside his friend. Antsley twitched, his face down, then reached his hand up to rub his head.

"I'm all right, sir. Grazed me is all. Get down yourself, sir." Antsley's helmet lay a few feet away. A shiny ding in the rim, just below the red cross, marked where the bullet had knocked it from Antsley's head. "But this guy—he's been shot."

Hansen was dead. A brace of .42 caliber machine gun rounds had hit his legs and caused him to crumple. A single rifle shot to his head had killed him.

Witt had a bullet crease across his waist.

Rogers had tripped, nothing more. He was shaking, his rifle in his left hand, his right hand fingering the rosary on the dog tag chain at his neck. Will waved him back so that he and Antsley could look at Witt's wound.

"We've got it here, soldier," they said to Rogers. "Go on. We'll take care of them. Ansley, cut his pants open."

Witt's wound was not deep. Will doused it with sulfa powder. "We're going to put a bandage on it, soldier. Antsley, put a bandage across there. I don't think it's in the muscle, soldier. If you can stand, fine. If you can't..."

"I'm all right, sir. Just a sting. Big sting, but just a sting."

"You want to go back to the hospital?"

"Nah. I'm okay. Glad you're here, Doc."

Will didn't wait to hear the rest. He left Witt and Antsley with the wounded and with Hansen's ragged corpse, then stood up and stormed across the last twenty yards of pasture, yelling, his musette bag flailing as he pumped his fists at the tree line, which by then had already been subdued.

"GODDAMN YOU. WHO TRIED TO SHOOT MY MEDIC?"

Altgelt, inside the hedgerow where the Germans had been hidden, heard Will yelling. He and his men had four German prisoners on the ground. One was gasping, a large stain spreading across the breast of his uniform. A second soldier lay in a heap, a pulpish mass of blood and bone coming out of the hole that had been his face. The other two lay on their stomachs, hands folded behind their backs, their helmets and rifles tumbled on the ground a few feet away. Will brushed aside the muzzle of Altgelt's rifle, which had been within an inch of the back of the head of one of the prisoners.

"WHO TRIED TO SHOOT MY MEDIC?" he screamed, and landed on the prisoner with both hands, grabbing his throat and beginning to choke the man as hard as he could. "ANSWER ME GODDAMN YOU WHO SHOT AT ANTSLEY YOU MURDERING— "

Altgelt stepped back and watched. Rogers, still shaking, guarded the other German. No one else moved. Will's German prisoner gasped and jerked as Will clenched his throat with both hands and squeezed, jerking his body up and down. Some of the men lit cigarettes. The whump of mortars from the distant ridge bothered none of them, nor did the thunderous blasts from the Shermans returning fire, fifty yards ahead of them, muffle Will's screams. Antsley, Witt, and the machine gun crew came up, just in time to see Will trying to choke the German to death. The other prisoner began to cry; he was only eighteen and, from the sounds he made, it wasn't at all clear he was even a German.

"YOU CAN NOT SHOOT MEDICAL CORPS," Will screamed again. "THE GENEVA CONVENTION SAYS...." He slapped the boy twice, hard, with his open hand, and then his voice trailed off. He looked up at Altgelt, then at Rogers. Both of them were certain that the doc was going to murder the prisoner. "They can not shoot at medical corps, Sergeant. They can't."

"Sir," Altgelt said, his voice more calm than the men expected. "Sir, we'll kill them for you. If you want." He paused and waited for Will to finish pounding the prisoner's head with his fists.

Then the rush of combat began to drain away. Altgelt and Rogers, Witt, all of them had experienced the rush, but it was Will's first time. He realized that he was choking a pimply-faced, skinny teenager, a dirty boy wearing a threadbare coat, and stopped. "It's against...." Will's voice trailed off to a whisper. The men smoked and waited to see what would happen. It was good for the docs to see what the krauts did, they all thought.

"I'll shoot them if you want, sir," Altgelt said again. "But if I shoot them, I can't question them. They probably don't know anything, but we're supposed to question them. But if you want me to...."

Everyone knew the Germans had been left behind to cover a retreat. One of them had been a sniper; that was how the Germans retreated, leaving a sniper to hide and shoot. They didn't know which of the four had been the sniper or who had shot at Antsley.

"You can't kill 'em, Sergeant." Rogers's drawl was clear. "That'd just be murder and you can't do that. God's on our side, and we do unto them what we would have them do unto us."

The men let Rogers have his say. When circumstances permitted, Altgelt let them all have a say before he decided what the platoon would do; the platoon had worked out its democracy long before it had got to Ste. Marie du Vire.

"Besides, Sergeant, I don't think they're the ones who shot at the medic." Rogers pointed to the dead German. "It was him, I think. Him, or that one." He pointed to the badly wounded prisoner. He really didn't know.

Will got up and made a show of straightening himself, adjusted his field kit on its strap, nodded at Antsley and then at the wounded German. They stooped over the casualty, ripped his jacket open to examine the wound. His face was ashen and he gasped for breath. His eyes were responsive but without much life. Will tried to concentrate on the wound so as to not want to finish killing him. The wound was bad.

"He's in shock, Antsley, pretty bad. Let's get some plasma in him. Oh, jeez." Will had probed the stomach wound; the tip of the probe came out covered by a green, foul, running mess. He pressed on the boy's abdomen and found it stiff, then removed his hand; the wound pulsed with a purulent ooze.

140

"He's going to be septic in about ten seconds, Antsley. Take a couple of men to carry this kraut back to Shorty. If you get him back to the field surgery he might make it. " Will hurriedly wrote a note and tied it to the German's uniform so that Garth and Morph could read what had been done, a full bag of plasma, two syrettes of morphine, a sulfa dust to a purulent bullet wound.

Sergeant Altgelt said, "No."

"Sergeant?"

"Sir, I need the men to stay in the line. And I need you and your medic here too. Witt, if you can walk, you take them back. But I need you and the medic here, Doc. Those tanks are moving out and we've got to get going. Witt'll take them to the rear."

"Okay, Sergeant. Antlsey, go with them as far as the jeep. Bring everything back you can carry, bandages, morphine...."

"No, Captain. I need you both here. Witt, when you come back, bring the jeep as close up here as you can." He faced Will a last time. "You can get your medical gear when he brings the jeep up."

Even though he outranked Altgelt, technically, Will knew that the sergeant had just ordered him and Antsley to stay put. He began to protest that if Witt stayed at the field hospital, there would be no jeep coming back and they would run out of supplies. Then he understood that it wasn't going to happen that way. Altgelt paused long enough for Witt to show that he could walk despite his crease wound. Witt cocked his rifle and swiveled it toward the Germans.

"Okay, Witt, go. YOU! YOU!" Altgelt pointed to the surviving Germans and gestured that he wanted them to carry their bleeding comrade back across the meadow to the jeep. "GO! NOW!" He motioned with the muzzle of his own rifle. The two Germans lifted the boy, then turned to walk. Witt limped along behind, his rifle muzzle no more than a foot away from them. The G.I.s watched them pick their way across the field. Altgelt called Lieutenant Campbell on the walkie-talkie.

"We're cleared here, sir," he shouted into the radio. "I sent Curtiss and the new guy ahead to catch up to the tanks. I've got the light machine gun over at the edge of the clearing, everybody else out on a line on either side. Sir? We lost Hansen. We're moving out, now. I think we're ten minutes behind the tanks." He paused and listened to Lieutenant Campbell's instructions, then acknowledged. "Yes, sir. And, uh, sir? I've got the doc and a medic with me. I'll bring 'em up." He put the walkie-talkie away and adjusted his field bag. The squad began to walk.

Bang.

Bang bang.

Bang.

They heard the rifle shots, fired from across the meadow, maybe as far away as the hedgerow where they had started half an hour earlier. A couple of the men nodded; one or two shrugged. Someone said that the krauts shouldn't have tried to overpower Witt. Altgelt used his hand to motion that they should wait a minute longer, to be sure.

Witt came back, alone, in the jeep, and took his place in the line. No one said anything. They just smoked, and exhaled, until Altgelt motioned for them to move out.

When darkness fell word was passed back to the company that the battalion commander wanted the dressing station set up at the command post. Will and Antsley worked their way up through the reserve company and found the major in a shattered pigeon coop in a farm yard. The house and barns were demolished, but a well near the ruins had not been hit.

"Captain Deere says you men are pretty low on supplies."

"Yes, sir," Will answered. "We've bandaged up about fifteen men, maybe twenty, down there. We can still sew some holes but there isn't much morphine left. We're down to one or two boxes of plasma. Then it's water."

The major's expression could have been concern, or just fatigue. Word had got round during the barrage that the Germans had finally snapped to the fact that there was a gap in their flank all the way back to Le Déversoir, and had closed it. The battalion, now completely cut off, was taking fire not only from the 88's above but from some Panzers that had come in below.

"I've told the squad leaders to strip medic pouches, Captain. That means getting them off the men's belts. Off the corpses. You're going to need them." To make the point, the major held up the field telephone, its wires screwed to terminals on the box. Will took the phone, pushed it to his ear. It was dead. The major continued. "We've been stringing wire as we go but the phone's dead. That means the Germans cut it. So, we're here all by ourselves. There won't be any more supplies. Make do."

Will and Antsley set up their dressing station at the well at the base of the farm lane. A battered sign said: *La Madeleine* and, in smaller letters, *Prefecture St. Lô*. By looking up at the Martinville Ridge they could see that the Germans still held the high ground.

"At least we've got well water, Antsley. There's a lot you can do just with clean water." Will spread out his poncho and his field kit. "We've got to boil it to keep the scalpels clean. We need some for shock. But we can't debride anyone, not if we can't send them back for Collins and Garth to finish up. So get ready to sew."

"Sir?" Antsley, laying out his own equipment, had waited until they were alone. "Sir, thanks. Thanks a lot."

"For what?"

"For beating the shit out of that guy. You saved his life."

Will did not want to be thanked for beating up a prisoner. He knew how close he had been to killing the boy and, if Antsley and Rogers hadn't been there, he thought, he probably would have. As for racing across the meadow to pick Antsley up, he knew it was more than panic; he had been looking for a German to murder. The barrage did not make him any more peaceable.

"I shouldn't have done it, Antsley. If you build a fire hole around the gas ring, put some rocks in it, you can get more heat with less fire, boil more water cans. And I suspect I didn't save his life."

"You pounded the shit out of him, sir. He looked just like the sniper. If you hadn't, someone would have killed him."

"*Like* the sniper? What are you talking about, Antsley? I don't know which one was the sniper."

"Not the Germans, Captain. Major Halliburton. That sniper you had on the ground back there today, his face beat to a pulp, I thought, 'Jesus, that's exactly what the major looked like.' When you brought him back from London. Every single guy back at Shrivenham wanted to buy you a round. We would have, too, if he hadn't confined us to quarters. That, and the short arms."

"What are you talking about?"

"When you beat the major up. In London. You're a hero as far as the men're concerned, sir. Even if he did try to get you killed in the landings, and me with you."

"I didn't beat the major up, Antsley. A buzz bomb hit a building. The wall fell on him."

Antsley winked and said, "Right, Captain. You had as much right as anybody. You got to him first or somebody would have killed him. Maybe me."

Antsley had no doubt what had happened. The guys knew that Halliburton had gotten a dose, probably the clap. Will had pumped him full of sulfa and penicillin that Douglas had swiped from the medical supplies. No one wrote it up in Halliburton's medical file but a week later the executive officer found a case of Pro-Kits, hundreds of them, in Halliburton's quarters. Pro-Kits were french letters, rubber contraceptives soaked in sulfa, given to the men to keep them off sick-call from venereal disease.

"The major thought I ratted on him about something, Antsley. I didn't. Not that it matters, but I didn't. And I didn't beat him up in London."

Halliburton had accused Will of leaking word about the venereal disease, then added Douglas to the accusation. "You little cocksucker," he had said. "I'll get you. And you, too, Hastings. Backstabbing motherfuckers." He had gone a little crazy, the way very short men do. He had ordered Will and Douglas to do short-arm inspections on the men every night, but that was not his downfall. It was entirely by chance that, three weeks later, Halliburton stumbled drunk into the Rainbow Club in London and found Will and Douglas there, waiting for Peter.

"Hey, it's the guys who like to look at dicks," he had yelled. He was drunk. Soldiers always insulted each other, especially when they were drunk. "Hey, you," he had yelled at the other men in the Club. "It's the short-arm doc and his right-hand man. Keep away from those two or they'll want to look at your dick."

That was a little strong, even from a drunk. Will had ignored him; the Rainbow Club was closing in a few minutes.

"Hey, Hastings!" Halliburton had gone on. "You seen the whores out there? I need me some rubbers. You know a lot about rubbers."

The USO staff had walked Halliburton out the door, but he didn't have enough sense to go away. When Peter didn't show up by closing time Will and Douglas left the Rainbow Club to find the Piccadilly tube entrance. Halliburton was waiting for them.

"Hey, cocksuckers! Those two guys want to take a look at your dicks," he had yelled, just as the first shriek of falling bombs pierced the air. The air raid wardens rushed to get everyone off the street and down into the tube entrance but Halliburton continued to shout.

Will had been shocked to see how efficiently Douglas had snatched the major off his feet. Douglas had grabbed Halliburton by his necktie and dragged him from the tube stop all the way to the corner of Wardour Street, near the Windmill Club. Will had been even more shocked when he caught up to find Douglas methodically beating Halliburton to a pulp.

Douglas's skill had been frightening in its technical simplicity. He hand-slapped Halliburton's face to make him gape, then punched a well-placed fist in an eye. He slapped Halliburton's face with his other hand, then punched his other eye. Douglas broke nothing, closed everything, and had reduced Halliburton to a whimpering heap when the Windmill Club exploded, the bomb shaking the building in front of them and heaving the street and sidewalk beneath their feet.

Rocks and splinters and dust settled on them as fire erupted from the Club's doorways. People screamed through the cracking sounds of fire and air raid sirens. When the smoke and debris settled, Will had gone to pull Douglas off but found only Halliburton, lying on his back, his face battered, his hands doubled into bruised claws, a whipped dog. Douglas was nowhere to be seen. But, through the confusion, Will heard a voice in the shadow. "Take good care of yourself, Will."

"Get some water boiling, Antsley. No reason to hide the gas ring now." Will studied the scissors, the scalpels, the spool of running nylon sutures, a pile of dead men's bandages and sulfa packets. The Germans had begun to shoot flares, illuminating the hillside to expose the American firing positions. Will could tell from the blasts that the major had ordered the weapons company to start firing the howitzers back at the Germans. The noise was deafening.

"The men were glad you beat him up. He had messed up one of their girls." Antsley busied himself with the gas bottle, attaching the hose and the gas ring. "She was going out with one of the guys and then she disappeared. One of her friends told us about her. We don't know if he raped her, gave her the clap, beat her up, or what. But the men weren't going to take it."

"Let's make that the sterile side," Will said, pointing across a low rock wall. "We can dump the contaminateds over there and keep the reusables on this side." He didn't want to talk about Halliburton. If he had been careful enough to not say anything to Shorty, Will certainly wasn't going to admit anything to Antsley. A round crashed into the farm house fifty yards away, then another, closer to the command post.

"He was always throwing his rank around, saying he was going to send you back to the infantry for having threads hanging off your pockets, canceling passes for nothing. We all wished you had killed him. I'll tell you this, sir, if you hadn't, we would have."

The thunderous explosion of the German .88s up on the ridge preceded by a few seconds the crash of shells just below them. Branches were ripped from trees and dirt flew, settling down over the aid station. The major ordered his howitzers to fire back; it nearly deafened them. Ten minutes later the first of the casualties was brought to the aid station, a gaping hole in his thigh and blood on his face. Shortly afterward more arrived, some on foot, some carried, some dead. Antsley didn't finish his story.

"We're going to get overrun, Antsley. Not by Germans, I hope, just casualties. We're going to have to do fluids by mouth when the saline runs out. The plasma won't last if we get some burn cases or something hits one of the ammunition carts."

"I know, sir. I know." Antsley was busy, cleaning wounds and organizing the men who needed the most urgent attention. *It'll wait*, he thought. *This battle's going to last a while. There'll be time later on to ask him if he saw that guy back there in the field with Sergeant Altgelt. I swear that guy looks like just like Douglas.*

It wasn't a buzz bomb but Will recognized the roar of an incoming shell. The shock was so intense that both of them were knocked on top of the men they were supposed to be treating. There was an electrical charge in the air, something that made hair stand up and, for a moment only, even the dressings in their hands felt as if they were about to catch on fire. Just as they heard a shout, it passed.

So, too, did the major.

"Medic! God, damn, oh damn, oh Jesus, MEDIC!"

Will crawled across the farm yard to the collapsed command post. The major's body was crumpled beneath a hodge-podge of ammunition boxes and light machine guns that, just moments before, had been the defense line for the battalion headquarters.

"Oh, jeez, oh shit, get over here, oh jeez," the executive officer panted, feverishly pulling debris off the major's chest. The pounding was so intense that Will couldn't hear what they were yelling, but it didn't matter. The Germans had already shifted their fire and, with the white phosphorous light of another flare, he could see what they were yelling about. "Oh, jeez. You, stop. Find D Company, get Captain Deere up here." He pointed to one of the runners. "Get him up here now. The Major's dead. GO."

There was nothing left for Will to bandage. He helped the perimeter guards pull the major's body from the debris, not to help the major, but to free up the ammunition boxes and disentangle the walkie-talkie from the roof tiles that had come down on them. When the body was clear and covered by a poncho, he scurried back to Antsley at the aid station and went back to work.

"Doc?"

"Yeah."

"The Captain says you've got as much right as the rest of the men. You and the medic here. To help carry the Major. You want to?"

They did. They hadn't been up at the command post with him more than an hour before the shelling killed him. But they and everyone else near the command post had heard the major's last message back to the regiment right before the shelling had started.

"We'll hold out," he had said. "Don't you worry about us. The only way we're coming off this ridge is to march into St. Lô."

If he had lived another twenty-four hours, the major would have done it on foot. Instead, he entered St. Lô on his back, his body strapped to the hood of Will's jeep.

The battalion, what was left of it, entered St. Lô from the east, on the Bayeux road. It picked its way toward the wrecked marketplace and the abbey church of Sainte-Croix, hidden under tons of blasted building stone and collapsed roof slates. Captain Deere set up a perimeter guard, then told his platoon leaders to send a couple of men from each unit to help erect a suitable platform for the Major's body. An hour later every man in the XIX Corps knew about him.

When the rest of the 29th Division followed the battalion into the city, every soldier marched by and saluted the major who had led them into the town. It was while Will and Antsley helped Lieutenant Campbell and Sergeant Altgelt to lay out the major's body and place a flag across it that Shorty spotted him.

Shorty paused. Two days had passed since he had gotten back to the field hospital to discover that Will had swapped with Collins; he figured that another hour or so wouldn't matter. Shorty sat on some debris across from the crushed marketplace and watched the men pass.

Popper's last message had said that once St. Lô fell the evacuation hospital at Isigny would be too far to the rear; a suitable site was needed, closer to the front, available to both divisions. Shorty didn't need Sergeant Prior to show him the drawings he had found in Will's things, another sketch of the abandoned monastery and an enclosed farm just beyond it. Shorty had seen them himself, and knew that they were exactly what an evacuation hospital needed.

Shorty watched the division commander accept the command of the city from Captain Deere. The men saluted. A unit flag was draped over the Major's body. The Stars and Stripes were hoisted up by a piece of lumber and strapped to the stub of the market cross. Many of the troops shook Will's hand, some saluted him. Shorty knew from the number of casualties brought to the apple barn that Will and Antsley had suffered under fire; they should be allowed to finish it. But, hero or no, it was time to rein Will in.

"Go back to Ste. Marie, Will. Get your gear from the service company, all of it. You've got twenty-four hours to report back here. Right here. Dismissed."

Shorty had been blunt. There had been no *esprit du apple barn* in his voice, no congratulations for the tired warrior who, with his dutiful medic, had performed under fire. "Take Antsley and Fouquet with you. You have a day to R and R, get your stuff, and detach from the field hospital." He and Antsley had hitched a ride back to Ste. Marie.

Will had gone straight to his cot; when he lay down, his head struck the box, the worn towel covering that was inside, some bread, a bit of cheese, and the bottle of wine. He took them out, one by one, and placed them on his foot locker, and shook the towel. There was no note.

His second uniform had been washed and folded, laid out properly on his foot locker. Antsley was the kind of kid who might have done something like that, but Antsley had been with him on Martinville Ridge. *It was the laundry ladies,* he decided, although he had no idea why they would have done it. *The laundry ladies. Them or Dr. Genet.* He closed his eyes, just for a moment, to think.

The next he knew it was daylight; he had slept through a night for the first time since the LST had made its first run to Omaha Beach almost two months before. He took his clean uniform and walked toward the unit's field shower next to the old *tuil* factory.

"Hey, Garth." His colleague stood naked under a drizzling hose when Will walked in.

"Hey, Will."

"Is Collins around? I might want to chat with him a bit. You know, this and that. Thank him for covering me with Shorty so I could keep his gutless ass out of the combat line."

Garth didn't laugh or sneer or do any of the things that a buddy would do; instead, he glared. "Listen, Will. I don't think any more of Collins than the next guy, but don't blame him."

"Why not? He wanted to keep his skin clean, so I went up the line in his place. The least he could have done was cover my back with Shorty. He looked sick enough when those mortars started dropping. Why couldn't he tell Shorty he was sick enough for me to trade with him?"

"Well, first, because Shorty went nuts when he came back from Isigny and found out you had gone up to the line. He said you violated a direct order. And broke a promise."

Will didn't reply; he had violated a direct order. And broken a promise. But, in Will's mind, that was between him and Shorty, and Shorty shouldn't have told anyone.

"This is the Army, Will, not some fucking boy scout camp. It isn't even a hospital. And Shorty isn't some stooge who doesn't really mean what he orders. He's as much in the Army as the rest of us, and if he has to go so far as to actually order one of us to do something, then we have to go so far as to not make him court martial us over it. You were wrong."

That stung, not because it was true or false but because Will had taken it for granted that all the men would be on his side. It was revenge for his brother that he had gone looking for, and they would have done the same. And it wasn't like he had run away from battle; when he came back there was no battle, and when there was a battle, he volunteered to go and let another guy be safe. Then he was under the gun when the Nazis had shelled the whole damned battalion at the base of some crummy ridge on the road to St. Lô. And, and....

"You want to know what really happened, Will? Let me tell you. When it turned out you were gone, Shorty sent Collins to the 115th. That's right. When the 116th got cut off there was no way you could handle the 115th, too. So Collins went under fire anyway. It wasn't your fault the 116th got cut off like it did, but for the last three days we've had docs from the evacuation hospital up here covering for you while you were out playing G.I. Joe. You know how many casualties there were? Do you have any idea?"

"No. Antsley and I had over a hundred. That's almost a whole company out of the battalion."

"In twelve days pushing on St. Lô, First Army had 11,000 casualties. That's a thousand a day. And right here, in this very field surgery, we had over three hundred of them in the last couple of days, just from our battalions and the rest of the regimental combat team. Three hundred! Not counting yours. So ease up on Collins. Ease up on Shorty. Another guy would have court martialed you. What did he do?"

"He fired me. I'm out of the 261st. 'Find a place for a new evacuation hospital, Will,' he said. 'Go look for some place, three or four places, I don't care, write a report.' Garth—do you really think there's a big empty hospital sitting out there somewhere just waiting for me to find it?" Will heard his own bitterness and knew that Garth heard it too. Shorty had invited Will to join the family; Will had let the family down. The family had thrown him out.

The more he talked, the more he knew he had screwed up, but he couldn't stop himself. "You know what Shorty said? He said, 'Not my problem, Will. Don't come back until you find a place. Then Colonel Seacom will decide what to do with your report. And with you.'"

Will apologized.

Garth nodded, then finished cleaning himself. Will showered and changed into the clean uniform, then went to look for Antsley and Fouquet. Sanders found him first.

"Sir? Are you still here? I mean I know you're here, but like on duty? The ambulance just brought in a kid you worked on last week, Newton. Gunshot in the leg, doesn't look so good. You sent him up to the evacuation hospital; they sent him back with an order releasing him for duty. He's sick as hell, sir, and, well, would you take a look?"

Newton did not look good. His chart said soft tissue bullet wound but his leg said something else. Collins's sutures had ruptured and the bullet hole was black, oozing purulent fluid across his ankle and foot. The leg was swollen to twice its normal size. His temperature was one hundred four and he was gasping. The return-to-duty note from the evacuation hospital said only recovery leave exceeded for condition, return to unit.

"Sanders, he's bad, we've got to get some fluids in him, fast. Get Antsley here, any medic. Run!" The drainage stank. Sanders ran, came back.

"Sir?" Antsley had appeared at Will's side. "Sir? I've got to tell you about him."

"What, Antsley?"

"Captain Collins wrote him up for three days' recuperation and then return-to-duty. We saw the leg going bad and I took it to Shorty, told him that the wound was infected and he was probably allergic to penicillin or sulfa. That was what his tag said when we sent him to Isigny."

"What'd Collins say about it?"

Antsley screwed up his courage.

"He didn't know, sir. We, that is, Shorty, he signed your name to it." He waited for the truth to sink in. "Shorty, that is, Lieutenant Carter, he signed your name to Newton's transfer. He thought Collins had screwed up when he said Newton was okay to go back to the line. Then everybody would be..." Antsley's voice trailed off. He wished that Will would hit him, or yell, or threaten him. Will did not; he continued to examine Newton.

Newton wasn't sick as hell for long. Will tried to drain the pus from his leg but it was too far gone. Newton groaned once, then stared blankly at Will until his eyes became glassy, then died.

Word of a disaster travels in the military even faster than gossip in a sewing circle. By the time Jefferson had put Newton's personal effects in a bag and Sanders had added Newton to the Graves Registration report, the enlisted men in the 261st knew that Antsley had tried to rescue Collins' patient, and had failed. The medical techs forged a confession and put it in Collins' personnel file; Will made Sanders tear it up. In the end the men settled for an anonymous twix to Major Hampton, Supply, in the 116th Battalion; their men would get the word around that one of the battalion's most experienced combat soldiers was dead because someone back at the evacuation hospital made Captain Collins's bad judgment worse by ordering the grossly infected man back to duty.

Will signed the death certificate, then returned to pack his personal gear. He rolled his sleeping bag into his poncho, strung them under his field pack, then jammed what little else he had into a barracks bag. The cot, the folding camp chair, the lantern, the plank he had used as a desk, all these he left for the next man. When he finished, he walked over to the laundry shed, then wrote out a V-mail to Virginia.

> *20 July – Still in Ste. Marie and have to hurry. The unit left an hour ago but I stayed behind to check on a boy who Collins had taken care of, a GSW in the leg. He was sent back to the evac. hospital five days ago but when I got back here some of the men told me that they wanted me to check on a soldier in the barn that someone at Isigny had returned to duty and sure enough it was the same boy, named Newton. He was dead. The gunshot wound looked like someone had injected the muscle full of pain killer and he probably didn't feel it when it got infected until it was too late. I think this is the boy Antsley had tried to put back on sick call and someone at Division Medical Office over-ruled us. If I had seen him yesterday I could have gotten him back to the evacuation hospital and also told them that some administrative officer somewhere F/W medical treatment. Instead, I'm being sent away to look at a site for a new hospital. SSDD. I'm sending this to you just in case. – Will*

It was late in the morning when he folded it and wrote: Virginia Sullivan, c/o general delivery, Tierra, Texas USA, on the address box. By then the women had finished the day's washing and the ducks were bobbing in the reeds at water's edge. He saw Dr. Genet, downstream, wading, flicking his thin line back and forth, three times, again, letting the fly settle on the water and waiting as the Vire carried it away.

Will gazed at the large trees that shaded the riverbank and thought of the quarry. He remembered the shed, the elm trees on the far bank, the diving rock, and wanted to go home. He closed his eyes and saw each of them clearly, Johnny, Hoyt, Molly, all of them, except Virginia—he could not make her appear. He had tried, even before Peter was killed, to remember what she had looked like there in the quarry, in the water, wet, inviting, the way she was the year that they were in love. That Virginia would not appear for him. Instead, the Virginia who walked down the school hallway appeared, and he stopped her outside the library door. That was an earlier Virginia, before the quarry, but only by a few months, when he was still Shirley's boyfriend.

"Mrs. Tarlton's asking me about your mother," he had told her. She listened to him, carefully. "Sort of the way anyone does, you know, how are you, how's Mrs. Hamilton, how's school. But not the same." He had paused so that she would understand that this wasn't just an idle comment. Virginia waited. "She came up to me in front of Reilly's and said 'Will, how are you getting along with Doc?' and then she told me Doc could be hard to get along with, and then she said she saw your mother go in to see Doc, and she said 'How is Mrs. Sullivan? You can tell me.' I told her I didn't know, I thought she was just fine."

Virginia had become very quiet, then answered him. "Well, tell me. How is she?"

He told her that he never listened to what Doc said to people in the clinic, or what people said to Doc, or read the scraps of paper that cluttered Doc's desk. He did not tell her that he had known for a long time that Emma Sullivan was sick in her head. Emma didn't talk anymore. When she looked at anyone, him, Doc, Mrs. Tarlton, she became very bashful and wouldn't speak, except to answer 'that's nice.' What Will did say was that when Doc walked Mrs. Sullivan back out to the waiting room and talked to Poppy, Doc mostly shook his head. Virginia knew all that.

One evening, a week later, after washing up and putting away the brooms and mops, he walked from Doc's over to Nona's Café to find her.

"I'll finish waiting tables in about an hour," she said, "if you can wait that long."

He said he could. When Nona closed up, Virginia walked to the courthouse square. Will was waiting for her under one of the trees by the big front steps.

"Doc called somebody today. I think it was in Lubbock. He said he was going to have to send a woman over there. I heard him say no, she didn't need a straightjacket or anything like that, but she couldn't take care of herself any more. He said it was more like she just forgot her mind, just left it someplace and couldn't remember where. He said he had done all he could do."

"Did he say it was Momma?"

"No." Will thought for a second, and knew that he had dissembled. "Well, yes, he did. Sort of. He said she's a real nice lady who's married to the newspaper man here in town. That was all he said. And he also said 'whenever they could.'"

Virginia had begun to cry, not loud, or wailing, or in gulps, but the kind of crying where you have a stream of tears from both eyes and you put a hand over them, as if that would keep anyone from seeing them. Will had told her he was sorry and, to his surprise, he had put his arm around her.

153

To his greater surprise, she embraced him back, wrapping her arms all the way around his chest, and laid her head in the spot between his shoulder and his neck. She held him, letting her tears flow and getting his shirt wet. He held her tightly, even though he hadn't gone to Nona's to ask her for a date, just to tell her about her mother. Even so, he could tell that Virginia wanted him to hold her. Shirley would never have done that. Shirley would have told him that the Flemings would never go to a doctor unless they were sick, and Shirley had never held Will. But with Virginia, holding was just natural.

Then Virginia had kissed him. He had not kissed her; she had kissed him. He didn't know much about kissing but he knew this was no peck in the back row seats of the Rialto or a hurried sneak attack on someone's back porch. She had kissed him wetly, her wide, full mouth taking him in, and he decided on the spot that Virginia Sullivan was all that he had ever wanted in life.

He no longer missed Virginia but he missed terribly the idea of her. He crossed his arms to ward off her absence but discovered instead that his arms remembered Géraldine Dupré, the sensation he had felt when she had held his arm with her hands, without asking, and walked along with him. He didn't know why but she had made it seem as if that was what they always did, and it was good. The trees rustled.

"*Bonjour?*" Dr. Genet shuffled his feet in the meadow.

Will got up from the floor of the laundry shed and went to shake his hand. Genet showed him two fish. Will showed him the box, then pulled away the cloth to expose the boule of bread, the cheese and the bottle of wine.

"Merci beaucoup, Doctor. Thanks. Do you want to drink this with me, right now? Let's drink it." Will glanced at his watch; it was almost noon. He figured that Fouquet and Antsley would probably come get him for the ride back to St. Lô just as he was about to dig into the picnic, but they could wait. *What's Shorty going to do? Fire me?* He handed the bottle to Dr. Genet, who set down his creel and the fishing rod and took the bottle with a free hand. "Do you know how to open this? I don't carry a bottle opener around with me. Not much used to wine, I guess."

He was not particularly surprised when Dr. Genet opened his creel and took out a folding knife. For a moment Will wondered why the Germans hadn't taken the knife, indeed, why they hadn't dragged Genet off to a labor camp like most of the other men of Ste. Marie du Vire, why they left just him and the priest and a couple of other old men. Genet flicked open a blade, cut a band from the cork, and by a casual sleight of hand trick, flipped the cork out as easily as if it had been a peanut in a shell. Will expected him to tilt the bottle back but, to his surprise, he instead placed it firmly, but carefully, into a tuft of grass, the neck open at the top. There were no glasses.

"*Respirer. Ahh. Attendons.*" He closed his eyes, opened his arms, lifted his head, and drew in a deep breath, sighing with a sort of middle-aged ecstacy that Will had not seen before. "*Le vin; il faut qu'il respire.* The wine has to breathe."

They broke the bread and cut up the cheese.

"Thanks, Doctor. For the bread. And the cheese. Well, all of it." He pantomimed a gesture of gratitude, to which his friend shrugged and seemed to indicate that he had nothing to do with it, nothing except to enjoy the sharing of it.

Will cut off a wedge of cheese, tore a bit of the bread and poked it into his mouth. Genet followed suit, his infectious aha and wiping of lips making Will glad that he had made one friend before being sent away. He separated his canteen from his canteen cup, poured some of the wine into one and passed it to the doctor, then poured a bit for himself, trying to not waste too much down the side.

"Calvados?" he asked.

"*Poof! Calvados, bah! Pas Calvados, c'est du vin! Un Sancerre. Sancerre.*" He acted like a school master or, perhaps, an uncle, giving a sly lesson to a boy. "*C'est le plus rare vin que j'ai ....*"

Will wasn't clear on the difference between Calvados and wine, whatever it was that Genet called it, nor did he care. Genet sipped, Will drank. He refilled his canteen, and Genet's cup, and drank again. He was already drunk from fatigue and anger, and in the hot noon sun it took very little for him to be drunk from the Sancerre as well. His few words of French were deadened by the time Genet poured the last of the bottle. They lifted their tin stems in a toast, then drank off the rest.

"I'm being sent off. Tell the priest goodbye. And, your nieces."

"*Á mes nièces. Á leur santé. Merci.*"

"Yeah. Merci. To friends." Will tilted his canteen, emptied it, and stood. "If I make it back this way."

He took Genet's hand, shook it, and said goodbye, then slung his pack over his shoulder and walked away.

Antsley and Fouquet were waiting in the jeep. Will climbed in the front, slightly drunk, content that Genet had toasted him as an *ami*.

"Stop, just a second." The jeep lurched to a halt in front of the barn and Will yelled for Sanders to come out. Some of the other men came as well, but Garth did not.

"Bye, sir. Take care."

"Yeah. You too. Keep your heads down."

"Right, sir."

"Sanders, a last favor. Mail this for me." He handed Sanders the V-Mail. "Take care of it. It's pretty important."

Sanders promised he would; it was the first time anyone could remember Will with any letters, coming in or going out. Sanders would tell the others, later, that Doc sent a Dear John letter back to that girl in Texas. *Good for him.* Will waved a last time and Sanders waved goodbye to the back of the departing jeep. None of them wondered whether they would see each other again. The jeep made its way up the street and past the square. Will, and Fouquet, and Antsley were gone.

"Here's the standing orders, Doc."

Will and his two medics met up with Captain Deere and the survivors of Lieutenant Campbells's platoon. Will swung his bag into Deere's jeep; Antsley and Fouquet piled into the truck with Lieutenant Campbell's men who would follow behind on the road out of Pont Hébert. Will tried to pay attention through his fog of Sancerre.

"You're attached to Lieutenant Campbell's platoon. They're going to escort you and this other guy around to find a new field hospital. Lieutenant Campbell's going to send a runner back to me every day so if you need anything, just give a message to the runner. Runner—no radio. Runner only. Got it?"

"Yes."

"Okay, second, and Lieutenant Campbell knows this, but there are a lot of little kraut units out there trying to get back into their lines. Basically it's because of them that you're to maintain radio silence. Do not mess with them unless they attack, and if they do, Lieutenant Campbell will know what to do. I think any little kraut platoon that survived the last six weeks would just be trying to sneak back through our lines and not pick a fight, but that's no reason to get on the radio and start broadcasting where you are and what you're doing. Make sure your men know that. Got it?"

"Yes, sir. Radio silence. Don't pick a fight."

"Third, and this is it. The lieutenant will maintain combat awareness, guard duty, outposts, that sort of thing, but I'm sending the platoon to get some rest. They've been in it since day one; there's only about a third of them left. They'll help you if you need something, but try to let them recoup. They're worn out. Got it?"

"Yes."

"Okay, see you in a week or so."

"Sir?"

"What?"

"Where are we going?"

The jeep bounced along on the road that led from Pont Hébert to Carentan. It passed dozens of wrecked guns and German field pieces, smashed trees and artillery craters, some smoking tanks with treads scattered across the fences. Exhausted troops marched in the opposite direction, men from the Fourth and Thirty-Fifth Divisions, moving to St. Lô to start getting ready for whatever came next.

"There's some places marked on a map, basically places up and down the river north of Pont Hébert. First one is an abandoned monastery a couple of miles from here. Next to a farm called Château Dupré. Lieutenant Carter was pretty clear that you go there first. That's where I'm leaving you. Fact is, on the map it looks like it's right across the river from where you've been the last week or so. This seems like the long way around to get there."

The wheels, hitting holes in the demolished pavement, forced the two men to sit in silence, their helmets slipping forward over their heads. After several kilometers Deere turned off the Carentan road and drove back into the hedgerow lanes in the direction of the Vire. There emerged below a peaceful scene, out of place in war-torn Normandy, an orchard on a hillside that led down to an enclosed farm and, beyond, the gothic walls and ancient tower of a religious community.

Deere steered down the lane to the chateau and turned in at the large gate on the south side, the troop truck following behind. They halted in the barnyard. Men got out, the lieutenant and the captain making note of the barn, the poultry coops and dovecote, a one-room house built into the wall, some small stock pens. At the far end there was the chateau itself, a small, classic, stone home, facing them, its broad steps framing a formal porch.

Will did not wait for Deere or Campbell. He left them in the farmyard and walked toward the house.

Géraldine stood at the top of the steps. He saw, but did not pay attention to Claudine, who stood behind her, or to her parents, in the doorway. Instead, he looked only at Géraldine who, as he drew near, left the others and walked down to him. She took his arm, just reaching her hands out to him, and they stood together, unsure what came next. Anyone looking would have thought they were going to walk to church, or window-shopping, a boy and his girl strolling, aimlessly.

The men lost track of the days. They settled into the barn and the one-room house. They wandered through the orchard and lay in the sun near the abandoned monastery. They swam in the Vire and drank Calvados. They carved yo-yo's out of the bung plugs of Dupré's wine barrels and played baseball inside the barnyard. They flirted with Claudine and avoided her mother's broom. They rested.

They ignored Will and Géraldine.

All of them forgot, for those three days, that Captain Deere also had said that soon they would be joined by another officer, an administrative officer, someone from the Fourth Division.

CHAPTER FOURTEEN

August, 1944

Something held him down.

Antsley? Is that you?

No.

It was Virginia, in the quarry. She swam up silently, behind him, and clutched him, clasping her arms and legs around him, her hair floating onto his shoulder, the curve of her tummy snug against his back. He was so relieved that it was her, that she was holding him, that the waiting for her was over, that even though he had waited longer than she said he would have to wait, now she was there, in the quarry, the soothing water covering their nakedness.

At the quarry's edge the water was cool and clean, but there were ducks bobbing alongside a laundry shed, rippling the surface as they followed Genet's fly casts, hoping to pilfer his dinner for themselves. Genet stood in the rushes, flicking his rod, lifting his grizzled head upward, turning to see what glinted in the morning sun.

It was a glider.

Will struggled. Something held him down.

It was a huge, powerless, green-brown glider, one wing falling away, fluttering back and forth, drifting, just beyond the trees. *'Jump!'* he yelled. *'Peter–jump! You're going to ...'* Then, Peter and the crew, arms raised. Germans. *Abwärts! Schnell!* Peter jerking, *a coup de grâce*, a priest. Will hiding in the trees.

A sting.

When the light returned it filtered through the leaded windows of the chapel, spreading into the cloisters of the monastery, the dust hanging in the evening rays of sun to make holograms against the paving stones that encircled a tiny garden. The cool air soothed him and he sat on the bench to trace the shapes on his sketch pad, lifting his head occasionally to study the colonnaded arcades that led away to dozens of tiny rooms. *Why am I here?*

It wouldn't come to him, why he was there. It was his duty. He could not remember what his duty was but he remembered he had a duty. With a fleeting thought he considered that he couldn't wake up because he was dead. Johnny Bradley was there, his arm around Hoyt, laughing. Virginia looked—he despaired because he couldn't see her, not anymore, but Géraldine was there too and she did not look dead. She looked like life. She smiled at him, gently, and took his arm to lead him away from the cloister and along the arcade. The rooms they passed were shabby, ravaged by birds and rain, tables overturned, benches upended, but they came to a clean room, a very small one, sparse, and he knew that she had prepared it for them. On a wooden table near the door there was a pannier covered by a towel. She gave him bread and wine and, when he touched her face, gently, she pulled him to her, and they sat on the floor. She lay his head in her lap and smoothed his hair and he slept very deeply, without pain, for a time.

'Sir? Sir? He's here.' It was Antsley. '*Sir, you have to come. Sir?*' He answered, "I'll walk back, Antsley, I'll go to the house. We'll wake them up," but when he lifted the latch string in the postern gate a noise exploded in his head. Hands reached under him. *It's okay, Doc, I've got you.* He knew the man's voice but couldn't see him. All he could see was Géraldine, who was lifting him, blood on her blouse. *Why do you have Peter's map? Why did you get blood all over it? Why...*

Another sting.

He decided not to sit up but, rather, to close his eyes. He could wait to swim until later, he had time, Shorty wouldn't check on him, not for a while. He wanted to vomit, and was thirsty.

Later, his eyes closed, he found that they were in the water, or back in the water, in the quarry, or in the river, near the meadow, he couldn't see clearly. It didn't matter because he could feel her, her nipples, erect on her firm small breasts, the first he had felt in his life, pressed into him. He reached behind him to clasp her but she held him tightly until, by a nudge, or a pause, or by mutual agreement, she turned him to face her and would not let him go, her legs around his hips. They had kissed, naked, clasping, wet, her thick hair over both of them, she kissing him eagerly, her hand

160

reaching for him, finding him, and lifting him, his body quivering with excitement, until a burst of noise exploded in his head.

A loud voice, angry, a memory, not a dream.

It was Bart, standing on the bank, watching them, shouting:

"*VIRGINIA! WHAT THE HELL ARE YOU DOING? JESUS!*"

Not even the morphine could stop him, and Will woke up.

Will opened his eyes but didn't speak. Out of habit he began the process of waking up, opening his eyes, gathering light, focusing, slowly lifting his head so as to not challenge the neck muscles, stiff from laying on a hard canvas cot. Every day, for as long as he could remember, he had awakened with a pain in his neck from sleeping with a steel combat helmet.

His helmet was gone.

He sat up in a rush, alarmed, and shrieked when pain shot through his chest. It ran up into his shoulder, and out through the back of his head, blinding him with a hot searing shock. Then, when he lay back on the bed, the landing sent another bolt flashing to the back of his head and down to his shoulder, through his shoulder blades, and into his lungs. Before he fainted he thought that the Germans had broken into the platoon and begun to shoot them, a bayonet had been rammed through him, that someone was killing him. He wondered if Antsley had gotten away, or Fouquet, or Halliburton. Then he blacked out.

The shriek brought Miss Garlock, Lieutenant Garlock. She was used to shrieks in the ward; that a soldier was in her ward at all meant he was badly hurt. She had been in the burn ward but, to her wonderment, the men whose skin had been seared away by white phosphorous or an artillery flash, some in simple accidents with a jerry can of gasoline—those men had been pretty quiet. They had no sensory nerves to tell them that their bodies were burned beyond repair, so they didn't feel the pain of their burns. Most of them had let out horrible sounds only when they saw their own plastically deformed skin, especially those with burned-away lips and noses, but theirs had been cries of despair, not pain. Lieutenant Garlock had worked in the burn ward as long as anyone, but she finally had succumbed and transferred into the ward of thoracic wounds, chest wounds, gunshots in the lungs. There were some disfigurements, not many, but all the men cried when the morphine wore a bit low.

Will had been shot through the upper back. Lieutenant Garlock knew from his chart that a large bullet had hit him somewhere just between his thoracic spine and the scapula. The surgeon, Captain Sheffield, had charted that the scapula had turned the bullet, which then passed through the muscles of Will's back and out his chest wall without hitting his heart. His pulmonary function was low but not, from what the surgeon could tell, from a complete penetration of Will's lungs. He also charted that he had no idea how it kept from killing the patient. Will, unlucky, had been very lucky indeed.

She gently lifted his wrist and searched for a pulse. His fingernails returned color. From a few steps away she patiently counted his respirations, eighteen to the minute, not ideal but high enough that she could ask for another few grains of morphine sulphate.

The doctor said no. Yes, it would be painful but, no, because so many days after surgery they needed to be sure he would wake up. His shriek had been a good sign, not a bad one, although he was pretty sure the patient wouldn't agree.

For the next few hours Lieutenant Garlock, then Captain Sheffield, checked on Will. He became more restless, he tried to move in the bed, he moaned, but his vital signs were stable. They could wait.

At four in the afternoon Will woke again. He opened his eyes and started to lift his head, then remembered how much it would hurt. He waited to see what would come into focus.

There were no trees, no tent canvas, no barn rafters, not the plaster ceiling of the great room of Chateau Dupré. The walls were green, not the green of trees or grass, but a soft green. There were round circles of light.

Slowly he moved his eyes from side to side and from the upper to the lower range of his vision. There was no steel helmet nor, below, could he see any uniform. He waited until he was satisfied he could endure the motion, then slowly lifted his head, not much, only enough. The shapes he saw weren't solid or in focus. He waited. It took some time before he could spot his feet far below the horizon. He counted them; there were two. He moved them; they didn't move. Eventually, with patience, he saw beyond them to the rounded rails of a bed. Beyond the bed rails, on the far wall, he could make out an intravenous stand, a bottle hanging from it, a tube going in the direction of the bed.

He knew he was in a hospital.

His mind was not clear but he reasoned that if he was in a hospital, he must be hurt.

He thought about this for a long time, then resumed his search. To his right he saw only curtains. The curtains also were green, stretched on a frame. To his left side, at the extreme corner of his view, there was a side rail and, beyond, another bed, five or six feet away. He rotated his eyes again to the right. It hurt to do this but he wanted so badly to know his surroundings that he was willing to endure the pain. There, at the highest edge of the right corner of his field of vision, he saw plaster. It was not a cast, not on his arm, bigger than a cast would be for a broken arm.

Will closed his eyes and began a self-examination. He wriggled his toes, slowly, but enough that several toes found each other. He was satisfied it was not the sensation of a phantom limb. He opened his left hand, closed it, touched his thumb to his forefinger, felt it. It was there. Then, when he tried to wiggle his right fingers, he felt nothing. He attempted to make a circle of his thumb and first finger, then his thumb and second finger, but there was nothing. He tried again, found nothing. He knew he had lost his hand. From the pain in his back he deduced that he had lost his arm as well.

Tears came, pity tears for his arm and hand. He shouldn't have lost them. They were a good arm, a good hand. They didn't always know to call a scalpel a scalpel or a rongeur a rongeur, but they were fine for a combat surgeon. He could have taken them home with him to be a doctor's arm and hand after the war. This was bad.

He waited for a half hour before he checked again for his left hand. It was still there. The fingers rubbed each other, producing a bit of pain in his chest, but not much, and he could make full circles with thumb and forefinger, thumb and little finger, any two fingers he wanted.

Lieutenant Garlock watched him. Most of the men in her ward needed intensive hands-on treatment, changes of intravenous saline bottles, cleansing of gaping wounds, debridement of dead skin, changing of sheets and mattresses and replacing of bed pans. Captain Hastings needed very little of that; her principal task was to see that he didn't develop a pneumothorax, a sudden leak of air from the lungs that would signal that the bullet wound had finally weakened the tissue enough to cause it to deflate on its own. When he had shrieked in the morning she was afraid that his right lung had collapsed and expelled air into his chest cavity. It hadn't. Captain Sheffield told her that if he continued with no changes, Will would get an x-ray in a day or two to be sure that both his lungs were filled and, perhaps, look for more bullet traces. But nothing more had happened with Captain Hastings until the late afternoon when, she realized, his eyes were open.

She had started to go to his bedside, to say hello, introduce herself, but then she saw his toes. The right toes moved, then the left. His eyes moved up and down, back and forth. Captain Hastings was awake and checking himself out. Something about him told her to let him have his privacy; she would talk to him when he wanted to talk.

For the next hour she watched Will move his toes and his left arm. He gently lifted his head, looked around, lay back on his pillow. He tried to see what the plaster was on his body but it restricted his motion so much that he could not turn his head far enough to get a good look.

At six o'clock in the evening a serving cart entered the ward. Will smelled hot food before the wheels and clatter of dinner approached his bed. His eyes flicked open and, remembering the pain of motion and sound, he lay still. Lieutenant Garlock saw him open his eyes and, when the dinner cart arrived at his bed, she raised a side table and set a tray for him.

"Would you like to eat, Captain?" She held the food tray where he could see some of the items. Chicken, potatos, gelatin. Soup. Tea.

He opened his mouth but words didn't come out. He didn't know why, but speech wasn't available. He tried to speak, failed. He clicked his mouth several times, then closed it. He looked at the tray and blinked his eyes.

"Should I try to raise the bed for you?"

He flicked his eyes back and forth; that or the panic on his face, she wasn't sure which, said no.

Lieutenant Garlock looked around the ward. *Five minutes will help and won't hurt,* she thought. She stood over Will and picked up the soup. He relaxed. She fed him with a spoon, one bite, then another, then more. Would he like some crackers in it? He wasn't sure. She tried one; he ate it. She fed him the rest. Chicken? No. Some potatoes? Will tried; it was too much. He sipped the tea through a straw. Dinner tired him, but helped. He blinked at her, smiled a weary smile, and closed his eyes.

She was pretty sure he wasn't asleep but he had eaten and, what's more, he had spoken to her. Blinks, opening his mouth, closing his eyes. She had helped.

The next morning Captain Sheffield returned, accompanied by a colonel from the 29th Division Medical Office. They hovered over Will until he awoke from the noise of their whispers. When his eyes opened and focused, they were reading his chart.

"Good morning, Captain. Are you awake?"

Will looked at them, then blinked his eyes up and down.

"How's your pain level this morning. Are you hurting?"

Will had a dull but persistent ache from his upper back, through his body and up into his head. He had heard of men losing an arm before; the ache was a phantom pain, injury to an arm that wasn't there. He was not willing to lift his head to see if it would cause the same searing pain he had felt the first time he had awakened.

Captain Sheffield looked at his chart again. Will had taken a single dose of morphine sulfate after dinner, then neither medicine nor complaints of pain the rest of the night.

"Feel good enough to let us wheel you down for an x-ray, Doc?"

This confused him. An x-ray of what? There was no arm to x-ray. He blinked at them.

"We'd like to take a look at your lungs. You sound good but sometimes these wounds trick you. You know that. You did a lot of these from what the Colonel says."

The colonel tried to look affable but, essentially, he was an Army doctor, more army than doctor.

"You're looking pretty good, Captain Hastings. You're going to pull through just fine. Captain Sheffield says if you don't have any more metal in there, if the lungs are okay, we can start getting you back on your feet in a day or two. Nothing fancy, just start a bit of rehab. How does that sound?"

It sounded confusing. What happened to his lungs? He drew in some air, let it out. Nothing special. He blinked again.

"You got shot in the back. Did you know that? Right through the back. Damned lucky you weren't killed, don't know why you weren't. Glad you weren't. Lost a lot of blood. But when the medics got to you, you were stable. Hole in your back big enough to drive a jeep through. Hole in your chest. But somebody knew what they were doing, and you were stable."

Who? A bit of the fog lifted. They had been at Château Dupré. Campbell's platoon was there. How long? Three days? Four days? A week? He couldn't think straight. Something had happened— what? He blinked at the colonel, at Captain Sheffield.

"Take it easy, Will. There's no rush. You've been out for a week. First thing now is to clear your lungs, be sure you can breathe. I think you're all right but that's why we've got this big machine here in Cherbourg. This hospital has been in business for what, Colonel? Two weeks? Runs as good as any place in the States. So, get some breakfast, go back to sleep. We'll come check on you in an hour and see if you're up for a trip to radiology." They patted his left arm and walked away.

He ate cereal for breakfast. At first he wanted to throw up, but after he overcame the gag reflex he realized it was Wheaties, with real milk. He chewed each bite as if he had never eaten Wheaties. Mrs. Franklin had always fried bacon and biscuits for Mr. Franklin but all Will ever got was Wheaties. He wondered where the Franklins were now, then remembered Virginia. Where was she? What was she doing? She wouldn't know anything about him being shot, he was glad for that. Then, for a moment, he became resentful—they had it easy in Tierra. No bullets. No bombs. Nothing but slow days, fresh air. Friends. Shirley. Molly. No, Molly had left when word came about Hoyt and Johnny being lost at Bataan. Well, friends, anyway.

Then he remembered Poppy. There was some reason Will was here, something to do with Poppy. No, that wasn't it. What was it? Poppy was not a very good person. In fact, Poppy was the only thing about Virginia he didn't like. *She was so beautiful, her thick auburn hair pulled to one side, her clothes clinging to her.* She would be doing all right because Poppy would be making money off everybody in town. Tires. Beef. Sugar. Gas. Ration books. Virginia wouldn't be starving. Why didn't she write?

Lieutenant Garlock helped him with his tray. He found that he could sit one-fourth way up with the bed adjusted. His left hand was just fine for eating, although a bit slow. He finally saw his body cast but he knew already what it would look like. There was a frame from his neck down across his left armpit, then to his waist, then around. It covered his right shoulder and back to his neck. There was nothing to the right of the shoulder. Everything under the cast felt numb.

"Want to talk?" she asked.

He looked up. She was clearing the tray. He looked at her. She was about thirty, maybe a little older, not heavy, not very much to look at either, but kind. Her face didn't have a sharp edge to it. Maybe he would talk later. He blinked. No, not now.

They didn't x-ray Will that morning or that day. He could tell from some commotion away from the ward that something had happened. He didn't know what it was but there was a surge of sounds outside, trucks coming, going, people rushing. He assumed that a load of men had been brought in; Will's x-ray could wait.

CHAPTER FIFTEEN

September, 1944

On the third day after Will woke up he heard Colonel Seacom coming, and remembered Halliburton. He remembered seeing Shorty talking with Colonel Seacom at St. Lô and figured it out—the colonel had agreed to send Will off with an officer from the Fourth; the officer turned out to be Halliburton. 'Shorty's surprise,' Captain Deere had called it. And then something had happened at Château Dupré.

The Colonel was talking to someone near Will's bed.

"I can let you ask, Major, but I don't think you're going to get anything. He's been awake for three days and hasn't said a word."

Colonel Seacom came into view. This time another man came as well, a major, a short, stocky man Will had never seen before. His branch insignia wasn't a Caduceus, nor was he infantry. Sometimes people confused them, the crossed rifles and the crossed snakes or whatever they were on the caduceus. His insignia was something else. He wasn't a doctor.

"Good Morning Captain. I'm Major Leatherman. How ya' feeling this morning?"

Something about the man troubled him. Will couldn't put his finger on it, but the major was not one of them. He was pretty sure he wasn't with the medical battalion and he wasn't with the 116th. Will blinked.

"Let me see how you're doing, Captain." Colonel Seacom acted as if Will was his patient and made a show of taking Will's vital signs. He checked his pulse in five seconds, then put a stethoscope on a part of the body cast where no sound could possibly have penetrated. He looked in Will's eyes and counted his breaths for less than fifteen seconds. He picked up Will's

168

left hand and dropped it. "No change." He turned to Leatherman. "No change." He turned back to Will.

"Captain, are you up to talking any? This man's from the MPs. He wants to know if you can tell him what happened at Chateau Wherever You Were?"

Will looked closely at Colonel Seacom. Something in the Colonel's expression said to keep his mouth shut. Or was Colonel Seacom just being himself, stern, not too friendly in the first place? It didn't matter—Will wasn't about to begin talking. He gazed at them with a blank stare, neither blinking nor communicating.

"He has some questions about the battle, Will. Do you remember the battle?"

The battle. Yes, there was a battle. What happened? *This man is not safe,* he thought. Will blinked; no, he couldn't remember.

"Let's try tomorrow, Doctor. Hate to bother you. We've got to get to the bottom of this."

"You're doing fine, Captain," the colonel said to Will. "We'll get you back on your feet, but first you have to rest. Rest, Captain. You get that, don't you?"

Will got it. Captain Sheffield had told him he could go to X-ray any time, that he could get on his feet in a few days. The colonel's hint couldn't have been clearer—stay here and keep your mouth shut.

Will stayed in the ward another week. On the eighth day he was taken to x-ray. His lungs were clear. There was a small trace of bullet fragment in front of his heart, probably from a ricochet off his third rib. If they left it alone it would probably work its way out some day. If it began to hurt, they could go back in and look for it.

Captain Sheffield himself stood on his left side and helped Will walk back from X-ray.

The next day they cut his body cast off.

To the right of his shoulder Will found, to his amazement, his right arm. It was puny, a much-reduced and shriveled right arm, but an arm. It was dead; he felt nothing. He couldn't lift it. And there was his hand. He couldn't wiggle it, or move the fingers, but everything was there. He began to cry, not wailing, but in the way men cry when they don't want to be seen.

"I thought you knew, Captain. You've done this procedure yourself, probably, to some of your patients. When you have something that close to the heart and lungs, immobilize. We just deadened your arm and wrapped it up with the body cast. If your arm was waving around out there it might have pumped bullet slivers right into your heart. Lung, artery, whatever, some place that a sliver shouldn't go, anyway. A bit of therapy and the arm will come right back. Sorry. Thought you knew."

Will was not an amputee.

At the end of the week they transferred him to a physical rehabilitation ward. Instead of lying in bed Will began a new routine. He walked up and down the hall. He sat in a chair and lifted five pounds, then ten pounds, on a pulley and rope. He gripped a rubber ball. He ate.

The colonel came to check on him every day, Major Leatherman in tow. Eventually the major concluded that if Will's color was returning and he could sit in a chair he could answer some hard questions, whether he could talk or not.

"Captain, we need your help."

Will blinked.

"Let me be straight with you. Something happened at Château Dupré. It's pretty serious."

Will asked for pencil and paper.

"What happened?" he wrote. His left hand scribble was almost illegible. The major figured it out.

"Major Halliburton was killed."

Will bowed his head and looked away. He made a show of lifting his right arm but could not bring it high enough to wipe his face.

"What happened?" he pointed to the sentence he had written.

"We were hoping you could tell us, Captain."

Will shook his head.

"Where are the men? What happened to them?" Will wrote something new.

"Ah, the men." Leatherman looked at Will, then the colonel. Colonel Seacom nodded and the major continued. "Most of the men are dead. The rest are wounded."

The answer was not a surprise, but it was brutal. *Most of the men are dead.*

"What happened?" he wrote. "Who?"

The major was not a cagey man. He knew that Will had been found on the floor of the great room of the main house at Château Dupré, bleeding, with a hole from a bullet that had come out through his chest. The medical people had told him that Will had probably been shot within an hour of the time they found him, that someone had cleaned out his wound, and that he was stable, if short of blood.

"Who wrapped up your wound, Captain Hastings?"

Who wrapped up my wound? Will couldn't answer that question. He blinked and shrugged.

"Captain, here's what we need to know. Write it out if you can. Who shot Major Halliburton? That's what we're trying to find out. Can you tell us?"

Will looked up at the two men, the medical commander and the investigator. The question jolted him, and he began to remember things. He called for pencil and paper.

"Where was he shot?" he wrote out.

"Major Halliburton's body was found in the chateau."

"Where were the men?" Will wrote again.

The major didn't know how to answer what Will asked. Will asked for more paper.

It took almost an hour for him to draw a pitiful sketch of the chateau. He began with the farm. The chateau lay in the bottom of a small valley. The buildings were enclosed within a wall that went around the house, the barn, the sheds, and a smaller house. They formed a rough square with an open courtyard in the middle. A small gate opened through the wall so that the family could lead livestock out to the pasture. On the west side, outside the chateau walls, there was an orchard. The orchard grew in orderly rows up the side of a slope toward a ridge that was traversed by a farm lane, on the other side of which there was a hedgerow. On the north side of the chateau there was a meadow. There was a very small cultivated field on the east side that was bordered by a canal. On the east side of the canal another slope led downward. Will hesitated; for some reason he did not want to draw attention to the monastery, and decided to not include it. On the south, the main gate to the chateau opened onto a small lane and a crossroad that itself was sunk between hedgerows.

On a second sheet Will sketched the buildings of the chateau. The barn was a series of open spaces separated by short walls. On one side there were stalls for the family cattle. On the other side there was a hay rick. Milking stalls lined the wall closest to the meadow gate. There were other small buildings for tools, poultry, some chickens and ducks and a dovecote. The small house had probably been used for the farm workers, but there hadn't

171

been any farm workers around when the platoon entered the courtyard for the first time. Lieutenant Campbell and Will had taken the small house for their quarters.

The home of the chateau was small compared to others he had seen. It was built in the shape of a rectangle. A large kitchen occupied half the ground floor. A single reception, a living room, occupied the other half. The family slept in rooms on the upper floor. Will had never been up there so did not sketch any walls or doors on the upper floor.

He erased some lines, made some notes to show where the gates and hedgerows were. When he was satisfied that he couldn't improve on the drawing he gave it to the major.

"Where was I?"

"Well, you asked me the one thing I don't know. No one told me where you were found, Captain Hastings. Do you remember being shot?"

Will shook his head no.

"Do you remember Major Halliburton being shot?"

He shook his head no again.

"Do you remember the attack?"

Will remembered some of the attack. A small German unit had appeared on the road on the ridge above the orchard. Lieutenant Campbell had an outpost in the orchard; he was isolated and stayed put when the Germans began to cross the road. Lieutenant Campbell had spread the rest of his men around the western and northern walls of the chateau and set up small arms and riflemen at the corners and in the upper floors of the buildings. He then sent a runner to find Captain Deere to report that there might be an enemy engagement.

"Do you know why he sent a runner?"

"Radio silence," Will wrote.

"What else do you remember?"

Something was wrong. Why, Will asked himself, *would this major be asking what he, a medical officer, remembered about a battle and what he remembered about another medical officer who had been shot?*

"Shell hit the barn. A big shell. Then another shell hit the wall and the courtyard. The chateau was way down lower than the ridge and they could shoot right down on us."

Château Dupré, in a valley, on no particular road, was a textbook example of a place of no military or strategic significance. It was such a bad site militarily that even the Germans had left it more or less untouched during four years of occupation. For days, the men inside the chateau had heard the thunder of guns and tanks several miles away at Hauts Vents, but no one had come near them.

"Then, all of a sudden, all hell broke loose, and there was a lot of shooting," Will wrote. "There was machine gun fire from the chateau and the platoon was shooting rifles and some other things, grenades I think, but the Germans lobbed big shells down on us. A lot of us were hit. A lot. Antsley, Private Antsley—my medic—he ran all over the courtyard trying to do what medics do. Then there was another shell that hit our headquarters house."

Leatherman read Will's notes and looked at the maps he had sketched. Will sat back in the chair. He was exhausted and surprised to find that he was exhausted.

"Anything else, Captain?"

Will shook his head no. He was very tired and, he realized, sweating through his pajamas. The house robe was not enough to keep him warm, and he began to shake.

Colonel Seacom and Leatherman stood up and waited while Will composed himself.

"My regrets, Captain. I know this is hard on you. I wouldn't do it if it weren't important. But it's my job. I have to find out what happened."

Will nodded.

Leatherman turned to ask Colonel Seacom: "How long is Captain Hastings going to be in the hospital, Colonel?"

"I can't say. He's doing pretty well physically. Obviously not well, you can see that. But the big thing is, he can't talk. Could be damage to his voice box, could be something else. We're trying to figure it out but don't know yet." The colonel explained.

Will knew what the colonel was implying—that he might have some kind of battle fatigue. Psychological neurosis. Shell shock. He could see the colonel raise his eyebrows and forehead, the military medical equivalent of tapping his forefinger to his temple.

"So when can he talk again?"

"We don't know, Major. You never know in these cases. We've had a couple of specialists look at him. Probably just a matter of time."

Will tapped the arm of his chair and they turned around to look at him again. He held out his hand to the major, who had the notes and sketches. He handed them back to Will. Will went through them one by one, handing each one back to the major until he found the one he was looking for.

"Where was Major Halliburton found?" The major had never answered Will's question. If he didn't know where Will had been found, at least he should know where Halliburton was found.

Leatherman nodded. He had forgotten to answer.

"Captain, if your drawing is right, he would have been found somewhere up here."

Will looked. It was as he feared. Leatherman continued.

"He was found upstairs in the main house, in a bedroom. Overlooking the courtyard."

Will arched his eyebrows, a thespian attempt to show that he understood something that he hadn't known before. The major looked at him carefully to see if Will was dissembling; Will showed him nothing.

"Anything else, Captain?"

Will shook his head. "No." The colonel and the major left. Neither saluted.

If Colonel Seacom was aware of how poorly Will had sketched the layout, he didn't show it. If he was trying to protect Will, he didn't show that either. Will felt that, once again, he was on his own.

CHAPTER SIXTEEN

O n the following Thursday Will received two visitors.

The first, a hospital administrator, brought him his personal effects.

"Good Morning Captain Hastings. It's a great day to be in Cherbourg, France, *n'est-ce pas?*"

Will smiled at him and nodded.

"It's a great day because you have your personal effects. *Voila!*" The administrator lugged out Will's duffel bag. It bulged with his uniforms, his spare boots, his books, his personal Army-issue field surgery kit. Someone had collected them, gotten them to the division medical staff, and they had found their way to the hospital. It was true; stay alive long enough and the Army will find you.

Inside the bag was Peter's silk map. Someone had stuffed it into an ammunition pouch but the top of the map bulged out over the edges. The map had been rinsed but the blood stain would never come out. Will acted as if he hadn't noticed it.

"Next, your orders." He handed Will a set of typed documents. Pending the reports of radiology, surgery, and the rehabilitation physician, Will would be put on a boat back to England by the next available transport, subject to the convenience and necessity of the command, and from there to a regional hospital near Birmingham.

"How about that, Captain. These mulberries are great, what?"

Will didn't know what mulberries were.

"Portable harbors. Floating harbors. The jerries wrecked every dock and quay in Cherbourg twenty-four hours before the grunts kicked 'em out. Three days later the harbor was back up and running. It's nearly full speed now. Mulberries. We floated them in and anchored them. We've got boats unloading everything the army owns, twenty-four hours a day. Busier than New York."

Will nodded in appreciation.

"And your mail."

The administrator handed Will two letters, shook hands, and left.

> *Dear Will: I know you're injured. I read it on the wire service at the newspaper and the news hurt so bad I fainted. I pray that you are all right and safe and not hurt very much.*
>
> *Will, I need you. I don't know where you are or what's happened to you but I need you to come home. Things here are going bad, real bad. I can't explain, not in a letter. I need to see you to tell you in person. I need you Will. I know you think I haven't written much and I'm truly sorry. I wasn't good at that but I'll be better, I promise. But please come home.*
>
> *Love,*
>
> *Virginia*

He read the letter through again, surprised at how it made him feel. She needs me? He wasn't exactly sure what day it was, just that it had become September while he was in the hospital. Somewhere after her last letter, more than six months ago, and this letter, he had lost the tug of Virginia Sullivan, and it surprised him. She had never been one to need Will, not in person and not in her letters. She had only told him once that she loved him and that had been just before high school graduation. After that, when he had said he loved her, she had smiled, or blushed, or turned her head, never answering more than "I've already said it." As for needing him, he had believed she didn't need him or anybody else.

He remembered the last time he had seen her, almost ten months ago. She was even more beautiful than before, her auburn hair, her long face with high cheekbones. She was tall and had filled out even more after high school. He thought of her, in the water, in the quarry, and could only imagine what she looked like now. But the thought of her didn't make him hurt, not anymore. His thoughts drifted back to how he got his scholarship.

"Well, Will. I understand you and Virginia...." Poppy hadn't exactly finished the sentence. Will had tried to splutter out something, but Poppy had shushed him. "I put a lot of thought into this, Will. You've got a lot to make up for, you know." Will had expected something harsh but figured it was just taking a while for Poppy to warm to the subject. "Here's my decision. No boy is going to marry my daughter if he can't do right by her."

Will remembered the perfect combustion of his guts. Poppy had decided Will was going to marry Virginia, something Will had planned to offer to do anyway. He was seventeen years old, helping out at the slaughterhouse, mopping at Doc Pritchard's, somehow between the two jobs he was going to find a way to be a husband, too.

"You're going to college. I've been on the phone. It's set. You're going. And you're going to study hard."

He had blacked out. Poppy hadn't noticed, probably hadn't even stopped talking, but for a moment Will had lost consciousness. The import of Poppy's decision, marry Virginia, go to college, everything Will had ever imagined he wanted, it was all happening, right there in the back room of the *Tierra Times*.

"You are going to study hard, that or you're going to be one unlucky sonofabitch. Understand me, Will?"

Will understood. He could feel Sheriff Hoskins fidgeting around behind him, menacing him, daring him to say something stupid. He wasn't exactly sure of the connection between the sheriff and Poppy, but everyone knew there was one.

"Sir, I—"

"Shut up, Will. You're going to college. Then you're going to medical school. And by the time you finish up, Doc Pritchard's going to need you to take over. He's getting a little long in the tooth, Doc is."

So it had all been arranged. The dean at Texas Western College had already written the admission letter. The dean at the medical school had wired to say that if everything Doctor Pritchard and Mr. Sullivan had told him was true, and the boy performed as they said he would, a place would be held for him in Galveston after his second year of college.

Money was never mentioned.

Poppy shook Will's hand. It would be more nearly correct to say that Poppy took Will's hand, and gripped it, and told him that they had an agreement. Will would go to college for two years. He would do well in college and then he would go to medical school. He would be Doc's helper between sessions, learn Doc's business and, when he finished, he would have Doc's practice waiting for him.

"And then you get Virginia, Will. Understand? Then, not now. And not before then. Not again." And Poppy didn't say it, but he might as well have added, 'Ain't that right, Hoskins?' because Will could practically feel from behind him the surge of Hoskins' enforcement of Poppy's will. He would have Virginia, and become a doctor, and have a future, and, unfortunately, while it was everything he had ever dreamed of, he would have no say in the matter. Instead of being jailed, or beaten up, or even threatened, he had been corrupted.

That was how it played out, except for three things. Virginia. The war. And Géraldine. Maybe Virginia does need me. Maybe she doesn't. Do I need her?

He turned to the second letter. It was not from Virginia.

> Dear Will:
>
> I'm writing to apologize if I have caused you any hurt. It was never my intention and I was wrong. Virginia's having trouble here. Poppy and Bart Sullivan have disappeared. I'm sure you know about it, she probably told you by now, but it's hard on her. She doesn't have a job now. People are helping her but she doesn't have much money. Is the Army sending her money? The church is doing what it can for her but everything is tight here.
>
> Some good news. Hoyt Carter is alive. He was with the Philistines for over two years and then got away. There's no news of Johnny Bradley. The Carters are really happy but Mr. Bradley is about out of his mind now. He said it was better when he didn't know anything.
>
> I'm sorry.
>
> Shirley

Reading Virginia's letter had given him a sniff of independence; Shirley's letter plunged the dagger back in. Trouble? What had Poppy Sullivan and that sorry brother of hers gotten into? And what about Virginia's job at the ration desk?

He had told Virginia in November that Poppy's business was going to get them all in trouble. *Stay out of it, Will; you don't know anything.* That was what she answered; being proved right didn't make him feel any better. Instead, Virginia sounded like a charity case. And why on earth would the Army be sending money to Virginia?

If it wouldn't have hurt his chest he would have laughed; Virginia and

Shirley were like comic book enemies. Shirley had never done anything for Virginia unless there was something in it for her, usually to do with Will. Virginia had never clung to Will unless Shirley was after him. That was probably it, he thought. Shirley could act like a cheerful giver at church, act like she was a friend, and still damn Virginia in letters to Will. *I apologize if I hurt you.* What was the scheming little bitch talking about?

He dug into his duffel bag. The old letters were still there. He pulled them out, one by one. There weren't many, four or five from Virginia. There was the last note he had gotten from Peter, and Douglas' twix from the clerk at Eighth Air Force setting him up to meet Peter in London. There was the last letter from Shirley, with the photograph of Peter and Virginia on the front porch.

Hoyt's alive. Will was overjoyed that Hoyt had made it out. *I'll bet Johnny's out there hiding, somewhere.* Hoyt and Johnny had been inseparable. Hoyt, Johnny, and Will had been inseparable, until Virginia, until that business with Poppy. *What does she need me for now?* Will wondered if Molly knew about Hoyt; she had gone off to San Angelo to work in a factory the day Mr. Bradley got the telegram. And Shirley again, stupid twit—she had never paid the least attention to Hoyt, the one guy who didn't care that she was a stuck-up snob. She should have thanked her lucky stars that Hoyt wanted to go out with her, and prayed to God to bring him home when he disappeared, but she wouldn't have. Tierra seemed far away and long ago.

It all made him tired. That Virginia wanted him to come home was hopeless—nobody just went home from the Army. He sure wasn't going home; he was going to England. And why did she need him? And why now instead of before? Poppy, of course, and her job, but what, exactly? *Virginia's letter didn't say anything about money—was that what all this was about, just money?*

It made his head hurt. He drifted back to sleep, his duffel bag open, his letters on the top, his last thought being neither of Virginia nor Shirley, but of a different problem he knew he would have to face.

God Damned Halliburton. What was he thinking?

CHAPTER SEVENTEEN

"Captain? Are you awake?"

Will was more restless than asleep, thinking about the men. He couldn't stop the vision of the barnyard. Shells hitting walls and roofs. Legs. Arms. Antsley. Lieutenant Campbell. Fouquet. Rogers, Altgelt, Shockley, all of them.

And Curtiss. How the hell had he wound up there? God damned Halliburton.

"Captain, are you awake? You've got a visitor."

Will opened his eyes, expecting to see Colonel Seacom or, worse, Leatherman. Instead it was Captain Deere.

"Afternoon, Captain. Sorry to... hope I didn't... well."

Will understood; nearly everyone he saw apologized to him for waking him up or bothering him. He smiled feebly at Captain Deere.

"Do you remember me, Doc? I was—am—the company commander, C Company, 116th. You came on with us at St. Marie du Vire. And Martinville."

Will remembered.

"I'm the one Shorty asked if it was okay to put you and the other doc with Lieutenant Campbell's platoon. I'm sorry, Captain. Really sorry."

"The other doc?" he scribbled.

"Yeah, the guy from the Fourth. The major."

"He isn't a doc. Just a major." Isn't. Wasn't.

Deere was a small man, compact, very fit. He looked like an infantry captain, the sort of tight young hero who could lead men through hell and high water. "I thought I was getting you out of the way, sending you all up the road away from Pont Hébert. The jerries were about to unload on all of us—they did unload on us at Hauts Vents—and I thought I was getting you guys to a safe place."

Will reached out his hand. His right hand was still smaller than his left, his arm a bit withered, but they acted like an arm and a hand. He fumbled across his chair to Captain Deere's hand and took it, shook it like a friend. He looked Deere in the eye and tried to express that he understood. It was the war.

"Captain, I don't like to bother you but I need some help."

He should have known. Deere was like the major; he wanted something.

"Listen, they've got Curtiss. I don't know if you remember him or not. He was one of the soldiers in Campbell's platoon. He was by far the best soldier in the whole company. Well, they've got him."

Will sat up, listened closely. He had not asked about Curtiss, not a word or a question from the moment Leatherman had begun to poke at him. Will had tried to be careful and lead them away from talking about anyone and they had never said a word about Curtiss. Now, here it was, in his lap.

"And I think they're going to shoot him."

Will took his pencil and note pad off the bed stand a second time and wrote: "What's going on?"

"Listen. First, I don't know for sure. I saw him in the lock up. He wouldn't say anything to me. Can you keep this under your belt?"

Will nodded.

"Listen. I'm his CO. I had to tell him that he didn't have to say anything to anybody and that if he did, it could go bad for him. He said he understood and that's all he said. So, let me say this to you, Captain. If you say anything, or write anything, they'll get it. If it helps them, they'll use it. They mean to shoot him. Do you understand what I'm saying?"

Will nodded again. All the time he had been in the hospital, ever since the Major had begun to prod him about Halliburton, he had thought about it. Curtiss and Géraldine had dragged him out of the courtyard and into the main room of the chateau. He had thought he was going to die; blood had soaked through the chest of his field jacket and he was faint. Curtiss had pulled out Peter's silk map to clean Will's wound. Géraldine had rinsed the blood out and wrung it dry, and then packed the map into his wound. They had stuck a morphine syrette into him and, from the morphine, from loss of blood and shock, Will had passed out. He was not going to write or say anything to Captain Deere.

"Lieutenant Campbell sent a runner back to get us. When we got to the chateau it was a mess. We found you in the main house. Rogers was stumbling around in the courtyard, fumbling with his rosary. Everybody else was well, accounted for. It was bad, Captain, real bad."

Will listened. Everything he had dreamed about the battle had been bad, and true. Major Leatherman and the Colonel had told him that the platoon was wiped out. How could it get any worse?

"Rogers took us into the house and up the stairs and that's where we found Major Halliburton. He had been shot in the head. Now listen. Don't say anything. Don't write anything. Just listen. Rogers said it was Curtiss who shot Halliburton. I asked him did he see it, he said no. He told me that he saw Curtiss chase Halliburton up the stairs, heard gunfire, and then he ran up. I asked him why he thought it was Curtiss who shot Halliburton; Lieutenant Campbell had set up a firing point in the main house as well as out on the walls. I thought maybe it could have been the Germans. Rogers said no, because the battle had been over for a while. That's when I realized—there weren't any Germans, not a single one, not inside the chateau. All the fighting had come from the outside. The Germans never stormed the place on foot."

Will nodded, then remembered that Deere had told him to just listen and not tell him anything. The Germans had never assaulted the chateau, not with foot soldiers. They had fired down on it from above and blown the place apart. When Will had been shot in the courtyard the Germans were still shelling the chateau and raining machine gun fire down into it. The men, those who hadn't been knocked out, were trying to shoot back. The barn blew up. The outer wall of the small house collapsed, leaving the chateau breached and exposed to the Germans.

"We looked all over the place, digging men out of caved-in walls and roofs. Nearly everybody we found in the barn was dead. There was one guy who had been up in some kind of poultry coop and he had about four rounds through his arms and leg but he was still alive. Rogers survived. But what we didn't find were krauts. Not a one, anywhere. We sent a patrol up past the orchard and on to the ridge. The Jerries had set up there and sighted in an anti-tank gun and a couple of MG 42's. There were shell casings everywhere. From up there they could look straight down and see every square inch of the chateau; I never saw a worse place to defend. But the krauts had disappeared. I doubt if the platoon hit any of them. It was a turkey shoot for them. And then, one more thing."

Will waited.

"Curtiss wasn't anywhere around—he had vanished. A couple of the wounded men said they saw him fighting during the battle, but Rogers said Curtiss disappeared after he shot Halliburton. We never saw a trace of him."

"Where did they find him?"

The croak of Will's voice startled both of them. It was the first thing he had said to anyone since he had been in the hospital. It was, he realized, the first words he had said since Géraldine and Curtiss had saved his life. He clamped his mouth shut.

Captain Deere looked at him. He looked around the ward to see if anyone had overheard, or noticed. No one was paying attention. He drew his head closer to Will.

"About a week later we finished putting the hammer down on Kluge's army at Périers. It was wrecked, I mean wrecked. There weren't two bricks left stuck together in the town, complete rubble. The 35th chased the krauts further south and west and a couple of days later they ran them down. They took a big group of prisoners somewhere about twenty miles south and—guess what they found. The Germans had about forty of our men, POW's. Curtiss was one of them. Now, listen. He had cut off his mustache, had on a medic's uniform, big white cross on the sleeve. No name tape on his field jacket, a bullet hole through his dog tags. Not a thing on him to show he was Private Curtiss. He said he was a medic in the 507th, that he had been part of the unit the SS shot up at Graignes. He would have gotten away with it, too, but they dumped all these men back in the pool at St. Lô so Army Intelligence could talk to them. Well, we were there. Rogers saw him, told the battalion CO. The MP's got him. He denied he was Curtiss. But they've had him ever since. They've got a court martial set up. They charged him with shooting Halliburton and desertion."

Deere sat back. The whole story was out.

Will tried to sift through it all. He knew that the best thing was to say nothing, write no notes. He folded his hands on his lap, tugged on his pajamas, waited.

"Listen. If you know what happened—no, that's not what I want to say." Deere paused to pick his words. "Listen. I don't know what happened.

183

I wasn't there. All I know is that Curtiss was in Lieutenant Campbell's platoon. We never had his personnel file; he joined the battalion a week or so before D-Day and his paperwork never caught up to him. He was the best soldier I ever saw. The best. Truth is he pulled Campbell's butt out of a crack so many times that I left him alone to be sure that the platoon could pull its weight. Campbell learned and by the time he...well...well, he was a damned fine platoon leader at the end, and I expect it was because of Curtiss. I don't know Rogers. He was just a name on the personnel roster. Maybe a good soldier, maybe something else. Don't know. But Halliburton was a piece of work. First minute I ever saw him he demanded that I arrest Curtiss for some nonsense. I told him to mind his own business. Every day you guys were with us Halliburton sent word back to tell me how to run the company, where Lieutenant Campbell was screwing up the outposts, the gun pits, the duty rotations. He was a real piece of work, the kind of guy who knows everything except how to keep his mouth shut. Shorty Carter said he was your friend; I have no idea how you put up with him. None of my business; he's dead. But what I do know is that if Rogers points the finger at Curtiss and says he went upstairs and heard a gunshot and then Curtiss deserted, well, Curtiss is going to need a miracle. There's not a thing you can do for Halliburton. There might be something you can do for Curtiss. That's all I'm going to say. "

He stood up, shook Will's hand, then, oddly, saluted. Will had never been saluted by a combat officer before. The doctors weren't considered Army, even in combat hospitals; they were just doctors with captain's bars. Deere looked at Will, his face saying something that he would not or could not put into words. He waited a minute, then turned and left.

Will tried to nap but could not. His chest hurt, as it often did, but more on the inside than usual. The exit wound was healing and he assumed that if the entry wound or any of the places where the bullet had rattled around had become infected Captain Sheffield would have put him on penicillin. He attended his physical therapy session but did little to advance the strength in his arm or hand. The inhalation exercises were painful.

Colonel Seacom had hinted that, in the absence of a medical explanation for Will not being able to talk, the next group of doctors he saw would be psychiatrists. The medical corps had made a lot of noise about staffing specialists to look at claims of combat fatigue and war neuroses. In fact, there were very few referrals to the specialists, at least not in Normandy.

Captain Deere's news put a new face on it, however. No one could or would claim that Will was exaggerating his wounds, but the merest suggestion that he was mentally off could cost someone his life.

His mind returned to Peter. What had it been like for him? Had a fighter come down from above and blown the wings off his plane? Flak through the belly? A direct hit in the pilot's windshield? A frantic attempt to bail out? Had it been fast or slow? Peter had been the stronger of them, the better one. If anyone could keep his plane in the air long enough for the rest of the crew to get out, it would be Peter. If they had made it to the ground together, he would have led them somewhere and got them out.

God, how I loved Peter.

No one paid attention to him. It was common for wounded soldiers to cry.

He lay quietly in his bed all night. The ward nurses checked on him, found him with his eyes closed, still. When the nurses changed shifts at eleven o'clock they wrote that Captain Hastings's respiratory rate was better, just at 20, and his pulse and temperature were nearly normal, but something seemed different about him. They made a note to check on him more frequently. When they changed shifts again at seven in the morning he appeared not to have moved during the night. His eyes were open, but he was quiet. He declined breakfast.

At eight o'clock he wrote a note and passed it to the nurse.

"Would you ask Captain Sheffield to come?"

Sheffield came around one in the afternoon.

"Everything all right, Captain? Are they treating you all right?" Sheffield handed Will a note pad.

Will motioned for him to bend near.

"My—voice." He was hoarse. "I'm—it's—coming back."

Sheffield was delighted.

"That's great, Captain. Let me look at you." He told Will to open his mouth, then stuck a tongue depressor in it and told him to say 'ahh.' Will did. "No redness, looks good. Don't overdo it."

"Feels, well, different."

Sheffield smiled, patted him on the shoulder, and told him he would be back soon. Will had guessed correctly; the Army was quite predictable.

In less than a half hour Colonel Seacom appeared, the first Will had seen of him in days.

"Will—Captain Sheffield says your speech is returning. Congratulations."

"Thank—you—sir."

"Great step forward. We'll have you back up and running before you know it."

"How—long? sir?"

"Before you're up and running? I don't know. Soon. What did you have in mind?"

"Soon." He paused to let the Colonel process it. Will pointed to his chest. The wound was almost closed. Betadyne and strands from his sutures were prominent above his somewhat sunken chest. "Back—to—work? Soon?"

The colonel did not know what to say and, as Will had expected, said nothing. He was beaming with pleasure. Captain Hastings had turned a very good corner.

They spoke a few minutes more. Colonel Seacom assured him that there was no hurry, that Will could go on back to England, heal up without the sound of artillery fire in the distance, rest up. "Chest wounds are serious things, no need to rush it. You know that."

Will nodded and smiled. "Back to Shorty?" He wanted to go back to the field hospital.

The Colonel said that Will was a "case for the books. Maybe they'll write you up in the journals." Will said that would be something. The Colonel stayed so long that Will decided it would help to wince, to sit further back in the chair and close his eyes a few times. At length the happy commander took his leave.

CHAPTER EIGHTEEN

T he next morning, as expected, Leatherman returned.

"Good morning, Captain. I happened to run into Colonel Seacom and he said you had made some remarkable progress. Wanted to stop by and say congratulations." He held out his hand, Will took it.

"Thank—you—sir. Better." Will pointed to his throat in case the Major was a dunce. "Won't—be—long."

"Long?"

"Back—to—work. The—men."

"That's great, Captain, just great."

"Tell—me—about—platoon?"

The major took the bait.

"Well, Captain, the platoon is pretty shot up. Do you remember Rogers? He got through okay, and the runner. Captain Deere has them back in the company. Not a lot of the others. Let me give it to you straight. Lieutenant Campbell. He's dead. Who else did you know? Banks was killed, and Shockley. Over half of the platoon, they were killed there in that barnyard. The rest, every one of them, shot up or injured one way or another. Most of them were taken to Isigny. I don't know of any who were brought up here to Cherbourg. The battalion is having to replace the whole platoon. The company's out of action for training."

Will sat back and listened. The Major's report was worse than he thought. He remembered Helton's complaining. Shockley was a daredevil, would run through anything like a wing back, always grinning. Even when Will had pulled a huge piece of split wood out of his arm back at Martinville Ridge, Shockley had picked his Browning automatic rifle back up and gone back into the line. Dead. Others, dead. Others still, mortar fragments and machine gun shells in them. And their mothers? Telegrams? Had the Army tried to send a telegram to anyone about Peter? Who would Peter have listed as next of kin? He hoped Halliburton was roasting in hell.

"My medics, sir?" He croaked, without acting.

Leatherman didn't know, not by their names.

"Sir?" Will motioned for the major to come closer, as if it would make it easier to talk. Leatherman bent down.

"I—remember—something."

The major waited. Will continued.

"I—saw—Major—Halliburton—after."

"After? What do you mean? After what?" Leatherman could barely conceal his excitement.

"I—was—shot."

"How? Where?"

"In—house. Main—house." He waited for Leatherman to show he understood, then continued. "I was in the—main—house. Wound treated. Major was there."

"Major Halliburton treated your wound? Is that what you're saying?"

Will shook his head. "No."

"Morphine. His. Then Major left."

"What do you mean? Left you? Left the house? What do you remember?"

Will found that it did hurt to talk, more than he had expected. His throat was dry; he took a glass and bent the straw, sipped from it.

"Major had morphine. Hurt."

"Major Halliburton treated you? Is that what you're saying? He gave you morphine because of your wound?"

Will shook his head.

"His morphine. Curtiss—pulled—me to—house. Put me—on floor. Halliburton—there."

"Then Halliburton left?"

Will nodded.

"Who treated your wound?"

"In back."

"The wound was in your back. You couldn't see. Is that what you're saying?"

Will nodded.

"And Curtiss? Was he there?"

Will nodded again.

"Where did Halliburton go?"

"Upstairs."

"What else, Captain? Anything else?"

"Curtiss. Went upstairs." He waited for this to sink in. "Then shooting."

The major could scarcely contain his excitement.

"Do you remember anything else?"

Will sat back in the chair, not merely showing Leatherman that he was tired but, in truth, very tired. The interview had gone almost as Will had thought it would. He rested, closed his eyes.

"No." He coughed, then held up a hand to indicate there was more. "A question."

"A question? Sure. What do you want to know, Captain?"

"What happened? Curtiss."

"What about him?"

"Killed too?"

"You think Curtiss was killed? Is that right?"

"Yes."

Leatherman smiled, a cat-has-the-canary smile. Will hated it, and looked away so that the major would not see Will looking at him.

"No, Captain. He got out."

Will said nothing. This was, he knew, the time to be neutral.

"Would you like to see him, Captain?"

"Yes. Like to see him. See others."

"I'll see what I can do, Captain. I'll see what I can do."

The major made a show of shaking Will's hand. Will knew he wouldn't salute—the major didn't think of Will as an officer, probably didn't even think of him as a doctor. Army lawyers are like the rest; Will was just a witness, a prize pig. He put on a show so that Will would know that he was glad Will was much improved. Will was a good man. The Army was grateful for him. He thanked Will. And, as he left, he told Will again that he would see what he could do so that Will could see the men and, to be sure, Curtiss.

The following morning, as he had expected, Will received a military order to appear at the court martial of Private George Curtiss. The hole in

189

his back and chest ached and it occurred to him that, not until this minute, not in the LSTs, or on the beach, or at Ste. Marie or Martinville or on the road into St. Lô, only now, holding his subpoena for Curtiss's court-martial, was he afraid. It had been Will's turn to be shot, and he didn't like it. Now it was his turn to stop someone else from being shot, and he didn't like that much either.

It was the risk of failure that scared him.

CHAPTER NINETEEN

October, 1944

"This General Court Martial has been convened and duly sworn in to try the accusations stated against you. You are charged that, first, on August 12, 1944, while under the command of D Company, 116th Battalion, and while detailed to a post at the Château Dupré under the command of Second Lieutenant Mark Campbell you did murder Major David Halliburton by shooting him in the head with a firearm, in violation of Article 92 of the Articles of War. Second, that on August 12, 1944, you did desert your post with the intent to avoid hazardous duty or to shirk important service, in violation of Article 58 of the Articles of War. Third, that on August 12, 1944, you did misbehave before the enemy by neglecting your post and endangering the safety of the post and of the soldiers at that post, which it was your duty to defend, in violation of Article 75 of the Articles of War. If found guilty of any one or more of these charges you may be punished by death or by any term of years of confinement, reduction in rank, forfeiture of all pay and benefits, and dishonorable discharge from the Armed Forces of the United States. How do you plead to these charges?"

The prisoner stood before them at attention. His counsel, Lieutenant Stanford, a second lieutenant of infantry who had graduated from law school a year earlier, stood beside him. It would have been difficult to tell which of them appeared to be more frightened. They remained silent.

The division commander had instructed the division judge advocate to locate a suitable building for court martials. He had selected a boys' school on the edge of Cherbourg. The students' desks had been removed but an exercise blackboard at the front of the room remained, faint traces of undecipherable irregular French verbs visible behind the five officers who had been appointed to serve as the members of the military jury. The high ceilings muted the proceedings and seemed to add a degree of dread.

"Your silence will be recorded as a plea of not guilty."

The law member of the court martial resumed:

"I'm going to outline this procedure for you, Corporal Curtiss. This court martial will follow the proceedings set out in the Articles of War. You have counsel appointed for you and if you want an additional lawyer, or someone else, tell us and we'll postpone this until you're satisfied with the counsel who defends you. You do not have to testify and if you do not testify, none of the members of the court martial will take your silence as evidence that you are guilty. You have the right to demand witnesses and if there is a witness you want to demand to come before the court martial we will find that soldier's unit and get that soldier here. Do you understand those rights?"

"Sir," his lawyer spoke up. "We do. At this time we have no objection to the members of the court. The accused is satisfied with me as his lawyer, or has not told me otherwise. And we will reserve whether he will testify."

"Fine. Well, Major Leatherman, do you want to make an opening statement?"

"Yes, sir, I do."

Will had seen Major Leatherman in the corridor. Leatherman had stopped, once, in his comings and goings, and patted Will on the shoulder to tell him that he had nothing to worry about as a witness. Major Leatherman now told the court martial the same thing.

"Officers, I want to summarize what the evidence in this court martial is going to show. Corporal Curtiss was a member of Lieutenant Campbell's platoon in Captain Deere's company. The battalion was in combat almost daily from the time it got off the beach on June 6. After the capture of St. Lô the battalion was sent across the River Vire to join up with the 35th Infantry Division. Now, Captain Deere's company had a second mission, to escort Major Halliburton to scout out a suitable location for a forward hospital to be set up after St. Lô was taken. Captain Deere will testify that he assigned that duty to Lieutenant Campbell's platoon. The prisoner, Corporal Curtiss, was a member of that platoon.

"Also in that platoon was Private Rogers. He will testify that they found a farm, Château Dupré, which Major Halliburton wanted to scrutinize as a possible hospital site. He will also testify that Corporal Curtiss did not like Major Halliburton. Now, as you all know, about five miles away the German VIIth Corps began a counterattack. Following orders, the platoon stayed put inside the Château. On August 12 the Germans attacked the Château. The attack was so devastating that there were few men who did not become casualties, among them Private Rogers and Corporal Curtiss.

"Private Rogers will testify that in this attack Lieutenant Campbell was killed and another officer, Captain Hastings, a doctor, was severely wounded. Major Halliburton manned a gun and fought with courage but, after the attack was over, Corporal Curtiss began to argue with Major Halliburton in the main house of the chateau. Private Rogers will tell you that he saw Corporal Curtiss chase Major Halliburton up the stairs of the main house, Private Rogers heard a shot, and when he ran up to see what had happened he found Major Halliburton, dead with a bullet wound to the head." He paused, drew up his chest, and let out his breath to deliver the dramatic finale to Major Halliburton: "To the back of his head." He paused again so that the compounded treachery would sink into the minds of the court martial officers. "And then he will tell you that Corporal Curtiss disappeared.

"Finally, and I have intentionally saved this summary to the last, you will hear from Captain Hastings. This fine young medical officer was shot during the attack and it's a miracle he's alive. Captain Hastings will testify that he was dragged from the courtyard of the chateau to the main house where Major Halliburton had taken up a position. Major Halliburton had medicine, particularly morphine, and was treating Captain Hastings when Curtiss came in. He will testify that he witnessed Curtiss and Major Halliburton argue and, as he was near death, saw Curtiss chase the major up the stairs, then heard the gunshot that killed him.

"This, then, is the case. After Major Halliburton was shot Corporal Curtiss disappeared until he was recognized by Private Rogers several days later and many miles distant, trying to hide in a group of liberated American POW's milling around in St. Lô. This man not only shot a superior officer, indeed at that point his commanding officer, he abandoned his surviving friends, the wounded and the brave, at his post. It is difficult, indeed impossible, to imagine a more criminal act under the Articles of War than for a soldier to murder his commanding officer in time of war, then flee his post in the face of the enemy. On the one hand, the supreme punishment of death is the only punishment that can redress a death so cowardly inflicted. On the other hand, to give any punishment other than death will be to send a message throughout the Army, to the allies, to soldiers everywhere, that the murder of an officer in time of war and in combat is no more serious than going AWOL during boot camp. It is the duty of a soldier to obey orders, to follow training, and to fully and unconditionally respect and support his officers. It is the duty of an officer, such as you gentlemen, appointed to a court martial, to listen to the evidence, to make a decision based on the evidence and, however unpleasant and unwelcome the duty may be, to decide a punishment based on that evidence and that decision. Gentlemen, the Articles of War are clear and the facts will be just as clear. Corporal Curtiss is guilty of murder, of desertion, and of cowardice in the face of the enemy, and the evidence will not lead you—it will compel you to find him guilty and to sentence him to the ultimate penalty, death."

"All right, you may be seated. Lieutenant? Do you wish to make an opening statement?"

"Sir, if it please the court, I would like to reserve my statement of the defense."

"All right, fine. If you change your mind, inform me, and if you wish to make a statement after Major Leatherman rests the prosecution's case, you will have the opportunity."

"Thank you, sir."

"Major, call your first witness."

"Call Captain Deere."

Major Leatherman was confident that the officers had heard the details of his outline. For that reason, knowing that the members would be listening for the story exactly as he scripted it, he departed from it with his first witness.

"Captain, what did you find on arrival at Château Dupré?"

"It was a wreck, sir. The west side of the courtyard had been demolished, probably by mortar fire. On the west side of the chateau there was an apple orchard. It grew up a hillside and up on the ridge there was a road, one of those small lanes that separate the farms. From up on that road you could look down on the chateau, see right inside the courtyard, see the fields on the east and beyond, maybe all the way to the river."

"Anything else, sir."

"Yes. By the time I sent Lieutenant Campbell there his platoon was down to twenty men. Of those twenty, when we got to the chateau, we found only two men who were uninjured, Private Rogers and Private Helton. Sergeant Altgelt was wounded; we found him in the remnants of a barn on the south side of the courtyard. One or two men were injured when the courtyard wall collapsed on them. Lieutenant Campbell was dead. Nine others were dead. Private Shockley was alive when we found him but he died before we could get him to an aid station. Ten dead, seven wounded, two not wounded."

"Did you go over the grounds with Private Rogers?"

"Yes, we did. First I sent a patrol up to secure the ridge. As soon as I was satisfied the chateau was secure I went up there. The whole ridge was full of shell casings, machine gun casings. There were some larger shells too, what I thought were PAKs."

"What is a PAK?"

"A German anti-tank gun. I figured that's what blew the walls out of the chateau."

"Anything else?"

"Well, I think what was worse was that there was not any sign of a dead German anywhere. Nothing."

"Explain."

"There was no blood on that ridge. No bodies, no helmets, no tattered uniforms. The only thing I found between the ridge line and the chateau was a bunch of limbs shot off the apple trees. Inside the courtyard there was not a single German. According to Rogers, the Germans never even came down."

"What else did you find?"

"Rogers took us to the main house."

"Describe that for the court."

"Well, it was like any of these old French farm houses. A nice stone house, several steps up the front to a main room, high ceilings, high windows. When we got inside we found Captain Hastings on the floor in the main room. He was unconscious, lost a lot of blood. Had a bloody bandage in his chest and some towels in his back. One of my medics was already on him and trying to get some blood or plasma into him. Rogers led us up the stairs to the second floor."

"Tell the court members exactly what you found."

"Well, we found Major Halliburton up there. He was dead. Shot."

"How, sir?"

"One bullet hole in the back of the head, front of his head blown off."

"Are you familiar enough, Captain, after landing on Utah Beach, after leading your company from Utah Beach to St. Lô, and fighting from Pont Hébert through a German counterattack, and from there to Château Dupré, to tell whether a bullet hole was an entry wound or an exit wound?"

"I think so, yes, sir."

"Objection."

Again Major Leatherman showed his experience. Captain Deere was not a forensic ballistics expert. He had no special training in muzzle velocities, in trajectories, in bullet deformation other than the practical experience of seeing a third of the one hundred sixty men in his company shot by small arms, of seeing over six hundred bodies of Germans his men had shot with small arms, and of seeing the blood, the bullet holes, and the guns that caused them.

"Your objection?"

"Sirs, with all due respect, I don't believe Captain Deere has been shown to be a forensics expert."

"No, I don't suppose he has. Major, I'm going to sustain that objection."

"Yes, sir. I withdraw that question and respectfully state that I didn't consider beforehand that it would have been controversial. I shall be more respectful–" and here he nodded respectfully and collegially to Lt. Stamford "–to the court and defense. Instead, let me ask this. Captain Deere, did you look on the wall beyond the major?"

"Yes, sir."

"What did you find?"

"A bullet embedded in the plaster."

"Where?"

"About head high. Right in line with the way Major Halliburton's body was laid out."

"How did you find it?"

"I saw it first when Rogers pushed the door open. Halliburton was on the floor but the blood splatter on the wall was right there in front of me. And the bullet hole was in the middle of the blood splatter."

"And the bullet?"

"We took the major's body downstairs and out into the courtyard, covered it with the other men. I went back up and dug the bullet out."

"And can you identify this, Captain?"

Major Leatherman handed the prosecution's first exhibit to the captain.

"Oh, that's it all right. That's the bullet."

"And what kind of bullet is it, sir?" Major Leatherman looked at the lieutenant to see if he would again object to the captain's testimony on forensics. His backup plan never came to light because, to the major's surprise, the lieutenant did not object.

"Oh, it's one of ours all right. Thirty ought six. I've dug enough of these out of walls, Germans, French, churches, barn doors, trees. I know what it is."

"Let me ask you this, Captain. This is a sort of hypothetical question and the defense may have an objection to it, but if the question is allowed, here it is. If a German soldier had taken one of our rifles as a trophy, and had fired it from up on that ridge west of the chateau, could that explain how Major Halliburton was shot with an American thirty ought six round in the head on the second floor of that farm house?"

Again the presiding court member looked to Lieutenant Stamford to see whether there was an objection. There was none.

"No, sir. The wall where we dug the bullet out was on the west side, the same side where the Germans had attacked. There was no window anywhere near. The bullet had to have been fired from the east side of the room to lodge in the west wall."

"Last question, sir. Did you find Corporal Curtiss there at the chateau?"

"No, sir. We did not."

"Your witness."

Lieutenant Stamford had far less to work with. *I may be the only lawyer in the whole Army who's defending a guy who won't talk to him.* In fact, the only source of information he had to work with was Captain Deere, whose testimony seemed to have tied his client to a firing squad post in the prison yard. However, Deere had whispered to him in their interview to ask two lines of questions. Given the choice between trusting a captain who seemed to want to help a client who did not want to help himself, or going it alone, he had made the decision to take the captain's advice, even if the questions seemed obscure.

"Captain, do I understand that only two men came through uninjured in the battle at the Château Dupré?"

"Yes, Private Rogers and Private Helton."

"Can you tell the court members how it was that Private Helton came through without injury?"

"Yes. He wasn't there."

"Explain."

"Lieutenant Campbell had sent him as a runner to find me."

"Why?"

"Well, he sent him as a runner because of the presence of a German unit up on the ridge line mid-day on the twelfth of August."

"And why did he send a runner at all?"

"Because I had ordered Lieutenant Campbell to observe radio silence."

The lieutenant paused for a moment and looked up to be sure that the court members were taking this in. Out of the corner of his eye he saw that Major Leatherman had folded his arms and was focusing very carefully. Leatherman, he knew, suspected something.

"Why did you order Lieutenant Campbell to observe radio silence?"

"Well, we were in a new zone. Our unit hadn't been west of the river. We were attached to a new division for the time being. We knew from briefing that the Germans were generally west and south but that didn't mean we knew where they all were. And this was not a combat- sufficient platoon. Like I said, it was down to twenty men. Their mission was, frankly, a reward for being in combat so much. They were supposed to go off into some very quiet rear area and look for a quiet place to put in a hospital. They were not supposed to go engaging the enemy."

"What did Private Helton tell you when he came running up?"

"Objection. Hearsay."

The law member of the court looked at Lieutenant Stamford with a bit of reproach.

"Yes, Lieutenant, that does sound like hearsay."

"I'll ask a different way, sir. Captain, were you expecting to see Private Helton?"

"No. We had been drawn in as the new left flank of the 35th when the German VIIth counterattacked. There had been a hell of a tank shootout up to within a mile of us and we were in support of a light weapons unit blocking their approach to the river. They wanted the bridge back over the Vire. The last thing I expected was a runner from the north, essentially behind our lines, coming up."

"Your reaction, sir?"

"I was worried. And Helton gave me a note from Lieutenant Campbell."

This was news for all concerned. No one had told Leatherman that Helton had delivered a note, nor had Leatherman told the court members.

"Did the note regard the situation at the Chateau?"

"Objection, hearsay."

Before the law member could intervene, Captain Deere continued.

"The note said that Major Halliburton had ordered Lieutenant Campbell to attack a German unit on the ridge."

"Objection, Captain. Sirs, this is hearsay. In fact it is double hearsay, to tell the court what Major Halliburton said to Lieutenant Campbell to say to Captain Deere."

"Sirs, if I may respond, I believe that this qualifies as an exception to the hearsay rule."

The law member and Major Leatherman both appeared dubious. "Please explain."

"I believe this is an excited utterance, sir. It's like the woman who screams, 'He snatched my purse.' It doesn't matter that it came by runner; it's Lieutenant Campbell and Major Halliburton who made the excited utterance and Captain Deere who heard it, sir."

"I disagree," Major Leatherman inveighed. "Most strongly, sirs. An excited utterance must be made in the course of an exciting event and must explain the event. This supposed note does not do so. Captain Deere was too far removed from the event for him to perceive Lieutenant Campbell's excited utterance. And the exciting event would have to tend to explain some element of the case for it to be admissible as a res gestae."

The law member again looked to the defense for a reply. The reply was, to his surprise, a smile.

"Sustained, Lieutenant. I believe that Captain Deere was too far removed from the event for him to testify to an excited utterance."

"Very well, Captain. May I then ask whether you heard an exciting event which tends to explain something about the case?"

"Yes. I heard Major Halliburton order Lieutenant Campbell to attack the Germans on the ridge."

Lieutenant Stamford was proving to be good at setting traps himself. Major Leatherman quietly fumed when his example of when to exclude evidence became the very reason why the court martial had to admit the evidence.

"What about the radio silence, Captain?"

"Major Halliburton violated radio silence, sir."

The courtroom went quiet. Lieutenant Stamford waited a full minute to let the point sink in.

"What did you hear? What did he say?"

"He said, 'We're about to be attacked. Lieutenant—fire! That's an order.' Then he said, 'Give me that gun.'"

"What else did you hear?"

"One of our machine guns fired a burst, and there were several rifle shots. Then the radio went dead."

"What did you do?"

"We followed Private Helton to Château Dupré."

"Captain, may I ask several questions about Corporal Curtiss?"

"Yes."

"What had he achieved in your company?"

At this point there was an unsettling edge in the room. Major Leatherman no longer trusted Lieutenant Stamford to be the innocent and inexperienced defense counsel he had anticipated. He expected a trick. The presiding member and the law member, on the other hand, had sat through so many courts martial that they were disappointed; was Lieutenant Stamford throwing in the towel and trying to use the company commander to put up the good soldier defense?

"He was a good soldier, Lieutenant."

"Objection."

"State it."

"The character of the accused is not relevant, certainly not in the absence of proof of habit or regularity."

"I withdraw the question and say that I asked it poorly, sirs." The lieutenant turned back to the captain. "What was his job in the company, sir?"

"He was a squad leader. He was under consideration for promotion to buck sergeant to be the platoon sergeant."

"And in your company, what did the squad leaders do?"

"Same as everyone. They were assigned by the lieutenant and led the men in their squad to perform the tasks of the mission. They could do anything—walk point, carry ammunition, man any of the weapons."

"No further questions."

This startled everyone. The court members had expected that the Captain would say something favorable about Curtiss; the prosecution had expected something vague, perhaps evidence that after Lieutenant Campbell was killed Curtiss would have been the ranking person in the platoon. They were all disappointed.

"Major, call your next witness."

He called Private Rogers.

"Private Rogers, how familiar were you with the main house?"

"I know it pretty well, sir."

"How did you happen to go up to the main house?"

"I crawled out through the broken rafters out there in the barn, sir. One of their shells brought the roof down, and some of the wall. That's when we got it. I was knocked down by a section of the wall. When I came to, it was over."

"The action?"

"Well, there wasn't any shooting. And I crawled out. It was bad, sir. Shockley was lying there in the door and I thought he was dead. Sergeant Altgelt was under one of those beams. I tried to move it off of him but it was too big and I thought he was going to get crushed to death. Then I found one of the medics there dead so I went to find somebody to help. There wasn't anyone in the little house where the lieutenant had their command post. Well, Lieutenant Campbell was in there. Something had blown the wall out, just knocked the whole thing in. Lieutenant Campbell was blown to bits and I got out of there. Well, there was wounded men everywhere, and I ran to the main house to look for anybody to come back to help me get that beam off Sergeant Altgelt."

"What did you see there, Private?"

"Captain Hastings was on the floor, sir. He was in bad shape, and Corporal Curtiss was there with him too and he was yelling at Major Halliburton."

"What was he yelling?"

"He was calling him names, sir."

"What names?"

"I don't like to say it, sir. He yelled it a lot."

The presiding member intervened.

"Private, why do you not like to say what you heard?"

"I don't like those words, sir. They are really bad."

"Private, are you a religious man?"

"Yes, sir."

"Is that why you don't want to say?"

"Yes, sir."

"Were they angry-sounding words, Private?"

"Yes, sir."

"The kind of names that would make you fight?"

"Well, I wouldn't like to be called that, sir. It would make me pretty mad."

"Listen to me, Private," interjected the law member of the court martial. He stopped Leatherman with a wave of his hand and spoke directly to Rogers: "I don't like to order this but because of the serious nature of the charge we've got to know exactly what happened and you were the one who heard what was said, understand? So, I'm ordering you to say what you heard Corporal Curtiss say. What words or names did he use talking to Major Halliburton?"

"It was 'mother' and 'fucking,' sir."

"Are you sure?"

"Yes, sir. He was shouting pretty good, but he said it two or three times."

"Major, you can resume. Private, thank you." The law member sat back, satisfied that he had got at the heart of it.

"Then what happened?"

"Major Halliburton turned and run upstairs."

"Where were the stairs?"

"Oh, just right there. A couple of feet away, kind of in front of the door like."

"And what did you do?"

"I was just standing there seeing if somebody would go back to the barn and help me with Sergeant Altgelt but instead Corporal Curtiss he jumped up and ran up the stairs too."

"And you?"

"I stood there until I heard the shot."

"The shot?"

"The shot. Then I ran up the stairs, too. That's when I found Major Halliburton."

Rogers said almost exactly what Captain Deere had said. Halliburton was shot, through the head, his body laid out with his head near a west wall. There was a splatter of blood on the wall. He saw no way for a bullet to have come in through a window from the German attack.

"There hadn't been any attack for a bit, sir. It was all over by then."

"When you were up there with Major Halliburton did you see anyone else?"

"No, sir. It was empty from what I could see. The main house."

"Did you see Corporal Curtiss, Private?"

"No, sir."

"In the main house, in the courtyard, anywhere?"

"No, sir. I never saw him again. It was like he disappeared."

"And what happened next?"

"Well, after a while the company come up. I showed Captain Deere what I had seen. That was about it."

"Your witness, Lieutenant."

Lieutenant Stamford was indeed frightened for the life of his client. Whatever else Private Rogers may have been, he was not a liar. The difficulty with such witnesses was not that they knew too much but, rather, knew too little. He knew that he would have to back away at any sign of Rogers guessing at facts he did not know.

"Private, first may I ask whether you saw a gun upstairs."

"A gun?"

"Yes, Private. When you saw Major Halliburton, was there a gun? On the floor, in the hall, on the stairs?"

"No, not that I saw."

"You said that you also did not see anyone upstairs. Did Corporal Curtiss pass you on the way down the stairs? When you ran up, did he run down?"

"No."

"Did you go all over the upstairs rooms to see where he was?"

"Nope. I ran up the stairs and Major Halliburton was laying there in the first room."

"How, then, did Corporal Curtiss get down the stairs?"

"I honestly don't know, sir."

The Lieutenant let out a breath of relieved air.

"How well did you know Corporal Curtiss, Private?"

"He joined the company right before we left England. Nobody really knew him; the rest of us had been together ever since they put the battalion together back at Camp Swift so he didn't really have any friends, not in the company."

"Well, how about after the landing?"

"I'll say this for him. He saved my life that day, and the Lieutenant's and some others. At the time we was so scared we didn't know what to do and he just dragged us right on up the sand dunes and through those bob wires. You know, a lot of men did the same thing, but Curtiss, he sure saved my life that day."

"And after that, how good of foxhole buddies were you?"

"Like I said, at first he didn't have many friends. He never did talk much, just did his job. But sooner or later you know everybody."

"Did you ever see him threaten anybody who wasn't a German?"

"No, no sir."

"Did you ever before hear him call people names, except for Germans?"

"Not as I remember."

"And by the time you were at the chateau did you figure you knew him as well as anybody?"

"I guess so."

"Did you all talk about home, family, what you would do after the war?"

"Sure. Everybody did."

"Did you tell him you wanted to go home and maybe get into a seminary?"

"Probably. That's what I want to do. I think everybody knew it."

"Did you tell him that you liked to see all those stone crosses there in the market squares here in France?"

"Same thing. I do like them. Calvaries is what they're called and they've been here for hundreds of years."

"And what about him? Did he tell you what he was going to do after the war?"

"Only thing I remember is him saying what everybody said, he was going to go home."

"Who to?"

"His wife and kids."

"He was married?"

"Yep, I think so. He said 'his wife and kids.'"

"So he had kids."

"Yes, sir, he did. I actually saw him looking at 'em once. Two of them, a picture he kept in his jacket. We all done that."

"All right. Thank you. Now, were you in the barn the entire time of the engagement on the twelfth of August? At Château Dupré?"

"No, sir. I was outside at first."

"Where outside?"

"I was back up in the orchard, the apple orchard."

"How did you come to be back inside?"

"There was three of us up there as a perimeter guard. Witt was up there with us and he came slipping down into the trees and told us there was a column of Germans coming down that track. Sure enough, in a few minutes, there come about twelve Germans. They had a worn out truck towing a gun and they were just edging along that road."

"Where exactly were they?"

"Oh, about two hundred yards up the road, to the north."

"What did you do?"

"Witt and I ran down to the chateau and told Lieutenant Campbell. Banks stayed up in the orchard."

"What happened next?"

"We watched 'em come up to the edge of the orchard and stop. They stayed off the road and it was a miracle they didn't stumble over Banks, he was that close to them. Well, we watched them and they was clearly looking down at the chateau and they had to have seen us."

"Is that when the attack began?"

"No, sir. They sat up there for the better part of an hour or two. They was probably afraid to cross that ridge with the chateau in plain sight, so they laid just to the right of it. So Lieutenant Campbell come over to the barn and ordered us all to set up. We put a machine gun in the corner of the loft. We had a couple of grenade launchers in the squads and we put those up in the edges of the windows. Then he sent Helton off to find the company."

"What happened next?"

"All I know is that firing broke out, sir."

"From where?"

"Lieutenant Campbell sent me to the barn where Sergeant Altgelt was so I didn't see it. We never saw what really happened but suddenly we were firing the light machine gun up at them and sure enough they set up a machine gun at the end of the ridge, right below it, and started shooting back. Then we tried to send a mortar round up there and the next thing I knew the Germans had rolled out that big gun on wheels and started shooting at us. Point blank."

"Were you with the lieutenant?"

"No, sir. I was in the barn. Sergeant Altgelt was on a machine gun set up near the milking stalls. I had my rifle at the other end of the barn. I never saw the lieutenant."

"Did you see the doctors?"

"No, sir."

"Did you see Captain Hastings when he was shot?"

"No, sir. What I seen was that he was running around in the courtyard, going from the barn to the house that Lieutenant Campbell had set up as his headquarters to the main house and all over, checking on the men. He was trying to do what a medic does."

"And Major Halliburton, was he acting like a medic?"

"I didn't see him."

"Did you see the other machine gun that the platoon had?"

"No, sir, but I could hear it. I think it was in the little house, the house where the lieutenant was."

"Did you see Corporal Curtiss?"

"Yes, sir. He was up on the roof of a little building where they had the chickens and all."

"What was he doing?"

"Shooting at the Germans."

"With his rifle?"

"No, he had a BAR."

"A Browning automatic? Was that what he usually carried?"

"After he was a squad leader, yep."

"Did you ever see him put the BAR down and use another gun that day?"

"No. He never put it down. It was his gun."

"Did you see it when you saw him in the chateau?"

Lieutenant Stamford gambled. Rogers did not play.

"Sir, to tell you the truth, I never thought about it until this minute. When I saw him in the front room yelling at the major, he was on the floor."

He paused again and closed his eyes. Lieutenant Stamford wished he had not asked but there was no turning back at this point.

"With Captain Hastings?"

"Yes, sir."

"Did you see a handgun?"

"No, sir."

"A regular M-1 carbine?"

Rogers thought some more.

"No, sir."

Lieutenant Stamford could feel the tension in the room. He knew without looking that Major Leatherman was writing out his next few questions, and he knew what they would be.

"You did not see Corporal Curtiss pull a gun and point it at Major Halliburton, did you?"

"No, sir. I will not say I did. I never did."

"Let me ask you one last thing, Private. You said you came to in the barn. Did the Germans ever attack on foot after they blew a hole in the barn and launched mortars down into the courtyard?"

"Not as I know, sir."

"Do you know how long you were knocked out?"

"A few minutes I judge. I don't know exactly. But when I come to it took a minute to figure out what happened."

"Who was the first person you talked to?"

"I think it must have been Sergeant Altgelt. He was under that beam."

"What did he say to you?"

"I can't rightly say, sir. He had a lot of trouble talking."

"Is it possible you had a lot of trouble hearing?"

"Oh, yes sir. I was seeing stars and hearing bells. At first it was like he was talking and no words coming out."

"And who is the next person you talked to?"

"I think it was in the house. I ran in and saw them and asked them would they come help me with Sergeant Altgelt. And then I seen they was yelling and standing over Captain Hastings."

"You 'seen' they were yelling? Was Major Halliburton yelling?"

"I don't remember what he said."

"Was that also because you were still having trouble making out words?"

"It might be, sir. I was shocked up pretty good."

"Private, you knew Captain Hastings was a doctor, right?"

"Sure."

"Do you know what morphine is, Private?"

"What the medics use when someone gets shot. They jam it in them."

"Or burned? Do they use morphine for that?"

"Yes, I've seen that."

"Or a leg blown off. Morphine for that, too."

"I suppose."

"Private, what would an officer in the medical corps like Major Halliburton have that a seriously wounded man like Captain Hastings might need? Something that someone trying to help him, like Corporal Curtiss, would expect him to give?"

Not a single person in the room looked around. Lieutenant Stamford expected Major Leatherman to object but, whether from a genuine concern about the facts that were unfolding or fear that the court members would hate the intrusion, he, too, listened.

"Morphine?"

"Morphine. That's right. No medical officer or combat medic in the United States Army would ever go without morphine in his belt, would he?"

"I don't know. I guess not, sir."

Everyone in the room, except Rogers, knew that Lieutenant Stamford had gotten the witness to agree with him so much that by this time all he did was echo Stamford's thoughts. Rogers only knew that if he couldn't disagree with the question, then he had to agree with it.

"Private, at this point you are in the room with a badly wounded man, Captain Hastings. Right?"

"Yes, sir."

"Corporal Curtiss has saved your life before, he's saved others in the platoon before, and he was on the wall there at the chateau as long as you could see him, with his BAR, trying to save the platoon again. Right?"

"Yes, sir."

"And he's trying to help Captain Hastings from what you can see. Right?"

"Yes, sir. I think that's right."

"And your hearing is not very good because you've had your head knocked in when a barn roof landed on it with a German antitank shell blowing up. Right?"

"Yes, sir."

"Private, did you ever consider that maybe you heard wrong?"

"No, sir. I didn't think of it."

"Until now?"

"Until now."

"And now that you have thought of it, what do you think you really heard Corporal Curtiss screaming at Major Halliburton?"

Rogers sat very quietly, confronting the fact he had made a mistake and hadn't thought about it. He considered that he might himself be in some ill-defined trouble for making the mistake; he did not consider that it might cost Curtiss his life.

"Morphine, sir?"

"That's right, Private. Morphine. Isn't that what you really heard?"

"I think it might be, sir."

"And one last question, Private. Did you see Major Halliburton give any of his morphine to Corporal Curtiss to give to Captain Hastings?"

"No, sir. I just saw the major turn and run."

In the excitement of defusing a bomb many lawyers think that they have won the case. Lieutenant Stamford thought so. He passed the witness back to Major Leatherman feeling confident that the court would not listen to another word. In this he was mistaken.

Leatherman asked Private Rogers the three questions he had written down—

"Did Major Halliburton have a gun?"

"No."

"Did you see a gun strapped across Corporal Curtiss's back as he ran up the stairs?"

"Yes, I think so."

"Was it his BAR?"

"Yes, sir, I'm pretty sure it was. I think so."

The court martial adjourned for the day.

Major Leatherman was convinced by the testimony of both Captain Deere and Private Rogers that Corporal Curtiss was so mad at Major Halliburton that he had raced up the stairs and shot him in the back of the head, then run away. Lieutenant Stamford was convinced that he had proved that Halliburton needed killing—he had broken radio silence, probably opened fire with a machine gun to start the entire attack, and he then had refused to give morphine to his friend, Captain Hastings. He had probably cost the Army a very good platoon. Major Leatherman, in turn, was convinced that even if the court members had any doubt about whether Curtiss had murdered Major Halliburton, they would have no doubt about his desertion.

Major Leatherman and Lieutenant Stamford gathered their papers and left the makeshift courtroom. Each of them passed Captain Hastings, who was sitting on a wooden chair in the hallway, waiting as he had been all day to testify. Each of them briefly said hello—"Captain Hastings, recessed until tomorrow." "Captain Hastings, sir. See you in the morning"—as they walked by. Neither wanted to appear too friendly with Captain Hastings for fear that the other would suspect him of being unduly friendly. Neither paid heed to the fact he was engrossed in reading a letter.

Lubbock State Hospital
109 West College
Lubbock, Texas

September 18, 1944

Dear Captain Hastings:

I am Mrs. Emma Sullivan's doctor at the state hospital where she has been for several years now since she developed senile dementia. I know her daughter Virginia well as she visits Mrs. Sullivan more than the rest of the family. She has told me all about your medical training and your Army service and I congratulate you.

I am writing to see if you know of some way you can help Virginia more. She came yesterday and she looked completely depressed. Her clothes were mended, as all of ours are these days, but also not well washed, ironed, or kept up. She looked worn out. She seemed to be distracted the whole time. On her way out I asked her if she would like to stop in my office and we talked. At length she broke down and told me what is happening. I'm sure you know all of this but

---

while you've been away she was living at home with her father who was a local businessman and her brother, the postmaster. Virginia was fired from her job at the courthouse. Then her brother was taken away for something to do with the draft and her father disappeared one night, as did the town doctor and the sheriff. I don't know how she survived these last two months but it wasn't until yesterday that she learned what happened—they put her brother in the Marines and the sheriff's in jail here waiting trial for some kind of corruption or something. No word from her father or her doctor.

Frankly, I don't see how she is getting by financially or keeps from losing what they have. I don't know what you can do. We are grateful for you boys and proud of you. I know the hardships must be impossible for us here to understand but life here is still pretty hard on some people, especially Virginia. Sometimes the Red Cross can help.

Dr. Richard Alexander, M.D.

Lubbock State Hospital

CHAPTER TWENTY

"Where were you shot, Captain Hastings?"

Major Leatherman stood at his counsel table as he asked the question. Will sat in a rigid chair in front of and slightly to the prosecution's side of the long table where the court members were placed. He realized that the odd placement of the witness chair made it easier for the court to see him than for him to see them. In front of him he could only see Major Leatherman and, across the room, at their table, the defense. He had thought he would be able to look directly at the court members when he testified, but he was mistaken.

"In the back, sir. It came out the front."

"How are you today, Captain?"

"Sore. My right arm is still weak. I'm getting better."

"When I asked where you were shot, I also wanted you to tell the court members where in Château Dupré you were when you were shot. Can you do that?"

"Yes, sir. I had been inside a small house where the officers were quartered. Lieutenant Campbell and one of the men were in there during the fight. Someone ran in and said that the barn had been hit and men were down. Private Antsley and I ran to the barn and it was destroyed. The roof was caved in, beams down, men in really bad shape. We bent down to work on them and while we were there a huge round hit the wall of the house, where the lieutenant was." And Fouquet.

"Captain, when you were in the hospital you drew me a map. Do you remember that?"

"Yes, sir."

"Is this the map?"

"Yes, sir. I'm not very good at drawing, but this shows everything."

"I offer these into evidence, sir."

The court admitted as exhibits the maps Will had drawn.

"Now, on this map of the entire chateau, would you mark a number 1 for the barn?"

Will complied.

"A number 2 for the house where Lieutenant Campbell was?"

He marked a number 2.

"And a number 3 where you were positioned when you were hit."

"I was about here, sir. I had run from the barn back toward the house after the round hit it. The wall was knocked in, the little house was blown up pretty good, and then I was hit. About here."

"How far is that from the main house?"

"I don't know, sir. Twenty or thirty yards."

"Describe what happened, Captain."

"I knew that Lieutenant Campbell and one other man were there in that little house. When it got hit I ran there and found them both. They were pretty splintered up with the blast, pieces of wood from the beams, stone. I had been in it like that before, on the beach, and again up on Martinville Ridge in the assault on St. Lô, but I was more used to men being carried into a field hospital and me going to work on them, not to men being killed outright just in front of me, not with a single blast. I staggered away from the rubble and was out in the barnyard when something hit me in the back, really hard, like a bolt of electricity or something. If it hasn't happened to you, I can't describe it."

"That was in the courtyard, where you marked the spot?"

"Yes. It knocked me down. I lay there a minute, then started to get up, and the front of my field jacket, there was blood soaking it right through here." Will pointed to an area of his chest to the right of his sternum and slightly above it. "Then, everything flooded in. I was cold, my head was spinning, I got to my knees and fell again, then I just sort of lay there, in the dirt and rubble. I knew I had been shot. I knew it could be bad."

"How did you get into the house, the main house?"

This was delicate. Will was not concerned about the truth so much as the whole truth. His delay in answering the question gave him the appearance of someone who was being deliberate to say only what he knew.

"I can't be certain about it. Someone lifted me under my arms and dragged me and walked me, sort of all at the same time."

"Who was that, Captain?"

"I can only say that when they stopped, I was on the floor of the main house."

"Who was there?"

"Major Halliburton and the corporal." And Géraldine.

"Corporal Curtiss?"

"I think so."

"Was it Major Halliburton who helped you to get to the house?"

"I don't think so."

Major Leatherman knew exactly what testimony he wanted from Will so he knew where he was heading. Where Leatherman was going was not Will's concern. The next question would reveal if Leatherman had figured out what Will was going to tell the court.

"What were they doing?"

"Arguing. Shouting."

"What about, Captain?"

"I was bleeding pretty good then. There wasn't anything left in my utility belt; I had used everything I had on the men in the barn, my bandages and the syrettes. I knew that my other medic, Fouquet, was dead too. He had been with the lieutenant, here—" Will pointed on the drawing to a place near the little house "—during the shooting. And I was getting faint from loss of blood and shock."

"Was Major Halliburton trying to help you?"

"It didn't look like it, sir."

This caught Leatherman by surprise. Will studied his face for a clue but from his expression Will was sure that no one had told Leatherman anything about Halliburton and Will, at least not about the Windmill Club or the short arms. On the other hand, Will knew that Leatherman wouldn't leave the subject hanging.

"Where was Corporal Curtiss while you were there on the floor during all the arguing and shouting? Was he between you and the major?"

"More or less, yes, sir. Curtiss was on the floor right in front of me and the Major was over by the stairs, maybe ten feet away."

"Did you hear Corporal Curtiss curse at the major?"

"I heard him curse. I don't know if he was cursing at the major. I mean, we had been under fire for some time, we had just taken a beating and the men out in the courtyard were dead or dying and there was dirt everywhere. They were both shouting."

"Did you see Private Rogers?"

"I think so. He came in about the time that the Major ran up the stairs."

Leatherman relaxed. He did not know where he had been, but he was back on track and knew where he was going.

"What did you see next, Captain?"

"The major ran up the stairs. Corporal Curtiss ran after him."

"Did you hear anything further?"

"Yes. A shot. From upstairs."

"What was your situation, Captain? Was there anything you could do?"

"No, sir. I was on the floor there. I was bleeding and I think I was beginning to slip away."

"Did you see Private Rogers do anything?"

"Yes, sir. He ran up the stairs after the shot was fired."

"And after that? Did you see Private Rogers again?"

"Yes, sir, I did. He came back down the stairs and said the Major had been shot."

"I have one last area of questions, Captain. Did you see Corporal Curtiss come back down those stairs?"

"No, sir."

"You've drawn this main house on your exhibit, Captain. Let me ask you to describe one more detail. Were you in the house at other times, such as before the battle?"

"Yes, sir."

"Was there a balcony, an outside porch upstairs that leads to the outside?"

"Yes, sir. The balconies were small ones, just kind of outside the two rooms upstairs, more like a place to stand to water the flower boxes than what I would call balconies."

"Could a man have gone from the front room upstairs and out on to the balcony you described?"

"Yes."

"And from there to the ground?"

"I suppose so. A man could jump. There weren't any railings or anything, but it wasn't all that high."

"Let me summarize. There is shouting. Major Halliburton runs up the stairs. Corporal Curtiss runs up the stairs. You hear a shot. Private Rogers runs up the stairs. A little while later, Private Rogers comes back down the stairs and says that Major Halliburton has been murdered?"

"I think he said shot but yes, sir. I'm following you."

"After that, did you ever see Corporal Curtiss again?"

"No, sir, not after that."

Major Leatherman turned to face the members of the court, briefly, but with an air of unctuous satisfaction. He then turned to face the defense and, with a completely different air, a visage of grim piety, he said

"Your witness."

Lieutenant Stamford didn't know what to do. Will had told him very little during the meeting the court had set up for him. Most of what he knew came from reading the notes Will had written to Major Leatherman.

"Captain Hastings, did you write a series of notes to Major Leatherman while you were in the hospital?"

"Yes, sir. I was having trouble getting my voice back after surgery."

"I understand. Was one of the notes about the fact that there was supposed to be radio silence?" Lieutenant Stamford went to the stack of papers in the court's file, opened it, and took out the notes that Will had written.

"I think I wrote that we were supposed to be under radio silence."

Lieutenant Stamford handed Will one of his notes.

"Did you write: 'All hell was breaking loose, and there was a lot of shooting. There was machine gun fire from the chateau and the platoon was shooting rifles and some other things, grenades I think, but the Germans started lobbing shells down on us.'?"

"Yes, sir. I wrote that note to Major Leatherman."

"Captain, I understand that you were in the hospital and maybe not in the best of shape to put this all together, but one way to read this note is that the machine gun fire from the chateau was the first thing that happened in the battle. Is that what you meant to say?"

"I don't think I meant to say that."

"What were you trying to say? This seems—to me, Captain—that there was machine gun fire, rifles and grenades, and then the Germans started lobbing shells. Do you see why I can read your note to say that the machine gun fire from the chateau—from our men rather than the Germans up on the ridge—was the first thing that happened?"

"Yes. But that wasn't the first thing that happened."

"All right. Explain the sequence of events if you can."

"The first thing that happened was that our two men from our outpost slipped down through the orchard and back into the chateau. They were pretty excited about seeing the German unit up on the road off to the north, to the right of the orchard and headed for the ridge. Lieutenant Campbell got some field glasses out and looked up there, but the Germans had stopped short of coming out on the ridge where they would be in the open. After a few minutes, a single German edged out and slipped down about five feet below the ridge and looked down on us with a pair of field glasses."

"What happened next?"

"Lieutenant Campbell asked the patrol, really it was just Private Rogers, what the strength was, how many Germans and that sort of thing. Rogers said that he thought they had a towed gun and didn't know how many men on foot. The lieutenant then got the squad leaders together and told them how he wanted to set up a defense, where to put who. Then he sent a runner out the gate on the east side to go off to find Captain Deere."

"Is that when the shooting began?"

"No. In fact, nothing happened. Not until Major Halliburton came in."

"Where was Major Halliburton?"

"He mostly was up in the main house. He came down to the small house after word got around about the Germans up there. He came in and demanded that Lieutenant Campbell do something about it."

"How did Lieutenant Campbell respond to that?"

"He showed Major Halliburton the ridge line up there. One German sitting below the crest watching us. Not twenty feet down the hillside from the German we could see one of our men burrowed into the ground up there behind a tree, the last man of our outpost that had been up in the orchard. He was tucked in pretty good and the Germans probably never saw him."

"What happened next?"

"Well, we all sort of stood holding our breath for a long time, and all that time Major Halliburton kept telling Lieutenant Campbell to do something."

"Anything specific?"

"Yes, he said to shoot that German up on the hill."

"What was Lieutenant Campbell's response to that?"

"He told the major no, that there was probably an artillery piece just out of sight and he wasn't going to get in a shoot-out with it, not with us exposed down below. The major argued with him, told him we were in a walled fortress and to 'act like a man.' That's what he said. 'Have some guts, act like a man.'"

The mood in the room had changed again. Major Leatherman had chosen to not object on the grounds that none of what happened before Curtiss chased Halliburton up the stairs was relevant; he now regretted that decision.

"May it please the court members, the only facts that are relevant are those that involve Corporal Curtiss's conduct toward Major Halliburton and what happened up in the main house, not what happened before the battle."

"Lieutenant, are you just fishing?" The law member of the court focused on the defense. "If you aren't out to prove something about Captain Hastings's notes to Major Leatherman, which is where you started this line of questioning, you should move on and I'll recommend to the court members to disregard the evidence about Major Halliburton and the Lieutenant. Are you?"

The Lieutenant didn't know. He had been fishing when he read Will's note and he was learning as much as anyone about what had happened.

"I didn't mean to get afield, sir. I did begin with the issue of Captain Hastings's notes and I will get back there." He turned back to resume the questioning.

"Captain, about your note regarding radio silence and the machine gun fire, why did you write that note to Major Leatherman?"

"I couldn't talk yet, Lieutenant. In fact, my arm was so weak after getting out of the cast that at first I couldn't write everything."

"What do you mean by 'everything?'"

"That Major Halliburton started this battle. He broke radio silence, then...."

The bedlam that broke out in the courtroom was not far short of the bedlam that had broken out at the chateau. Major Leatherman shouted objections to the line of questioning as irrelevant, to Will's answer as 'nonresponsive,' and to Lieutenant Stamford's questions as character assassination of Major Halliburton. The members of the court martial, infantry officers and artillery officers, shouted questions at Will without regard to the procedure: "Are you saying this doctor grabbed a radio and started talking?" "What was he doing with a walkie-talkie?" The law member was silenced by the other members. The presiding officer looked from Will to Leatherman to the court members to the recording clerk and back, torn between the duty to preside over the trial in an orderly manner and the duty to find out what happened in a battle that had wiped out a combat platoon. The duty to preside prevailed and he banged on the table with a gavel that until then he had thought was purely ceremonial.

"Stop! Silence! Stop! I demand order in this court and I demand that you sit down and be quiet. All of you." He banged the gavel again for effect, then turned to the members of the court. "Members of the court martial. I ask that you be patient. I want to know as badly as you do what happened. We will find out what happened. The evidence you just heard is surprising to me, to say the least, and sounds like it was surprising to you. Please bear with me a minute and we'll resume. Major Leatherman, Lieutenant Stamford, take your seats. Now, I want to ask you two men this question. Do either of you have any objection to my asking Captain Hastings about his last statement? I'm not sure if what he said is relevant to the three charges against Corporal Curtiss and, if they aren't, we'll stop that line of questioning in this proceeding and refer that investigation to General Baade to deal with the right way. But for the moment, I just want to know if it has anything to do with the charges against Corporal Curtiss. Do you two men object to my sorting this out in a neutral way? I'm not trying to help you, Lieutenant, and I'm not trying to help you, Major. I just want this sorted out without another outburst."

They knew they could not object and they did not object.

"Captain Hastings, you said Major Halliburton started this battle by breaking radio silence?"

"Yes, sir. That's what I saw happen."

"Does that have anything to do with what you saw happen between Corporal Curtiss and Major Halliburton later, after the battle?"

"I don't know how to answer that."

"Well, was Corporal Curtiss present when Major Halliburton broke radio silence?"

"I don't think so, sir. He had been sent up to the dovecote."

"Then he could not have blamed Major Halliburton for breaking radio silence, could he?"

"I don't think so. I think what set him off was when Major Halliburton fired a machine gun at the Germans but instead he shot our last scout up there on the side of the hill. And that's when the battle started."

"He did what?"

"Major Halliburton was pretty mad at Lieutenant Campbell. The major grabbed the unit radio we had, turned it on, and started trying to call Captain Deere on it. Lieutenant Campbell turned away from the window and tried to grab the radio from Major Halliburton. They wrestled over it for a second and then someone said to get to the window. There wasn't room for all of us to crowd around the window at the same time, but the lieutenant looked out and said some pretty choice words. He was mad, and scared, too, I think, because some more Germans had run out onto the ridge when the major was on the radio. The next thing we knew, Major Halliburton had run outside toward the dovecote where Corporal Curtiss was, up on the roof. The lieutenant had sent one of the men up there with a machine gun and it was pointed out the gate that they used to let the cattle out. The next thing we knew the major had taken over the gun and fired off a burst."

"Captain, are you saying Major Halliburton broke radio silence by taking the unit's radio and tried to call Captain Deere, then took over a machine gun and fired it?"

"Yes, sir. That was what started the battle, at least that's what I think. And that's when Corporal Curtiss screamed at Major Halliburton that he was crazy, that he had just shot our man up in the orchard."

Halliburton had started the battle. He had ordered Shockley to step aside. He had unlocked the light machine gun and, before anyone could stop him, he had fired a fifteen-second burst up the hill. Bullets pocked up around the tree where Banks was hidden. At the end of the burst, Banks bounced twice, then doubled over.

The Germans then ran down below the ridge about five steps and returned fire. Rogers and Altgelt shot back at them from the barn with their carbines. Another man in the barn sent a couple of grenades up the hill with a grenade launch attachment to his carbine; the grenades landed short, in the tree-tops. The Germans set up their own machine gun and raked the courtyard. Men began to fall. Curtiss and Shockley tried to chase the Germans back up to the ridge but, at that point, the barrel of the German anti-tank weapon poked out from behind the trees. They rolled it out onto the ridge, then turned to aim it at the chateau. Shockley sent another burst of machine gun fire at the weapon crew but the plate shield protected them. The first anti-tank round went through the wall of the house where Lieutenant Campbell was trying to direct the defense. The second round went through the barn roof. A third round collapsed the barn wall.

Will was troubled at how clearly he remembered it. It had happened in slow motion, the way people say things happen right before you die. Antsley and Will ran across the courtyard to the barn. Altgelt, his leg broken, was under a huge beam that had supported the near end of the heavy roof. They bent to try to get the beam up when another round hit the small house again; Will looked up to see the roof collapse and the courtyard wall cave in. He ran to see if he could get Lieutenant Campbell out when he was hit in the back and knocked to the courtyard ground.

"As I fell I saw Corporal Curtiss up on the dovecote roof. Major Halliburton was running toward the front door of the main house."

"What happened next, Captain?"

"Nothing, sir. It was over."

"What do you mean, 'It was over,' Captain?"

"The shooting ended. I just lay there. It seemed like an awful long time."

"And the next thing you can tell us are the events that happened inside the main house, is that right?"

"Yes, sir."

The presiding officer turned to the lawyers.

"I'm going to let you resume the questioning at this point. I am going to let Captain Hastings's testimony stand in the record." He turned to the members of the court. "Officers, as I told counsel, I am going to let the testimony stand. You may consider it for any purpose or for no purpose. While it does not necessarily explain the events inside the house that resulted in Major Halliburton's death, you may consider that it has some bearing on whether Corporal Curtiss had a motive."

Leatherman beamed at this turn of events; it had not occurred to him that anyone was thinking of Halliburton's recklessness as a cause for motive.

"Or," he continued, "you may consider that it might have some bearing on an overwhelming sudden passion, something so shocking that it overwhelms someone's mind and prevents him from acting as he ordinarily would act."

Leatherman sagged back in his chair. The presiding officer had just told the members that Curtiss could be justified in shooting Halliburton for his recklessness in starting an unnecessary and suicidal battle.

"Lieutenant, resume, please."

"Yes, sir. Captain, let me direct your attention to the events after you heard the shot, after you saw Private Rogers run up the stairs. Are you with me?"

"Yes, sir."

"Was it your testimony that Corporal Curtiss fled the scene by jumping off the balcony?"

"No, sir. It was my testimony that Corporal Curtiss ran up the stairs. It was my testimony that a man could conceivably jump off the balcony. I don't believe Corporal Curtiss did that."

"Why not?"

"Because he came back into the front room where I was laying and helped get a dressing on me."

"I thought your testimony was that you never saw him again after he ran up the stairs."

"No, sir. I thought I said, and what I intended to say, was to answer Major Leatherman's question whether I saw him again after Private Rogers came downstairs."

"Do you mean to say that Curtiss came down and tended to you *after* you heard the shot and after Rogers ran upstairs but that Curtiss left before Rogers came back downstairs?"

"Yes, sir. I do mean to say that. That's what happened."

"And what do you mean by 'tended to you'? What did he do?"

"He cleaned my wound, dressed it, and dusted sulfa powder on it."

"Anything else?"

"He didn't do anything else." Will tensed, bracing for the next question, the natural question, trying to hide his fear that the Lieutenant would stumble onto the secret.

"And then he left?"

"To the best of my knowledge, after he dressed my wound, I didn't see him again."

Nor had he seen Géraldine again. She was gone. *Maybe, after the trial.*

"Until today?"

"Sorry?"

"Until today. Maybe I asked the question badly. Today is the first time you have seen Corporal Curtiss since August 12. Is that right?"

"No, sir."

"When did you see him again?"

"I haven't seen Corporal Curtiss since he tended me there on the floor in the chateau."

"I don't understand."

"I've never seen Corporal Curtiss after that."

"Until today. Here." The lieutenant vaguely nodded at his client, embarrassed at not making sense with his simple question, unaware that finally he had asked what Will had waited for.

"The soldier next to you? Are you saying he's Corporal Curtiss? That's not him."

For the last time, the court went silent as the court martial members, the lawyers, the recording clerk, as all of them absorbed what Will had said. The Lieutenant's stomach rolled, the natural fear of a lawyer who has just heard evidence that will clinch a case, but that is so good that the witness must be crazy.

"Corporal Curtiss, Captain? That's what you're being asked. Do you see Corporal Curtiss here in the courtroom?"

"No, sir."

"This soldier beside me is not Corporal Curtiss?"

"No, sir. That's a soldier named Douglas, sir. He was Private Douglas when I knew him in England. I guess he's Corporal Douglas now, the two stripes on his arm."

"Just a minute! Stop!" The gavel banged again. "Captain? Are you testifying, under oath, that this prisoner—YOU! STAND UP!—is not Corporal Curtiss? He is—who'd you say?"

"I'm pretty sure he's Private Douglas or Corporal Douglas, sir. He was a clerk back in the field hospital training school at Shrivenham when I was there."

"Look carefully, Captain. This is no joking matter." The presiding officer glared at Will with an intensity he had never seen before, not from Poppy, not from the Sheriff, not from anyone. Will settled his guts and looked back at him, as if it was the most natural thing in the world to sit through a trial without the man on trial being in the courtroom. "If you're lying to this court, and I understand fully how a man can be grateful to his

223

fellow soldiers for their valor, for saving your life, and you may think that's what Corporal Curtiss did, but if you're lying, whatever happens to Corporal Curtiss, I'm warning you that charges will be brought against you. Do you understand me, Captain?"

"Yes, sir."

"Now, who is that man?"

"I am pretty sure it's Douglas, sir."

"Bring Captain Deere back in here. Rogers, too. Get them in here."

The men were brought back into the courtroom.

"Men, the prisoner's identity has been questioned. I won't tell you who questioned it, or how, but I want you to tell me if you can identify..."

"Sir?" Lieutenant Stamford stood up and addressed the court.

"What, Lieutenant?"

"I need to raise a law point. In fact, I respectfully object and ask the court members to withdraw so that we may address a law point."

The presiding judge was exasperated. He looked at the Lieutenant, then at Leatherman, whose prosecution had led to such a mess, and then at Will. No one looked ready to back down.

"Sirs, members of the Court, witnesses. You must retire while we take up a point of law. Be outside when we resume." The officers rose, looked at the judge and the lawyers, then filed out of the classroom. "Now, what is it, Lieutenant? This case has turned into chaos—no reason I should expect you to let it get straightened out, is there? What?"

"Sir, I respectfully object to this procedure. What you've done is the same as a lineup, but with only one person to pick from. If the police have a lineup, at least they get three or four or five men out of the cells and make them stand up next to the man they arrested. Here, you just have the suspect standing out, the accused."

"Look, Lieutenant, you can stop all this right now. Turn and ask him if he's Curtiss or not. If he admits he's Curtiss, we move on. If he denies it, we'll let Captain Deere and Private Rogers tell us."

"No, sir."

"What do you mean, no? That's an order."

"Sir, I object. To order me to communicate about a critical fact with my client, then tell the court the content of our communication, which might tend to incriminate him, that is wrong. It is self-incrimination, or at least asking for the possibility of—my client—incriminating himself, and it puts me in an ethical dilemma. I cannot comply."

"Listen to me, you…"

"Sir?" Leatherman had stood up and now he, too, interrupted.

"What? Leatherman? What?"

"Sir. I agree with the lieutenant. I can't ask him to supply the missing identification against his own client. And I agree that we have been surprised, to say the least, about this issue of identification, but if it comes to a lineup, it needs more than one man."

"I don't care. This is not some civilian court, Goddamnit, and I don't want to hear a bunch of Boston lawyer stuff out of either of you. Get everybody back in here."

They returned.

"Captain Deere, is this man Corporal Curtiss or is he not?"

"Sir, this man is smaller, thinner than Curtiss. He doesn't have a mustache. It may not be him."

"Private?"

"I never thought about it until now, sir. But, I mean, he's smaller and thinner and all, but he looks like Curtiss to me."

"Sir?"

"Who is that talking now?" He looked around the courtroom, his temper getting the better of him, the orderly proceedings a thing of the past.

"Captain Hastings, sir."

"What now, Captain?"

"I'm pretty sure I can tell you if I'm right or not."

"You already told me, Captain."

"Well, you can tell for yourself, then, sir."

"How?"

"Private Douglas had certain, er, physical characteristics."

"What do you mean, Captain? Be plain."

"He had a medical condition."

The major turned to face him. "What? What do you mean, a medical condition?"

"Cryptorchidism."

"What does that mean?"

"Basically, sir, that he has no testicles."

"What?"

"Just that, sir. No testicles."

"How would you know a thing like that?"

"Short arms, sir."

"Short arms?"

"That's what the men call them, sir. There were so many cases of vene-real disease in England that a memo came down to the medical corps that we had to do inspections of the men. Their, uh, genitals. For signs of VD. At Shrivenham we usually did them before and after leave and random times at night. Then it changed to every night."

He didn't mention that it became every night right after Halliburton had accused him and Douglas of telling the commander that Halliburton had gotten the clap. After that, the men in Douglas's group were subjected to a short arm inspection every night at midnight. Will performed them. Not even Douglas could hide from Will that there were no testicles in his scrotum. It was never discussed.

The presiding member glared at Will. "So?"

"Sir, the condition is pretty obvious. If a man has no testicles in his scrotum, his doctor will see it on an exam. Douglas couldn't have hidden it if he wanted to."

"You mean he has no balls?"

"Yes, sir. No balls, sir. Not that I could see." Will had hoped to avoid the question, but he was in too deep at this point to go into details about the fine line between undescended testicles and a complete absence of tes-ticles. He had no doubt that, if need be, the man standing next to Lieuten-ant Stanford would be able to suck his testicles up into his chest to avoid a firing squad.

"What about Curtiss?"

"I never examined Curtiss, sir. The only thing I know is that he had a couple of children. I took it from that he had—testicles. Sir."

The presiding officer was stumped. He had not gone to law school, nor had he landed on Utah Beach with the Fourth Infantry Division, nor fought his way up to Cherbourg, nor conducted the court martial, to look at a man's scrotum. He looked up and saw Rogers.

"You! Private! What do you know about this?"

"Well, golly, sir—I don't know. I mean, he's got the two boys. Corporal Curtiss did, sir. Ronald. And Albert."

The presiding officer smelled more fish than he wanted, but had no way to cook it. He finally made a decision.

"Captain, I don't know whether to believe you or not. I'll say this—I'm not going to be the one to take a look at this man to find out. But here's what I am going to do. Counsel, listen. Here's my decision. I'm going to call someone from the medical battalion and send you, Corporal Curtiss or Corporal Douglas or whatever your name is over to the hospital for an examination. If it turns out that this man has no balls, strike that. If it turns out that this man has the condition that Captain Hastings says he has, then I'm going to recommend that this prosecution be dismissed. If you ever find Corporal Curtiss, Major, you can start over. But, and you lawyers listen carefully. You too, Captain. If this man turns out to have—if the report shows Captain Hastings is lying, this trial will resume. We'll be back here in an hour and we'll stay until it's over. Then, and regardless of the outcome, I'm going to recommend to the Judge Advocate General that he start proceedings against Captain Hastings." He turned to face Will. "I'm going to charge you with perjury first. And I'm going to get the Division S-2 to go out to that chateau and dig up every shell and bullet and broken needle and anything else and if there's anything that looks like you had something to do with starting that battle, Captain, perjury will be the least of your trouble. We're in recess."

The presiding officer turned to a military policeman who walked forward and took Curtiss, or Douglas, by the arm, and escorted him back to the cloakroom that was used as a holding cell. Curtiss, or Douglas, did not look at Will. Will did not look at him. The presiding officer watched them both, and saw nothing. He then left to find the colonel in charge of the hospital, to set up a short arm inspection, for one soldier only.

CHAPTER TWENTY-ONE

November, 1944

A brown heron swooped along the Vire, passing so close to Genet's head that he had to duck to avoid a collision. The laundry women laughed at the top of their lungs.

"Ay! Genet! Why don't you do laundry and let us do the fishing?" They laughed again, one of the ladies mocking his fly-casting with an imaginary pole, another snickering that he came that close to really being tetched in the head. The doctor, twenty yards downstream, turned to send an insult back their way when he noticed that the current had pushed the aft end of the rowboat away from the bank. It pivoted on the worn dock rope, causing the boat to float against the sluice and block the flow of rinse water.

"Not a lot of water getting in the way of your washing, Ladies. Are you debutantes too dainty to tow a boat?" he yelled back. "Afraid to get your hands wet?" 'You old goats,' he muttered by way of finishing the insult. 'Pests!' He wasn't sure whom he meant by the pests; they were interfering as much with his fishing as the rowboat was with their washing. But there were other pests, too.

Not until early October had the river become clean enough to fish in, or do the laundry for that matter. The Americans had blocked off the Vire long enough to lower the water. It had taken weeks to dig out the cows, goats, collapsed bridgeworks, paving stones, and Germans before they re-opened the sluices; the last of the dead and dying fish, a few horses, and the rotted marsh plants broke free at last and drifted on their way to the English Channel. Genet had only resumed fishing a week or so ago.

On the good side, children had begun to play again, venturing out to snare rabbits in the meadow and pick green apples and berries in the forests, much as they had done before the first jackboots had clicked on Ste. Marie's cobblestones. He had forgotten what children were like—noisy, stomach aches, full of life, oblivious to the shell holes in the school roof and the wrecked square in front of the church. He was sure that some of the boys had taken the rowboat and tied it up at the wrong end of the laundry.

Or, he admitted, it could have been himself. He clomped in his waders, climbing out of the reeds and muck to walk to the laundry shed and fiddle with the dock rope.

"Ay, when I move it," he said, "the water will flow back through the sluice." He untied the line from the corner of the hut, let it out so that the boat would float out into the river, then walked it along to re-tie it on the downstream corner. "What are you going to do then?"

"What do you mean?" one of them, the grouchiest, threw back at him. "Of course the water'll go through here. It's the rinse water."

"I mean when the rinse water starts flowing again you won't have any more excuses for taking your drawers home dirtier than when you brought them here to wash. Six hours of gossip for a couple of shirts and a table cloth."

The other women roared in laughter. "The old doc's still got a mouth on him," one said. "Ay, Bernice, your old man'll say 'whose clothes are these? They're clean!'" The shrieks were so loud that even the ducks swam away. Genet won the round, and they did keep score.

It was dark in the village by the time he walked out of the meadow and up the cobbled street to the square. The clinic door was still closed but one of the windows had been filled in with slats scavenged from the departing army's debris. He walked around back to the kitchen door and let himself in.

"Perch," he muttered. "There used to be river eels in there, and some trout." He had caught a few larger fish, bottom dwellers, but threw them back for fear of eating whatever the carp had eaten while the Vire was flushing the stinking corpses away. "A bit of pork would be nice. Ahhh...." He had no salivary memory of pork or sausages, just the notion that he used to have them, and mutton, too. He cursed the Germans a moment, then began to clean the meager supper with a dull scalpel. He had picked some morel mushrooms from the woods, some wild onions in the meadow, and with a few more strokes he sliced his vegetables into a common skillet that was barely hot enough to cook on. Evening dinner had devolved into a necessity, no longer a pleasure.

There was a tap on the front door. He walked through the hallway, into the clinic, and listened. Someone tapped again.

"Doctor? Genet, are you there?"

"Who is it?"

"Marie Osmont, Doctor. It's Paul; can you see him?"

"Come around to the kitchen. I'm in there. Come on. This door's locked."

Paul Osmont had an earache. It was nothing special, just a bit of pain when he swallowed. Genet took the boy and twisted his head sideways, up, down, moving the lamp across the kitchen table to get a better look. The onions and fish cast a lovely aroma into the kitchen; he wished that boys would go home and complain as soon as their ears began to ache instead of waiting until suppertime.

"It's not draining. I don't see any wax, but there's not much light. You, boy, are you washing your ears?" He said yes, he washed them, which Genet doubted, the buildup of dirt inside the outer ear being a contrary witness. "You go swimming? Get water down in your ears? Hear any bubbling when you swallow?"

The rest of the story came out. Paul, Henri Pommeroi, and David Eglise had been playing inside the apple co-op barn where the men were getting the distillery ready for the harvest; Paul had found something American.

"Open your mouth. Wider. Tilt your head." A penny was lodged in the back of his mouth, hard against his tonsils, behind the jaw. Genet went to the clinic and held a lamp to the cabinet; as he suspected, the long, slender dog-leg forceps had disappeared long ago. He found a tracheal tube and brought it back to the kitchen. "All right, here's what we're going to do. I'm going to pour some water into your mouth and try to dislodge it. Don't swallow, for God's sake, or you'll choke to death. Okay? I'm going to go right behind you and when I say rinse and spit, swirl the water around and cough and spit the damn thing out. Understand?"

Paul said he did, but he did not. When Genet said rinse and spit, the boy swallowed, choked once, and began to gasp. His mother screamed, Genet clutched the child from behind, and squashed him as hard as he could. Paul coughed twice, swallowed, and then blinked his eyes.

"I'm okay."

"Open up," idiot, Genet thought. "Let me look. Wider. Tilt. Let me look."

Paul had swallowed it. The water was gone, the tonsils and jaw were free of one American feather penny, and the air way was not obstructed.

"It'll come out in the bed pan. One more thing to remember the Americans by. Ear feel better? Thought so. Bring him back tomorrow if it hurts any more. You're welcome."

The fire had gone even colder and, although it had cooked, to some degree, even the fish and onions were cold by the time he wiped Paul's mucus off the table and set his plate on it. He ate in silence, then cleared the table and scraped the dishes. He thought of walking across to the parsonage to listen to Father Jean's radio but decided against it. As the number of foreign soldiers in Ste. Marie decreased, Father Jean's sanctimony had increased. *Old goat says he understands everything on the BBC. Hah, six months ago he wouldn't let them plug the radio into the church's electrical wire for fear of the Germans coming to get him in the night.* Genet blew out the candles and trudged up to the second floor. He put on his nightshirt and opened the window, then gazed out at the dark town before crawling into bed. He listened for sounds in the night, in the town, nearby, and even inside the house. There was no rumble of tanks, no roar of artillery or the rattle of machine guns. No planes flew overhead. There were no whispers in the dark, nor the slamming of doors. The house sparrows slept. What Genet heard was the sound of nothing, not exactly peace, he thought, but an absence of war. He slept.

BAM BAM BAM

Genet jerked awake.

BAM BAM BAM

'Oh God,' he thought. 'They've come."

The hard knock on the door was the sound everyone knew, the German art of arrests. Before his sleeping brain unscrambled, Genet thought that they had come for him. Then he remembered it could not be the Germans, which only made it worse.

He held his breath for five minutes, thankful that he had closed his bedroom window. He wondered whether they would crash down the clinic door or charge in through the kitchen. He wondered what form the interrogation would take.

Instead, the next thing he heard was the unmistakable sound of a gasoline motor, a four-cylinder engine, no muffler. There was a clash of gears, the revving up of the motor, and then the clank of a jeep bouncing across the square in front of the church. The jeep's headlights shone on the *epicerie* window opposite, then against the wall of the post office. He expected the lights to turn and pierce the bedroom window, then a bullhorn shouting, "Genet, come out." Instead, the jeep drove away, down the south road. The last sound Genet heard was a wheel that bounced on the stone base of the *calvaire* at the end of the village. The gears clashed in a downshift, the engine revved a last time, and the American authorities drove away into the night. He lay awake for two hours, neither breathing aloud, nor moving, nor even shifting the covers, waiting until the roosters perched on the drying racks at the old tile factory down past the apple barn began to crow in earnest.

BAM BAM BAM

"Genet! Wake up, you old goat! Wake up!"

What does he want?

The priest stood under Genet's bedroom window and yelled, then walked the two or three steps back to the clinic door and pounded on it again.

"What do you want?" Genet threw open the window and shouted down at the square in general. "It's not Sunday. Go away." It not only wasn't Sunday, it wasn't even seven in the morning. "There's no mass for a half hour,' he shouted, "if anybody shows up," he went on, wondering why the priest was out proselytizing on a weekday for a mass that never drew more than two or three widows. "What?"

"Come down here, Genet. I thought you were dead. Everybody in the village woke up last night, except you. Are you deaf?' Father Jean cupped his hands to shout, magnifying his annoying squeak. His black robe flapped in the cool air, his broad black hat adding to an appearance that Genet thought made him look like an enormous crow. "You need a new stethoscope!" The priest doubled back in laughter. Genet wanted to pour water on his head.

He pulled on a shirt and pants and walked down the stair way and through the dusty clinic rooms at the front of the house. The front door was so out of use that it was stuck; when he finally broke it free, he charged out to the street ready to grouch and almost broke his leg by tripping on a large wooden crate that had been propped against the wall adjacent to the front door. When he picked himself off the stoop he was staring at a white cross painted on cheap pine slats. Above the cross there were stenciled the words U.S. Army.

Below the cross was the title: Number 2 Field Medical.'

Two more boxes were stacked beside it. There was a smaller box labeled Field Laboratory Number 8.' A third box was carefully positioned on top: Warning: Perishable Medicine. Use before___. There was no date. The only word he was sure of was medicine.

"Genet, you're rich!"

The doctor was speechless. Even if the crates were only half-filled they would contain more medical supplies than had passed through his hands in the last five years taken together.

"Genet, what a time to be deaf and rich! Now that you've got a box of medicine, you're so old and deaf that you're the one who needs a doctor. Get dressed; you need to clean up."

"What do you mean, clean up?"

"You, first. Then your house. When was the last time you had a patient in there? I'm going for the mayor; he's the only one who has any tools. We need to open your boxes." The priest left as loudly as he had arrived, shouting through the nearby streets on the way to the *mairie*, "Wake up, wake up! God has opened Genet's clinic!" In a half hour he returned with the mayor and old Varnet. They pried the lids off.

The Number 2 medical boxes had changed since the first shipments were dropped on the beaches at St. Laurent.

"Ay, Genet. What's this?" The crates were partitioned into sections, their contents divided into separate compartments for medicines and goods to treat the most common wounds.

"Slings. Splints. If there is a God, and if Father Jean tumbles out of the belfry, I can use this to line up his broken leg and this to wrap around his mouth." Genet fished out an assortment of slings and splints and a canister to mix plaster for casts.

"There is a God, Genet. Where do you think this came from? Eh?"

Another section contained a ready-made emergency surgery kit.

"My Heavens—hoses, bottles, what is all this? Do you have any idea what to do with this stuff? Have you ever done a transfusion?"

"Maybe cow's blood," someone snorted. "Or a sheep," the mayor added. "'Genet the Sheep-Fuc....'"

"Quiet! That's blasphemy. I don't care if you were joking, stop it!"

"No, it's not for transfusions. I saw the Americans do it. It's saline water. You put in a needle, then let it flow, and then mix in the medicine so it goes right in."

Varnet, who had spent sixty years wearing wooden shoes and fifty years carving them, had never heard of such a thing. The mayor suspected that Genet was saying more than he really knew, and might injure someone if he used it wrong.

Within a half hour they had carted everything inside the clinic.

The clinic itself was as shabby as its proprietor. With neither medicine nor supplies during the German occupation, most of Ste. Marie had come to learn that there was very little Genet could do for most problems that people couldn't do themselves with herbs and boiled water. His glass instrument chest had filled with dust, the discolored shelves holding tarnished tools. The rubber hoses of his old stethoscope, the bulb of the blood pressure cuff, all had cracked with disuse. His examining table was coated with dust. Even the disrobing screen had withered from abandonment, there being few patients in the last five years for whom undressing for an examination would lead to any treatment that Genet could provide, regardless of the diagnosis. He had had little to do for a long time and, so, gazed at his treasure.

My God, he thought. Where did this come from?

Between the mayor, the priest, and the carpenter, everyone knew before ten in the morning that the old doctor had been blessed by the fortunes of war. Three women and two girls from the primary school arrived at his door with mops and cloths. The postmaster showed up to help the mayor carry the examining room furniture outside, first to clean, then to air. Someone brought up a pot of tisane. Apples appeared in a box on the stoop. A geranium pot was tucked into his front window.

Varnet trimmed the rough edges from the planks that had filled in the front windows where the artillery blast had taken the glass out. By the middle of the afternoon, a sign had been painted on the trim board that was hung from the door bracket: *E. Genet – Médecin.* For the rest of the week Genet's front door was blocked by a queue of fluttering hearts, growing moles, and bowels that had not moved for months. Sprains ignored for five years now needed an American splint. Blood pressures that had withstood the anxiety of field grey uniforms and the roar of artillery now must be tested properly by the elegant, compact glass instrument that had a proud place next to a clean cabinet full of thermometers, lances, and an otoscope that illuminated by flashlight batteries what the doctor wanted to see. By five o'clock each evening someone had stopped by the green grocer for a few potatoes and some peas, or searched out the baker for the last crusts. To their unspoken pleasure, everyone in Ste. Marie knew that Dr. Genet would not starve in the coming winter.

Then Madame Osmont brought Paul back.

"The penny came out. Ugly thing, too. What do the Americans do with them?"

"Not much, I think. What's the matter?"

"It's still his ear."

"Show me your mouth." The otoscope was lighted. The mouth was red. "And your ears."

It was his ear or, more correctly, an infection of Paul's mastoid. A sickly pus oozed out the canal, turning the swab green and staining the stick beneath the cotton.

"Good. There, jump down. Pull up your shirt. Put this on your ear." He handed the boy a cotton ball. Let me talk to your mother." When the child turned away he said what any other doctor would have said: "Your child's ear is infected, and from the size, probably in the bone."

"No it isn't. It's wax."

"It isn't wax." He lifted his stained fingers to the mother's nose; she turned away. "It's not wax; it's pus. He has to have an operation. Now."

Within an hour the postmaster had called out the telephone operator who had, in her turn, called the prefect in Bayeux, who left to find a doctor. When the prefect returned he gave the instrument to the mayor who asked the postmaster, in earnest, how old the young man was and whether he had been in the military service, then hung up.

Within two hours the parents had spoken with the priest who assured them that, despite the common knowledge that surgery only delayed death from an infected ear bone, they had to choose only between death by operation, which would employ an anesthetic, or death by meningitis at home, which would take longer but was quite acceptable in the eyes of the Church.

"You told them what?"

The priest reiterated to Genet that he was on quite good ground, theologically speaking.

The doctor told the priest that if God wanted the Americans to do intra-abdominal and thoracic surgery on a spinster splintered in a dairy barn, then God didn't want an eight-year old kid to die from an earache. The priest put a curse on him, but not a very strong one, and when Genet confessed that while he had faith in medicine, he didn't know how the Americans used everything they had given him, the priest relented. They agreed, against Genet's instincts, to go find some Americans. Thus, that evening, after mass they, Madame Osmont, and Paul rode in the back of the only Citroen still running in Ste. Marie, bouncing along as the mayor drove the wrecked country roads that led to St. Lô.

CHAPTER TWENTY-TWO

―――――――❦―――――――

"Mail call, Hastings." Major Fondren flipped open the canvas flap of Will's tent. "You're either the luckiest SOB I ever knew, or the unluckiest. Want some hooch?"

"What've you got?"

"French white lightning; what else is there?" Fondren didn't wait for an answer; he sat on an empty Field Medical Number 2 that was Will's desk, chair, and dressing table, then poured a generous Calvados into Will's canteen cup and another into his own.

"I meant 'what have you got for mail call,' not what have you got to drink. Hard to say if I'm the luckiest or the unluckiest until I see what it is."

"Well, luckiest, I suppose. Here's three letters. Nobody else in CA gets anything. If it wasn't for you, the clerk wouldn't have enough to do, I'd send him back to the infantry." He handed over the letters. They were, in fact, letters. They were not orders. "But unluckiest, too. Not a word from Division. How'd you get on their black list, anyway? I mean, I've seen guys on a black list, but you? You're buried. But you know what? Being on a black list in CA in St. Lô is a hell of a lot safer than being promoted to the top of somebody's hero list over in Belgium. You know what they're doing over there? Looking for Germans to kill in some god-forsaken forest. Krauts don't take too kindly to us chasing them into their own trees."

"Krauts didn't take too kindly to us chasing them out of France, either. Look outside the tent."

CA was Civil Affairs. Word had come back to the schoolhouse within a day—the man in custody did in fact have cryptorchidism or, as the adjutant had told the waiting participants, the accused has no balls. Will had asked if he could be sent back to his division; Leatherman objected. "There is still some investigation to finish up, sirs. I request on behalf of the judge advocate that everyone be held in place until the military police have done with their work at that chateau."

Will had wandered around the Cherbourg docks, watched the constant flow of unloading boats, drank Irish whisky in the bar of the Hotel Bassin, and waited. After two weeks, he asked the Division Medical Office to let him go back to the 261st, to the rehabilitation hospital at Valognes, to an evacuation station at the port, anything. He was told that he was still on temporary duty. "Word is you're t.d.y. to the division until your commander requests you back, and no duty until your doctor gives you a full duty chit. Sorry." Will had nothing to do until he met Fondren, himself in Cherbourg for a day and night up from St. Lô.

"Come back with me," Fondren had volunteered. "Nothing left of the old hospitals—they look like an artillery practice range. I can send you over to the mental hospital every day to get the locals off my back. They think we took 'em to raise. I'll fix it up for you."

"Okay," Will had said. He bought Fondren a bottle of Bushmill's and the next morning the adjutant gave Will a new temporary order to assist in the civil affairs effort in St. Lô until Leatherman or the court martial were done with him.

"You know where St. Lô is, Doc?"

"Yeah, I was there for a couple of days. It's not too far."

St. Lô was about thirty-five miles from Cherbourg. It was about five miles from where he last saw her. He showed Fondren the view outside the tent. St. Lô was still as wrecked in November as it had been when Captain Deere had driven them away from the city at the end of July. The civil affairs garrison had created its own tent city across the Vire from the train station, an unrecognizable wreck of bomb-blasted rails, a splattered switching yard, sheds and a station house that was pure rubble. The piles of shelled rock that rose up the hillside from the train station had been the center of town, a market square that for nine centuries had stood in front of the cathedral, all destroyed. No house was left with more than two walls, no shops or public works had roofs or windows. The water, electricity, and gasworks could not be found beneath the ruins. That was what General de Gaulle called it—the Capital of the Ruins, he had declared for the newsreel. He promised to rebuild the city on new ground; the inhabitants insisted on rebuilding it where it stood. It looked more like an enormous open-pit rock quarry than a city, and each morning Will trudged up the hill to the old mental hospital to watch the local doctors tell the queue of patients that they had so little medicine and implements that the government had to decide who would receive treatment.

"So, no," Fondren answered. "Nothing from Division, Will. Sorry. I think anybody who wants to go back to combat is nuts, but whoever you pissed off isn't letting you go anywhere."

The first letter was from Hoyt's parents.

Dear Will: Hoyt is back in the Army now. Well, he went back in August when his leave was up, but he was just over in Clovis where he was teaching pilots about the jungle. He came home on the bus a lot and they said in town that Shirley was after him, but we didn't see much of her, but they could have gone to the movies I guess. Anyway, last week he told us he was being sent off to sell war bonds and he didn't like it one bit. But he has an Army address so if you want to write him he is at Army Post Office 40, San Francisco, California, and you're supposed to say Military Bond Drive and /Ninth Special Unit Command Continental US. He's on a train a lot. The cotton looks real good. We heard you are better and hope you take care of yourself. And he's a sergeant!

Will smiled, a genuine, deep happy smile. Reading the letter was almost like being at the Carter farm. "You boys get those cows down to the creek," Mr. Carter would tell them; Mrs. Carter would add, "There's water in the creek, don't drown, watch for snakes." He could imagine them at the table, deciding to write a letter to the Hastings boy about Hoyt. "Tell him what Hoyt's doing." "I am." "Don't tell him about Shirley Fleming, she's just leading him on a chase." "I didn't. I'm telling him Hoyt's address." "You've got to say Military Bond Drive." The Carters finished each other's sentences; Will liked that people finished each other's sentences, people who really were married to each other.

Mr. Bradley didn't write at all; he just sent an envelope with clippings from the Lubbock paper. **Sheriff to go on trial in January** the first began. Federal officials had charged former Tierra County Sheriff Hoskins with hiding the gin engine and separators from the building in a shed out in the country, then making a mess of the fire investigation so that any signs of arson would be gone before crop insurance agents could check out the

239

scene. The price of cotton sold to the federal government went up after the loss. Will was glad to see that Hoskins might finally roast for shipping Johnny and Hoyt off to the Army. He wondered why the sheriff had burned the cotton gin down.

"You okay?" Fondren asked.

"Bad news from home. Read this." Will handed over the second clipping. **Missing doctor found near Odessa.** An oil field worker had discovered Doc Pritchard slumped over in the back seat of his Chevrolet on a lonely stretch of road, still clutching a near-empty whiskey bottle. He had been dead for a week.

"That the guy you worked for?"

"Yep. Grouchy old coot, delivered every person in the county. Told me once I'd never be any good. 'You knothead. You'll never be a surgeon because you don't think your God—you're supposed to think you can walk on water. And you'll never amount to spit with women—your fingers are too short.' Doc used to go out to the adobes where the Mexican farm workers live, and just stay out there for days at a time, delivering babies, sewing them up after knife fights, just sitting with sick people."

"Why?"

"Because they weren't supposed to come into town for things like that. He said that if any of the old ladies in town ever saw a Mexican come out of his clinic he might as well close the doors."

Fondren poured another cup of Calvados; Will declined.

The third letter was from Virginia. She had written more in the last month than she had written in the seven years after he went away, first to college, then to the war. The tone of her letters, however, had changed.

> *Dear Will: It was nice to get your letter. I'm relieved that your wound didn't amount to much but it's hard for me to understand why you want to go back to the infantry hospital if the Army says it isn't ready for you to go back. There you were in a hospital bed wounded and saying that the only thing you wanted was to be with the men who were there when you got shot. Will, I'm going to admit that I don't think I knew that side of you, even though you ran around all the time with Hoyt and Johnny, but I just took it for granted that everybody was a friend without knowing how much of a friend you were in your heart. I'm just glad you weren't with them in the war and I'm more*

glad that someone was there to take care of you. I'm not trying to make it hard on you but I don't know what I'd do if you weren't coming back.

We're doing all right and I promise not to worry you any more. Mrs. Stuart finally got to where she couldn't work as hard so we fixed up Poppy's shed and put in a wash-tub and some wringers and some hoses and we're doing laundry for people. This boy Sandy I told you about, he helps me a lot. He's here all the time looking after us and carrying the tubs of wet clothes for me and won't take a penny. And then the cotton came in pretty full so, guess what! Molly's family was short of hands and we went out to their fields and picked cotton! If Poppy was here he'd be shocked at me working like that but if Poppy was here I probably never would have learned I could do it. Will, I don't think Poppy's going to turn up. It's been a long time since any federal agents came around asking and I think they gave up too. The one thing I wished Poppy knew is that Bart has been shipped out. They put him in the marines and sent one of those To The Proud Parents of A Marine cards from San Diego and now he's on a boat going to the Pacific. Mrs. Tarlton stopped me and said, 'Hmph! Hope you're happy now!' She thinks I'm the one who turned him in and so do a lot of other people. I don't think she cares what happened to Bart—she's just had to do without a lot since Poppy disappeared, and so have a lot of other people. (I don't get everyone's laundry, that's for sure). Well, I'm going to go; I'm dead tired, but, to answer what Mrs. Tarlton said, yes, I'm happy. I don't mind doing without except for doing without you. I know you can't come home now, but you will. Take very good care of yourself and don't go back to the men until you're well. Write me.

Love, Virginia

"That her?"

"Huh?"

"The letter? That the girl back home?"

"Yeah."

"So, what are you going to do?"

"I don't know. Don't have to worry about it until time to go home. That might not ever happen."

"Smart. I was in love with a gorgeous girl once. Problem is, she knew it."

"She knew you were in love with her?"

"She knew she was gorgeous. I guarantee you, it was like dancing, the whole time we were going out she was looking over my shoulder to see if someone better was coming up behind me."

"What happened?"

"She ditched me. Well, not really. Okay, she did, I guess so. She caught me with a girl who wasn't half as good looking and that was that. She was pretty pissed off, I can tell you that."

"So what happened?"

"I married her."

"I thought she quit you."

"Not her, the other one."

"Captain Hastings?" Someone outside the tent called through the canvas. The silhouette of a soldier could be seen from the inside. "Are you in there, sir?"

"Yes. Major Fondren's with me. Who's there?"

"Orderly, sir. Jenkins. There's some people up at the gate. They're asking for a doctor. I told them we don't treat civilians."

"So, what's the problem? Except that we don't treat the civilians?"

"Well, they said it was urgent and the hospital was closed."

"The hospital isn't closed, Jenkins. It's destroyed. Everybody who needs to see a doctor lines up in front of the mental hospital all day. Tell them that." Will sat on the bunk, tired of the charade of sitting in front of the mental hospital all day, watching the French authorities tell the French doctors who among the patients would be treated and who would be sent away. Fondren had been clear about one thing—CA did not treat civilians.

"They know that, sir. They just want somebody to tell them how to treat somebody. Can you do that?"

"I don't know." Will turned to Fondren. "What do you think that's all about? They know we can't lay a hand on them, so they want us to tell them how to lay a hand on themselves?"

"You go out there, Will, and we might as well let them line up right inside here instead of at the crazy house. That's why we make them go there."

"They've got the interpreter with them, sir, from the hospital." The orderly had done his job; that was clear. "He says he wouldn't bother you but they seemed to know you, sir."

Will ignored Fondren's inquiring look and did his best to appear nonchalant as he stood up, tucked in his blouse, and put his helmet on, then slipped out of the tent before Fondren could argue about it. The orderly followed him back to the wire gate at the front of the garrison. Will was looking for her long before he could make out the shapes in the fast-falling twilight. When he saw only Genet and the priest he had to hide his disappointment.

"Sir," the interpreter began, "it seems that this is a matter that is between..."

"*Bonsoir, Docteur Genet,*" Will volunteered. "*Monsieur le Curé. Comment-allez vous?*"

"My goodness, Captain, I didn't know that you spoke French."

"I don't. That was about all I know. I thought I should try."

"*My goodness! Is it you? We thought....*"

Genet and the priest broke off speaking to the interpreter or anyone else, then huddled for a few moments before resuming. The translator was suspicious.

"Do you know these men, Captain?"

"I do. They were pillars of the community in Ste. Marie, when the Germans were there and then when the fighting went through there." He hoped the translator would repeat it to Genet, but he did not. "Very good men. I'm glad to see that they are well." The translator missed that softball as well. Instead, he asked the two what they wanted so badly that they had to bother the Americans after dark. The priest took charge, to Genet's relief, and the translator repeated:

"Good evening, sir. We're very sorry to... it's like this. It's this boy. He needs surgery. My friend, Genet here, says he can't do it." The interpreter explained to Will what the priest told him.

"I'm afraid that I'm not permitted to do surgery either, Doctor," Will said. "Have you told him that? The most they allow me to do is watch the doctors here. What kind of surgery?"

"It's for his ear, Captain. What did you call it, Docteur? Mastoid. It's infected. He doesn't have the tools."

Will had wondered how long it would take for Genet to question his treasure; the answer was less than a week.

"Does he have any tools? For surgery? A speculum, and perhaps a small retractor? Something to nibble at the bone. Nibble is to take a small bite. Nibble."

The translator had to work at the words; the daytime queue was filled with broken bones, a few pregnant women, endless consequences of malnutrition and chest complaints, but no one brought their children to the

243

mental hospital for an ear infection. The translator was surprised when Genet answered that, yes, he had some tools for surgery.

"But he hesitated, Captain, when he tried to describe them. It was like he didn't exactly know all of them. Like they were unfamiliar. I don't think you should...."

"Is it all right if I take a look at the boy? Or maybe he would show us the examination he has done."

They tried to examine Paul first by the headlights of a jeep, then on a table in the orderly tent. The child suffered greatly, Will a bit more. Father Jean prayed; Genet tried to make himself look invisible.

"He's infected, Doctor, no question about it. If you had the right things, surgery wouldn't be such a good idea. Tell him." The interpreter translated it to Genet; the priest responded.

"It is one of the two choices, Captain. Hurt the boy with surgery, or not. The Church will not blame anyone."

"Tell the priest that isn't what I meant. Try to explain this to the doctor, please. Exactly as I say it." He paused while the interpreter did so. "If it was my patient and if I had penicillin—tell him." He paused again. "If I had penicillin, I would try that instead. Ask him if he has ever used penicillin."

Genet had not. There was no penicillin in France before the war; any that made its way into the country afterward, from Switzerland or Spain or Sweden, was exclusively for the Germans.

"I would use a syringe to put 80,000 units of penicillin in the boy's arm muscle two times a day for at least three days. Tell him that."

"Why? He doesn't have any penicillin. If you were going to give some, it would have to be approved by the authorities."

"I know. The doctors at the mental hospital ask me if I have some medicine, some penicillin or something, for someone. If it's something CA says we can let them have, then whoever is in charge tells the doctor whether the patient is high enough on some list to get the medicine. If the patient's a prefect, he gets it. If he's Resistance, he gets it. The wife of the prefect and the wife of the Resistance, they get the medicine. But, if he's a *plouc*, he doesn't get a damned thing. *Ploucs* sure don't get penicillin, not from them. I'm not blind."

"Where did you learn *plouc*?"

"Eighty thousand units. That's about fifty milligrams. In the muscle. Twice a day for at least three days. Tell him."

244

The translator did so. They waited for ten minutes while Will left and returned, Fondren in one hand, a box in the other.

"We can't give you any of this unless the prefect approves, Doctor. Come back tomorrow and ask for approval. But this is what it looks like." Will opened a small, well-sealed box labeled 'Warning: Perishable Medicine. Use before___.' He took out a smaller carton and opened it; inside were a dozen glass bottles with rubber stoppers. A wooden box with a clasp contained a glass syringe with measurements from twenty to one hundred milligrams and two needle sets to screw into the base. Will removed the glass syringe and pointed to the line that indicated 50 mg. "Fifty. Twice a day." Then, if that didn't seem to be helping the patient, maybe think about surgery. The doctor should bring the child to the mental hospital to see about it. It's a bad infection. Do you understand?"

It was understood. Genet only, perhaps the priest, understood everything, but Fondren and the interpreter, even the orderly, suspected there was more to the story.

"Tell me, Will, just how well do you know these people?"

"Pretty well. We were there more than a week. The doctor showed me about fishing. That was before they had to drain the river. And the priest, he took me to the churchyard one day. He had taken care of the burial of some British pilots shot by the Germans. They went out of their way to come to the field hospital every day, see if we needed anything. Like the Calvados we were drinking in my tent. Their Calvados. When they came up."

"Don't get all preachy on me. If there's something I need to know, I don't want to know it. For Christ's sake, Will, the last thing you want in your personnel file is something about, I don't know, the natives, whatever."

"Got it. If there's something you need to know about me and the natives, I'll make sure you don't know it."

"Thanks. Carry on." Fondren was sure enough of what he didn't want to know that he decided to go back to his own tent. Dealing with the French was hard at best, impossible when he actually knew some of them.

Genet carried on, too.

"You look skinny, Captain. Are you well?"

"I was wounded. At a chateau across the river."

"I think I heard something about it. It seems you are recovering."

"I am. How are... my friends? Are they at home? In Ste. Marie?"

"Your friends?" The priest was not aware that anyone, even the mayor, had so much as spoken to the Americans more than once or twice. "The laundry women? They're fine."

"No, not them. I seem to remember two *particular* friends. Doctor?" Will wondered how much the priest knew, and suspected not much. He wondered how much Genet knew, and suspected that Genet was keeping it to himself. "They came back and forth to the field hospital. I did something for a relative, I think."

Genet also studied the priest. He had been afraid to come to St. Lô in the first place but it had turned out well, not badly. He didn't want to cause a reversal of fortune at this point, and measured his words.

"They are not at home. I spoke with them, it has been a long time ago now, and they said the war had come too close and were going to leave."

I know that, he thought. *There's no one there. Not even the cows and the ducks. It looks like a farm that the Germans shot up from the hilltop and then the Army combed over the barns and walls and house for every bullet case and scrap of army material they could find and then like someone else took every living thing and put it on farm wagons and left. There was no one home. Fondren doesn't want to know about that.*

"Well, if you hear from them, tell them I hope they found some place away from the war. A safe place."

"I will, Captain." Genet stopped for a moment and did some mental calculations. The priest was stupid; he could handle the priest. The translator was not stupid, but he seemed to be willing to act as an intermediary for more than just a medicine consultation. In the end, he concluded that Will had taken a chance; he would take a chance. "They said you would know where they are."

Will didn't answer that. Genet didn't know where they were and he didn't know why Will would know. *How much English does that girl speak?* he wondered. *And when did she speak it? It was only a couple of days.*

Will hadn't replied but the priest did. "Who are you talking about, Genet? I know everyone in Ste. Marie and where they've gone. Who does he want to see? I'll know where they are."

For the last time, that day at least, Genet decided to take a chance.

"My sister, Padre. The Duprés."

"They don't live in Ste. Marie. She left to marry Dupré, I don't know, it must be thirty years now. It's your mind, Genet. You're not just getting

246

deaf; you're losing your memory, too."

"That's it, Father. That's it, exactly. Thank you, Captain. I will bring the boy tomorrow." He knew, Will knew, that it was a lie for the benefit of the translator; the priest didn't know but he wasn't paying attention. Father Jean was trying to sort out how often it seemed that Genet was forgetting things these days. "And if you have a chance to fish a little, you know where to come."

"I do, Doctor. I do. You're welcome."

It was not until the tired Citroen neared Ste. Marie that the priest sorted it out.

"Genet? It wasn't your sister he wanted to see. It was...."

"Yes, you old goat. Hush."

"He was asking about...."

"Don't talk about it. Better we don't have anything to say about it."

"And the box? Is that why you have the Number Two Field Medical?"

"I don't think so, Father. That, I think, came from God. Better we don't question God, don't you think?"

"But if we don't know where they are," the priest worried, "why did you tell the American he would know where they are?"

Fondren had gone, but not quietly. He was not in Will's tent, but Will found what he had left on the rolled blanket pillow. There was the letter Virginia had written and, with it, the picture of her and Peter that Will had tacked to the tent pole. A foot or two away on Will's bedroll, in the direction of the tent flap, he had placed a drawing taken out of Will's sketchpad. The girl was not beautiful, a bit plain even to someone who didn't know how to look at her, solid, and with a full mouth, high cheek bones, and clear eyes. They had talked about the drawing before and Fondren had said what he liked about it.

"How'd you learn to draw like this? I like this one, not like some girl you just want to go play around with." Will had drawn her looking directly at him, eyes calmly gazing at him, a very slight smile that could have been bashful, or tentative, or ready. "Plain pretty, you know, not a knockout, but like there'll be something there after the looks are gone."

Fondren had left a note, too: "There's a war on, Will."

Will cleared the papers off the bunk and sat on it, thinking what to do, then making a decision. They had not been able to say a lot of words to each other, but he was pretty sure they had an understanding. It didn't matter that he didn't know exactly where she was; Genet had told him where to look.

CHAPTER TWENTY-THREE

"Âllo?" The boy was probably thirteen or fourteen, still young enough to have a clean face and thick hair, but old enough to wear someone else's grown up pants and sweater. He tapped on the window and called out again. "Âllo? Anyone there?" He held a switch in his hand, flicking it back and forth against the ground. He had tied one of the cows to a broken cart wheel near the path that led to the cottage. "Monsieur Martel? Are you there?"

Jean-Claude peeked out through the curtain, saw it was only the boy, and opened the door just wide enough to peer outside. From the doorway he had a clear view of the lane beyond the jumbled yard and up to the road that led to Carentan. The groves of trees opposite, those that had survived the fighting, stood at the edge of the marshland, the bases of their trunks still under water from the ruptured dikes. It was there that Jean-Claude peered most carefully, looking for someone who might be hiding in the trees. There wasn't anyone. It was safe, but the habit had kept him safe from the Germans and he would keep the habit now.

"Are the cows all right? Something the matter?"

"No, the cows are fine. Both of them. I drove them to the asparagus meadow and they grazed where the goats hadn't been grazing. The goats eat everything. They eat the grass, they eat the milkweed, they eat the tin cans from..."

"Why did you bring the cow?"

"I was through milking the other one."

"Why didn't you bring both of them? Or milk this one and...." It was exasperating to talk to the boy. He might have been retarded or, probably, just a plouc, a farm boy. "Why are you here? That's what I'm trying to get you to tell me."

"Oh, because I was milking this one. Well, I wasn't. I was just starting to milk this one and I had taken the other one back to the asparagus meadow and brought this one in and he said to me, 'Ay, dere, bone jure.' Just like that. I didn't understand him and so he said it again and...."

"Who?" The hair on Jean-Claude's neck stood straight up. "Who said it? Who are you talking about? Did he follow you?" He ducked back into the cabin, instinctively checking to see if the back door was open and that his Garand was leaning against the window frame.

"The American. He said, 'Ay, dere, bon jure.' and I said, "Bonjour, Monsieur,' and he said, Oo aye... and then I didn't understand the rest because he was an American. So I said, 'I don't know' and 'not here' and 'nobody here with that name.' Just like you told me." He held out his hand, palm up. Jean-Claude ignored him.

"This was in the asparagus meadow?" It was. "How long ago?" The boy didn't have a watch; no one did. The Germans had their watches. He thought it was fifteen minutes ago; he had left the milked cow in the asparagus pasture and gone back to the barn and taken this cow out of the stall and walked all the way over here through the trees, like Jean-Claude had told him, not by the lane, and he had stopped once because he saw a rabbit, but couldn't catch it, so came to the cabin, like he said. "What kind of American was he? Was there just one or were there a lot of them? Were they in a jeep? Or a truck? Did you look at the helmet, or the armband? Specifically, did his armband say 'M.P.?'"

"I didn't really see it—I was kind of afraid to go up close. I don't know if there was anybody else. You know how that asparagus pasture has that old cistern back there by the road? He might have left 'em back there."

Jean-Claude gave the boy a franc. It was an old one, but the boy didn't seem to care and left, pausing to let the cow bellow at him for want of milking, then disappeared back through the edge of the marsh and into the trees. When he was out of sight, Jean-Claude climbed up the attic ladder, draped the blanket over the opening, and climbed back down. He pulled the ladder away and took it out the back door, then fetched the rifle and locked the cabin.

It took five minutes for him to slip across the marsh and over the still-submerged dike to the woods, then another five minutes to glide quietly to the edge of the asparagus meadow. It was not, in fact, an asparagus meadow. It was part of the old Bois de Perce estate that had been treated as commons for a hundred and fifty years, a place where any boy could graze his animals if he was willing to risk being set upon by the Perce spirits that were said to haunt the unsettling dank fog that hovered over the wet grass below the level of the marsh. Few did.

The asparagus, called Rommel's Asparagus, were the thick tree trunks that had been chopped down, stripped of branches, and stuck on end in this meadow and others all around Carentan to puncture any Allied planes or gliders that attempted to land there. Only one glider had crashed there, and little of it remained. There were not any Americans in the meadow, not where Jean-Claude could see them. He edged around the tree line that bordered the meadow to get a better view of the barn and cistern beyond.

His network had bicycled hidden messages and Molotov cocktails past the Germans. It had not dissolved when the Germans were pushed out, nor had all the people it had hidden come out in the open. It was still intact in late October when the postmaster at Pont Hébert had told the priest at Carentan, who had told the baker in Montmartain, who had told the farmer in La Planque, who had reported to Jean-Claude that a dozen or more military policemen had arrived to swarm over Château Dupré.

The men who had picked its apple orchard, in the name of the regional cooperative, had told the Americans that, no, the place had been empty since the Germans had attacked some soldiers there—everyone was dead. The American in charge, a major, had followed his soldiers around for days, digging bullets out of walls, trees, and rafters. The neighbors had watched the Americans collect a sack of rusted shell casings, a few pock-marked apple tree branches and window frames, and the carcass of what turned out to be nothing more than a stinking hare. They drove away in a thick cloud of dust, leaving the gates ajar to hang on their hinges and the house open to the elements. Wind and rain blew in through the windows to soak the rugs and furniture. Animals had gotten at what was in the cellar. The watchers reported that, if anything, by the time the Americans in October had left the place it was more destroyed than when the Germans had attacked. Jean-Claude thanked them.

Still, the watchers who tended the jail in Cherbourg passed word that the one American soldier was still in custody under American guards. Jean-Claude had decided it was too soon to relax.

He moved quietly from tree to tree, always looking at the meadow to see if anyone walked into it. He didn't expect anyone; more than a half-hour must have passed since the cowherd had seen the American. He crept around to the far side of the meadow to see the milk shed where, apparently, the soldier had appeared.

"Hello *bonjour*," someone said behind him. Jean-Claude jumped, turned, and gripped the Garand in a single motion, startled that he had not heard anyone in the trees and more startled that when he stopped spinning he was aiming his rifle at an American soldier who stood not five feet away.

"*What do you want?*" Jean-Claude answered. "*You startled me.*" He lowered the Garand but did not relax his grip.

"*Excusez-moi.* I don't speak French very well. *Je ne parle pas...*" He held his hands at chest-level. "*Je cherch, search-ay,....*"

"No English. No Germans." Jean-Claude brusquely shook his head, his heart pounding. He hoped the American wouldn't try anything, then realized the soldier was not armed.

"I'm not looking for English, or Germans."

"What you look?"

"French people. A family."

"No here. No this place. Go wit' me."

Jean-Claude led him all the way to Carentan and found the priest, who left them at the walls of the church, then returned with the school teacher, who had been their translator.

"Yes, I speak a bit of English. Who are the French people? Is that right, you are looking for French people? Who are they?"

"I'm looking for a family named Dupré."

"Dupré? I don't think so. There isn't a family of that name in Carentan. A moment, please. Let me ask the priest." He spoke in rapid-fire French to the priest, who nodded, then shook his head. "No, the priest says there is not a family Dupré. Sorry."

"They come from near Pont Hébert. Their farm was attacked in August."

The school teacher made a show of asking the priest, then Jean-Claude, and then the telegraph operator who had arrived.

"No, no one has come here from Pont Hébert. Is it possible you mean Deschamps? Or Duplain? There is a family Duplain who farm on the road to Isigny." The school teacher turned again to explain himself to the priest and the telegraph operator; they nodded, shrugged, agreed.

"No, thanks. It's Dupré."

"My regrets, sir. But I've been a teacher here for twenty years. Carentan isn't so big that a family could come here, even now, and we wouldn't know them." They shook hands, and the American walked away from Carentan.

Fifteen minutes after that, the cowherd found them, still at the porch of the church. He reported that the American had taken the path that ran alongside the canal, and continued until he was out of sight. Shortly after, an acolyte who lived on a farm near Rougeville arrived for evening mass; he reported that an American had left the canal path and gotten into a jeep, then had driven away. They waited until evening fell before Jean-Claude returned to the cabin.

Will was already there.

"You. Go. *Allez!* Go!"

"*Cousin, is that how you greet a guest?*" Madame Dupré had been behind the door; she now loomed out into the room. "*Where are your manners? Put that gun down.*"

"*What is he doing here, Cousin? I spent the afternoon sending him away!*" Jean-Claude clenched his teeth and his fists. "*Do you think I hid you here so that anyone who asks a few stupid shepherds if they want some chewing gum can follow them to my house? You're crazy.*"

"*We didn't ask him here, Jean-Claude. He knocked on the door and we could see him from the vent window, standing in the yard. We thought he was dead.*"

Will stood at the door, listening, understanding almost not a word of the exchange but understanding clearly that Jean-Claude had not been happy to be outsmarted. He didn't care. *What can he do to me that's worse than getting shot in the back?*

"I came to thank you."

"Not understand." Jean-Claude would not let Mrs. Dupré speak directly to Will. The ladder groaned; Mr. Dupré appeared. "*Merci pour quoi?*"

"They took care of me. When I was shot." He thought it unlikely that Jean-Claude would know the story or understand the English, so he carefully unbuttoned his army jacket, then his shirt, and opened them to show the scar in his chest. "They..." And he pointed at the Dupré husband and wife, certain they would not deny it. They didn't.

"*Vous n'êst pas mort. Nous croyions que vous étiez mort.*" You're not dead. We thought you were dead.

"No, not mort. Not dead."

He shook their hands and made to leave, but stopped. He could feel Jean-Claude bristling behind him. Mr. and Mrs. Dupré seemed somewhat bewildered but he sensed that it would be a mistake to come to the point directly. "I came to thank Géraldine. And Claudine." He waited a moment, then attempted with his fractured skill: "Mercier a Géraldine et Claudine. Pour this." If they had noticed that he had raised his voice, they didn't show it. "*Ici?* Geraldine o Claudine? *Ici?*"

"Non." Jean-Claude answered too quickly.

"Where? Oo aye?"

"Not here. To church."

That seemed unlikely; he had been at the church when Jean-Claude had walked him to the town and held him somewhat under guard with the priest and others for a half-hour trying to persuade him that no one in Carentan had ever heard of anyone named Dupré. He didn't believe she was in the church. He was pretty sure she was in the attic.

"To church. Bien. Good. Tell them I was here. I go to make a hospital." He waited a moment to let the word sink in. "A hospital." Their expressions showed a bit of comprehension; the words were similar in English and French. "At the monastery. Le *monastère*. I will be at the monastère." He had studied for this possibility, and hoped he had got it right. He said, again, loudly, slowly, "I will be at the monastery every day." He then repeated it in purposely-mangled French, in his best stage voice: "*Je vais attendre au monastère.*"

They smiled, they said they were pleased he was not dead, and said *au revoir.*

He left.

CHAPTER TWENTY-FOUR

The only time Major Popper, of the Twenty-ninth Division Medical Office, and Major Leatherman, of the Fourth Division Judge Advocate General Office, had occasion to meet each other was in Paris. General Blakeley's aide told them to sit on the wooden bench in the hallway and wait: "The general said for you two to settle it. If one of you makes him take five minutes to fuck with this, heads'll roll."

"Look, Leatherman—I don't care what you believe. We've let you keep the guy for four months. We want him back."

"Not until someone answers a lot more questions about that shootout, Popper. He was there and, frankly, I think he's lying."

"The Twenty-ninth lost a whole platoon of battle-seasoned troops in that shootout, Major. Plus our doctor. Your division lost one guy. If Major Hampton is right, the one guy you lost is that idiot who started the shootout."

The aide came outside to tell them to keep their voices down: "The general said if you two interrupt him one more time, you're both headed for a rifle platoon."

They could hear the general better than he could hear them. The door opened and closed as a series of planning officers, supply officers, and executive officers walked in, were told what to do, and walked out.

"I want a convoy of gasoline up this road by 0500 and I want you personally to escort it all the way to Liège. And there better not be a dry gas tank in Liège by 0800. Got it?" A colonel got it, and left. "I'm not trying to replace four battalions. I'm trying to replace a thousand combat infantry we lost in two days and I don't want a thousand replacement soldiers filling up four battalions. They wouldn't last an hour. Who was the idiot who sent this? Listen—I want every platoon in this division to absorb those men equally, train them on the run, and they better not miss a beat...." Another colonel got it, saluted, and left. "Tell air support that I don't care if it's snowing at 20,000 feet and the planes are flying upside down and backwards..."

A stream of cigar smoke blew out the doorway every time someone opened it. Grizzled soldiers with handguns strapped to their waists were elbowed out of the way by clean-cut young officers with hands full of reports. There was no heating in the cold hallway. Leatherman wouldn't give up.

"Besides, Major, our doctors haven't cleared him for duty yet."

"Hastings has been on active duty as a civil affairs liaison for a month, Popper, dicking off in France, while we're swamped in Belgium. Can you hear what the general's saying in there? They're losing a thousand soldiers a day. The Twenty-ninth is down fifteen hundred men. And do you know where they take 'em, Major? Right through my hospitals. Turn the guy loose."

"No. Not until one of two things happens. Either he comes clean and tells us what really happened out there at the chateau, or we find this guy named Curtiss. If the kilroy we've got in jail in Cherbourg really is some guy named Douglas, then you find Curtiss in your outfit and we'll turn the doc over and you can have this guy with no balls to boot. Otherwise, no dice."

At almost eleven o'clock at night, the heavy oak door swung open for the last time. The aide was astounded to find the two men still there.

"Listen, for God's sake, what the hell's so important about one damned captain?"

"He wants to go back to combat duty, Colonel," Popper answered. "One of the best combat surgeons we had, a purple heart with a combat wound through his whole body, and he wants to go back to work in a field surgery. He's not even in your division."

"He's holding out on what he knows about the murder of a senior officer. That trumps your bleeding purple heart."

The colonel shook his head, drew in his breath, and walked back into the general's office. He came back out a moment later but, before he had a chance to say anything, General Blakely roared at the two waiting men himself:

"This better be good you two. I'm going to belgium in three minutes. You've got two of them. And one of you is going to regret making me give it to you."

Leatherman and Popper walked gingerly into the lair and gave the general the problem. It took him longer than three minutes, but not by much, and when he was through both of the trembling officers wished he had simply taken a sword and cut Hastings in two, giving each of them half. The general really didn't care who was right.

CHAPTER TWENTY-FIVE

"Going fishing?"

"Yes."

"Don't you think by now you should at least have a fishing rod? I mean, come on, Will, this is like when I was in high school and we'd go out behind the gym and smoke cigarettes. We smelled like Lucky Strikes and the coach could see we weren't carrying our homework around, so it was pretty hard to claim we'd been outside reading Shakespeare."

"Okay, I'm not going fishing."

"Where are you going?"

"I'm going to Martinville, then to Le Déversoir, then to Ste. Marie du Vire. They're all in the St. Lô prefecture. They were overrun by the Germans. Nobody knows what the medical situation is out in those little towns."

Fondren suspected that if anyone knew what the medical situation was in those little towns, it was Will. Will disappeared every day, usually at dark, sometimes at three or four in the morning. He had never missed a single moment of duty at the mental hospital in St. Lô, filling his days by watching the local doctors beg for medicine and supplies and the local officials tell them which patients they could treat.

"You know, Fondren, it wouldn't be so bad if they'd just let me do something, or if they'd let us give them enough medicine so they could take care of these people themselves. Can you imagine back in the States if some government guy tried to tell the doctors who they could treat and what they could prescribe? There'd be a riot. We wouldn't stand for it. But here, the doctors are under their thumb. Some guy who used to be in the resistance, now he's a 'police captain.' He says, 'See that woman? See her hair? We shaved her head for sleeping with a bosch. Send her home. That farmer, he put Germans up in his farm, send him home. This fellow, the Germans threw him in jail; give him whatever you've got.'"

"Not my orders, Will. I'm trying to get the gas works running and figure out how to get the water supply cleaned up. My job is to keep them from freezing and starving this winter. Yours is to tell us if there's an epidemic."

"I'm through with today's epidemic in St. Lô. I'm going to go see if there's an epidemic in the countryside. If that's okay."

It was twilight by the time the jeep lurched to a halt in front of Genet's house. He knocked on the door; Genet answered.

"Bonsoir, Doctor. How's the little boy?"

They joked for ten minutes, long enough for Genet to figure out that Will wanted to know if Paul was still alive. Paul had spent the afternoon kicking a soccer football with the other kids. It was also long enough for Will to be sure that the priest and everyone else in the village saw the jeep and could prove that he was there at the doctor's office. He left by the back door.

In the dark he could not make out the ducks until he startled them, then saw the splashes as they jumped one by one off the wring shelf and into the slow-moving water. The rowboat was tied to the downstream end of the laundry shed. He gently drew in the docking line and eased himself into the craft, then released the rope and let the current carry him to midstream. He crossed the river with only a dozen strokes of the flat oars.

The monastery was quiet. He passed through the arched entryway and walked along the columns to the courtyard. She was sitting on a stone bench, facing the garden, her head covered by a shawl. She turned as he neared her, stood, and took his arm in her hand, then held him.

"I t'ot you dead," she said. "I don't know you living." She touched his face, brushed his hair away from the corner of his helmet. He took the helmet off and let it drop to the ground. "Dey take us away. I tink you not to live."

"I had to find you," he said. "You saved me. I couldn't just let you go away."

A scant bit of light from a hazy moon glowed through the arches, enough that he could see tears streaming down from her eyes. He brushed them against her scarf, then pushed it away from her head. It was the first time, he realized, that he had seen her hair without a scarf or a shawl; it was thick, cut short, not like he had imagined. Not like Virginia's hair. Géraldine reached her face up to his. They remembered the last time they had been in the monastery, before the attack.

They had slept together but that is all they had done. On his second day at Château Dupré Will had gone to count the number of rooms in the monastery, to measure the size of the chapel and the church, to make sketches for his report. He had found Géraldine waiting for him near the kitchens, in a small room that probably had been the cook's quarters. They had talked, not speaking each other's language well, but enough to know that they enjoyed being together. "My friends Hoyt and Johnny, we went everywhere together. There was this guy named Bart, and he made fruit brandy that's a lot like Calvados, and we used to sit out by the cemetery on weekends and drink it and think we were on top of the world." "My mother's family was from Ste. Marie but my father's family has always been here. The Duprés gave the monastery to the church. That was centuries ago. The Germans took some of the monks. I come here to be alone."

It hadn't mattered what they said or whether they had understood each other; couples rarely do, at first. They were becoming familiar.

On the third day she had brought a pannier to the monastery. They had eaten together, for the first time. She showed him how to take the strong cheese, not in slices or chunks but in small bits, on a piece of thick bread, with a bit of the plonk wine. He told her that back home the Hamiltons cooked a lot of okra, and green beans when they had some. She understood the word cotton. He understood that she had a cousin, not a close cousin, but a cousin, named Jean-Claude, but he hadn't understood that it was a man's name.

On the fourth day they had talked, and eaten, and fallen asleep with full stomachs, when Antsley had found them.

"Sir, you've got to come. Hurry. You've got to come."

That had been the end of their beginning. That had been months before, and now they were going to begin again.

She reached her face up to him and he bent his to her, and they kissed each other, an exploration, a cautious kiss, neither of them certain it was what the other wanted. It was. Then it became something more serious. He lifted his right hand over her shoulder, his left hand beneath her arm, and drew her to him by instinct, and she opened her mouth to him. Her arms found their way around him; she smiled because he moaned when she spread her fingers across his back and pressed them, each of them apart, into his skin. He put his fingers deep into her thick hair, touched her head beneath, gently, but with purpose.

She slipped her hand inside his jacket, and inside his shirt.

"I hear you," she said. "Is right say, I hear you? In de house."

"I knew you were there," he answered. "I didn't know if you could hear me, but I knew you were there."

"I hear you, when you dere."

Jean-Claude had heard as well. He had locked them in the attic for the next three nights. It was not Géraldine, nor Mr. Dupré, nor even Claudine who engineered her departure; it was Madame Dupré.

"*Jean-Claude, put up the ladder.*" Madame Dupré had waited for him, but after five minutes, she had yelled down at him below. "*Jean-Claude, put up the ladder!*" He had refused.

"*You have a chamber pot.*"

"*You left it outside. I'm coming down.*" Madame Dupré had begun to climb out of the attic door and dangle her ankles in the air above the tiny living room. Jean-Claude yelled at her to wait. He went out to get the ladder and the chamber pot. When he returned, Géraldine was gone. He did not discover the ruse until morning.

"I tink he trow dem out. When he know."

"Why?"

She didn't answer. She took his hand in her hand and drew him back down to sit beside her.

"Will Hastings, what you want?"

"To do?"

"Wit' me. What you want wit' me, Will Hastings?"

Someone had finally asked him what he had not asked himself. He was afraid to answer, not because of him, or her, but because when morning came he still would be in France, in the Army, and he didn't know where that would end.

"I want to be with you. That's all. I just want to be with you."

"Why?"

He had hoped she would ask him, *what does he mean, to be with her?*, or *where?* or even, *for how long?* He could have answered those questions. He had to think about why.

"You went to St. Lô, for Claudine. You brought her back, and your

261

aunt, and even some more people." It took him a number of tries before she understood what he was saying. He continued. "They were your family, and you were willing to walk through a war to take care of them. That's what I was trying to do."

It had come to him in the hospital. He had loved Peter enough to go AWOL in a combat zone to look for him. She had gone through the German lines to find her sister and her aunt and bring them home.

"You love your family. Your family loves you."

"Is *normale*."

"It's normal if you have a family. I don't have one." That was all he said.

She took him by the hand again and held it, smiling, turning to face him and smiling again. The next time she kissed him it was not so much tender as full and passionate.

"No here," she said.

She led him out of the monastery and up the hill toward the chateau. The back gate, the postern port that led from the meadow into the front court, had been left ajar and she led him through it. The chateau itself, the Dupré home, was empty and open, the shutters and windows still broken from the battle. She led him, not to the front porch and through the main door but, instead, around to the kitchen door. He had not been in the kitchen before and expected that when she led him across the stone floor through the next door they would pass into a dining room; instead, the door led to a small back stairway he had not seen before. Then, instead of leading him up to the floor above, she led him down.

The room, a servant's chamber in more prosperous times, was small, space only for a small bed, a chair and stand, a tired armoire. It was clean. The bed was made, the linens fresh. There were towels on the chair.

It was dark in the room. There were no windows, no lamp, nothing more than the scant moonlight in the stairway.

He felt her take away the shawl and lift her faded sweater over her head, drop it to the floor. There was nothing beneath her cotton shift. She took the straps off her shoulder and lifted it, too, away from her.

"Don't hurt me, Will Hastings." She said it softly, not in a whisper, more of a plea. "I never do dis before. But now I do." She was not afraid that he would hurt her in making love; she was afraid he would hurt her by taking her, then not keeping her. He did not know what she had given up for him.

"I won't hurt you, Géraldine." For a fleeting instant, less than a second, he remembered the quarry, how near it had come. "I never have done this, either. I don't think I knew it, but I waited, too. To find you. I won't hurt you."

"Not ever, Will Hastings."

"Not ever, Géraldine."

It did hurt, both of them, just a little, but they found their way, and it was what they had waited for.

They woke at four in the morning.

"Shhh." She put her finger on his lips, sat up to listen. He listened.

"What?" He whispered. He was very good at listening for trouble, in the dark, in the strange French countryside. He heard nothing. They lay back down, together, and began to discover something only imagined, the sense of finding themselves entwined, naked, in the dark, seeing by touching.

She explored him, placing her open hand against his neck, touching the scars on his back and his chest, gently, tracing the curve of his body and his hips. He was afraid of touching her, despite her strong, compact body, but she took his hand and led him to trace her in the same way, gently, but with purpose, without reluctance. What he had learned in clinics, soldiers' stories in barracks, none of it had prepared him for such intimacy, no more than girls' whispers at St. Agatha's or the breeding of livestock had prepared her. She put his open hand against her, and she kissed him again, below his ear, against his neck, then turned to take him to her.

"What do you want, Géraldine? What do you want to do with me?"

"*Tout.* Evert'ing, Will Hastings." She wanted to say it more clearly, but people rarely can. "*Toujours.* Be wit' you, Will, *toujours.*"

"You won't leave me?"

"No."

"I won't leave you. The Army will take me, but when it does, I'll come back. I won't leave you."

They would sort out the rest when they had to.

Will slipped out of the bed before the sun was up, to return to St. Lô before the line of patients formed at Bon Sauveur. He returned in the night, leaving the jeep at Ste. Marie du Vire, rowing across the river from the laundry shed.

They learned some French, some English, not much. She asked him about Texas; he told her what he knew. He asked about France; she told him about the farm, of having been sent away to St. Lô, for school, of cousins near Cherbourg and Caen. Hers was not the France of Paris or fashion, nor his the America of Broadway or Hollywood. It was what they knew. Each wanted more.

They were together only a week.

CHAPTER TWENTY-SIX

Major Leatherman couldn't help himself. He was a lawyer, not a soldier. He did not grasp that General Blakely was running a war, not a courthouse. Wars require soldiers, not trials. He used his one minute to try to persuade the general that the next trial would come out right.

"..., and shot Major Halliburton in the back of the head... the entire platoon, that's right..., ... says he's not... Another doc, yes, sir... can't say... back to their units pending."

"Shut up, Major. Let me read this." The General made a show of reading the division judge advocate's report of the trial. "Is this true, you already sent the court martial officers back to their units, 'pending resumption of the proceedings?'"

"Yes, sir. The presiding officer told them at the recess that if the medical test came back, well, if there was a question of identification, he would recommend charges be dismissed. So when the test came back, they were sent back to their units. But that was before we learned that apparently this Captain Hastings knew the man back in England during training."

Major Popper was no fool. He wanted to point out to the General that, according to what he had been told of the court martial, Captain Hastings had to have known the soldier on trial back in Shrivenham—how else would he have known that Douglas had whatever he called it? But Popper was a soldier and he had faith in generals. General Blakely's facts were fuzzy but his decision wasn't.

"Tell me, Leatherman—do you believe in God?" Pause. "You, Popper? How about you? Well, good. I do too. Now, listen to me. I don't know if this soldier shot this medico or not. If he did, someone might give him a medal for stopping that sonofabitch before he got a whole company killed, a whole battalion. I never heard of a doctor taking over a goddamned infantry platoon and starting a battle it couldn't win and in this case didn't win. If the Lieutenant had survived this thing I would have made him bring that goddamned major up here and we would have shot him together. But he didn't. So, does that mean a private can go around shooting officers? Hell no, of course not. But Jesus Christ, Leatherman, you can't even prove it was the same man. And now you want to go after this other doctor who was a genuine goddamned hero with a bullet through his chest and laying there on the floor bleeding and the only suspicion you have is he told you some crazy thing about this guy's balls and it turns out to be true? This doctor who got shot, he set records in this theater for saving men on the operating table, and you want to go after him because he seemed to know too much?" The general glared at them, both of them, but Leatherman knew he had got the worst of it. "Well, let me tell you what, both of you. You said you believe in God and so do I. So we're going to let God sort this out. I'm not pulling another half dozen officers away from killing Germans for a couple of days to decide whether you can shoot a couple of damned fine Americans. This thing is over. Now, I don't know who this private is but you stick his ass in a uniform and if he's the man you think he is, balls or no, he'll do just fine marching along behind Patton's tanks with a BAR on his arm. You get his ass on a truck headed to Belgium tonight. Am I clear? And this Captain Hastings—he says he just wants to go back to his field hospital, by God, you get him on a truck back to his own unit tomorrow, you hear?"

The general paused to stare at his aide, then nodded at him, and the aide began to handwrite a couple of lines on a personnel form. The aide handed it to the General. The General signed it.

"God's going to fix this. We're getting clobbered in the Ardennes. It's a long way to Berlin and it's going to be a cold winter. Here—you get that doc's butt back to work; there's going to be some more damn fine men for him to save on an operating table somewhere. And if he or that guy with no balls had something to do with killing that sorry damned major, let God punish them. There's damned sure enough bullets flying around for Him to do it. Get out of here."

Leatherman slinked out, holding a carbon copy of an order transferring Douglas to General Patton's Third Army infantry replacement pool. Popper saluted, then left, gripping the order transferring Will back to the 261st of the Twenty-ninth immediately.

The General did not leave, not that moment. He instead turned to the aide and said, "Fix their records, you hear? I'll be God damned if I'm going to let something like this fuck up the reputation of my unit, you hear? "

Blakely's aide had worked it out beforehand; all that remained was the typing. He stayed past midnight, entering additional notes onto the official orders that sooner or later would find their way into the two men's personnel files, Will's and Douglas's. No soldier who killed a major, even a sorry one, would spend ten minutes of this war anywhere except in the front of the front lines. No officer who helped him cover it up was going to get a chest full of medals, not for being wounded or for bravery or for anything else.

After he finished putting Will and Douglas firmly in God's hands the aide spent another half-hour composing a fit eulogy for Halliburton. When an officer in Blakely's command died in combat, his home town newspaper got a full account of the General's praise and grief, honoring the sacrifice to a greater cause, the loss of a gentleman soldier who was a casualty of the good war. The aide typed one final order, promoting Halliburton to Lieutenant Colonel with a silver star for valor, then handed the records to the headquarters clerk before going off to follow General Blakely's race to the bulge the Germans were putting in the line in Belgium.

CHAPTER TWENTY-SEVEN

———⟡———

*P*énicilline, sulfa. Penicillin, Sulfa."

"I understand."

"*Des pansements*. Bandages."

"Yes, of course. They are necessary."

"*Aiguilles de suture*. Suture needles."

"Oui. Of course."

"*Sang et plasma*. Blood and plasma. *Iodine*. "

About fifty French civilians had begun to line up before dawn. They stood, wet and shivering, in front of Bon Sauveur, the abandoned mental hospital that was St. Lô's emergency room, clinic, waiting room, and hospital. The local doctors formed a queue on the porch behind a tired wooden table where a nun wrote each person's name and malady before passing the patient forward for an examination. One-by-one the doctors turned to tell Will what they needed. In his first days in St. Lô they had believed that the Americans had sent a doctor to do what Fondren had not, help them with medical supplies. After a few weeks, they considered Will to be just another flunky.

"*Please, Captain, you must explain to the major that he has to give us stores of medical supplies; you can see for yourself that the patients who come here are critical.*"

Will turned to the translator:

"They say that they are grateful for everything you are doing."

"I'm not doing anything. The Civil Affairs officers here don't have the authority to release supplies until someone from the Division Medical Office signs an order. The division is two hundred miles from here in some Belgian forest. Until they give us an order, we can't do it."

"They know that."

"Then tell them I said they're welcome." Will wanted to tell them that they should just sneak around behind the CA garrison and cut the barbed wire some night. The medical supplies were stacked up in boxes by the fence and the guards slept soundly after drinking a bottle of Calvados.

"Please ask him whether he can inform us of exactly when we might receive penicillin."

"And disinfectant."

"And plasma."

"Tell him it's critical here in Calvados."

The translator told them he suspected that the nice young American was after a local girl and too tired to worry about the sick and afflicted. They said they had seen a girl hanging around that morning; maybe it was her.

"A bit young, don't you think?"

"Must have been pretty, before....."

The doctors shrugged. The translator shrugged.

"First patient, step up."

A boy of twelve or thirteen years was brought forward, his face bleeding. *"He was helping to clear rubble from the docks at the river. A piece of iron struck his face when a chunk of stone slipped."* The nun jotted down his name and passed him on to a second woman, who might have been a nurse or a doctor or someone who simply wanted to help. This woman rinsed a strip of cloth in Calvados, then cleaned the blood away. The child did not flinch, his eyes blinking straight ahead as the cuts were re-opened. Will observed, made a note. The next patient moved to the table.

"His skin is red and itching. He's covered with scales—do you agree, Captain?"

The translator paused so that Will could step around the nun and look. Crawling midges and mites covered the child. He agreed with the diagnosis. The child's mother was told to rub Calvados on the exposed areas until the rash disappeared. Will wondered whether the bugs would get drunk and die before unleashing typhus on the town.

A woman limped to the front of the line.

"She fell in her cellar. Her right leg seems to be swollen and she cannot turn her foot. Can you remove your shoe, Madam?" They gave her a glass of Calvados to hold her while they took her shoe off. It was obvious that the foot was broken. The nurse helped her past the table and into the Bon

Sauveur in search of a doctor who might try to set her foot without an x-ray, then splint it without a plaster cast.

The patients in line did not try to advance or give way regardless of who was more ill or injured. A woman was carried by two neighbors in the back of an ancient truck, her pregnancy coming to an obvious termination. A farmer arrived on a stretcher, dead, his arm blown off by an unexploded shell he had knocked around while clearing brush under his apple trees. A nun had injured her back while attempting to rescue a relic that was lodged in rubble near the altar at Notre Dame. All were treated with Calvados, rubbed on or, in some cases, ingested, including the party which had borne the farmer's mutilated body to the hospital in faint hope of saving his life.

Will watched it all, moving only when on occasion he was invited to look in a mouth or an ear, to tap a knee or to concur with a diagnosis. The French doctors no longer tried to conceal their resentment.

At about four in the afternoon Major Fondren lurched his jeep up the hill from the river bank and jerked to a halt in front of the hospital. By the time he was out of the jeep the doctors and nuns had left their patients and formed a line in front of the porch, all chirping and quaking in anticipation.

"*Tell him welcome back.*"

"Welcome back, Major. The doctors have been asking after you."

"*Tell him this one,*" and they inclined their heads in Will's direction, "*doesn't do anything but make notes on a clipboard.*"

"*He doesn't get his hands dirty.*"

"*He's chasing a girl.*"

Fondren's French was even worse than Will's, the Army not having required CA officers to be able to communicate with the civilians whose affairs they managed. The translator was more diplomatic:

"They welcome you back, Major, and ask if you have brought any supplies? It is even worse now than when Captain Hastings took your place."

"'Fraid not, Pierre." The translator's name was not Pierre. "Came with some orders for Captain Hastings."

"Orders? From the Division? Have they finally released the medicine?"

Fondren did not answer. Instead, he called Will to walk back to the jeep with him.

"Will, how about a toast? Good news from Division."

"What's to toast? They don't have any morphine, no ether. No sulfa.

270

No blood. They don't even have their own surgical instruments. And they think I'm the one holding out."

"Thought you'd like to toast your travel agent—your orders came through." That made Will slow down and listen. "Fun's over."

"What do you mean?"

"Fourth Division threw out the court martial. Case closed. Governor stopped the execution. Your boy's free. And you're going back to your field hospital. In Belgium." He waited for Will to say "hallelujah," or, "at last," anything to acknowledge that Will had finally got what he wanted. It didn't come.

"When?"

"You're welcome. Thought that's what you wanted." The look on Will's face did not look like someone pleased to be getting away from a bunch of angry French doctors and their untreatable patients. "You're going out of here on the next supply truck that comes through. Probably tonight. Maybe in the morning. When it rolls, you roll. So, how about that toast? A bottle of champagne? It's Calvados, of course, but I thought we'd celebrate."

"Sorry. Thanks. But I have to find someone."

"Find someone?"

"Find someone. Listen, thanks, Fondren. You're right, I got what I asked for. You came through and I appreciate it. But I figured it would be like everything else in the Army—here's your orders, hurry up and wait."

"Not this time. Took three days for your orders to get here, but they want you out on the next chassis that has a working internal combustion engine."

"I'm taking the jeep." Will didn't even ask if he could take the civil affairs jeep; he just climbed into the driver's seat and started the engine, as if he was Fondren's superior rather than the reverse. Fondren laughed, a dry, confused laugh. He wasn't stupid, just surprised.

"You're in deep, aren't you, Will? Jesus Christ, how long have you been here? A couple of weeks?"

"A couple."

"And you got in that deep? That fast? Didn't anyone tell you about playing the field? Cherché la femme? Peggy the Pin Up Girl? You're supposed to look for them, not catch them."

"Sorry, I'm going. I'll be back. List me AWOL if you want. Or just keep the truck waiting for me until I'm back."

"Tell her I said goodbye. And you will be on that truck when it rolls out of here; I don't care if it's tonight, tomorrow morning, or five minutes from now. Got it? I'm out of excuses."

"See ya."

He drove the jeep through the wreckage of Pont Hébert, then over the same roads and ruts that Captain Deere had taken in July. Will had worried all along how he would tell her goodbye. They knew that sooner or later the army would send him away; he had promised that it would be only until the end of the war, and then he would be back. When he crunched into the farmyard of Château Dupré he still was trying to compose the sentences in English and translate them into meager French.

"It's time," he would say. "The army," he would say. "Belgium, they're sending me to Belgium," he would say. And he would tell her that he loved her enough to not let himself be shot again, enough that he would come back to her immediately when the war was over. She would cry and he would hold her. At four in the morning he would pull himself apart from her, put on his dirty uniform, and touch her face. He would drive back to the camp before the sun came up. And she would know he was coming back.

It was the first time he had seen the chateau in daylight. There it all lay before him, the tidy walls ruptured, the barn crumpled where Antsley had died. Fouquet and Campbell had been killed in the caved-in bunk house not twenty yards from the spot where he stood. Even Hércule had been shot beneath the walls of the dovecote. He left the jeep in the forecourt and entered the house.

The house was empty.

The bed was ajar against the wall. The thin sheets and cover were tumbled onto the floor and the armoire had been wrenched into the middle of the room. The chair was tumbled over. The bedside table lay on its side on the floor.

He walked through every part of the house, then back into their bedroom. He took the sheets, opened them, looked at them, folded them, and lay them on the foot of the bed. He straightened the dresser and table, then got on the floor to look for any sign of her. There was none. The only evidence of her was the smell of her, in the thin slip of cloth that had covered the pillow. He put his face deeply into it, then put it inside his shirt and left the room.

The only clue was the postern gate. It was left open, swinging on its hinges. She had left that way.

He ran to the monastery but knew that she would not be there, and she was not. The boat was where they had left it last, and he rowed across the Vire.

Ste. Marie the village had done little more for the church than the field hospital had done for it. The belfry had been covered by rough boards but rain leaked down into the chancel and formed a puddle on the stone floor. A half-dozen votive candles burned in a stand near the tired, cold altar. He hoped that Father Jean, someone who might know something, would enter with his predictably aggravating timing, but the priest did not. Will waited alone until dark, hoping for some unknown sign, a message, anything, but at last he knew: she was well and truly gone.

At nine o'clock in the evening he knocked on Genet's door.

"She's gone, Doctor. *Elle n'est pas là.* Do you know where she is? *Où est-elle?* Where?"

"*I don't know, Captain. She is not here. She is not in the village.*"

"Do you know anything?" It took Will several attempts to say this and he was not sure Genet knew what he wanted. Genet did not know anything.

"Did you see anyone? At the monastery? Vu quelque personne aux monastére? Anybody?"

"*Non, Captain. Non.*" He could tell that Will was suffering, and suffered with him. "*Desolé.*"

Will sat down on Genet's floor. He put his back against the wall and faced the treatment table, the disrobing screen, the wicker creel and Genet's fine old fishing pole. He took out his sketch pad. He worked hurriedly, but methodically. As he left he gave Genet two sheets of paper.

On the first sheet he had written:

> Géraldine Dupré—I have to go to the Army, in Belgium. Géraldine, I will come back for you. I will not be killed.
>
> I tried to find you. I looked for any sign of why you were gone. If it is because you don't know how you feel about me, that's all right—I love you enough for both of us. If it is because you do not want me, tell me when I come back and then I will let you go. And if you were taken,

I will bring you home. The only thing I ask is, when I come back, tell me why you left. If you want me, I will stay here with you. Or we will go where you want to go.

My whole name is Woodrow Wilson Hastings. I was born December 9, 1919. I am an orphan. I went to the University of Texas Medical School in Galveston Texas. In 1943 the Army drafted me as a doctor. My Army serial number is 29-1919-Tx-00287. My army address is Army Post Office ETO, 29th Infantry Division, 261st Field Hospital. I will come back.—Will.

On the other sheet of paper there was a drawing. Genet recognized his niece, but not as he had ever seen her. The drawing made him wish that he was young, that just once he had traded his miserable life as a country doctor for a woman like that. Géraldine was lovely, not changed by some artist's soothing of jaw or cheek or eyes or mouth, but lovely from something Will had seen inside her. Her skin glowed, even through the pencil drawing. Her eyes were open, her lips full and inviting. It struck Genet that she had no scarf. He had never seen his niece, not since her childhood, with her head uncovered. Her thick hair blew gently away from her head, and there was no doubt that she was a woman in love.

There was no doubt that the American loved her.

Genet put the two pieces of paper inside the small wooden syringe and medicine box. It was empty now, the medicines long since removed to a more secure place. He opened the clasp and parted the halves, then laid each sheet inside. He made sure the edges were straight, the paper not crumpled or smudged. He carefully closed it, sad but also pleased that, once again, the box Will Hastings had given him held the possibility of making someone better.

CHAPTER TWENTY-EIGHT

Claudine shrugged, gallic, her startling beauty tempered by events and by months of hiding. She looked unwell, swollen, her clothes ill-fitting. She seemed miserable.

"*Âllo Monsier Capitaine.*"

"*Âllo, Claudine. Ça va?*"

The guard had called for the charge of quarters at ten o'clock at night and told him a girl was there looking for Captain Hastings. "She won't go away." The c.q. had shrugged and gone off to find Will, who had run to the gate hoping for Géraldine. He had gotten Claudine, almost unrecognizable.

"You know this girl, Captain?"

"I was on her farm. It was destroyed in an attack. Excuse us for a moment." He didn't wait but, instead, took Claudine by the arm and walked around to the side of the guard tent, then sat with her on a pile of rubble that had been stacked up along the riverbank.

"Claudine—where is Géraldine?" He paused, then made a stab in French. "*Òu est Géraldine?*"

"*Elle a été prise. À l'église.*" She looked at him; he didn't understand. She said it again. "*À l'église.*" The church.

"The church? Here? In St. Lô?" He had the wild hope that Géraldine was nearby, maybe in the ruins of the cathedral, maybe in the wrecked abbey church where months before he and Antsley and the entire division had laid out the major's body after the capture of the city. She dashed his hopes.

"*Pas ici. Pas ici à St. Lô. À l'église.*"

"Where? Where is she?"

She didn't answer him. Instead, she took from inside her jacket a wad of cloth and stuck it in his hands. He looked at it, startled, as much by its feel as by the act itself.

He knew it was her scarf. It was bundled, thick and pliable, and he knew what was inside. He gently untied one of the corners and laid it open. Hair, roughly cut hair, came out in his fingers. She had cut off her hair—why?

He felt something else. Claudine had shoved something into his hand, a piece of paper, a note. He walked a dozen steps away to the light of the guard tent, stepped inside, and opened it.

> *Will Hastings: I write this and pray I not ever give to you but if you have this, I say these things. I love you. I go, but not like to go. I not free. Toujours, Géraldine Dupré*

He read it again, his stomach rolling over, eyes fighting against the moisture. He carefully folded the note and the scarf and put them inside his jacket, then walked back outside the tent.

Claudine was gone as well.

"Did you see her, Corporal?"

"The girl, sir?"

"Yes, the girl, of course the girl. Where did she go?"

"Don't know, sir. She was there, then I looked up and she was gone. I thought she was with you."

Will peered out through the barbed wire gate of the civilian affairs camp, down the jeep trail toward the bridge that crossed the Vire, then in the other direction, along the river bank. Claudine had disappeared as easily as he himself used to do, gliding through the French night, gone before he could ask what they meant, the note, the scarf. Before he could ask why Claudine had brought them. Why her instead of Géraldine.

Why had she cut her hair?

Where is she?

"What do you want, Géraldine? What do you want to do with me?"

"Tout. Evert'ing, Will Hastings." She had wanted to say it more clearly, but people rarely can. *"Toujours. Be wit' you, Will, toujours."*

"You won't leave me?"

276

"No."

But she had.

"Ready to go, sir?" The driver, a corporal, let the truck idle in the dark. He watched Will and Fondren shake hands. Fondren helped Will toss his barracks bag into the back of the truck, then stood aside as Will climbed into the cab. They waved goodbye.

"As much as I can be. We've gotta make one stop on the way." Will waited while the driver lurched forward in the dark, drove past the officers' tents and the enlisteds' tents and all the way to the sentry at the barbed wire gate of the civil affairs garrison. The driver slowed for the gate but Will told him to turn right instead, inside the compound, and drive back along the fence. He directed the truck to the supply tents at the back of the camp. "One last thing, Corporal. Promised to get a load of supplies out tonight. Not my place to ask why."

"Me neither, sir. I's just told to pick up this officer, that's you, sir, and then high tail it back to rejoin the convoy on the road to Caen."

"Keep your lights off, no need to wake up the guys in those tents."

Will told him to halt at the medical stores. From there it was possible to see across the Vire River bridge to the vestiges of St. Lô. Notre Dame was, in the driver's words, spooky. A clouded moon was visible through the vestiges of the church's tower where, months before, artillery had knocked the bells out. Below the bell tower a stone gargoyle peered out over the remnants of flamboyant arches that had supported the cathedral roof, giving the ruined city a haunted look by moonlight. A quartermaster clerk walked out of the medical supply tent; Will handed him a requisition form.

"Don't know him myself, Private. A major. Just handed it to me and told me to bring it."

The clerk shrugged and, by the glow of a flashlight, began to load the boxes that were listed on the form. Fifteen minutes later the truck rumbled back past Will's former tent, then past Fondren's, and ground to a halt in front of the sentry at the barbed wire gate. The driver handed the sentry a chit for the supplies. The sentry neither studied the list nor counted the boxes stacked high in the back of the truck, so overloaded that it looked like they would spill off the sides and hit the ground at the slightest bounce. He glanced at the form just long enough to see an officer's signature releasing the supplies. He took a copy, gave a copy to the driver, and waved the truck out through the gate. The truck inched out onto the main road, crossed the bridge back into St. Lô, and disappeared into the night.

Must be new, the sentry said to himself. *That way just goes into St. Lô—he'll have to turn around to get to the Caen road. Damn, it's getting cold.* The sentry looked again, across the bridge and down the road in each direction. The truck wasn't coming back. There were no headlights, no one on foot, no sergeant coming around to mess with him. He pulled out a bottle of Calvados, tilted it, swallowed hard, cleared his throat, and looked again at the signature on the requisition form; it wasn't just the driver who was new. *Wonder who the hell Major Halliburton is and why he's taking all those medical supplies off in the middle of the night. Oh well, not my problem. Here's to you, Major Halliburton, whoever you are. Hope you're keeping warm.*

The sentry stuffed the requisition slip into the strong box at the barbed wire gate, then marched a few steps in each direction, looking out in the dark for anyone trying to break in to steal something, and tried to stay warm. Satisfied there was no traffic, he took another swig, then put the bottle away. It was a cold night but, as far as he was concerned, it was still better to freeze in St. Lô than be shot at in Belgium.

CHAPTER TWENTY-NINE

Will had hoped for more of a briefing but all he got was that the Germans were making some kind of push back into Belgium. Then Major Popper was called out of the room and a few minutes later a scrubbed lieutenant came in to tell him that the major regretted not being able to come back but would Captain Hastings follow him out to the jeep; a driver would take him as close to Siersdorf as they could get. Will bundled his letters and orders and hoped that the lieutenant would offer to hump his bag for him, but the boy did not. Will followed him outside to a jeep waiting across from the Pont du Fragneé.

"Hello, sir. You a new doc?" The jeep driver looked like he was fifteen years old. Will nodded. "Out to the 76th, sir? Get ready, sir. It's not like anything back in England. Mostly tents and mud. It's about ten minutes from here."

"No, I'm not assigned here, not in Liège. We're headed to the 261st, somewhere near Siersdorf."

"Nobody told me that, sir. You sure?"

Will decided not to argue. He wasn't new, he hadn't just come from training in England, and he wasn't assigned to a muddy evacuation hospital in the rear. Popper had gotten that much across to him before he was called away. Will reached inside his winter coat and fished out his letters and his orders to report to the 261st. He handed the orders to the driver and, looking across the bridge to the other side, had no doubt about the reason for the boy's alarm.

Belgium, on the east side of the Meuse, was a wreck. Someone had taken pains to shoot at the winged messengers atop the columns that lined the bridge, without success, and at the fine old buildings opposite the quay, with great success. Anyone would be scared to drive thirty miles into the war zone, but the driver would have to learn about war on his own terms; Will could not ease it for him. They drove away from the old city, toward Germany, passing through a swath of rubble, burned farms, and abandoned tanks and trucks.

The first letter was not a letter. It was from Mr. Bradley and contained no more than his usual clipping from the Lubbock newspaper. Cotton Gin Foreman Testifies Against Sheriff. The story reported that a man named Clayton had helped Sheriff Hoskins and some wetbacks take a Bessemer engine out of the cotton gin and hide it in a shed out at a quarry the night before the cotton gin burned down. Will tried to remember someone named Clayton but could not. He turned to the second letter.

> *Dear Captain Hastings: We thank you in our grief for your letter about Micah. He was a good son and he wrote many times that he was proud to be in your service. He told us you could draw but we never thought about it. The picture you made of him whittling that yo-yo up out of a piece of barrel wood is better than any picture and we are glad of it. We know you did your best.*
>
> *Matthew and Sarah Antsley*

They had been in the barn at Ste. Marie and, from behind a screen partition, Will had watched Antsley walk the dog for a dozen wounded soldiers. He had found the unfinished drawing in his barracks bag at the hospital in Carentan, and mailed it to Antsley's family.

As for Virginia's letter, his impulse was to throw it away. He remembered back in college, getting a letter from Shirley, knowing that Virginia would be mad if she knew Shirley was writing to Will behind her back. Now, when it was Virginia writing, and it was Géraldine's back, Will felt a vague unfaithfulness reading about life in Tierra as reported by a woman who, without saying so, had taken him back into the fold of her life. Even so, it was not so easy to throw away. He opened her letter.

> *The Secretary of War expresses his deep regret that your son Bart Sullivan was lost at sea aboard the S.S. Renegade in the South Pacific on November 14, 1944...*

He read it a second time, unsure whether he was supposed to be sad for the loss of the prick who had sent Hoyt and Johnny to the Japanese or sad for Virginia's loss. He could not muster sadness on either account. He unfolded her V-mail and began to read:

> Dear Will: I received this telegram for Poppy. Of course, it came from the Western Union so Arnie told everyone in Tierra right away. Three or four came to give me condolences but a lot more of them started in all over again, saying it was my fault. At first I was going to have a service for Bart but then Mrs. Tarlton yelled at me in the post office, said some very ugly things, and I decided that I had made amends for Bart for the last time. I did not tell the draft board about him. I do wish I knew how to find Poppy because he should know, even if he blames me, but I know he's never coming back.
>
> It would be better still if you were here, Will. I think I can handle anything that comes, but I don't want to handle it alone, not anymore. Will you come home to me? Please take care in all things. All my love,
>
> Virginia.

The flag on the ridgepole said '261st Field Hospital.' The clerk inside the tent, however, was not anyone Will knew. He had a haggard look on his face. A small pile of medical tags had stacked up on the wood crate desk, along with some dog tags. Medics raced in and out, ignoring both Will and the clerk. Through the tent flap he saw jeeps churning in the cold mud, leaving casualties, then turning around and going back into the forest. Will had not heard artillery fire for almost six months and was surprised that it made him jump, as if he were indeed a new doc.

"Okay, sir. Just drop your stuff anywhere. We're short-handed. I'll get you sorted out as fast as I can."

"Thanks. Is Shorty around?"

"Shorty?"

"Lieutenant Carter? Admin?"

"Not anybody here by that name. Sorry."

"Captain Garth? Captain Murphy?"

"Sorry, Captain. We're a pretty new unit. Most of us came on when they rebuilt the 261st. After Brittany." He didn't say why they had rebuilt it or what had happened in Brittany. "We're just now getting up to speed."

"I didn't know. I was with the unit in France. In Normandy." It had not occurred to him that the men might not be here; he wondered what the machinery of promotions and transfers had done to the fast and slender forward surgery unit he had been with before St. Lô. "Who's in charge?"

"Lieutenant Prior, sir. He's over at the ward tent. Said he'd fill the new docs in when he can. It's kind of busy; I guess you can hear it out there." The .88's crashing in the forest were uncomfortably close. "It's sort of like being in Hell."

The field hospital, less than a mile to the front, was a bit like Hell. Will had forgotten the constant sound of artillery fire and the whump of mortars. Now they were back, not as heavy as at Martinville or even as at Ste. Marie, but very nearby. The tree trunks around the field hospital were splintered at head level, testament to the return fire.

"Lieutenant Prior? We had a staff sergeant back in France, man named Prior."

"Yes, sir, that's him. Field commission. Unit's been under fire a lot since, when did you say were with them? With us, I mean?"

"July."

"That was a long time ago. Covered a lot of ground since then, sir."

"Are all the old docs gone? Major Popper told me that they had changed everything, but I thought he meant just moving the surgeries around, something like that. More evacuation hospitals or something.

"Don't know, sir. Maybe Major Collins can fill you in when he gets back from Charleroi. Don't know when he'll be back. If it's all right with you, Captain, can you just go on down to the ward tent? I'll keep your personnel file. The ward tent's the only one that doesn't have an ambulance in front of it. Lieutenant Prior'll get you started. There's some other new docs on board, too. You can all learn on the job."

"Thanks, Corporal. Thanks." Will left his barracks bag on the ground in front of the ammunition box that doubled as the personnel desk. He handed his orders and personnel file over to the teenager and went outside.

The air was cold, almost freezing. The mud between the headquarters tent and the ward tent had crusted on the ground to make a sea of icy ruts that was almost impossible to cross. Will pulled his winter jacket close around him and re-buttoned the collar, then shifted his field surgery bag to his left hand to ease the dull ache in his right. An ambulance passed him, bouncing back toward the Liège road, its springs sagging with the load. A jeep drove off the path in the other direction and continued toward the ward tent.

The ward tent, indeed the entire field hospital, looked like a frozen ant hill, bundled soldiers racing in and out with quiet urgency, men on litters, medics holding intravenous lines and bandages, the air filled with puffs of frost from their breathing. A round shrieked over, a high explosive, and erupted thirty yards away in the trees, sending men scrambling for cover.

It was deafening, the conflict, and no matter how hard he looked, Will could not see beyond the shattered tree trunks and into the forest. He walked on, looking up from time to time, and lowered his head into the cold wind. It was, he knew, all that stood between him and the rest of the battle.

CHAPTER THIRTY

July, 1945

The watchers at Chateau Dupré, the same men who had picked the surviving apples the previous autumn, reported to Jean-Claude that the American had walked around the chateau, rummaged through the rooms and the wreckage of the barns and outbuildings, then gone out the back gate to the monastery. He eventually returned and drove away in the jeep. They said that the American officer was gone. Jean-Claude was not satisfied.

The school teacher and the priest in Carentan reported that he had gone to the cottage near the asparagus fields and found it to have been abandoned. They also said that he had found no trace of them in Carentan or in any of the hamlets nearby.

The postmaster at Pont Hébert told the school teacher in Carentan that it was true, he had seen the officer cross back over the Vire and drive toward St. Lô. "And not just that," he added. "The cousin of my wife's uncle is the father of the priest who is the new abbot putting the monastery back in order. He says the officer walked around, talked to the monks cleaning the place, poked his nose in all the rooms, finally left. He's gone."

The sous-préfet of St. Lô, formerly the translator at the old mental hospital, knew the officer well from the previous autumn "when he was a worthless civil affairs officer. Tell Jean-Claude that the postmaster is right—the American showed up at Bon Saveur. He wanted to know about some girl, that's all, but she wasn't from here. No one knows her. He left to go bother the laborers at the market place, the churches, even the Irish charity workers. Then he drove away."

Will had discovered a construction site at the east side of St. Lô, near the old stud farm. A painted sign said *Hôpital Irlandais*. A tall, gaunt Irish-

284

man translated for the French laborers, and for Will.

"Yes, it is a hospital we're building for them, a Red Cross hospital. God knows they could use it."

"Who?"

"The Irish, and happy the Irish are to come to the aide of the Capital of the Ruins—that's what De Gaulle calls St. Lô—the Capital of the Ruins. We found someone even more miserable than the Irish. Thank God you Americans didn't liberate Galway, there'd be nothing left. You know anything at all about these people?"

Will told him of his time at Bon Saveur. The translator told Will he was the only American he had seen in St. Lô in months. "Not sure they want any Americans for a while, it is a long time they'll be cleaning up after you." Will told him about Géraldine and the fellow called for his wife, who was French. She knew how to find out what Will was asking and would make inquiries. The following day they told him.

"It is not in St. Lô you'll be finding her, nor her sister. The aunt is here if it's the aunt you'll be wanting, but the aunt has not been seeing the girls since the Army was looking after her at a hospital. At Isigny. She does not have any news of the sisters. Or her parents."

Will left.

The *sous-prefét* sent word to Carentan that Will was truly gone, and everyone except Jean-Claude believed him. Still, it was not until Father Jean, in Ste. Marie, sent word that Jean-Claude believed it was safe to claim his due.

Will had haunted Ste. Marie a final time, no longer hoping that he would find Géraldine but that he might find someone who could find her. He had gone to see Genet and, finding him absent as well, he went from door to door, to the laundry women at the river, to the co-op men in the apple barn, the mairie, the post office, asking. Eventually the prefect of police relented and told him, truthfully, that Genet was in Paris. "Seul." By himself. He could tell Will nothing of the family Dupré or of their abandoned farm across the river.

The only thing that had given Will any comfort was that, while Genet was indeed gone, he knew also that Genet was coming back. His electricity was switched on. His gas was working. His medicine cabinets were clean. And the drawing of Géraldine had been framed and was hanging in Genet's hallway. Will wrote his name and military address on a slip of paper and dated it, July 23, 1945: "Write to me. Tell me how to find her. Will Hastings." He left it where Genet would find it—between two plates in Genet's cupboard.

He had done all he could to find her, and had failed. He drove away from Ste. Marie for the last time, followed as far as the calvaire by the priest, who stopped and made the sign of the cross when the jeep turned east toward the road that would lead back to Caen and the American Navy port at Le Havre.

"I assure you," Father Jean had written, "that he is gone. He was a nuisance for a few hours. The police told him that Genet was gone. No one here knew any more than that, and he learned no more than that." Jean-Claude had sent a reply; Father Jean answered. "Yes, he came to the church. I told him I did not know anything about her." Then he added as a post script: "He did not go into the cemetery. He saw nothing."

The following day a former resistance footsoldier who now organized dock workers in Le Havre sent word by the postal route carrier to Caen and, in turn, to Ste. Vire and Carentan. "Captain Hastings is listed on the boarding orders for the Sea Robin. The vessel departed the harbor at ten in the morning, bound for Southampton, then America."

Only then did Jean-Claude tell Monsieur and Madame Dupré to gather their things and to bring Claudine, that they were returning to the Château, all of them.

"And the child?"

"No."

But the priest in Carentan already had spoken with Father Jean in Ste. Marie. Together they overruled Jean-Claude.

"Géraldine is no longer your concern. But the child—he goes with the family."

So, after an absence of almost exactly one year, Chateau Dupré received its owners from hiding in exile on the very day that Will dropped his barracks bag onto the deck of the troop carrier Sea Robin, leaned back against the king post rigging, and stared back at the disappearing coast line of his life in France.

CHAPTER THIRTY-ONE

"**N**OW HEAR THIS. NOW HEAR THIS. ALL ARMY OFFICERS REPORT TO..."

Will had responded to three announcements to Army officers to report to the captain's wardroom. Each time he was told the announcement was not for him: "Sorry, Captain. It's for the unit officers on board. You're unattached. How'd you get on the transport list anyway?"

In this manner he had learned that he had not been given a berth in the cabins with the other officers, that he had not been assigned to a mess hall rotation with the other officers, and that he was not on the list for the officer's club, a cramped cubbyhole where the officers could sit and drink whatever they had stolen in the war. Will would have tried for a glass anyway except that while being refused admission he had picked out Blackwell inside the room, entertaining a cadre of other medical officers with a bottle of Scotch. "Proud I served under him," Will heard Blackwell say. "Not surprised when it came out he was killed leading an infantry unit against the jerries at some chateau in France. A tough bird, but a good one."

Will had left the officer's club and returned to his solitary post at the deck rigging. That had been two days ago, south of Iceland. He sat on the deck, studying a snapshot Fondren had given him, his only souvenir of France.

"Okay, pick two cards..." The *Sea Robin* rose, then slammed down onto the North Atlantic, drowning out the sound of whatever was said next. "Okay, you got 'em? Don't show me. This is something I picked up from a guy in Germany. Or was it Belgium? Don't show me the cards."

Will smiled, despite himself. He turned slightly to look over his shoulder; Cheadle was shuffling the deck, trying to keep the homeward-bound wind from blowing the cards out to sea. Six or seven grizzled men sat cross-legged on the deck, their backs against their barracks bags. One of them, his wool cap perched over his forehead, had his face six inches or a foot from Cheadle's head in what Will knew was a futile effort to see how the trick worked. A young infantry officer dropped down on the deck beside him.

"Space taken, Captain?"

"All yours, Major."

"Tucker."

"Hastings." They shook hands.

"Monster?" Tucker peered over Will's shoulder at the snapshot, a beast staring out from a perch over the wrecked roof of a gothic church.

"Gargoyle. Wards off evil."

"Good luck with that. Cigarette?"

Will decided Tucker was right; the gargoyle in question had failed miserably, perched above St. Croix near the porch where Major Howie's body had been placed in honor.

"Thanks. Meeting over?"

"Yeah. You skipped it?"

"I'm not on the list, whatever the list is. Of officers. It's just for you guys in charge of troops going home. What was the emergency this time?"

"Debarkation. We'll get a radio signal in a day or so with procedures. How to march the men off the boat. 'Listen up, Gentlemen. It is your duty to keep the men in order until all are ashore. You will be assigned to....' and then a bunch of stuff about putting them all on a train or something until they get to Fort Wherever. Then they'll get discharged or sent to Japan. Points."

"Japan for me, then. I'm short. Seventy-five."

"Too bad. Should have got to the war sooner."

Will didn't try to explain. He had gotten to the war sooner than most, stayed longer than most, and had fewer points than any of them. Collins had become a lieutenant colonel before the 261st made it to Germany. The new docs who had come on board with him in Belgium had become majors before reaching the Elbe. Even Prior had become a major. Will's rank was the same as the day he entered the service in San Antonio—captain. He had seen Major Popper again, once, near Cologne: "It's out of my hands, Will.

You're doing a great job." Not until he was sent to Le Havre to wait for a boat to Norfolk did he see his personnel file. *Non-promotable, by order of the Commanding Officer.*

"It'll be all right. At least I won't have to go look for a job. You?"

Tucker was going back to Denver to work in the family chemical factory. "Cereal. I'm tellin' ya, you know what we learned the last couple of years?" Will didn't know. "Shelf life. That's right. Shelf life. The army wanted cereal that would keep a year or two on the shelf. Some years the farmers grew too much wheat, oats, corn, whatever, and it rotted in the silos, some years not enough. But if you turn it all into cereal, sprinkle in a few chemicals, it'll sit in a warehouse until the next century. We got contracts with Kellogg's, I think Post, all of them." Will agreed with him that it was good. "Bread, next. It's how you do the flour. Anyway, good luck." The major stood up, faced into the salt air breeze and stretched, then wandered away.

The wind blew the queen of clubs onto Will's face.

"Sorry, sir."

"Hey, Cheadle. How's it going?" Cheadle retrieved the card, then studied Will, searching his memory for a captain who knew his name. Will helped him. "LST. June 6. The Big One." He waited a moment, then added "Halliburton? Captain Blackwell?"

"Oh, hey, sir. Took me a minute, been a while. How ya' doin' sir?"

"Doing all right, Cheadle. How about you."

"Alive, sir. Alive. Doing just fine."

"You stay with Captain Blackwell? He's on board. I guess I should say Lieutenant Colonel Blackwell."

"Captain Blackwell's on board? That's great. But naw, no such luck, sir. Last time I saw Captain Blackwell, he was headed off somewhere at Southampton and I was headed off to the replacement depot. How's Captain Blackwell doin'?"

Not bad, Will thought, not bad at all.

"Spent the rest of the war in Scotland, from what I can tell. At a rehab hospital." *Telling his fellow desk doctors that he had served under the great Doctor Halliburton, the fallen hero who had led a charge against a battalion of SS at some chateau in France.*

Cheadle didn't know what to say to that, and said nothing.

"And how about your medic, Captain?"

"Antsley."

"Yeah, that's right. Antsley. Any idea what happened to him? We watched you guys run off that ramp and I figured Holy Cow, that's the last we'll see of you guys. You see him after Southhampton?"

"Antsley's fine, Cheadle. He's fine."

"That's good, sir. Hey, it's good to see you, sir."

"You too, Cheadle. Take a little care with your cards, okay?" Will nodded at the cluster of combat veterans who waited fifteen feet away for Cheadle to come back and trick them out of a dollar. "These guys look like they've spent the last year shooting guys for less than a buck."

Cheadle grinned and left.

The following day the officers again were ordered to the ward room. Will waited until they all returned to the deck, then went to the companionway outside the captain's cabin. There he found taped to the wall the debarkation orders for the units: "The 264th Regimental Combat Team will debark at 0800 via Gangways 2, 3, and 4 and proceed in order to Norfolk Naval Station Shed A, in column of companies, First Battalion lead. The 385th Hospital Training Section will debark second via Gangway 2 and proceed to Norfolk Naval Station, Shed C..."

As with the rest of his military career, Will found himself accounted for but unassigned. "Unattached personnel will debark last, officers via Gangway 3, enlisted via Gangway 4, and proceed to Shed D for in-processing and transit orders...."   He thought of the day in Southampton when Halliburton had thrown him and Blackwell off the LST. They had made their way along the pier, watching Halliburton stand beneath a crane-load of machinery suspended above the deck, wishing at the time that it would drop onto his head, wondering now what would have been his lot had the crane been so inclined, then realizing it didn't matter. Will had gone to France not to lose Halliburton but to find Peter, and had failed at both. He made the decision that, having nowhere else to go, he would expect less of Japan and thereby keep it from being so bad.

The *Sea Robin* stood off the roads in Chesapeake Bay for six hours waiting for a berth but, by 10:00 the morning of August 1, 1945, eight hundred soldiers cheered when the anchor chain groaned and the vessel swung toward home. At 12:00, only four hours late, the troop carrier came to rest against against the pier of the Norfolk Navy Base. Huge docking lines snugged home and, one by one, gangways began to connect the deck to the dock. Hundreds of dirty men shoved against each other, hit each other with barracks bags and pushed with arms, looking less like an army of conquerors than a swarm of enormous canvas ants racing for the queen.

"TWO SIXTY FOURTH, ATTenTION! First BATTalION, A CompanY! FORward, MARCH!"

The deck was no place to march nor had anyone in the 264th Regimental Combat Team marched in parade drill in over a year. The men shoved and pushed and almost killed each other as they forced their way down the gangplanks. Will stood well clear and watched, not from a sense of complying with his vague debarkation orders so much as that the men on deck had a right to their urgency; they were going home as soon as they cleared the Norfolk processing center and there was no reason for Will to get in the way of even one of them.

He watched Tucker at Gangway 2, ordering and cajoling his men without enthusiasm or success, finally abandoning his voice and authority to the unit sergeants who themselves were standing well clear as the men made for land. The 264th was off the *Sea Robin* in two hours. Blackwell's medical squad was gone in fifteen minutes. By three in the afternoon, only Will and a half-dozen men of all ranks were left.

"Can we go now, sir?"

"Pardon?"

"Go? sir?" A specialist, technical fourth class, and a few other privates and corporals stood near Gangway 4. "Ain't nobody left is there? All right if we go onshore?"

"Sure. Let's all go. Hoist your bags. Ready? Go." For the first, and last, time in his career, Will was a commanding officer.

That was it. The six men straggled down the gangplank, trying to not fall in the water as they balanced their bags on their shoulders. Like him, they were not members of any of the units shipped home on *Sea Robin*, nor ambulatory wounded men, nor essential technical personnel, just six stragglers from the war. He wondered if he should try to write something on their orders to give them a claim to go on leave, then decided against it. He followed them into Shed D.

The debarkation shed was jammed with men; the six unattached soldiers disappeared in a crowd of troops standing in lines. Stenciled signs with unit names, sub-unit names, and no unit names told them where to queue. It took Will a half hour of slow shuffling to make it to the front of "Unattached Personnel," where he learned that he was indeed unattached but, as an officer, he should have gone to a different line. Another fifteen minutes passed before his pushing and shoving and being told to wait his turn got him into the unattached officers' line. A half hour later he made it to the front.

"Orders, sir." Will handed the clerk his embarkation orders. "Got your personnel file, sir?" Will opened his barracks bag, dug it out, and offered it to the slightly chubby corporal. "Hang on to it, sir. Don't need it here. Don't lose it, though. Okay, Hastings, medical officer. Stand by."

Will stood by for a long time. The clerk thumbed through a wooden box of index cards, vainly searching for Will's name before leaving to find a superior. He returned with an even chubbier sergeant who was chewing him out. "I don't care, Idjit. If he's in this shed, his card is in that box." The sergeant looked at Will and rolled his eyes to communicate how bad things were in the army, a constant struggle against idjits who couldn't find an index card. Will's card was not in the box. The sergeant accused the corporal of losing it, then wondered aloud if Will had gone to the wrong shed. As a last resort he looked at Will's orders, thumped them with a forefinger, and told Will to stand by again. "I sees the problem, now, sir. Should have said so." The sergeant disappeared. Ten minutes later he returned with a brown paper bag.

"Ain't found your orders yet, sir. Sorry about that. But the lieutenant he said this bag had your name on it so here." He thrust the sack at Will, then told him to stand by again. "Just wait there, Captain. I'll find the idjit that screwed this up and get your orders. Be right back." Will watched him disappear. The bag was full of letters.

> October 27, 1944:
>
> *Dear Will. I hope you are doing okay over there. It came out in the Lubbock paper about your being wounded and all but Virginia told us....*

It was signed by his high school math teacher, a man Will had not seen or thought about in years. He told Will he was proud of him, the whole school was proud of him, and they all hoped he was safe. Another letter, signed by all the ladies in the First Baptist Church, revealed that they had been praying for him. The Sanger brothers, who owned the butcher shop, wrote a one line note: 'Hurry up and come on home, Doc!'

Will wondered how all the letters had shown up in the debarkation shed at Norfolk.

There was a V-mail from Molly Cochran, tucked inside a larger envelope that contained a regular letter. The V-Mail was dated March 1944. In much-reduced handwriting she said that she was working in a munitions factory in San Angelo and hoped he was doing okay.

The regular letter, only five days old, was easier to read.

> *Dear Will: I hope this finds you safe and well. Virginia told me about you being wounded but that you had gone back so I hope it wasn't real serious, but it sounded pretty serious. We've all been praying you are okay. Well, I guess you're going to be surprised to get this V-mail. I sent it off last year and it came back in June this year, never got to you because it was on a boat that was hit but it didn't sink but somehow instead of sending the mail on to you they must of sent everything home for us to send again because when I got it back the war was over already. Well, in Germany, not Japan I guess. I have moved back home because Momma is sickly and Daddy can't run the place by himself. Maybe you'll take care of her when you get home. I hope so. Well, I suppose Virginia already told you everything but I thought I should tell you myself. I'm going to get married. You don't know him, he's from San Angelo too and of course we met at the plant. He was too old for the Army at first and by when they was taking his age in the Army after all he was in charge of fuse calibrations and the plant asked for him to be essential. So he fought here....*

"Hey, Captain—got your card." Will looked up from his letters; the officious sergeant was standing over him, waving an index card. "Stand by and I'll find your orders. You ain't with no unit, right? It's just you. 'At's why we couldn't find your card. When a guy comes through what ain't got a card I always tell the clerk he ain't with his unit—go look in the..." Will wanted the sergeant to go away, and he did. Will opened the next letter, from Nona.

> *Hey Will, I guess Virginia already told you but a B-24 blew up that shed by the quarry and they found your army box...*

"Here you go, Captain. New Orleans." The sergeant was back. "Your orders. You got 'til August 8 to get to New Orleans." He handed Will a thick wad of carbon-copied pages, directing him to report to Camp Plauche for advanced training in tropical medicine. Will was headed to the Pacific. "So, not enough points huh, Captain? Too bad. We aint' got a lot of guys in here that go to New Orleans." He pronounced it 'New Orleens.' "Most of 'em goin'home, of course, unless they's like you and ain't got enough points. Most of you like that goes straight to the train and on to San Fran. Don't seem right."

Antsley had guessed wrong; if he had gained fifty pounds he could have stayed in the States and been a clerk. By being a conscientious objector he had guaranteed himself a place in combat, as a medic. Will didn't blame the clerk; he just wanted to get out of the shed.

"So, take these orders out the front there...." He pointed to a door cut in the opposite wall, leading out to the rest of the United States. "... and they's a Transportation Command out there and you give 'em your orders and they'll fix you up to get on a train. But, hey, Captain—you must of done somethin' right, you got more'n a week to get to New Orleans."

Then he was gone. Will was on his own. He put Nona's letter away, put the paper bag of letters in his barracks bag, and slung it over his shoulder.

The Transportation Command was just another hut, hastily built on the other side of a chain link fence that separated the Norfolk navy sheds from the Army bus depot. Hundreds, perhaps thousands, of soldiers jammed toward the wooden shack. The men were so familiar to him—they walked a certain way, drooped their heads a certain way, clustered in groups of twos and threes. In the inexplicable manner of armies, units metastasized, disintegrated, re-formed, NCO's yelling *listen up you fuckers* to men who were not listening, the empty threat of some vague military discipline unequal to the sound of an .88 or the sight of a Panzer crunching over a frozen hillock and into your outpost, its barrel swiveling, hunting.

Will wondered whether Douglas had survived Germany and concluded that he had. Standing in the line of the Transportation Command it occurred to him that he didn't really know Douglas's name. When he had awakened on the train between Stranraer and Birmingham to find Douglas handcuffed to him, wearing Will's Class A jacket and rifling through his barracks bag, he had said his name was Bell. When he popped up at the school at Shrivenham it was Douglas. In France he had become Curtiss. *Of course—airplanes! He names himself after airplanes. Why didn't I think of that?*

The assembled Army units weren't the only people crushed against the chain link fence. Girls, women, mothers, families, hundreds of civilians, American people, farmers, housewives, businessmen and preachers, infants, gaping boys and squirming girls, all had jammed up against the fence, their fingers poking through the links, shouting. *Joe Bob! Hey—Mickey! Scooter, over here, we come to get you!* They squealed, yelled, jumped up and down, and to his amazement, soldiers found their families in the crowds and broke ranks, running to touch a wife, a mother, a baby never before seen, trying to claw and touch through the thin links of fence. He made it inside the building.

"Orders, Captain." Another clerk, efficient, exasperated, busy, held out his hand.

"New Orleans, Camp Plauche." Will handed him the new orders. "Not sure what I'm supposed to do, Corporal." He stood patiently while the corporal looked at them. "For transportation orders."

"Do, sir? You don't have to do anything. But you've got eight days before you got to be at New Orleans. Where you wanta go?" He lifted a pen over a form, looked up. "Where's home? You want a train back home, Captain?"

Will didn't answer, not at first. Instead, he tried to remember where Shorty had lived. Was it Dallas? Fort Worth? What was Shorty's wife's name? He could find her. Then he decided.

"Have I got time to go to Iowa? I'm afraid I don't know much about trains anymore, Corporal."

"Don't know exactly, sir. Where to?"

Will rummaged into his barracks bag and found the letter from Antsley's parents.

"Davenport? In Iowa? How long does that take?"

The corporal had never heard of Davenport, Iowa. He said that he could send Will to St. Louis or Chicago but he'd have to get a local train from there, then get himself back down to New Orleans.

"You from Iowa, sir? Timin'll be close."

"No. Not from there. I thought I should try to go see these people."

The corporal was patient, polite, but efficient. He wanted Will to answer him and get his transportation voucher and go away so that he could go on to the next confused combat veteran, then the one behind him.

"Tell you what, sir. How about I send you to St. Louis and then on to New

Orleans? You get to St. Louis and you can see if you got enough time left to go to wherever it is. Then you go on to New Orleans yourself. No sweat."

"How about if I just take you home with me, soldier?"

The room stopped. Men arrested in place, their arms poised in mid-air, knees bent. All sound was muffled and the room became quiet, the soldiers and their scuffing boots and clanking bags and caps and paper orders suspended in time. Will could see, but only in front of him, making out the disbelief on the clerk's face. The only sense he trusted was his hearing, and it heard her say—

"Will, I've come for you. I've come to bring you home." She was behind him, and he knew it was her.

He turned to see her. Virginia, tall, her thick auburn hair brushed long over her shoulder, her gaze soft, eyes lifted to him, head tilted slightly forward in earnest. He saw her full mouth and high cheekbones and perfectly formed nose and from her lips she was saying that she had come for him. With her left hand she reached to take his right arm, gently, but with purpose, and without looking at any other thing in the room and without seeing the corporal or the queue of soldiers or the men who wanted to get to the front of the line, she put her right hand behind his back and drew him to her.

"We can go to St. Louis, Will, if that's what you want. Or we can just go home. We'll do whatever you want." She offered, more by her looks and by her openness than by what she was saying, to let him make the decision.

He could not make words come out. He only could look at her, see her, older now, grown up in some vague way, but very much the tall, commanding, auburn-haired girl he had wanted for as long as he could remember. He heard her tell the clerk to make out the transportation form for Tierra, Texas, and then to New Orleans. Then he let her lead him away.

The waiting for Virginia was over.

CHAPTER THIRTY-TWO

From the day in September 1944 when she had written a desperate letter to Will at his convalescent hospital in Cherbourg, then all through the long year of motherhood and picking cotton and denying that she had brought ruin on Tierra, Virginia had planned how she would tell Will. She had accepted that he might know anyway; the tone of his letters had been more polite and less ardent after he had been wounded and since he had returned to combat. Shirley may have told him everything, or even done so little as send him the Tierra Times elopement story. Either way, whether Will knew or did not know, she prepared herself just as she used to do with Poppy—she planned what she would say and what he would say and what she would say in reply.

In her mind it most probably would be: Will—I have to tell you this. I didn't wait.' 'I figured that.' 'I had a baby.' 'A baby?' 'Yes, Will. Please sit down, and let me tell you the whole story. Then you can judge me. It won't be easy, but here's what happened.'

She would then tell him that she had found out that she was just like hundreds of thousands of other girls all over America, and their soldiers, struck by passion and love, an overwhelming emotional turmoil of longing and separation on the eve of war. She would say she was sorry that she had given in, sorry it had not been Will first, and sorry that she had to tell him. But she also would tell him that she had come for him, and she would mean it.

He would be hurt. He would be angry. He would say she was wrong. She would answer as Poppy used to answer her, saying, "Will, what's done is done. I can't undo it. But I came to tell you the truth. I came to ask you to come home. And I came to say I'm sorry, that I wish I had known how

297

to love you better before you left and to say that I do love you. If you will have me, I'm yours."

She hoped he would say yes, and that he would take her back.

She also considered that he might pick up his barracks bag, say goodbye, and get on a train going anywhere else.

In either event, long before she used Poppy's old printing press to make up enough train tickets to get her to Norfolk, she had made up her mind that by the time she got back to Tierra and back to her baby, she would have done right by Will Hastings. Nothing afterward could be as hard as the year she had just passed, even if Will said no and never returned to Tierra and she had to tell the rest of the town the whole story.

Virginia had planned for everything except what happened.

They boarded a full train bound for Greenville, North Carolina. There, wedged in between soldiers, local laborers getting on and off at each whistlestop, farmers, and war workers headed for California, she told Will about Tierra in the last year of the war. He had been so polite, so quiet, that she wondered whether he had forgotten everyone she mentioned.

Virginia told him that the quarry where they had gone skinny dipping, and where they had been caught by Bart, had been overrun because a B-24 had blown up the shed and all of Poppy's hidden tires and oil cans and cigarettes had come tumbling out into the open. After that, the green sedan had sown panic at Reilly's Grocery Store and at the courthouse each time it glided into Tierra, its government men snooping for witnesses for the sheriff's trial. Mr. Fleming had testified that the bank had paid $25,000 for the damage to the cotton gin and another $5,000 for the burned cotton bales. Bob Clayton testified that he had helped carry the old gin engine out to the shed the night before the fire. The sheriff denied it all and said if anyone had done it, it had to be Bart or Poppy, a story the jury seemed ready to believe until Mr. Bradley testified. After losing his own Johnny at Bataan, Mr. Bradley had let Mrs. Tarlton handle all his mail and he never opened his box again, not until he heard about some goings-on the Sheriff and Bart had to do with selling jug liquor to the high school boys. Then Mr. Bradley produced the big brown envelope that had been hidden in the bottom of his mail box since the night of the fire. Inside the envelope there were negotiable certificates for the cotton bales, with Bart's fingerprints on the envelope, and Hoskins's on the certificates, all hidden away to cash in on the next year's bumper crop. The jury took less than an hour to send

Hoskins to the pen.

She told Will about working in the cotton fields, of doing laundry with Sandy Clayton, of going to church, of Shirley's pursuit of Hoyt Carter, who had fled to California to sell war bonds as a model soldier. Will listened to every word but said little in reply. Virginia had heard that soldiers coming back from the war did not talk much, and she made herself be patient.

Then she told Will that she had seen Poppy, one time.

"He was waiting for me across from the Lubbock State Hospital when I went to see Momma. When I came out he followed me back to the bus station. I was so happy to see him but all he wanted was to blame me over Bart. 'You told them this and you told them that and if you hadn't said anything to them he'd be home today and I would be too. But no, you shoot your mouth off and they pick him up.' I told him it wasn't like that but he called me a liar and a tramp and said that instead of a son all he had was a son lost in battle."

Will had said he was sorry, that there isn't a good way for people to lose a son in battle.

"Bart? Lost in battle? He wasn't lost in battle. Let me show you what I showed Poppy." She brought out a newspaper clipping and gave it to Will. "I asked him if he had actually read the telegram and he said he had; I suppose Arnie must have known where to find him. So I said, 'Did he get the newspapers?' and he said, 'No.' Then I showed him this, from the day before. Right there on page 1, big picture."

Will looked at the picture. It was captioned GI's land on Mindoro and portrayed soldiers getting off a boat and wading onto some island. He did not see what she wanted him to see.

"Look close, Will. Right there on the boat, see the name? Renegade. Bart's boat. That was the first time that boat was in battle. Poppy looked at it and said, 'What is this?' and I said, 'Read the telegram again, Poppy. It didn't say Bart was lost in battle—it said he was lost at sea. Someone threw him overboard. No one could stand him, Poppy. They hated him as much in the Navy as they did in Tierra.' And Poppy said to me 'Get out of here you little bitch.' And I said goodbye."

She had not seen him leave the bus station and had not heard from him since.

In Greenville they left the train and found a room for the night, a small, humid, hot little square of peeling wall paper and a bare light bulb, where Virginia finally realized that she had failed to plan for what would come first, the chicken or the egg, the truth or the intimacy. She chose the truth.

"Will, can you sit down here beside me? Please?" She sat on the sagging mattress and patted a place beside her, unsure whether she sounded business-like or seductive. He sat down.

She knew it was time to tell him but, equally, she was prepared to let him make love to her first. It would have been easier if he had tried to do so. He did not.

"Will?"

"Yes."

"There are some things I have to tell you. Some other things."

"Is that why you rode the train from Texas to Norfolk? To tell me some other things?"

"Yes, Will."

"Not to come for me, or to take me home?"

"Yes, Will. I came to get you and, if you will come with me, to bring you home." She waited for him to say something but, when he didn't, she plowed on. "If you want to. But there are things and, there are things. And, after the....things, you might not want to come home. But I do want you to, Will. I came to ask you to come home with me."

"And no matter what the things are, Virginia, you might not want me to."

"What?"

"You might not want me to come home with you. Like you said, there are things." He looked at her, carefully. She did not understand. "I fell for someone. In France. Her name is Géraldine. Géraldine Dupré."

Virginia heard her own pulse, pounding in her ears. The room was quiet, the click of a ceiling fan rotating down the hall, in the lobby, click, click, a drone of flies buzzing at the window pane, the air thick and hot. She could not see, and closed her eyes in hopes it would go away. It didn't.

"I'm very sorry, Virginia, but I'm not going to lie to you. You have the right to know."

"What, Will? What on earth happened?"

"Happened? She was there, when I was shot. If she hadn't been there, if Curtiss hadn't been there, I would have died." He did not think about, much less mention, that Virginia had not been there for him, then or for a long time.

"She's a nurse?" Virginia had heard what everyone else heard, that men fell in love with army nurses. Doctors had flings with nurses. It was happening to her.

"No, she's not a nurse. She's a farm girl. It was her farm. Where I got shot."

"And you fell for a farm girl who was there when you were shot?" Virginia knew when she said it how unfair it sounded, but she couldn't help herself. "You ...." She almost said: You could have written to me, then realized that Will had done no more than she had done, nor had he been any more unfair with his letters than Virginia had been with hers.

"Yes. And she's gone."

"Gone?"

"Gone. She was gone before they ever sent me back to my unit, before Belgium and Germany."

"Gone? Like, she left?" Virginia wasn't quite sure why she wanted to know, but she did.

"I don't know. She's gone. We were supposed to meet the day I got my orders to go back to the unit and she wasn't there. I couldn't find her. I never heard from her again. That was last November."

To her astonishment, Virginia heard only the grief in his voice. He wasn't throwing some French girl in Virginia's face to punish her for not writing to him. He wasn't marking his territory like a man of the world. This was her friend Will, the boy she had grown up with, the boy she had teased and nearly given herself to; now he hurt for having loved someone else, and for having lost her. Virginia found herself putting her arm around him and holding him.

"It's all right, Will. It's all right. It could have happened to anyone." And then, for the first time, she understood what it meant to care for someone else more than she cared for herself. "It could have happened to me. I'm here, Will, if you want me to be. I know it hurts, but it'll be all right. I'm right here."

He told her that before he boarded the *Sea Robin* he had stolen a jeep from the motor pool in Caen.

"I went to the cottage at Carentan, to the chateau, to St. Lô. I went back to Ste. Marie to find Dr. Genet. No one would tell me anything. She's gone, Virginia, she is well and truly gone."

"I'm sorry, Will." She meant it. "Back home, whenever something happens, we always say, it's the war. It's changed everything, the war. I don't know why I didn't think the war would change you, too."

They sat in the quiet room and let the evening light turn to dark. Virginia's mind raced, trying to decide what to do with herself. She had been foolish, she decided; she should have written Will from the first minute and turned him loose. She should not have scrimped pennies and printed fake train tickets and persuaded Molly to keep Peter with her at the farm while Virginia traveled across America in a vain attempt to fix everything that she had messed up before the town learned the whole story. She did not see how she could fix this. Will got off the bed and put on his shoes.

"Where're you going?"

"Well, away. I mean, I had to tell you. I should have told you in Norfolk but I was so astonished that you were there, I just didn't know what to say. But now, well, now I've told you. Gin, I'm sorry. I know I caused a mess." He slipped his uniform jacket on over his shirt, straightened his tie.

"You don't have to go, Will." She swallowed hard, not quite looking at him, not quite looking away. "I mean, unless you want to. But I'm not asking you to go."

"Well, it's not right, Virginia. I mean, you know."

"I did come to get you, Will. You don't have to come home with me, but I'm still asking you to. And I'm sorry about Géraldine. But if she's really gone, well, I'm here. It won't be the same, but I am here. If you want."

She asked him to wait until the morning before he made up his mind for sure. He said he would. Neither of them slept but, at four in the morning, Virginia folded open the bedsheet and the cover and gazed uncertainly across to him, sitting in the dark. He got up from the chair and sat down on the open bed. She took off his shirt, his undershirt, and helped him out of his clothes. He slid in beside her and, wordlessly, they took each other, almost nine years after they had gone to the quarry for that very purpose.

In the morning, in their nakedness and uncertainty, she told Will what she had come to tell him, that while he was gone, she had had a baby.

He said that he had thought so. No one had told him, but he had seen her changes, and he knew it.

He knew also that it was the war. He told her not to tell him anything else, that it was all right, that he didn't need to know. The only thing he let her say was that the baby's father was a soldier, and that he had died.

Will and Virginia were married in Greenville, South Carolina, on August 3, 1945. They found a justice of the peace and asked him to hurry because they did not want to miss the train.

CHAPTER THIRTY-THREE

The federal investigators found no evidence that the box was anything more than what Arnie had told them it was, a military footlocker that belonged to a local soldier who had been stationed in England, sent back home for safekeeping until after the war. Thus, on the day that Hoskins' appeal was denied, the former sheriff had been handcuffed to a guard and put on a train bound north to Leavenworth at more or less the same time that the box was put back on a train headed west to Tierra. It arrived in the afternoon of the day that Tierra celebrated Will's safe return with a picnic on the courthouse lawn.

The town had besieged the returning couple at the train station, given them twenty-four hours of privacy, and then plied them with fried chicken and salad and iced tea and bragged that the war would soon be over. Will was indeed the man everyone wanted. Talk swirled of what would happen after the war—rebuilding the cotton gin, a new house, a new clinic. He denied that his wounds were serious, just a bullet that didn't hit anything important.

In full view of the assembled well-wishers, Will picked up Peter and chucked him under the chin. Peter cried. Virginia rocked the toddler and put him on the lawn, where he crawled directly toward Molly Cochran and hugged her leg. When at last the couple alleged fatigue Will found himself, his wife, and the child escorted to Poppy's worn stucco cottage three blocks away. There, waiting for them, was Sandy, a claw hammer, and Peter's footlocker.

"What's this?" Virginia asked.

"Peter's things."

They opened the box and began to go through the bits and scraps that were important enough to Peter Hastings to keep them for his brother to find.

"Listen up. Just because we bombed 'em into the Stone Age doesn't mean they're finished. You gotta look behind every rock."

Sluggo didn't feel like looking behind every rock. In fact, Sluggo didn't feel like going on patrol at all.

"The war's over, Sandy. We won. Let's do something else."

"The war isn't over, not until they surrender."

There was not much doubt in Tierra that Japan would surrender. The news that a single bomb had destroyed an entire Japanese city had raced through Tierra even faster than had the news of Pearl Harbor almost four years before. The farmers drinking coffee at Nona's were already talking about it when the boys had lugged the bundle of newspapers to the café. "Japan's whipped," the men agreed.

"We patrol until the order comes to stand down." Sandy pulled himself up to his full height, then jogged across the highway to the cotton gin yard. The piles of lumber and gravel there were known to be favored by the Japs as forward bases, although even Sandy had to admit that as the new cotton gin got bigger, the stacks of building materials got smaller. There were fewer places for the enemy to hide, and it was harder every day to get Sluggo to help fight.

"Let's just go throw passes, Sandy. Come on. Hey, you know about practice?"

"Whattaya mean? Stay down—I'll check out that redoubt." Sandy dropped onto his stomach and began to crawl across the parking lot toward a cement mixer. "Cover me," he yelled back.

"They're going to start football practice at the high school. Next week."

"So? Get down. Take cover. You're exposing our position."

"So, there's a sign in the window at Reilly's Grocery Store." Sluggo did not get down. He stood in the middle of the cotton co-op trailer lot and watched his friend grind on his stomach toward the construction site. "The schedule."

"What schedule?"

"The football schedule. First game's at Cochise. In three weeks."

"Yeah. So?"

"The game's at Cochise. That's forty miles from here. People are going to go. In their cars."

"And?"

"Cars, Sandy. Gasoline. My dad went to Homer's yesterday and filled his tank up with gas. No stamps or anything, he just bought it."

The war was over. Even if Japan didn't know it, if Sandy didn't want it to be over, Sluggo had figured it out. It was hard to play like there was still a conflict.

"So, come on, Sandy. Let's just go throw the football. We'll be old enough to play next year. You want to make the team, don't you?"

Sandy sat on the ground with his back against the legs of the cement mixer. It no longer looked like a captured gun pit, or a secret radar installation, or an artillery battery. Sluggo had made it look like a cement mixer, and Sandy looked like a thirteen year old newspaper boy.

"So, Smart Guy, if the war's over, why was Captain Hastings getting on the bus at six thirty in the morning?"

Sluggo didn't know why Captain Hastings was getting on the bus. Sluggo had gotten up and gone with Sandy to the bus stop at the courthouse square at six-thirty in the morning because he had called Sandy a fibber. Sandy had claimed that Nona always gave him a cup of hot chocolate when he brought the Lubbock papers to her at six forty-five in the morning, and Sluggo didn't believe him. He had watched the bus driver hand Sandy the newspapers and had watched Sandy lug them to the courthouse lawn to count out Nona's order. Captain Hastings had appeared out of nowhere, with his barracks bag, and climbed up into the bus without a word. The bus had driven away from the courthouse square and turned back up toward the Lubbock highway, then disappeared.

"Because there's still a war on, Smart Guy, that's why. He's going back to the war."

Nona had given Sandy a cup of hot chocolate, and given one to Sluggo too. They had sat on the wooden step behind her kitchen and sipped it while it cooled, watching the men come in to talk about the bomb. Sluggo remembered something he had heard at the picnic on the courthouse lawn the day before.

"I heard Mr. Bradley talking to him and he said he was going to be here until Friday."

"Who?"

"Captain Hastings. At the picnic yesterday. He was talking to Mr. Bradley and Mr. Bradley said, 'Well, Doc, you going to get to stay home?' and Captain Hastings was playing with that baby and all and he said, 'No, sir. Just here until Friday, then...,' and I don't remember what all he said but he had to report somewhere. And today's not Friday; it's Tuesday."

Sandy didn't know either. He knew that when they were going through that box there at the house last night Mrs. Hastings had told him, told Sandy, he better go home. Sandy had figured that there would have been some bayonets, or a captured flag but, instead, they had taken out some letters and pictures and started to look at them. Captain Hastings had gotten awful quiet and handed the letters to Mrs. Hastings. She had said something about her having tried to tell him something but Sandy had been holding the baby and not paying much attention to them. Then the next thing he knew Mrs. Hastings was telling Sandy he better go on home. He didn't understand grown-ups.

"Well, that just proves it. It proves that the war's not over. The Army must have called him last night and canceled his leave and he had to get back right away. They're still fighting."

Sluggo didn't think that sounded right but he didn't care about Captain Hastings, who had turned out to be a failure as far as he was concerned. He wasn't a pilot; for that matter, he wasn't really even a captain. Old Bradley said that he was really just a doctor, that the Army just made the doctors into captains so they could order people to take their medicine. If Captain Hastings wanted to get on the bus a couple of days before he was supposed to, that didn't prove the war was still on. If anything, it just proved that Captain Hastings was leaving sooner than he said.

Sluggo left Sandy by the cement mixer to walk back across the Clovis Highway toward the town. They couldn't have played war much longer anyway; the workmen were starting to show up at the cotton gin to work on the new building, laborers to move the rubble out of the way and carpenters to build the new sheds in its place. Sluggo waited at the edge of the pavement and looked at the highway, just for a minute, before going on. *Don't want to get killed now that the war's over,* he thought. There were a lot more cars than there used to be and now, he figured, he had to watch both ways before trying to cross the road.

The End

307

ACKNOWLEDGEMENT

I could not have written *Engaged in War* without extraordinary assistance. The Second World War, one of the most thoroughly-documented episodes in history, poses special challenges to writers. I have attempted to pay special respect to every man, woman, and civilian who was caught up in the war with attention to accuracy in details of the campaigns that form the background of this story, yet not overwhelm the narrative with details of unit numbers, medical procedures, and similar matters. All characters in this story are fictitious but the background events did take place, from the field surgery in a captured German fortification on Omaha Beach to the tragic entry of the body of Major Howie into St. Lô, France on the hood of a Jeep, and from the use of French schools for courts martial to the construction of a hospital in St. Lô by the Irish Red Cross. Writing fiction from such histories invites errors and, if such be found, I regret them and accept the criticism that is their due.

The authenticity of *Engaged in War*, however, is a different matter. First, this novel could not have been written at all but for the kind and patient advice of Dr. C.E. Atkinson of Sheffield, England. His first-hand knowledge of medical practice, implements, treatments, and the emergence during the War of penicillin and sulfa was given to me generously and with patience. Dr. Atkinson passed away during the final revisions of the manuscript of this novel. His kindness, skill, and generosity are legacies that go far beyond these pages.

For the more precise problems of military medicine, I was given excellent technical advice and corrections by Dr. Dan Witt and by Dr. Keith Black, former military medical officers themselves. My errors in French and German were graciously read and corrected (with undoubted amusement) by Nanou and Paul Knisely and by Pat and Birgit Robbins. They and Philip Schmandt and Steven Nagle gently helped me in the details of life and living in France. Mrs. Marguerite Knisely (a lovely French woman who easily could be and may well have been someone's Géraldine) opened her war-time letters, her photograph albums, and her memories to help me understand what life in rural France under the German occupation meant. Their wisdom may be found in every page, and to them I acknowledge very special gratitude.

Special acknowledgement goes to Mindy Reed, Editor, who has patiently assisted from the first page to the last.

Finally, I thank my dear wife, Alice, whose encouragement and support keep me going, in this project and in all.

ABOUT THE AUTHOR

The **French Letters** series of novels are widely praised for their sense of America in the 1940s, both at home and in the Second World War. *Virginia's War* was a Finalist for Best Novel of the South and the Dear Author 'Novel with a Romantic Element' contest. *Engaged in War* won the silver medal at the London Book Festival for General Fiction and earned Author of The Year Honors for Jack Woodville London. The third novel in the series, *Children of a Good War,* is scheduled for publication.

Jack studied the craft of fiction at the Academy of Fiction, St. Céré, France and at Oxford University. He was the first Author of the Year of the Military Writers Society of America. He is the author of a number of published articles on the craft of writing and on early 20th Century history. His craft book, *A Novel Approach,* a short and light-hearted work on the conventions of writing, is designed to help writers who are setting out on the path to write their first book. *A Novel Approach* won the E-Lit Gold Medal for non-fiction in 2015.

Jack's work in progress is *Shades of the Deep Blue Sea,* a mystery-adventure novel about two sailors and a girl on a Pacific island that, instead of a tropical paradise, turns out to be a land of prisoner of war camps, cannibals who believe that God is singing to them from a military field radio, and an inconvenient Komodo dragon.

Jack lives in Austin, Texas. Visit him at jwlbooks.com or contact him at jack@jackwlondon.com.

CPSIA information can be obtained
at www.ICGtesting.com
Printed in the USA
LVHW041107280820
664156LV00002B/239

9 780990 612179